THE DRAGON AND THE EAGLE

A JAMES CHASE MILITARY THRILLER

BOOK TWO

TONY PEREZ

DRAGON PUBLISHING

Dedicated to Tayler, Connor, Parker, Gage,
Aden, Hunter, and Martha Miller

Thank you, Karyl

And a special thank you to Christina Garcia for putting up with me.

CHAPTER ONE

THE ATTACK

2005 HOURS—02 DECEMBER 2025

CAPTAIN NOAH WILLIAMS STOOD ON the fly bridge of the *USS John S. McCain* as he peered out across the inky waters of the South China Sea before him. The night was calm and quiet, typical for this time of year. A mild breeze tugged at his green and black camouflage-patterned Navy Working Uniform Type III and cooled the thin sheen of sweat on his lined forehead. Had it not been for the Malaysian littoral ship performing routine exercises a half-nautical mile away from them, the night would have been perfectly still. The *KD Keris-111* was in clear view because of the stars and bright moonlit night, and Williams knew that once it found its position, their training exercises would resume.

For now, however, Williams was perfectly content to gaze out across the sea at their country's mutual ally. His thoughts went to his family back home. They had been sending him broad hints that they wanted to see him home for the holidays, but he couldn't put in for leave as they weren't home ported. He, like the remainder of the crew, had to remain on the ship for the entire duration of their deployment at sea.

The terse email from Maggie, his wife of nearly fifteen years, on his laptop below deck played over in his mind as he watched the shimmering array of lights of the *Keris* shifting positions. In a moment, the *McCain* would get a message from the vessel, letting them know they were ready to continue.

Williams had been the captain of the *McCain* for the better part of the past three years, having earned that role through his commitment to the

United States Navy, not to his family. Sometimes he wondered if he were more married to his job than his own damned wife. Many people would have killed to be in his shoes, and he knew that he hadn't earned his rank by asking for assignments that didn't have multi-month deployments. Maggie would simply have to understand that him being home for the holidays wasn't going to be possible.

Securing his position on the *Arleigh Burke*-class destroyer had been his lifelong ambition, and he'd be damned if he'd trust it in anyone else's care. It wasn't so much that he didn't think anyone else could do as good of a job taking care of her as he would. In fact, he knew that he was easily replaced, as there were a number of equally qualified officers vying for an opportunity to command such a prestigious vessel. For Williams, though, it was more than just a job. He was curiously protective of the *McCain*. It was his home, his crew, his second family, and the long deployments were all part of the role he played on the vessel. Some of the crew might have called the *McCain* their second home. To Williams, the condo he shared with Maggie was his second home and this ship was his true residence, and the truth was, he was more familiar with it than with his own home.

Sprawling across 154 meters in length, the destroyer was the very definition of lean grace when cutting through the South China Sea. Though she was fairly hefty, clocking in at 8,900 lean tons of displacement, she was only twenty meters across at the beam. When moving at maximum speed, she could easily cover thirty-five kilometers per hour, powered by four gasoline turbines affixed to two powerful shafts. A dull matte shade of gray, she wouldn't be winning any beauty contests any time soon, but she was unquestionably a sight to behold.

Williams had to admit he loved the ship, loved working aboard her, and loved being deployed to exotic places in the Pacific. Nights like these reminded him of how much he loved his job as a naval captain. Even though it was early December, the air was balmy and comfortable. Overhead, the stars dazzled bright against the backdrop of the evening sky and the full moon cast the distant *KD Keris-111* in stark relief. The air was fresh and clean and had a hint of a salty aroma wafting off it. The only thing that would have made it better would have been a hot cup of coffee, but he knew that if he had a cup of the brew after lunchtime, he was guaranteed to get a poor night's sleep. As it were, he was looking forward to a restful night and confident that he'd get it too.

He always rested well after these training exercises. While they may have invigorated other men, they lulled Williams into a peaceful repose. There was something about the natural rhythm of the rapport he had with his crew and seeing them work toward a common goal of maintaining the security of the United States, even this far away from home. Watching his men learn and grow beneath his instruction was a job he took rather seriously. Keeping his men safe and the *McCain* at peak operational ability was a matter of personal pride. Knowing his crew respected him was the icing on the leadership cake.

The radio on his instrument panel on the flybridge crackled, and he stood upright, instantly alert for the incoming message from the *Keris*, letting them know they were in position. Williams squinted at the vessel in the distance. The littoral ship was still at a forty-five-degree angle, not quite perpendicular to them yet, but they'd be in position soon. Then, the voice of Communications Petty Officer Third Class Alexander Wyatt filtered into his ear.

Wyatt's voice was strangely tense as he said, "Captain Williams? I'm getting a message from the Chinese destroyer *Kee Sung*, and I don't know what to make of it."

"The Chinese?" Williams furrowed his brow. "What are they saying?"

What the hell did the Chinese want? He was acutely aware a Chinese Type 055-class destroyer had been shadowing them since they'd started their training exercises with the *Keris*, but it had kept a good twenty-five nautical mile distance between them. Even though the vessel was one of China's deadliest destroyers, it hadn't made any overt threats to them… yet. Williams was content to pointedly ignore them if they would continue to extend the same courtesy to him. The largest of its class in the world, the surface combatant vessel featured over one hundred vertical launching silos—112 of them, to be precise—in addition to their decoy launchers, an HQ-10 short range surface-to-air missile launcher, and two torpedo tubes for the lethal Yu-7 torpedoes. The last thing he wanted was to needlessly antagonize the Chinese destroyer. Was something about to change between them?

There was a pause, then Wyatt said, "Sir, they're telling us that we're in Chinese waters and demanding that we leave right now."

Williams scanned the horizon as he considered the communications officer's words. The *KD Keris-111* patiently waited a half-nautical-mile away. From his vantage, he could see that the Malaysian ship had finally moved into position. There was no visual indication of any other vessel in the water with them, but the *McCain* had been closely tracking the trailing Chinese destroyer since their discovery of it several days before. "Well, tell them that we're exercising our Freedom of Navigation in this region."

"Yes, sir," Wyatt replied.

Williams heard the note of uncertainty in the young petty officer's voice and matched it with his own puzzlement. There was no logical reason that the Chinese should have been accusing them of trespassing. Under the United Nations Convention for the Law of the Sea (UNCLOS)—which the United States had not signed but unequivocally recognized—Williams and his crew had every right to expect safe passage through these international waters. China's reaction was neither justified nor reasonable. His message back in that response would be loud and clear. *We're not in your waters, so kindly go to hell.*

His frown deepened. It had to be an honest mistake. Surely China knew this, and their message would be relayed back to them, and they'd go back to quietly shadowing them like they had been before. What other possible recourse could they seek? Their position was in the Spratly Islands archipelago, but even that was in international waters.

His hand went unconsciously to his face, and he rubbed at his jaw as he considered the message. This wasn't the first time the Chinese Navy had pulled such a stunt. Some five years ago, they had done the same thing back when the *McCain* was under the command of a different captain. The Chinese frigate had issued a total of ten curt messages to the commander before he had briskly reminded them of their routine operations in the international waters off Mischief Reef. China had finally backed off, but would they be so compliant tonight?

"Sir?" Wyatt said over the radio, a hint of anxiety in his voice. "I relayed your message to them, and they doubled down on their warning. Sir, they've issued what sounded like a threat against us."

A chill coursed down Williams's spine. "What the hell do you mean, a threat?"

"I'm not sure, sir." Wyatt's voice was uncertain. "They said that if we don't leave their waters, they're going to have to take action against us. I'm not sure what they mean by that."

Williams could think of a few things that China might do. If they tried it, though, he would retaliate just as firmly. *Who the hell do they think they are? They have no right to claim these waters.* "Thank you, Petty Officer. Please contact Okinawa. Let them know what you're telling me. And be sure to let me know if you have any additional updates."

"Yes, sir." Wyatt turned to face his communications panel.

Damn it. Williams's face turned down in a scowl. *The night was going so well too.* He wondered briefly if he needed to reach out to the Malaysian ship to inform them of China's threat and decided against it. There was no need to put them on edge too. While there was a fairly reasonable likelihood that China was merely trying to scare them off with their warnings, he wasn't feeling particularly eager to call them out on the bluff. But until the Chinese actually attacked them, there was little he could do.

Williams contemplated the Rules of Engagement (ROE) as he gazed across the waters at the sparkling lights indicating the *Keris's* position. The ROE were fairly straightforward in their expectations of how he would be required to respond were China to actually fire upon them. In no uncertain terms, as the captain of the ship, he would be obligated to defend his vessel at all costs. If China released a missile in their direction, he would be duty bound to fire upon them in return, even if it meant destroying the aggressor.

The thought of someone attacking his ship and his crew filled him with a cold fury. His anger was wholly justified. The naval exercises performed by the *USS John S. McCain* and the *KD Keris 111* were over twelve nautical miles away from Gaven Island and even farther from Johnson Island, the only two sections of real estate in the region that were both claimed and occupied by the Chinese Navy. Whether China had any right to these plots was still up for debate, but it was unambiguously clear that they had no jurisdiction over where the *McCain* and the *Keris* currently performed their exercises.

He let his gaze go back out to the blackness of the South China Sea.

This time, it no longer looked tranquil. Instead, it had taken on an ominous undertone, and the cool mist of the December evening was now a chilly shroud instead of a soothing balm on his sweaty skin.

⸻ ⸱ ⸱ ⸱ ⸱ ⸻

On the bridge of the *McCain*, within earshot of the captain but just out of visibility, Petty Officer Alexander Wyatt sat frozen in place. Unsure he had understood the message from the Chinese military correctly, he replayed it in his mind, hearing the clipped and tense voice, heavy with a thick Chinese accent, informing him of the impending danger of remaining in Chinese waters. "*Attention* USS John S. McCain. *You trespass in Chinese water. We advise you to evacuate immediately or we will take action against you for your trespass.*"

Sweat beaded on Wyatt's brow as the warning echoed in his thoughts. He frowned, considering the radio in front of him. He had little recourse in this situation. As the saying went, he was just the messenger, but he was dreading having to relay this particular one to the naval base in Okinawa. He sighed and depressed the transmit button, then waited while his radio connected with the base.

A moment later, a man's crisp voice spoke through the radio, "This is Naval Base Okinawa."

"Fleet activities, Okinawa?" Wyatt spoke quickly, letting the words tumble out of his mouth as concisely as possible. "This is the *USS John S. McCain*, current position approximately ten-point-two degrees north, one hundred and fourteen-point two degrees east, stationed about twenty-one clicks from Gaven Island. We've just received a warning from the Chinese Navy and wanted to inform you of our current situation. They stated if we do not leave their waters, they will take action against us."

A momentary pause followed Wyatt's message, then the communications officer some two thousand kilometers away replied, "Are you sure of this, *McCain*?"

Wyatt shrugged, then remembered that the radio operator in Okinawa couldn't see the gesture. He said, "That's what was communicated to us, Okinawa. Granted, his English wasn't that great, but it seemed pretty clear to me. Please advise."

"Standby, *USS McCain*." Silence followed this instruction as the radio operator went to relay the message to the Officer on Duty. Once he had his instructions from his OOD, he could follow up with Wyatt.

Despite the unease nipping at him, Wyatt knew he had to be patient. The hiss of static filled the void between them, and he stepped back from the radio to glance around the bridge of the *McCain*. Upon seeing Captain Williams pacing on the flybridge a few meters away, probably feeling as anxious as he did, he looked back at his station. Various lights flickered on the communications system before him, indicating that signal was coming through loud and clear. The helmsman stationed to his left, a stocky man with close-cropped blond hair, was focused on keeping the *McCain* steady in their current position. Next to him, the radar operator, a man by the name of Garcia, stood with his arms crossed over his chest. Behind him, the sonar operator held a similar pose. They had been manning their stations before the call from China had come in, but both had been eyeing Wyatt once they realized the context of the message.

Garcia now raised a questioning brow at him and asked, "What do you think all that's about?"

Wyatt replied, "China," then shrugged helplessly at him. What else could he say? They both knew the threat the contentious country posed. "I don't think they're bluffing this time."

"Well, let 'em try," Garcia said flatly, his dark eyes narrowed. "We'll blow those bastards out of the water if they pull any shit."

The sonar operator exchanged a glance with Garcia, shook his head minutely, then scratched the back of his neck absently as he said, "They're just blowing off hot air, man. It's probably nothing. Hell, they'd be idiots to even try such a stunt. Garcia's right, though. We'll turn their ship into scrap metal if they *do* try."

Wyatt opened his mouth to answer, perhaps agreeing with him, when his radio clicked and a staticky hiss filled his ear. He held his breath. Was it Okinawa already? His hopes were dashed as a familiar and unwelcome voice flooded his ear once more.

"*USS John S. McCain*, People's Republic of China now warn you twice of your trespass in our water. We give you final warning now. We give no other communication after this message. Please confirm message and leave immediately from our water."

They did not wait for Wyatt to reply. Static followed the message.

A churning bolus of acid churned in his stomach, and he considered the communications panel before him before looking at his captain. On the bridge, Williams had paused mid-stride and now stood frozen, his eyes fixed upon Wyatt. Up until this point, he had only gotten a third-party relay of what China had been telling them. Now that he was closer, he could hear it for himself. He stood in a strained at-ease position as he considered this newest message from China.

Wyatt met the captain's eyes uncertainly, his own expression questioning. "Captain?"

"Still nothing from Fleet Activities?" Williams asked. It was a rhetorical question. Had they already responded, Wyatt would have promptly told him about it. The communication's officer was far too diligent to not relay critical information to the captain.

"No, sir." Wyatt shook his head.

Williams sighed. His furrowed brow betrayed the tension headache probably forming already. "This isn't the first time China's pulled this crap before, so I'm not too concerned about it. But do me a favor and keep a watchful eye on the sonar and the radar. Just in case."

Troubled as he regarded Captain Williams, Wyatt nodded at the instruction and then said, "Should I go ahead and try contacting Okinawa again?"

"Yes, go ahead." Captain Williams turned away, his feet guiding him once more across the bridge.

Wyatt suspected that by the time the night ended, the captain would wear a groove onto the metal surface of it from his restless pacing. He sighed and settled back into his seat at the communications panel. This night was getting worse by the minute. He cleared his throat, then depressed the button on the radio. "Ah, Okinawa? This is the *USS John S. McCain…*"

CHAPTER TWO

SELF-DEFENSE

02 DECEMBER 2025

CAPTAIN WILLIAMS'S FACE WAS A dark glower. He had been looking forward to this evening with the *Keris* for several weeks, and now China had to demand they leave their waters. Rather than getting a peaceful night of rest after their training exercises, he would instead be trying to prevent an international incident. A dull ache was already starting to form at the base of his skull, a foreshadowing of the tension headache developing there. In a few minutes, it'd blossom into a full-on migraine. At least he could justify that cup of coffee now. The boldness of the People's Republic of China didn't surprise him in the least, however. The nation evidently had all the self-restraint of an aggressive little chihuahua. Their brash words were just another clue of their lack of diplomacy and civility.

"Sir?" The voice of the radar operator, Petty Officer Garcia, rose to meet his ears from across the bridge. "We're tracking two incoming cruise missiles from Gaven Island! They appear to be the Chinese YJ-100s!"

"Come again?" Williams's words sounded hollow in his ears as he still struggled to make sense of what he was hearing.

It was one thing for China to threaten them, and another one entirely to actually fire at them. Garcia repeated his message, the tense words tumbling rapidly out of his mouth, but Williams had tuned him out. If—and it was a strong if   their defensive systems sprang into action in time, then they might have a chance to defend themselves against the Chinese cruise missiles. If they didn't? They were, to put it mildly, dead in the water.

There was no time to think. Williams instinctively drew a deep breath into his lungs. Spittle flew from his lips, his voice unwavering and clear as he barked out his orders to the crew. "All personnel, battle stations. I repeat, all personnel, battle stations. Johnson, activate ship defensive systems!"

Williams mentally detailed the specifications of the missiles as he scanned the horizon for any indication of their pending arrival. The YJ-100s were a subset of the Chinese CJ-10 missiles, and while they were not supersonic, they were still pretty damned fast, clocking in at a rate of Mach 0.9, approximately 700 miles per hour. That meant they would be upon them in less than a minute.

He didn't have to glance around to know that his orders were being followed. The sound of boots thumping on the bridge were enough to tell him his crew had sprung into action. Fractions of a second counted, and any delays could result in the missile successfully striking the ship. Distantly, as though the radar operator was miles away and not standing on the bridge a few meters away from him, he heard Garcia's frantic voice cry out, "Defensive systems activated! Locking onto the missiles now."

Williams stared tensely out onto the horizon, searching for any sign that the threat was zeroing in upon them. There was no time to linger, though. With his crew manning their respective stations, Williams moved quickly to claim his captain's chair on the bridge. Once the defensive systems had been activated, there was very little they could do until they knew it was either a success or failure. All they could do at this point was collectively hold their breaths and pray. A second later, the thunderous report of two missiles departing the ship sounded and heads jerked in the direction of the noise.

Dear God, please…

Twin trails streaked the sky as the anti-ballistic missiles sought their targets. Williams's breath caught in his throat. The YJ-100s were coming in fast, and with only a distance of slightly over twelve nautical miles separating them from Gaven Island, the source of the attack, they would be upon them in mere seconds.

A moment later, he saw it. Quite close to the ship, a brilliant fireball lit up the night sky, and then a second fireball. The *McCain's* defensive systems had worked. The intercept missiles had successfully neutralized the threats, stopping them just before they could make contact with the ship.

The *McCain* swayed from the percussive blast, and Williams found himself feeling uncertain if the wave of dizziness he felt was related to the rocking of the ship or the close call they had just encountered.

He released a quiet sigh. *If China wants a fight, I'll give them a fight.*

The pair of YJ-100s had fortunately been powerless against the defense systems aboard the *McCain*. The destroyer's slick-32, a powerful radar system that was part of the vessel's electronic warfare suite, had been able to detect the conventional cruise missiles almost instantly after the system was engaged. Then the *McCain's* SeaRAM had destroyed both missiles without a problem. Williams knew that the system's ability to quickly recognize and assess threats and then engage them had saved the crew aboard the vessel. There was no doubt the missiles would have blasted a hole through the body of their ship.

Williams closed his hands into a fist, then spun in his chair. His gaze found the Weapons Petty Officer seated at his battle station with his spine erect as he locked eyes with his captain. He seemed to have anticipated an instruction was coming, his focus wholly upon Williams and a brow raised in expectation.

"Johnson."

"Yes, sir," Johnson replied with a half-smile on his face. The rest of the captain's words were unnecessary, but he waited patiently for them nevertheless.

Williams was about to unleash holy hell upon their enemy, and as far as he was concerned, it was unquestionably justified. He was ready to follow through and play his part in seeing that China received missiles in return. He held up his hand, exposing his open palm and splayed fingers to Johnson. "Prepare five cruise missiles and target the cruise missile platforms on Gaven Island. I don't want to give China any chance to think about attacking us again."

"Yes, *sir*." Johnson turned back to his station with practiced precision, his fingers punching buttons on his console in rapid succession as programmed the order into the computer.

With that key task assigned, Williams turned away from the weapons officer and looked around the bridge for Wyatt. The communication's officer was also at his station and, like Johnson, seemed to have been anticipating a command was forthcoming. His finger hovered over the communication button on his console as his eyes met with Williams's. All he had to do was say the word, and Wyatt was ready.

"Wyatt, I want you to contact Okinawa." His voice was resonant and carried clearly for all the crew around him to hear. "Let them know that China has just fired upon us with two cruise missiles. Let them know that we will be returning fire."

During this exchange, all five missiles fired in rapid succession out of the aft portion of the ship and straight up several hundred feet before pivoting toward Gaven Island, their smoke trails punctuating their flight toward the targets.

"Yes, sir," Wyatt said obediently. He turned to his radio, picking up his handset, and brought it up to his mouth. "Okinawa? *USS McCain.*"

Glancing around the bridge, Williams focused briefly on each of the faces of his crew, all mirroring his own. Unbridled outrage and fury reflected from them, the sentiment seeming to be collectively shared between them. The night had gone to shit, and righteous anger thumped in Williams's head. Instead of blotting out reason, though, it made it more acute. Was he exacting revenge for their attack? Hell yes, he was. But he was also following the ROE, as he was obligated to do. The sense of satisfaction that would follow as he destroyed the missile systems on Gaven Island was only part of his motivation.

The *McCain* was still afloat. Unlike the *Titanic*, this vessel was actually all but unsinkable. Nobody had dared to utter that sentiment aloud, of course—maritime suspicion had all but forbidden such comments, even in this modern era—but she'd had her share of skirmishes throughout her prolific thirty-year career. Sure, she had been taken out of operation a few times over the past three decades, but it was never anything she hadn't been able to bounce back from.

"Captain?" Johnson's voice matched the annoyed expression on his face. "China's defensive systems on the island were able to intercept and destroy our missiles. What do we do?"

Hell yes, they would be firing more missiles at them. Did the Chinese Navy simply think they'd give up because their first barrage had been taken out? Williams had a response for Johnson ready on his lips, but they were cut off by the radar operator behind him.

"Uh, Captain." The high note of concern in Garcia's voice was unmistakable as he broke into the conversation. Williams froze at the sound of it, then turned swiftly to face him. "There's, uh…there's another incoming missile, sir, and it's coming in extremely fast."

"Another missile?" He thought of the ship's defensive systems. The YJ-100s had been clocking something like 700 miles per hour, and with Gaven Island just over twelve miles away, it had closed the distance between them in just over fifty seconds. Mounting horror rose inside him as he realized what the petty office was saying. If this new threat was even faster, then that meant there was only one thing it could be. A DF-100. "Johnson."

"I'm on it, Captain," Johnson said. He turned back to his computer console, verifying that the ship's defensive systems were active and tracking this new threat. When the SeaRAM fired off another round of three defensive missiles at this new incoming Chinese cruise missile, he raised his eyes to Williams. "Missiles fired. It's moving awfully fast, sir. I don't know—"

"Sir?" Garcia interrupted frantically. "The intercept missiles failed to hit the incoming missile. Sir—"

The deafening roar of a hypersonic missile colliding with the *McCain* blotted out all sound, and the night instantly transformed into a maelstrom of fear, pain, and confusion. The DF-100 rammed against the port side of the *USS John S. McCain* with devastating force, sending steel shrapnel and human debris flying through the air.

⸙ ⸙ ⸙ ⸙ ⸙

As it turned out, China had indeed wanted to deal them some damage. And by all accounts, they had unquestionably succeeded. The SeaRAM would not have stood a chance against what China had had in store for the *McCain*. While the infrared surface-to-air missile system had been designed as a defensive mechanism for a number of military vessels across the globe, the one time it mattered to the crew of the *McCain*, it didn't have the capabilities to do its job against hypersonic missiles. Despite having the potential to fire off up to eleven rolling airframe missiles at any one time, none of them could compete with the unfathomable speed of the DF-100.

Williams had been halfway across the bridge when a booming explosion on the port side of the *McCain* knocked him off his feet. A deafening blast had filled his ears, then a high-pitched keening followed. He'd tumbled to the metal body of the *McCain*, his head slamming against the surface.

Stars flashed before his eyes, blotting out his vision with their dazzling light. *What the hell...?*

Pain coursed through him, and the captain was acutely aware of a wash of heat and a brilliant light coming from his left. He turned his head in the direction of the searing heat, ignoring the surge of pain shooting down from his neck. At the bright, blinding light radiating from the port side of the *McCain*, Williams found his mouth falling open in stunned disbelief. The sons of bitches had actually done it. The impressive speed and power of the DF-100s had somehow managed to overcome the destroyer's defense systems, and now the entire left side of the ship was a blinding fireball of sooty smoke and suffocating heat.

Something trickled from his ears, and Williams raised a hand to the left side of his head. He pulled it away, rubbing his fingers together. He didn't need to see the dark liquid on his fingertips to know they were coated in a thin film of blood. Whatever had caused the explosion had also ruptured his eardrums. He struggled to push himself to his elbows, but another jolt of searing pain kept him flattened on the ship's surface. He lay on his back, staring up at the twisted metal of the ceiling looming over him. Despite the fog of confusion trying to blot out any coherent thought, cold suspicion about what had just happened dawned upon him.

Before the missile struck them, he had realized—all too late—it was one of those Dongfeng-100 missiles. The realization of its remarkable destructive force sucked the air out of his lungs. He had read intelligence reports about them but obviously never been on the receiving end of one before. Through the pain and the shock, Williams searched his memory, trying to recall everything he knew about the DF-100s.

Initially revealed to the public in late 2019, there had been little doubt what the intent of a DF-100 was. It had been built to sink ships, namely American carriers, but any large American vessels were fair game. If it sunk anything else? Well, all the better. The missile, called the "Long Sword," had been revealed to the public in a social media ploy to drum up jingoism toward the country. But was it merely just a move to bolster patriotism in the People's Republic of China (PRC), or was it actually a new and viable threat to the security of the United States camouflaged as a marketing ploy?

The American government had scrambled to learn as much as they could about the DF-100 and, in a fairly short amount of time, come up with a bulleted list of notes. They knew it was a hypersonic missile, meaning it could travel at Mach 5 speeds—or higher. Having a missile that could move at over five times the speed of sound was extremely dangerous. While the SLQ-32 electronic warfare suite on the *McCain* could detect and track conventional supersonic missiles, it had difficulty tracking a hypersonic missile. The Long Sword had been designed for one reason and one reason only: to destroy United States naval ships.

And, as Williams—and the rest of the crew aboard the *USS John S. McCain*—had just discovered, it was evidently damned good at it. As its lethal force met against the body of the destroyer, he realized with a vague tinge of regret that Maggie would never get an email reply back from him, nor would he be spending any other future holidays at home with her.

⊁—⊁——⊁——⊁——⊁

Wyatt's death had been swift and merciful, but the same couldn't be said for all of the bridge crew. The rest of them were flung carelessly from the destroyer, their bodies pinwheeling in the air before hitting the water.

A discord of panic immediately followed the explosion. Shouts arose in the chaos, lending to the confusion and fear. The sounds of dying sailors were drowned out by the wailing emergency alarms echoing throughout the body of the destroyer. The explosion had been cataclysmic, ripping through the engine room with a sort of fury that left no chance for the ship to remain afloat. The nose of the ship dipped, weighed down by the oily water flooding throughout the ship. Efforts to manually release the fiberglass-encased life rafts dotting the side of the vessel were at first optimistic, then frantic, as the flames engulfed the sinking ship. Men, their bodies incandescent torches flailing along the deck of the *McCain*, first fell into the brackish waters, then voluntarily jumped into it to put out the flames swallowing their bodies.

Those aboard the destroyer had erroneously believed it couldn't get worse, but they were terribly wrong. The flames navigated their way along the inside of the ship, searching for purchase on the sinking destroyer. Many rooms held little interest to the seemingly sentient fire, containing nothing more than basic naval supplies and equipment. A few held sailors, those souls instantly perishing in the hungry flames. Then the fire made its way into the engine room and licked at the fuel reserves stored there, and the *McCain* lost any chances of survivability.

While the *McCain* had been sinking at a leisurely pace before, it now sunk rapidly beneath the burning waters of the South China Sea. The encapsulated life rafts that had stubbornly refused to deploy minutes before now activated in rapid succession. The pressure of the water at twenty feet below the surface was enough to send the now-inflated rafts to the surface, but there were very few survivors remaining to cling onto them. Nearly a dozen empty rafts bobbed alongside where the *McCain* used to be, and those who hadn't been instantly killed splashed frantically toward them.

A massive plume funneled out through the wound on the side of the destroyer's body, questing tendrils of flame and burning air toward the night sky. The glow from the burning devastation turned the evening light into a twilight haze, illuminating the bobbing corpses floating face down in the water.

In the distance, the crew of the *Keris* watched helplessly as the destroyer they'd been performing routine exercises with just minutes before was engulfed in flames and being claimed by the burning sea. Quickly recovering from the initial shock, the captain commanded the large patrol vessel into action. These were their allies in the water, and they were duty bound to try to rescue them. They had barely started closing the distance between themselves and the drowning *USS John S. McCain* when the Chinese Navy turned their sights onto them.

The message sent to the *Keris* from the Chinese Navy was direct and to the point, stating if they did not leave Chinese waters, they would be subject to the same fate as the American destroyer. The Malaysian ship dismissed the transmission. Whether they didn't believe they could suffer the same fate as the *McCain* or thought their responsibility to the American crew prevailed remains largely unknown. Perhaps they had sincerely believed they could at least lend support to the flailing sailors treading water.

They navigated as quickly and carefully as they could through the floating debris, edging their craft ever closer toward the survivors and life rafts. As the *KD Keris-111* closed in on fifty meters from the survivors, its defensive systems activated, alerting the crew that a threat was closing in.

The five surface-to-air missiles they released in response wasn't enough to save them, though. Their defensive missiles were no match for the Chinese DF-100 cruise missile heading for them.

The anti-ship cruise missile collided with the *Keris* at the same rate with which it had impacted the *McCain*, exceeding Mach 5 as it blasted into the body of the ship. The projectile tore through the sleek exterior of the Malaysian ship, ripping the unsuspecting craft into two large fragments. The littoral vessel, which was much smaller than the *McCain*, didn't stand a chance against the anti-ship missile. Just as flames had torn through the *USS John S. McCain*, the fire instinctively engulfed the *KD Keris-111* as well. Bodies careened into the water, their screams piercing the air as they landed in the inky waves below.

Less than an hour before, there had been a total of two hundred and eighty-one sailors aboard the *USS John S. McCain*. Thirty-three of them had been officers, thirty-eight had been chiefs, and the remainder of the men had been enlisted personnel. The *Keris* had their own complement of forty-five men on board, with a total of eight officers and thirty-seven enlisted men. Of those numbers, seventy-five of the surviving crew of the *McCain* thrashed in the water, struggling to stay afloat as the bodies of the rest of their crew floated face down around them. Nearby, eight survivors of the *Keris* watched in dismay as the Chinese Navy destroyer sailed toward them.

It was fully dark now, the stars overhead blotted out by the thick black smoke that had poured out from both vessels. The chilly water enveloped the remainder of the victims as patches of oily water burned like bleak lanterns in a sporadic pattern around them. Despite themselves, many of them raised an arm to hail the approaching Chinese vessel homing in on them. Unfortunately, the sharks in the South China Sea were faster than the Chinese vessel. Bodies bobbed and jerked on the surface of the water, then abruptly disappeared. Screams punctuated the air briefly and then were silenced as these unlucky men were yanked beneath the surface by the hungry predators.

The Chinese Navy had seemed to anticipate this assault as they flung canisters of shark repellent into the ocean on approach. It did little against the feeding frenzy, but it was enough to keep some of them at bay. Battle weary, shocked, and frightened, the hapless survivors waited resolutely in the ocean for either a swift death by shark or a possible lingering one from their enemy. All in all, the Chinese Navy fished a total of eighty-two men out of the water. From their vantage aboard the Chinese ship, they watched as the *KD Keris-111* slipped beneath the chop and finally disappeared beneath the water.

The survivors huddled together on the deck, guarded by armed Chinese sailors. They knew their salvation from death was not a gift, nor was it mercy. They were now hostages, captives, the prisoners of a war that had not yet officially been initiated but was sure to result due to the actions of the Chinese Navy that night. As they stamped their feet and rubbed their hands together briskly in the cool night air, a collective shiver coursed through each and every one of those men—a chill that was not brought upon them from the brisk air of the night but from the fear of what was going to happen to them at the hands of their newfound enemies.

CHAPTER THREE

James Chase was dying. The bullet wound in his gut spouted hot blood through his fingers, and no amount of pressure applied to the site could stanch the flow. He could feel the thick liquid seeping through the black fabric of his tunic. The material clung wetly to his abdomen, tacky from his blood. The dazzling November sunlight bounced off the yellow sand of the Iranian desert, blinding him, and he blinked salty sweat out of his eyes. He didn't dare lift his hand from the sticky wound in his stomach, though, to brush the limp tangle of dark curls out of his face. A dull roar crested in his ears, drowning out the sound of his own heartbeat pounding in his head.

Yes, James was dying, and there wasn't a damned thing he could do about it. He had done his best to hold off the Islamic Revolutionary Guard Corps (IRGC) soldiers and, up until the fateful shot that had threaded his gut, managed to convince himself he still had a chance of surviving this ordeal. But then the captain of the IRGC had appeared out of nowhere, and with a jeering laugh, pointed his AK-47 into James's abdomen and pulled the trigger. The sensation of lead ripping through his flesh, ricocheting off his vital organs and pulverizing them, had been excruciating. James knew it would all be over soon and silently prayed for the warm embrace of death to put an end to his suffering.

Blackness descended upon him, wrapping him in a cold shroud. Despite the heat of the sun beating down upon him, he shivered violently. The chill seemed to permeate his bones, and he realized his teeth were chattering. Was it more from the cold or the shock of the blood loss? He didn't know. The sweat clinging to his body was now cold, icy cold, and the blood oozing from the wound in his stomach had clotted and congealed. When James pried his hand away from his stomach and peered down at it, a new horror flashed across his face as he realized the blood was now thick, like ichor, and matted to his fingers. He opened his mouth to let out a cry, and the sound wrenched from his throat, weak and panicked. He didn't like the unmistakable note of fear in it, but he couldn't help it—he was afraid. He was terrified. He couldn't breathe. He couldn't shout. All he could do was die.

With a start, his eyes flew open. The Iranian desert fell away, and he sucked a deep breath of air into his lungs. Despite his eyes being wide open, he couldn't see. Blinking rapidly, he tried to clear his vision. A faint glow off to his right drew his attention. A numerical readout next to his head informed him that it was 0334 hours, and as he watched, the digital clock changed to 0335 hours.

James was back in his bedroom. Safe. The threat had been neutralized, but not by his own accord. The only thing that had separated him from imminent death was the thin filament of reality, the end of the nightmare that had plagued him for the past decade. The dream was almost always the same, or a similar variation thereof. Knowing that it was just a nightmare did little for his sense of relief. He knew that the next time he closed his eyes, there was a chance he would have to relive it all over again.

Operation QuickSand was supposed to have been a routine "capture if possible or kill if warranted" mission, but to James it had been so much more than that. Even though nearly eleven years had passed since the fateful mission that had seen the death of nearly all of his friends—almost an entire team of elite Delta soldiers, slaughtered by an unexpected ambush and a betrayal from their intelligence source—James couldn't erase the memory from his head. Even if he wanted to, though, he knew it was the price he paid for surviving when so many other men had died.

He sighed. Already the cobwebs of the nightmare were fading away and the shivers were starting to subside, but he wouldn't be getting any more sleep that morning. James rolled over onto his side, pulling his bedsheet up to his chin. A thin dew of sweat had erupted over his body, but now the cool air coming from the vent overhead was causing a new chill. His eyes stared out into the darkness, fixed and distant. The dream was a blurry haze now, though his shoulder and thigh throbbed in the memory of his time in the Middle East. A white, puckered scar rested high on his chest, its twin lingering on his leg. A third one streaked across his bicep, an ongoing reminder of the series of bullets that had greeted him that November day.

James pushed himself up into a sitting position and swung his legs out from beneath the covers. His bare feet landed on the hardwood floor, and he yawned, his thoughts already moving to the day ahead. His hand swept across his face, wiping the last vestiges of sleep from it. These days, he wore his hair neat and trim, far from the shaggy growth that had adorned his face and scalp back during his Delta days. More silver lingered at his temples than he cared to admit, and it seemed as though the lines etched into his face were growing deeper by the day.

James rose to his feet, then turned back toward his bed and tugged the comforter up to his pillow. He grimaced at the damp bedsheets beneath his fingertips. Damn it. He had sweated through them *again*. That meant he'd need to do laundry again tonight. He felt like he was doing it more and more often these days, another unfortunate side effect of these steadily worsening nightmares. With a resigned sigh, he pulled the comforter back down. The last thing he wanted was to sleep on musty sheets. Maybe if it wasn't a long day, he thought he would have time to stop at the Exchange at Fort Belvoir and just purchase five sets of sheets so he could avoid doing laundry so often.

His thoughts went to the day ahead of him. He needed to be at the secretary of defense's house by 0500 hours to escort him to his office in the Pentagon, and traffic in DC was notoriously bad anyway but, during the tourist season, significantly worse. If he wanted to make it to the SecDef's residence on time, he'd have to get an early start. As much as he wanted to catch an extra half hour of sleep, he knew he needed to get moving. Already his stomach was growling, a reminder that he hadn't eaten enough after his session in the gym the night before.

Breakfast it was, then. James padded across the floor into his modest kitchen and flipped the switch on the coffee pot. It rumbled to life, and a moment later, the aromatic scent of Black Rifle Coffee filtered through the apartment. He opened his refrigerator and let his dark eyes sweep over the contents within. How long had it been since he had gone grocery shopping?

He made a mental note to swing by the Commissary on his way home that evening. Two eggs sat in a cardboard carton on the middle shelf, and next to it, the last couple ounces of his pumpkin spice flavored coffee creamer. It would have to do.

James turned on the burner and slipped two slices of bread into the toaster. The coffee pot gurgled as the carafe filled with the heady brew. He cracked the two lone eggs into the skillet and peered sleepily into it as the egg whites simmered in the pat of butter that enveloped them.

James Chase had never been much of a morning person, and despite sticking to his routine for six years now, he still hadn't grown accustomed to waking up before dawn. If it were up to him, he'd preferably not roll out of bed until closer to 0800. Even with an acute sense of discipline firmly instilled into him by his twenty-nine years in the military, James still couldn't fully commit to rising before the sun. Uncle Sam frowned on those who couldn't pry themselves out of bed in the early hours of the morning, and as a Criminal Investigation Division special agent in the US Army, sleeping in was far too similar to being lazy. James could reluctantly agree that he was anything but.

Lean and muscular and slightly above 5'8" in height, James was quiet, observant, keenly intelligent, and—according to the number of ex-wives and girlfriends he had left in his wake—sharply intense in his presentation. His calm demeanor and ruggedly striking appearance drew the women in, but his track record proved he couldn't maintain any of these relationships. Work always prevailed, his one true and loyal mistress. James had seen many casualties during his military career, his luck with women among them. Oh well. He couldn't win them all.

James didn't bother with a plate. He fished a fork out of his silverware drawer and stabbed the eggs sizzling in the skillet and put them in his mouth. He chewed automatically, mulling over his schedule for the day. As a CID special agent, he always had to remain mindful and alert while onshift. The first leg of his job started at Secretary Michael Andrews's house. James provided executive protection to the chief executive officer of the Department of Defense, also known as the secretary of defense. This duty had been bestowed upon him after five years of grinding away behind a desk in a small windowless office, and while it was certainly a prestigious opportunity, there was no question as to how grueling and taxing it was on him.

Other CID agents would eventually rotate through Protective Services Battalion (PSB) a few times in their career. Such a responsibility was assigned out of PSB, located in Fort Belvoir, Virginia. Like all higher-ups in the United States government, there was a certain level of authority that came with each assignment. The more elite agents would find themselves assigned to the SecDef himself, but less demanding details were still considered a prestigious responsibility. James had proven himself capable above all of his other peers. While there were other CID agents on the protection detail for Secretary Andrews, James's proven leadership skills had awarded him the coveted PSO role for the SecDef, code name Cobra.

James would be lying if he didn't acknowledge that he was proud he had been assigned as the Personal Security Officer (PSO) for Andrews, but it didn't change the fact that it was the most demanding of all protection details available to CID agents. Other agents were content with the smaller protection details, protecting the chairmen of the Joint Chiefs of Staff or Army Chief of Staff. James's outstanding work had caught the eye of the higher-ups in the battalion, and his progression from being a CID agent supervising a CID office, to being the PSO of the protection detail for the SecDef was a natural one.

Still. James wouldn't trade the opportunity for a lesser responsibility. Even if he hadn't been told who he would be protecting, he would have volunteered for the assignment. It was just part of his nature. If there was a hard job to do, he couldn't simply sit idly by and wait for someone else to step into the role. He not only had a keen sense of personal responsibility, but he also had an innate tendency to want to also look out for others as well. With his training and skills, as well as a pressing desire to challenge himself, it was only natural that he would assume such a role. And over time, he and the secretary got to know each other and became friends.

James scraped what was left of his breakfast into the sink, then placed the skillet in the sink as well. A squirt of soap and a stream of hot water was sufficient to satisfy his need for cleanliness and order. He'd hit the pan with a sponge before he left the house, but for now, it could sit. He swigged down the rest of his coffee, then placed the empty mug into the sink next to the skillet. He turned back toward his bedroom, weaving his way through and into his bathroom. He deposited his boxer shorts into the laundry hamper in the corner of the room as he made his way to the shower.

Moving automatically, he adjusted the dials of the shower, then stepped in. The steam from the hot water plumed up around his body, shaking off any remainders of sleep that may have clung to him. He quickly lathered up his thick, dark hair with shampoo, then rinsed it off beneath the stream from the showerhead. The rivulets of soap trickled down his tanned skin, dragging over the white puckered scars on his abdomen and thighs. He glanced over them briefly, his lips dragging down in a quick frown before he turned off the tap. There was no point in lingering over them. They already occupied enough space in his mind and in his dreams. James didn't particularly like being scarred up, but they became interesting talking points with the ladies.

James dried off, then got dressed in front of the bedroom mirror in a crisp black suit, complete with a matching black belt and a solid red tie. The starched white shirt he wore beneath the plain suitcoat didn't dare mar his appearance with a single wrinkle, and its long sleeves skimmed over his broad shoulders and muscular arms comfortably thanks to the precise work of his tailor. The bullet resistant vest beneath his coat was stiff and unwieldy, but he was used to its comforting weight. He tucked his two-way radio earpiece behind his ear, securing it with a firm push of his thumb, then clipped the radio on his belt. He clipped the speed-draw holster on and slid his Sig 9mm pistol in, then double checked both. The M18 gleamed dully back at him in the light of his bedroom, as he slipped two full 17-round mags into the magazine holder on the belt, completing the ensemble.

A final sweep around his kitchen confirmed there would be no dirty dishes or utensils waiting for him when he got home that evening and, with a glance back over his shoulder to make sure he hadn't left any lights on, he stepped outside into the frigid morning air. Immediately, a sharp gust of wind probed at his jacket, ruffling his close-cropped hair. In the distance, a robin quietly sang its lonesome song, the only sound other than James's feet moving almost silently over the icy parking lot of his apartment complex. One of his neighbors had strung twinkling holiday lights along the perimeter of the apartment building, and the cheerful hues reflected off the layer of snow in his driveway.

He rounded the front of his tuxedo-black Ford F-150 Super Crew 4x4 truck propped up on Wrangler off-road tires while he glanced appreciatively over the rugged, hulking body of the vehicle. Some men had girlfriends, but James had his truck. The black brush guard protected the front of the pickup, and a flat black remote-controlled winch rated to tow up to 15,000 pounds was attached to the center of the brush guard. He gripped the ice-encrusted handle, pulled the door open, and slipped behind the wheel.

Almost automatically, he flipped the radio on with a twist of his wrist, and the familiar sound of the talk radio host's voice filled the cab. The morning was still and quiet, and James kept half an ear on the morning news as he drove, his thoughts on whether or not all government agencies would be taking the day off because of the snow. The snowplows had already been through this neighborhood, leaving heavy white mounds of snow piled up on both sides of the roadway. Even with his heater running full blast, James could still see small puffs of his breath every time he exhaled.

As he navigated the frozen roads, his thoughts went once more to the day ahead of him. His first duty of the day would be to rendezvous with the secretary of defense at his residence. After meeting with him and moving him in the motorcade to the Pentagon, the second leg of his job would start. Most of the time, James could be found sitting behind a desk at the Pentagon, slogging through the seemingly endless stream of Non-Commissioned Officer Evaluation Reports and Officer Evaluation Records as well as all the mandatory online training. Even as a CW4, James wasn't off the hook for these tedious performance evaluations and training courses. Staying on top of them was necessary for contributing to the perception that he was a good leader.

No, the idea of chipping away at the Threat Awareness and Reporting Program (TARP) later that day didn't excite him either, but why should it? Frankly, he liked the predictability of it. However, he couldn't help but wonder if he had made the right choice to give up his position as a Delta team member. Being part of the unit was in his blood, and it wasn't something that could be given up easily. The camaraderie forged there was unbreakable, and James still sent both Ginger and Tex —as well as his other friends from the unit—regular correspondence. Ginger had been pestering him to meet up for karaoke, and while the man had a voice that would put a banshee to shame, James was looking forward to seeing him again.

Still. One perk of the job as a CID agent, though, was not having to dodge bullets anymore. So that was a good thing.

Traffic was as to be expected, but James still made good time getting to the secretary of defense's home. The route was a familiar one from his apartment complex in Lorton, Virginia. The I-95 North was packed with the usual morning commuters, his E-ZPass gave him access to the toll road and allowed him to bypass most of the rush-hour traffic. Sure, it was a little pricey, but it was worth every penny to help keep him from sitting in deadlocked traffic. He arrived at the Washington DC residence of Michael Andrews a few minutes early, then turned off the engine of his truck. James sat in his parked pickup, listening to the engine click as it cooled, as he scrutinized the house looming before him.

From the exterior, it looked just like any other vintage colonial house in the neighborhood, with a fresh coat of white paint on its exterior and eaves jutting out from beneath the dormer windows peeking out over the second floor. Someone had evidently been feeling the Christmas spirit at the Andrews household, and white icicle-style lights rimmed the rain gutters. A squat snowman, complete with a carrot for a nose, completed the whimsical décor. James had no doubt that Andrews's wife had a hand in seeing the house transformed into a winter wonderland, though he had an inkling suspicion she had somehow wrangled a CID agent into assisting with the makeover. One of the agents loved to decorate for the holidays, and James was sure Agent Sharp had single-handedly raised the stock price of Amazon a few dollars during the holiday season. And, no doubt, she probably had a hand in this as well.

The house, erected over a century before in the early 1920s, was surprisingly well maintained for its age. James swept his eyes over it as he stepped out of the car, swinging the door shut behind him. Its thud was almost inaudible in the morning calm, but James knew that the personnel inside the house had already spotted his presence over the camera that scanned the driveway and part of the road.

He strode across the driveway, his feet crunching over the snow as he navigated toward the rear entry of the house. As he crossed the driveway, he glanced up at the lip of the white-frosted eaves. The solitary red eye glowed from each surveillance camera, acting as a subtle indicator as to their location. Pinpointing their location was not an easy task for the untrained eye, but James knew where to look to spot them. He made eye contact with the cameras hidden up there, nodding briefly at the agent who was watching his arrival in real time from the feed.

There were several cameras installed around the perimeter of the house, sending a constant stream of video feed to the agents who monitored it from within the home. While there were no cameras inside the house, a safeguard for Andrews's privacy, that didn't mean that he didn't have sentries monitoring the residence around the clock. James knew that there was at least one pair of eyes watching him over the feed as he stepped through the three-and-a-half foot gate that was in front of the house. A cheerful cardinal sang its morning tune as he approached, not bothering to pause their interlude to announce his arrival. He angled his way to the right side of the house to a taller, six-foot privacy fence that led to the backyard. He strode through that gate and to the backyard, making his way down the three steps that led to the back basement door. He paused, listening for any sounds of activity inside the house. From James's vantage, the house was quiet.

Even before James stepped through the door, he knew what he was going to find. James had the layout of the house memorized. He could navigate it with ease, even with his eyes shut. It wasn't so much his eidetic memory that helped him; it was part of his training when he was in Delta. That internal memorization had saved his life when he was in Mehran. He hoped he would never need to recall it in the SecDef's house, but he knew he could count on this ability if he ever needed it. Being able to swiftly and safely usher Andrews out of the house—or any building, really—was a skill that was mandatory in his line of work. While the threat of bodily harm against him was slim, it was still a viable risk, and James was ready to move into immediate action should it be required of him in an emergency.

James turned the handle of the door and stepped through. The door sensor chimed at the motion, broadcasting his arrival, then the door clicked shut behind him. The two men inside the basement control room glanced up at the tone, then resumed their tasks. A single man stood in the room James had entered, and he nodded in greeting at the man standing in the basement kitchenette. The friendly, open face of Agent Sam Peters acknowledged the nod with one of his own.

The basement behind the SecDef's house had been converted into a command post, complete with a cozy kitchenette. That's where Sam stood, an easy smile on his face as he recognized his friend standing in the door-way. Behind him, a door led to the rest of the security post. If James craned his neck to peek behind Sam, he'd see a spartan office, unassuming in its decorations. It sported two desks, three computers, and two typical, land-line phones. Beyond that, there was a small bathroom, finished in plain, beige tile. Two bedrooms were tucked away in this downstairs space, giving the PSO and the communicator a place to sleep on their overnight shifts. They both needed to be with the secretary twenty-four hours a day, seven days a week. There were three CID agents that worked as PSOs for the sec-retary, and three communicators as well. They worked on-shift three days and were off for three days, and other days were designated for training. It was a complicated schedule, but they made it work.

The air force communicator had the responsibility of making sure the secretary had the ability to communicate with the Pentagon, and the White House, in times of crisis. In addition to providing several different means of communication to the Pentagon and the White House, as her title sug-gested, Audra Blake was also responsible for downloading all of the latest classified information from the Pentagon. This was part of her morning routine, and she had become quite efficient at it. All information of global importance that had occurred the night before would be downloaded onto the computer, and being able to ensure that it remained classified was criti-cal. When the SecDef awoke and came downstairs from his living quarters, he would then have access to his morning intelligence briefing. Audra was usually meticulous about making sure she downloaded the secretary's morning classified briefing on time.

"Good morning, James." Sam turned a white ceramic coffee mug in his hand, and James's eyes lit upon the mug with sudden interest. "How's your morning going so far?"

"It's going." James raised his hand to his face, stifling a yawn that bub-bled up in his throat. He pointed at the mug in Sam's hand. Sam nodded at the stone countertop behind him, where a fresh pot of coffee rested in the carafe. James followed his glance, giving the younger man a half of a nod in acknowledgment of his unasked question. The nonverbal communica-tion was part of their easy rapport. The ability to convey messages back and forth without saying a word had been earned from working long shifts together for almost a year. "How was your shift last night?"

"Uneventful." Sam took another sip from his coffee cup. His face widened into a grin. "I told you I was watching the Harry Potter movies, right? My son kept telling me to see them, so to get him off my back, I started watching them. Turns out, they're actually pretty good. I was just finishing up the last movie when I saw you pull up and walk around the side of the house. Perfect timing, buddy."

"No spoilers," James warned. He poured some coffee into a cup, then reached into the mini fridge on the counter next to it. His fellow CID agents also liked the fancy creamers, and James wasn't about to say no to the sweet peppermint flavoring for his steeped bean beverage. He poured enough into his cup to turn the drink a wan shade of white, then returned the bottle to the fridge. "I always thought those movies were so unbelievable, though. I mean, what about those little gnome-like things running around the joint? How are they able to keep them as slaves in this day and age? I mean, that's a gross civil rights violation. Surely somebody would put a stop to that crap, wouldn't you think?"

"The house elves, you mean?" Sam shook his head. "I'm not going to ruin it for you. You need to watch it for yourself, man. I was surprised I liked it as much as I did. Yeah, it's a kid's movie, but it was pretty smart overall."

"I'll take your word for it." James took a sip from the mug, letting the warm beverage bathe the back of his throat, sweet and strong, then he glanced back up at Sam. "So a pretty quiet night overall, then?"

Sam nodded. "Yep."

James leaned back against the counter, savoring the coffee. In a few moments, he would greet Andrews and they would begin the process of escorting him to the Pentagon. There would be small talk, idle chatter about the day ahead of them and perhaps some speculation on what might await them at the office. It was shaping up to be another routine, uneventful day as a CID special agent, just as he liked it.

CHAPTER FOUR

THE PENTAGON

J AMES FINISHED HIS CUP OF coffee and turned back toward the stainless steel sink of the kitchenette. He twisted the dial and held his hand underneath the flow until the liquid was hot, then let the water pour into the ceramic mug. Keeping the communal area of the basement office was a group effort, and no single agent had a monopoly on doing chores. If they wanted to keep it tidy—and understandably, they did—then they needed to do it themselves. James added a drop of soap to the mug, washed and then rinsed it out, and placed it on the folded tea towel next to the sink for it to dry. They were, after all, military men and women, not children and certainly not slobs.

Even though, he noted wryly as he smoothed out a rogue fold of the terrycloth fabric, *some* did *behave like slobs and needed to be told to clean up occasionally.*

Turning to his friend, James asked, "Is the morning briefing ready?"

Sam nodded and produced a manila folder from the counter behind him. He leaned forward as James reached across the room, accepting the file that enveloped a thin stack of printed out paperwork. This was everything that had been downloaded from the computers just a few minutes ago by the air force communicator, a fairly unorganized sheath of paperwork that would command Secretary Andrews's attention for the majority of the car ride to the Pentagon.

James accepted the folder and leaned back against the counter, drumming the thick cardboard sheath against his thigh. Despite Secretary Andrews's pleasant demeanor, he was particular about having everything ready to go when he appeared downstairs. Having it ready was necessary to help keep his morning running smoothly. While the secretary would never raise his voice against his security detail, his quiet disappointment was almost worse than any reprimand he might give to the team.

James turned the folder over in his hand. "Anything good in here?"

"You know better than to ask me that," Sam said as he shook his head. "It's fresh, though. Ms. Blake got distracted by Harry Potter and was scrambling around at the last minute, trying to get it all printed out."

"That so?" James raised a brow in Sam's direction. Audra Blake was the air force communicator, and the ebony-haired woman was usually disinterested in the antics of the overnight team. Somehow Sam had managed to convince her to watch some of the movie with him. "Those movies are that good, huh?"

"You'd be surprised." Sam pointed at the folder in James's hand with a shake of his head. "I'm telling you, you need to watch it sometime. Be careful with the file, though. I think Blake forgot to staple it together, so the files are running around loose this morning."

"Oh, for crying out loud." James turned away from Sam, pulling a drawer open. He rummaged around, then fished a small stapler out of the drawer and held it up for Sam to inspect. "How hard is it to get things organized on time?"

"Next to impossible," Sam intoned dryly. His hands moved to his hips, a posture of defensive bravado in response to the reprimand from the senior CID agent. "Hey, how long's that stapler been in that drawer anyway? Does the SecDef know we have an unauthorized weapon on the premises?"

"I'll staple your mouth shut. How does that sound?" James returned with no malice in his voice, his exasperation largely exaggerated, an almost fraternal quip. He pulled the files out of the folder and, with a firm squeeze, stapled the sheath of documents together. Then, with a flourish, he dropped the stapler back into the drawer and closed it with his open palm. Satisfied, he held it up for Sam to see. "There. Much better."

"You should get a promotion for that." Sam pointed at the folder in James's hand. Mock admiration replaced the mild irritation there a moment before. "That's called thinking on your feet, James. I mean, I'm pretty sure you just made Secretary Andrews's day that much better by stapling those pages together. I have no idea what he would have done if he had found the paperwork loose in the folder. I'll be sure to let him know what you did for him today. He's going to be very grateful for your hard work. You know that, right?"

James opened his mouth to reply, but a chime sounded overhead, stopping him before he could offer a retort to his friend. He glanced up. The sound meant only one thing: Andrews was working his way down the stairs and would be materializing in the doorway any moment. His remark to Sam would have to wait. He straightened his face into a reserved, polite smile and stood in a casual stance by the doorway of the control room.

Sam grinned at him from across the room.

Secretary Andrews made his way down the stairs to the basement. "Good morning, James. Sam," he said as he descended the last step. Despite the early hour, his steely blue eyes were alert and intelligent, his suit was crisp and neatly pressed, and his silver hair was carefully parted on the side. No cowlick or rogue hair dared ruin his hairstyle. At his full height, the SecDef stood at a modest five-foot-nine, but neither age nor fatigue had taken any of his powerful bearing away from him. Slim and muscular, Secretary Andrews easily appeared a decade younger than he actually was.

"Good morning, sir." James cleared his throat and shot a pointed glance at Sam.

Sam squared his shoulders in response, his face settling into a quiet mask. Playtime was over. Moving forward, they needed to remain focused and on their A game.

Secretary Andrews extended his hand toward James, and James transferred the file into the secretary of defense's grip. His other hand clutched the handle of a black leather briefcase. The man glanced down at the sheath of papers, then back at James. "You ready to go?"

James nodded and, with a final glance back at Sam, turned toward the stairs. He raised his left wrist to his mouth and said clearly into the radio transmitter, "Cobra is en route. Go ahead and pull up next to the driveway for us, please."

He led Secretary Andrews up the basement stairs, through the kitchen, and to the front door. Pausing on the front stoop, James scanned the front yard. The sun was already starting to peek over the horizon, and although it hadn't fully broached the tree line, the yard had already taken on the flush pink glow of early dawn. He then moved aside, allowing the secretary of defense to take the lead. He followed closely, his eyes sweeping back and forth beyond Secretary Andrews as he walked.

Ahead of them, the two-vehicle motorcade sat staged in the parking area. A driver sat in the front seat of the lead vehicle, his face turned forward. He glanced over, his expression unreadable as he peered at them, and nodded minutely in acknowledgment of the secretary's arrival, then returned his gaze ahead of him. James knew the man was already keeping a vigilant watch of the driveway and surrounding area. While the risk of incident was low, it was something they all remained careful of while on-shift.

The secretary paused, and James moved ahead of him, circling around toward the rear passenger side door. He reached out, gripped the door handle, and swung it open. The Chevy suburban was heavily armored, and the weight of the door never ceased to surprise him. The up-armored reinforcements—including bullet-resistant glass, ballistic panels on the doors and undercarriage, and a similarly reinforced engine compartment—were another of the necessary defenses in place because the strategic value of the SecDef's life couldn't be overestimated. An assault on him could be devastating to the very structure of the American government, and James was acutely aware of this every morning when he completed this routine.

Secretary Andrews afforded James another nod and, lifting his leg and gripping the sturdy handle above his head, hoisted himself into the black SUV. James waited for him to settle into the seat, then put his weight against the door, shutting it without having to slam it. The catch clicked as the door thudded shut, then James stepped to the front passenger side of the vehicle. He took a final glance around the yard, then opened his own door and eased into the seat of the suburban.

James could see the second SUV in the rearview mirror, but he didn't dare touch the mirror. The driver had already adjusted it to his own height, and James could see a hint of the bespectacled face in the corner of the reflection. James buckled his seatbelt, then glanced over at the driver. "Morning, Marc," he said. The man was lean and nondescript, but despite his stoic exterior, James knew he was a hard-working family man. When he wasn't chauffeuring the secretary of defense, he could be seen bringing pictures up of his daughter on his cellphone.

Marc Kovacs turned toward James and regarded him with a wide grin.

"Good morning, James." There was an expansive kind of energy to the man, even this early in the morning.

James had no doubt that Marc had been up almost as long as he had, but unlike James, he would have arisen early by choice. The man was the very definition of warmth and exuberance, and to some, the gregariousness could be almost off-putting. However, what Marc lacked in social awareness, he made up in keen attentiveness and an almost nonchalant approach to his job. Working as a CID agent came naturally to the man, and Marc was admittedly damned good at it.

James glanced back over his shoulder and met Andrews's gaze. The man was buckling his seatbelt, and his briefing folder was already resting across his lap. In a moment, he would prop it open and peruse its contents. James turned back toward the windshield and touched the transmit button on his radio. "Limo is ready."

There was a hiss, then a reply came back over the radio. "Chase is ready."

"Traffic?" James countered.

The answer came back without hesitation. "Minor traffic. Roads are clear."

"Let's go, Marc." James leaned back in his seat.

The personnel within the protection detail followed their own language rules, and to an outside audience, the technicalities could quickly become overwhelming. To James, however, it was all part of the nuances of his job. Learning the terminology of executive protection had been second nature to him, thanks to his experience of performing similar duties in Delta. He had become proficient in less than a week, much to the surprise of the personnel who had been assigned to train him.

The lead SUV in the protection detail had been dubbed the "Limo," and its nomenclature made perfect sense. The role of limousines was to transport high-profile persons from Point A to Point B, and there was no question as to the value of the secretary of defense. Indeed, with just a handful of people more important than him in the nation, his codename needed to match his station. What more fitting name was there for him than Cobra? While his duties may have garnered him less media attention than the president, the responsibilities of Secretary Andrews were numerous. As the primary decision maker only second to the president himself, the secretary was the voice of the Department of Defense. Virtually all weighty decisions in matters of defense went through him, and because of his position within the Department of Defense, he was also a prime target.

James knew his job as Personal Security Officer (PSO) put him directly in harm's way on a daily basis, and he accepted this with a sort of quiet dignity. Everyone eventually needed to face their own humanity on the mortal realm, whether they wanted to admit it or not. Throughout his life, he'd had plenty of opportunities to stare down his own fragile existence and had long since come to terms with his mortality. If such an event arose that he had to serve as the only shield between the secretary and a rogue bullet, it was a strike he was ready to take. It would be his honor.

James wasn't exclusively a human shield for the SecDef, however. As the PSO to the secretary, he was also sort of a liaison for him as well. Marc was the driver of the Limo, and unless Secretary Andrews addressed him directly, he was to remain silent throughout the entire ten-mile route to the Pentagon. This often proved to be a problem for the outspoken Marc, who wanted to chime in on conversations whether he was invited into them or not. James often had to shoot him sharp glances to keep him from saying anything in front of the secretary.

Despite being able to easily follow the rare conversation that occasionally occurred within the vehicle, Marc never let his interactions negatively detract from his ability to drive the Limo. The up-armored Limo made it much heavier than a standard SUV, and he knew the vehicle like an equestrian might know their favorite horse. He knew its quirks, its mannerisms, and how exactly he needed to control it. Keeping a trained eye on the flow of traffic around him while operating the Limo was almost second nature to him.

The other SUV in the detail was called the Chase vehicle, and within it were three personnel, two agents and an air force communicator. The driver of the Chase was an experienced CID special agent assigned to the detail, and in the front passenger seat was the shift leader. Their duty was to take charge of managing all the various aspects of the security detail in order to help ensure everything went smoothly. Any issues they encountered on the trip, whether a traffic accident or construction delay, were directly conveyed to James. Even mundane status reports needed to be relayed to the PSO, and James was careful to understand this intel and determine its value. The shift lead was also responsible for reaching out to the Advance Team to get status reports in case there needed to be a change in the route or a complete change in plans.

In the back seat, Air Force Communicator Staff Sergeant (SSG) Audra Blake was responsible for acting as the primary communicator to the SecDef, and despite her minor slip up that morning, she was typically regarded as a highly reliable and trustworthy individual. Her job didn't stop at just printing out classified morning briefing information from the computer and failing to staple it together. She could often be seen with a heavy backpack full of equipment, which was comically large on the petite woman's frame. Regardless, she hoisted the backpack around without complaint, and having it on hand made it easier for the secretary to connect with the Pentagon and the White House from anywhere in the world.

Unlike the Chase bringing up the rear, the Advance Team was responsible for scouting the route ahead of time. This team consisted of an additional two experienced CID special agents, both of whom operated out of a similar black SUV to the Limo and the Chase. In the hour leading up to the arrival of the Principle, the Advance Team carefully navigated the route to ensure there were no security risks that the Limo or the Chase needed to know about. They followed the same route the security detail's motorcade would eventually take, and during their drive, would make observations of any possible issues for the detail. If anything of concern was observed, it was promptly conveyed to the shift lead. The Advance Team also had the responsibility of coordinating with other law enforcement agencies at any events the SecDef traveled to, whether in the National Capital Region nationally, or internationally.

Together, the Chase, Lead, and Advance Team were key to keeping Secretary Andrews safe at all times. There was a sort of harmonious synergy between each group, and they operated like a well-oiled machine. Damned proud of his team, James realized how much he liked being part of a larger, more cohesive organization of soldiers. Having men and women he could depend upon and being part of a group that equally relied upon him gave him immense satisfaction. No, it wasn't the same as being back in Delta, but it was still pretty damned close.

James reached for his radio again, the mic clicking in his ear as he pressed the transmit button. "Moving out. Cobra en route to the Pentagon. We're about ten miles out and are expected to arrive in approximately twenty minutes."

"Got it, Limo," replied the security team at the residence.

Behind him, James could hear the sound of papers shuffling. He afforded a glance back over his shoulder at the secretary. Andrews was peering intently at the stack of classified papers on his lap. With something like dismay, James observed a thin filament of metal resting on the corner of the SecDef's knee. Unlike the hundreds of briefings before that had remained firmly affixed together, Andrews had chosen this day to pick out the staple from the briefing report and fan the papers across both his lap and on the seat next to him. He made a mental note to relay this to Sam. The younger man would get a kick out of this unexpected turn of events.

"Twenty minutes, huh?" Andrews glanced up from the documents on his lap and brought his thumb up to his mouth, wetting the digit, then turned to the next page in the stack. "Should be just enough time to get me through this briefing."

James nodded at him. "Sounds about right with this traffic, sir."

"That is if Marc here doesn't get us lost again?" An impish gleam twinkled in the secretary's eye. The corners crinkled, and he fixed Marc with a grin. "Should buy me another five or ten minutes, at least."

Marc's reaction was subtle, but James saw the man flush a deeper shade at the remark.

He had been on this route for nearly a year, but during his initial attempt at maneuvering the route from the SecDef's house to the Pentagon, Marc had accidentally made a wrong turn. Whether it had been nerves or his relative newness to the region, his innocent error had caused an unexpected fuss that morning. Ultimately, they had arrived with only ten minutes worth of delays, and Andrews had made an offhand joke about him taking a detour to pick up breakfast for the entire team.

The case might have been closed completely on the subject, but Secretary Andrews had brought it up the next day by producing a carefully wrapped croissant from his briefcase. With a deadpan expression on his face, he'd informed Marc that there was no need to detour from the prescribed route as he had brought his own breakfast that morning. The joke had lightened the mood and established the tone of their relationship moving forward. Despite his rank in the government, Andrews was still a human being. Marc was aware that he wasn't just protecting a valuable government asset but a person too.

"That's right, sir," Marc said, and a hint of a smile played at the corner of his lips, hinting at the easygoing man beneath the cleanly pressed suit. "If you need an extra few minutes, though, I do know of a fantastic donut shop up ahead. Just say the word."

Andrews returned the smile, then returned his focus to the paperwork on his lap.

Silence prevailed once more inside the Limo, and James continued scanning the road ahead. The shift lead agent had been correct. Traffic was light, and James recalled how easy it had been even during his drive over to the SecDef's house. The sun was almost fully in the sky now, and the heavy gray clouds were already starting to spit flurries down upon them. By sometime in the afternoon, it was projected to turn into sleet, but for now it was almost pleasant. Maybe he would be able to get home on time that night, after a short trip to the Exchange and Commissary. Hell, if he had time, he might even give his kids a call before he folded for the evening. He was sure they wouldn't mind hearing from their old dad, even if it were only for a few minutes.

The drive to the Pentagon progressed without incident, and even as the Limo was pulling up to the north entrance, James reached for his seatbelt. The hefty SUV rolled to a stop as he finished unbuckling. Marc hadn't even shifted the Limo into park, and yet James was gliding smoothly out of the front passenger side door. He swept his gaze across the parking lot, his eyes lingering across each quadrant of the unloading area. Satisfied there were no suspicious parties loitering in the parking lot, he turned back toward the Limo. Sometime during the commute, Andrews had finished reviewing the morning briefing and tucked all of the files back into the manila folder. They were secured in his briefcase now, and Andrews waited patiently as James opened the right rear door to let him out.

"Thank you." Andrews slid off the leather seat, lowering his head to duck out of the open door.

James nodded in reply. Even though this was part of their routine and James had been holding the door open for the secretary every morning since he'd assumed the protection detail as PSO, Andrews never failed to acknowledge him. Keeping the secretary of defense safe wasn't, at least, a thankless job.

Andrews brushed off the front of his suit with the flat of his palm, knocking the tufts of paper and lint from its freshly pressed wool surface. He then rose to his feet, his polished black shoes planted firmly on the ground outside the Limo, and glanced around them. At this hour, the Pentagon access was uncannily quiet, and there was almost no competing traffic coursing along the I-395. As the day progressed, the Mixing Bowl would become more convoluted. Already, traffic was starting to double in volume along the Springfield Interchange.

James left the heavy door hanging open—a security precaution just in case somebody decided to stage an attack on the secretary and he needed to turn Andrews around and rush him back into the Limo. The SecDef gave him a nod, and they both turned in unison toward the entrance of the Pentagon. Their heels clicked on the pavement as they strode across the walkway, echoing hollowly as they mounted the steps to the entryway. A Pentagon Force Protection Agency (PFPA) officer waited patiently at the doorway, holding it open for James and the secretary. Andrews stepped through the door first, and the PFPA officer moved aside to grant him enough space to enter. James waited until Andrews had cleared the doorway and, with a final glance back over his shoulder, strode through behind him.

The walk to Andrews's office was quiet. Small talk wasn't necessary, and James had no doubt that the secretary's mind was already on the pile of papers in his folder and the day ahead. He paused as he approached the wooden door that separated his office from the hallway. "Well, here we are, sir."

"Very good." Andrews turned toward the door, then glanced back at James a final time. "Thank you. Have a good day, James."

"You too, sir." James waited for the secretary to slip through the door, then he thumbed the transmit button on his radio. It would possibly be the last time he would see the secretary this morning, unless something came up and he had to go somewhere. "Cobra is in." This signaled to the team outside that they could close the Limo door and move out to the Pentagon garage area to park the Chase and Limo SUVs.

He turned back toward the hallway and let his legs lead him down the rest of the passage and then down two flights of stairs. The CID office was plainly decorated, free from unnecessary frill and ornamentation. The only décor, if one could call it that, was an assortment of photographs lining the walls. Each image featured the secretary, depicting various meetings between him and state leaders from other countries. Andrews was in his trademark pose in each picture, a polite yet genuine smile on his face as he gripped their palm with his right hand and patted their shoulder with his left. The minimalist approach suited James just fine.

Other than a solitary photograph of his kids, his desk was immaculately free of clutter. Order and structure were cornerstones of his identity, but they weren't the only facets to his psyche. Trying to calculate who he was through a peek over his oak desk would only lead to more questions. His other noteworthy skills, such as his knack for improvisation and his ability to think on his feet, he kept to himself.

Even though James knew he had a long and boring morning of online training ahead of him, he was grateful to be inside the comfortably heated CID office. While he always preferred to be out in the field, he had to admit that the heated office was a welcome relief on brisk winter mornings. He settled in at his desk and booted up his computer. Yes, the day was undoubtedly going to be dull, but that was all part of this job and he had grown to accept it. Routine. Safe. Mundane.

His gaze went to the picture of his kids on his desk as he leaned back in his chair, locking his fingers together over his abdomen. Yes, being a CID agent was markedly less exhilarating compared to being a Delta operator, but James knew exactly why he had chosen this job over being back in the field. He had all the evidence he needed in the picture frame in front of him.

CHAPTER FIVE

EMERGENCY BRIEFING

JAMES PROPPED HIS CHIN ON his fist and gazed blearily at the illuminated computer screen before him. A yawn slipped out of his mouth, and he stifled it with his palm. He read the sentence on the screen quietly, then clicked Next with his mouse. One slide completed. God only knew how many more to go. The Army Accident Avoidance courses were, ironically, not something he could avoid. Fortunately, they only came around once per year, and when he finished this round of training, he would be done with it for another twelve months. He just needed to slog through one more training course after Accident Avoidance, the Threat Awareness and Reporting Program (TARP), and he'd be good to go.

Around him, four other agents sat at their own respective desks, in front of their computer screens, their monitors showing the same or similar training scenarios. Marc sat directly to his right, and based on the pained expression on his face, he was probably at a similar position on the training course as James. He pinched the bridge of his nose with his thumb and his forefinger, his lips turned down in an expression of distaste. Audra bore a similar, sour expression as trudged her way through the Air Force Cyber Awareness requirement and, once she was finished with that, she would next tackle the Defense Travel System online training course. Across from him, a CID agent by the name of Liz Springer wasn't even pretending to be taking the required online training courses. Her hands were rested behind her head, and her face was turned toward a television monitor mounted to the wall in the corner of the room. To her left sat Charles Trent. Charles, like Springer, was watching the television.

"Y'all believe this bullshit?" Charles asked suddenly.

James glanced up from his computer screen.

Charles extended his hand and gestured at the television monitor.

"What's that?" James rubbed his eyes. They felt grainy and fatigued from staring unblinkingly at the screen for so long. He wasn't quite ready for reading glasses yet, but at this rate, it would only be a matter of time before he'd need them. He blinked at the television where some daytime reality program was playing at a low volume with the subtitles on, and he squinted at them.

Charles pushed away from his desk slightly and turned toward the other men in the room, a look of incredulous outrage positioned on his face. "This show. How are we supposed to believe that paternity of the child belongs to this fella? He doesn't even look like that man's son. And we're supposed to be buying this?"

"Oh my God." Marc let out a groan. "Who let you choose what channel we watch? You know reality television is going to rot your brain, right?"

"No worse than our TARP training," Charles pointed out. He shot a look at James. "What do you think, James? You think there's any snowball's chance in hell that this man is the baby daddy?"

James looked up at the television where a stringy-haired man was arguing his case. The last three of his visible teeth hinted at only a nodding relationship with a toothbrush. If the boy were his child, hopefully he inherited his mother's oral hygiene. "I think Marc may be onto something. Why don't you change the channel, buddy?"

Marc cast a glance at James, then at Charles. "You heard the man. Better get back to work. Don't you still have some paperwork you need to be doing?"

"Did it already." Charles raised a brow at Marc, then returned his focus back to the show. "C'mon now. Lighten up, man. I don't need y'all telling me what to do."

"Pretty sure we can," Marc countered. He ran his fingers through his hair and leaned back, fixing Charles in an amused gaze. "It's that thing we call 'having a job.' You should look into it some time, buddy. Hear it can make your life a little bit easier, with paying bills and all that."

"Not my fault you're a slower reader than me." Charles flashed a grin in Marc's direction. "Was just trying to start a conversation. No hard feelings, huh?"

"Speak for yourself," Marc said. He turned away from Charles. Evidently, his TARP training was more interesting than this conversation with his fellow agent.

"Whatever you say." Charles stretched his arms behind his head, then stood and glanced around the room. "I think I'm going to head to the food court for a few minutes, grab a coke or something to get my energy up. Chatting with y'all is as boring as watching paint dry. Anyone want anything?"

James shook his head, but before he could answer, the phone on his desk trilled. While phone calls to the CID office weren't entirely unheard of, they were still relatively uncommon.

Charles paused at the doorway, an expectant look on his face.

James shrugged and picked up the handpiece, bringing it up to his ear. He held up his finger, and in the background, he heard the television click off. "Chase here."

"James?" The voice of the secretary's administrator filtered through the phone. There was an unmistakable flatness to his tone. "Secretary Andrews just got word that he needs to report to the Situation Room in the Control Center for an emergency classified briefing."

"Say what?" The administrator's words made no sense. The Unified Combat Pentagon National Military Command Center, also known as the NMCC, was an area the secretary visited very infrequently. While the twenty-five hundred square foot facility had been recently renovated with state-of-the-art technology to make briefings—especially emergency briefings—as efficient as possible, it was always secretly hoped that it would go unused. Reporting to it suggested something had happened globally, which usually wasn't good.

"Then I think he's going to head on over to the White House," the admin continued, and James could hear the hollow resignation in his voice. Whatever had happened, he would probably have to meet with the president. "We're going to need you to get your team ready to go."

"I'll get the motorcade ready, and I'll meet the secretary in the hall outside his office. Let him know I'm on my way, please." James set the phone back on the receiver and quickly rose to his feet without waiting for the administrator to answer. Around him, the men stared at him in surprise. He reached behind him, snatching his dress coat from the back of the chair.

"What was that all about?" Charles asked with incredulity at the blank expression on James's face. One foot still halfway through the doorway, the man seemed frozen to the spot.

James didn't answer him right away. His eyes swept across the room, looking at the faces of the personnel in the room. "The secretary is going to an emergency classified briefing in the Situation Room in the command center."

"What??" Liz glanced at the other men in the room, then back at James. "Are you serious?"

James shot a steely glance at Liz. Now was not the time to question him. He shrugged into his suit coat as he spoke, his words coming out of his mouth in a crisp clip as he moved toward the elevator door at the back of the office, placing the radio earpiece into his left ear. "We're going to the White House. Get the motorcade ready. Now. I'll advise you on the radio if anything changes."

Charles stepped aside, his eyes wide as he stared at James.

"Got it," Marc's voice was distant as his fingers went to his earpiece and shoved it back in his ear.

The other team members put on their suit coats and placed their earpieces in as well. They knew not to ask James any more questions. The conversation with Andrews's administrator had been short and he had revealed to them everything he knew already, which wasn't much. But whatever it was, it was urgent and the concerned note in the administrator's voice told James everything he needed to know. As he turned away from the surprised agents and strode out of the CID office, he forced the turning thoughts out of his mind. It would do him no good to speculate upon what was happening, and he knew the secretary would fill him in on the details later.

The two-story ride up in the elevator seemed to take a brief eternity, and James tapped his foot impatiently against the red carpet as it ascended to the main floor. When the door chimed, James slipped his hand through it even before it fully opened, shoving it wider to provide a quicker exit. He wedged his broad shoulders through the door as they slowly eased apart.

Down the hall, Secretary Andrews stepped through his office door, his eyes flickering down to the watch strapped to his wrist as it swung shut behind him. His own face was undoubtedly a mirror of James's own, tense and drawn.

"Sir," James called out. He tried to walk briskly down the hall, but his impatience won over and he found himself jogging the final half-dozen feet to close the distance.

Andrews glanced up as James approached him, and something like relief washed over him at the sight of the familiar face. "James."

James searched the secretary's face with his eyes. "Is everything okay, sir?"

New wrinkles had formed on Andrews's face since he had left him that morning. Deep furrows channeled between his eyebrows, and his blue eyes were anxious as they met his gaze. Then he turned away from James and started down the hall.

For a moment, James was certain Andrews hadn't heard his question, but then the secretary started to speak. His voice was low and urgent, but James heard every word with sharp clarity.

"I can't tell you out here in the hallway, but you should know that the president is going to remote into this briefing." Andrews glanced up at him.

James considered this as his feet propelled him forward in contemplative silence next to the secretary. Andrews's words had chilled him. Finally, he said, "Well, that's not a good sign."

"No." Andrews's gaze remained fixed at the doorway at the end of the hallway. His voice dropped to a hoarse whisper. "It's not."

I wonder what could be going on? James pondered as they continued their journey down the hall. He arrived at the door first and found himself trying to suppress the growing impatience developing inside him. He lifted his finger to the intercom button and pressed it, the request for access ready on his lips. Before he could speak, however, a resonant buzz sounded. The heavy metal door unlatched, granting James and the secretary access.

James cast a glance up at the camera stationed above his head. Protocol mandated he give his security access code, but the air force officer on the other side of the door must have recognized the new arrivals on the security monitor at his workstation. Instead of wasting time waiting for him to enter the access code, he'd overridden the system and buzzed the door open. Bypassing protocol was not normal, so it underscored the urgency to what was happening. James's thoughts went back to the Middle East, when he was with Delta and all the different missions they had gone on together. One of the missions had involved retrieving a tactical nuclear device. Perhaps a terrorist had finally gotten hold of one and used it? The idea was unsettling, and he shoved it aside.

James drew in a deep breath, willing his racing heart to calm down. It was pointless to dwell on the what-ifs. Yes, something bad must have had happened somewhere. He knew that. The concern radiating off the SecDef was almost palpable. But until James knew for sure, he couldn't risk jumping to conclusions. Still, the air force officer overriding protocol to grant them immediate access was unnerving in itself.

Andrews reached out and gripped the handle on the door, then pulled it open. He slipped through, holding it open behind him for James, who followed the secretary closely, letting the door swing shut behind him.

James's gaze swept the room ahead of him as he entered it. He had been in the Pentagon National Military Command Center (NMCC) before, but the sheer size of it—as well as the colorful video monitors lining the walls—was admittedly a little daunting, even for a man with James's advanced technological background. It wasn't the technology itself that made him uneasy. It was what the room was used for that left him feeling unnerved.

The NMCC was a vast space, sprawling across some twenty-five hundred square feet. And square it was. The area was perfectly geometric, with sharp, clean lines running throughout its architecture. None of its real estate was wasted on frills, instead preferring spartan lines and architecture. In lieu of frivolous decorations, every square inch of it was packed with either advanced technology or accommodations for guests who used the facility.

On the north side of the room, thirteen monitors ran along the wall. The first of the monitors started at a mere two feet from the floor, and they climbed the vertical expanse in a neat line. The layout of the monitors on the wall wasn't just efficient, either. It was practical too. One large monitor dominated the center of the layout, spanning approximately ten feet in both height and width. On either side of this primary monitor were six more monitors, clustering together to give a panoramic view of the global happenings they broadcasted to the men and women working in the command center. These smaller monitors were almost a third of the size of the large one in the center, claiming only about three feet in both length and width.

What good were monitors without any personnel to observe them? To help facilitate this, the monitors faced row after row of stadium seats, each row rising gradually up the floor of the NMCC and ending as they neared the south wall of the room. The arrangement of these seats provided military personnel an unobstructed view of each of these monitors, affording them the opportunity to see each screen at a glance.

The stairs led to rows of workstations, twenty-four in all, and each one of the workstations was manned by officers from every branch of military service. In addition to the military staff, one civilian also joined their team, providing additional support to the command center. This individual was provided with direct access and information from civilian intelligence organizations: the Federal Bureau of Investigations, Central Intelligence Agency, National Reconnaissance Office, Defense Intelligence Agency, Homeland Security, and several other organizations that made up the intelligence community, known as IC. It was a highly complex arrangement, carefully thought out, and it worked quite well.

These screens were watched on a continuous, twenty-four hour rotating basis. When one of the staff ended their shift, another one took their place. Manning the Pentagon NMCC without interruption was critical as information of missile launches, troop deployments, submarine locations, and other global military operations was fed to it in real time. Furthermore, if anything of consequence happened to any branch of the military globally, it was promptly routed to the personnel stationed inside the NMCC, and that information would be quickly directed to the proper leadership.

If the NMCC was vital during peacetime, during Combat Operations, its value amplified dramatically. If a military incident occurred, the secretary and the deputy secretary could engage in an almost real-time battle rhythm from the security of the command center in the Pentagon. They would be able to provide operational guidance to all the different commands without needing to depart from the source of all of their intel.

Andrews paused for a moment in the entryway, his eyes brushing over the activity unfolding inside before lighting up on his target. A knowing nod jerked his chin up as he recognized the deputy secretary and the chairman of the Joint Chiefs of Staff, and his stride was steady as he approached the pair of men. From James's distance, he couldn't make out the words of their conversation, but the drawn expression on the SecDef's face was enough to cause concern.

Throughout the room, other clusters of personnel had formed. James could see several other director-level personnel talking, their heads tilted toward one another as they spoke. Their words were a cresting rumble in the room, but James could hear snatches of their conversations and it was evident they were all tense. A thrumming energy coursed through the room, echoing the trepidation he felt.

"Why do you suppose he called us in here?"

James heard the voice come from his left and turned his head to hear it more clearly. It was doubtful the owner of the voice would know what had happened, but James couldn't resist eavesdropping. He strained his ears, listening in on the soft-spoken conversation. The other person in the conversation seemed to be in the same boat, though. Their reply was inaudible, but the original voice's answer mimicked James's current assessment of the situation.

"You think it could be a nuclear incident? I heard the president himself is going to call in…" The voice trailed off into a whisper.

"Gentlemen."

A new person stepped into James's line of sight, and he recognized him immediately as Major Collins, one of the military analysts. Collins was in the air force, and his rank stood out on the lapels of his blue uniform, the golden oak leaves flashing in the dimly lit room.

Collins's face was drawn down in a frown as he approached the side door. "Why don't you come on in? The briefing is about to start."

Andrews glanced up from his conversation with the deputy secretary and the chairman of the Joint Chiefs of Staff at the sound of the major's voice. Collins rested a hand on Andrews's arm, acknowledging his presence, then turned away from the men. Andrews offered a brief handshake to the deputy secretary and the chairman, then stepped away from them. James watched the SecDef's back as the man faded into the crowd, then he took a step toward the Situation Room himself. A stream of a dozen individuals trailed ahead of them, and after a moment's consideration, James allowed himself to get caught up in the flow of pedestrian traffic working their way into the Situation Room.

The briefing was about to begin, and James again felt a thrum of tension course through him. In a moment, he would finally find out what had drawn them all together in the Situation Room. Whatever it was, it was surely something bad, and he couldn't avoid the icy fingers of uncertainty tickling the base of his spine. In all of his prolific, multi-decade career, he had never seen military leaders react like this. Sure, he had been privy to numerous dire situations throughout his term in the military and witnessed a multitude of briefings, but none of them had been like this, that was for sure. James knew with cold certainty that their lives were about to undergo a dramatic shift, and he was not looking forward to what he was about to learn in the briefing.

He had no idea how right he was, but if he had, he might have hesitated before following Major Collins into the Situation Room. James was moving inexorably toward an ultimatum that he had no idea had already been dealt. In just a minute or two, everything he thought he knew about domestic security would be forever changed. Relations between the United States and China had been irreparably damaged, and his actions over the next few hours could very well spell out the fates of hundreds—perhaps even thousands or more—innocent lives.

CHAPTER SIX

THE BRIEFING

J AMES CROSSED THE SITUATION ROOM, his feet moving silently across the carpeted floor as he took care to not bump into anyone while finding a spot in the back corner of the room. There he stood, his arms folded across his chest and his gaze fixed on the scene before him. A glance around the room confirmed he was the only person propped against the wall. The other various personnel, who also happened to be the top twelve military leaders in the Pentagon, claimed twelve leather chairs at a large, solid wood table that ran the length of the rectangular room. Unlike the NMCC, the Situation Room was a smaller, more rectangular space. The floor covered a surface area of about fifty feet by forty feet, allowing ample room to accommodate those who were seated at the wooden table.

Andrews leaned forward in his seat and let his eyes lock on the screen at the far wall of the room. The monitor was still dark, but in a few moments, the president's face would occupy part of that screen. His body was tight with anticipation, his eyebrows drawn together in a frown as he fixed his focus on the monitor. James could see the thumb and forefinger of his left hand reach automatically for the heavy ring on his right ring finger, twisting the black metal back and forth around the digit, a nervous gesture that was a trademark behavior to the man. Just as quickly as it began, however, it immediately ceased. Not everyone who knew the secretary was aware of this tic, but James had grown quite familiar with it throughout his tenure with Andrews. It was all the evidence James needed to gauge the emotional climate of the man. The SecDef was extremely upset, but he was containing himself with remarkable composure.

James followed the gaze of the secretary to the large video monitor attached to the back wall. The four-foot by four-foot screen was dark, and James could see the subdued faces of all the men and two women seated at the table reflected in it. The blackness of the screen exaggerated their features, making them appear haggard and drawn. It wasn't much of an optical illusion, and James had no doubt they all felt as old as they looked in the dark screen. Nobody dared remove their eyes from the monitor, lest they miss some important message coming from the lifeless screen. Somebody coughed, and someone else tapped the end of their pen on a legal pad in front of them. Other than that, the room was silent.

From the corner of his eye, James could see Major Collins navigating his way across the room. James couldn't read the expression on his face. Whatever the major knew, he was keeping it to himself for now. In a moment, however, they would all be privy to these private, troubled thoughts. Collins stopped at the head of the table, positioning himself in front of the Secure Video Tele-Conferencing (SVTC) screen. His voice was stark as he said, "Good morning, ladies and gentlemen."

There was a quiet murmur in response to his greeting. A few people exchanged impatient glances with one another, as though they could mentally will him to finally start talking.

Be careful about what you wish for, James thought. He felt it himself, the dueling desire to know what had happened and the mounting dread at what he was about to learn.

Collins tapped a button on a computer in front of him, and the SVTCs screen lit up behind him. A second later, President David Thomas's face flashed up on the bottom right corner of the screen. Another ripple moved through the room. It was one thing to know they would be privy to a classified briefing with the president. It was another one entirely to see him already waiting patiently, ready to begin speaking. If he were anxious, he didn't let on. Unlike the drawn faces of the men and women in the room, the president's expression was reserved.

Major Collins reached down and grabbed a small black remote sitting on the sideboard beneath the monitor. He pressed a button on it, and the lights in the room dimmed. Another click on the keyboard in front of him caused a picture to flash up on the monitor. James watched as an image of the ocean filled the screen. The water was a deep shade of blue. Intermittent cloud cover dotted the sky, and no daylight illuminated the dark expanse overhead. Several looming shapes in the background appeared to hint at the presence of islands. The picture itself was remarkably high resolution, clearly pulled from a satellite image.

"This image," Collins said, raising his right arm to point at the monitor behind him, "was taken from one of our satellites over the South China Sea. It was taken approximately two hours ago."

A hush fell over the people in the room and they collectively held their breaths, waiting anxiously to hear what the major would say next as they stared at the clear picture on the monitor before them.

Collins took another step closer to the image and turned his body slightly toward it, his eyes sweeping over the various landmarks displayed on the monitor. "At right around the same time this picture was taken, the naval base in Okinawa received an emergency radio call from the *USS John S. McCain.*"

Heads nodded at their awareness of the naval base in Okinawa.

Major Collins pressed a button, and the picture changed. This new image was identical to the first image, albeit a zoomed in picture. The resolution of this image was of slightly higher quality, and James could make out the outlines of two ships in the foreground.

"In this next photograph," Collins said, taking his eyes off the image for a moment to glance back at his audience, "you can see two ships in an area with several islands."

A low gasp rippled through the room. One ship was in severe distress, with flames and smoke billowing out of its body. A smaller ship some distance away appeared from its wake to be in the process of turning toward the larger one, possibly trying to lend support to the larger vessel.

Collins said, "The ship that's on fire and has smoke coming out of it is the *USS John S. McCain.*" He paused for a beat, allowing this information to sink in. Then he said, "The other smaller vessel is the Malaysian littoral-type ship, the *KD Keris-111.* According to the intercepted communication, it was trying to move into position for a rescue operation."

It was trying. That implies it wasn't a success. A chill coursed down James's spine. His eyes narrowed as Collins changed the image.

"This next photo…" Collins said as he turned back toward the monitor. His brow creased at the image. Even though he had known what it would be, it didn't change the gravity of the content featured in it. The *McCain* was no longer in the image, and the only sign that it had ever existed was a burning patch of oily water on the left-hand side of the image. Now the *Keris* was nearer the oily water and engulfed in a fiery explosion. He cleared his throat, then continued, "With this image, we know that the Malaysian ship was also hit by a cruise missile."

James cast a glance over at Andrews. The secretary had a deep frown on his face. His body was tense, and he leaned over the desk as he stared at the image. His fingertips were pointed at the monitor as though he could reach through the screen and rescue the men floating in the black waters of the South China Sea.

James was certain the man had no idea how his pose appeared, but James felt a wave of compassion for the man. It was clear that it pained him to see these men, American sailors, dying so brutally. Before he had been appointed to Secretary of Defense, Andrews had worked his way up to being a marine general. The corps and the navy had been like a second family to him, and his tough-as-nails exterior hid a soft spot for these service members. James understood the sentiment and felt it reflected on his own face. These weren't just random dots in the water. They were Americans, young men with mothers and wives and families.

"You can see the blur of the missile here," Collins said. He extended a finger toward the screen, pointing out the faint shape in the corner of the monitor. "With this knowledge in mind, we suspect the *McCain* was also hit by the same type of missile."

The image changed to show a grim timeline of events that immediately followed the attack on both ships. The first image featured a Chinese destroyer moving toward the bodies floating in the water. James could see the black dots in the infrared image, which undoubtedly represented the men who had either jumped overboard or been thrown from the convective force of the explosion.

Major Collins swept his hand in small circles in front of the monitor, pointing out various items of interest in the picture. "As you can see from this image, after the explosion, the Chinese naval ship was moving in to start rescue operations."

He changed the image again. It was similar to the previous image, showing the vessel closing in on the men. The next image revealed the Chinese vessel methodically collecting the living bodies from the sea. The dead were left to bob lifelessly in the waters. They were of no value to the Chinese Navy and were, sadly, ignored by them.

James issued a silent prayer for these lost souls. *May they finally be at peace now.*

"Okinawa Naval Base received a distress call from the *McCain*, stating that multiple missiles were fired from Gaven Island." Collins tapped another button on the computer keyboard, and a new window popped up on the screen. The loading screen for an audio file buffered, then waited patiently for the next command from Collins. He said, "A few seconds later, the radio went silent. I will play that message for you now."

"Okinawa? *USS McCain*. We were fired upon." The voice in the recording was high and tense. "There were two missiles fired from Gaven Island. I repeat, *we were fired upon*. There were two missiles fired at us from Gaven Island."

"Copy that, *McCain*." The communications officer in Okinawa sounded deceptively calm by this transmission, his own tension masked by his outwardly composed demeanor. "What is the SITREP, *McCain*? Were you able to prevent a strike?"

"Yes, sir. Our SeaRAM intercepted the two incoming cruise missiles and destroyed them!" The *McCain's* communications officer sounded uncertain, and there was a moment's pause that followed his message. Then he said, "We are returning fire now, Okinawa. We are, ah, we're now in the process of firing five cruise missiles at Gaven Island. We're trying to target their missile platforms and other assets."

"Copy that. Notifying the fleet commander now, *McCain*." Okinawa replied briskly. There was a muted shuffling sound as the officer reached into his desk drawer for his emergency contact list, barely audible over the dull roar of background noise. "Give 'em hell, *McCain*!"

The message from Okinawa cut off and was replaced by a booming explosion. Stunned silence followed the deafening noise, spanning several interminable seconds before the communications officer in Okinawa spoke once more.

"*McCain*?" There was a new note of urgency coming from his voice.

Whether the petty officer aboard the *McCain* had been stunned into silence or had something else distracting him was unknown, but several seconds of silence followed this single word. His stoic façade was now forgotten. "*McCain*, do you copy? I repeat, can you hear me? *McCain? McCain…?*"

Static hissed relentlessly in the comm, and it was all the answer Okinawa needed to determine the *Arleigh Burke*-class destroyer's fate.

Major Collins's gaze swept over the room, silently gauging the reactions from the personnel in the room. After a pause, he said, "As you can probably determine from the silence that followed that final transmission, Okinawa lost comms with the *McCain*. From that point, the ship activated its Voyage Management System, marking its location. A few minutes later, several EPRBs were activated."

An uncomfortable stillness fell over the room. James's gaze flickered to the personnel seated around the table, then to the president's face. His lips were pursed, and his eyes were guarded. Seconds passed, and his careful contemplation seemed to have a lulling effect on the personnel in the Situation Room. None of them dared speak, lest they inadvertently talk over their commander in chief. Finally, he said, "Can we verify for certain that the missiles came from Gaven Island, beyond what that young man in the audio said?"

"Yes," Major Collins replied without hesitation. "In addition to the verbal report from Petty Officer Third Class Alexander Wyatt, which we cross-referenced with Okinawa, we also have telemetry information from the onboard defense systems from the *McCain* before it was hit."

"And?" Thomas prompted.

"The telemetry shows the missiles did come from the vicinity of Gaven Island." Collins shrugged. There was nothing more he could say on the subject. The data supported the hypothesis, and there was no question that China was responsible for this violent act against the American Navy.

The president considered this. "When did it happen?"

"These images are from approximately two hours ago," Collins replied. He clicked on the computer keyboard several times, reversing the images on the monitor to the picture of the flame-engulfed *McCain*. Another keystroke zoomed into a series of numbers in the bottom right of the image, revealing the coordinates of the vessel and what appeared to be a date and time stamp. The printed numbers were indeed from approximately two hours before, accounting for the adjustment from China Standard Time, confirming his statement. Collins glanced at it, then back at the president.

"I see." Thomas reviewed the image. His expression was inscrutable, but James recognized the growing displeasure in the president's eyes. He wasn't just angry. He was livid. "Why would the Chinese fire upon and sink an American warship?"

The unstable accord between the United States and the People's Republic of China was no secret, and the mounting tensions between the two nations had been steadily escalating over the past few years. China was bound to make their move sooner rather than later, but what was their official catalyst for the attack?

Major Collins spoke up, his eyes trained on the president's image. "On the record, they're saying it's because both ships were inside the twelve-mile limit of Gaven Island and Johnson Island. We suspect the *USS McCain* and the Malaysian ship had received a warning before they were sunk. But as you and I both already know, this attack was bound to happen eventually, Mr. President. We just didn't know *when*."

"Do we know this for sure?" All eyes in the room turned to the secretary, then Andrews's voice rose to be heard by both Major Collins and President Thomas. "Is there anything to prove both ships received a warning before being fired upon by the Chinese?"

Collins nodded. "I was advised there were multiple warnings given by the Chinese, but it appears that we have since lost the recording."

"Can we recover them?" the president asked.

"We've reached out to Naval Base Okinawa to see if they can recover that digital recording for us," Collins said. He met Thomas's gaze evenly in the feed. "We're still waiting to hear back on that one."

President Thomas nodded slowly. "Do we happen to have any imagery from before the *McCain* got hit by the Chinese missile?"

"No, sir, unfortunately not." Collins shook his head, then he turned his attention back to the burning ruins of the *McCain*. "We tried to get that imagery from the satellite, but it was scrambled. We suspect the Chinese were jamming that specific satellite to prevent us from obtaining any imagery. The only reason we have what we have is because the satellite automatically changed frequencies outside the jamming frequency range of the Chinese."

"Hmmm." Thomas leaned back in his chair, his face now drawn in contemplation. "And what about the survivors, what do we know about them?"

Collins seemed to hesitate before answering. "There were survivors, yes. As to their fate now, though, that's still undetermined as of yet. The closest naval ship was another *Arleigh Burke*-class destroyer, the *USS John Paul Jones* (DDG-53). She was approximately 500 miles south when she received the distress signal from the *McCain* and shifted to flank speed to assist her."

The president nodded, his face stony and unreadable as he listened to Collins's report.

The major continued, reciting the intel from memory. "The fleet commander in Okinawa, Admiral Miller, was awoken and briefed on the situation by the OOD. Upon hearing it, he realized that the closest ship, the *John Paul Jones*, would be assisting with the recovery. However, the Chinese had already recovered all of them from the water, so unfortunately, we're not sure how many made it. They also warned us that any other naval ships trespassing in Chinese waters would also be destroyed, just like the *McCain* and the *Keris*. Because of this, Admiral Miller ordered them to hold their position to avoid putting them at risk of winding up like the *McCain*. Then Admiral Miller notified the Pentagon and reported the incident and asked for guidance."

"I see." President Thomas seemed to consider this. "Well, either way, we have to formulate a military response to this attack. Secretary Andrews, I want you to give me three military response plans by twelve noon, here at the White House."

"Yes, sir, Mr. President," Andrews said along with a head nod.

James had no doubt he was already formulating those plans in his mind.

"During that time," Thomas said, as though he hadn't heard Andrews's reply, "I will meet with the Chinese ambassador to demand the release of our American sailors." He steepled his fingers underneath his chin, his eyes distant and pensive. "I will also find out why this attack occurred."

More nods. The president's confident tone was reassuring. The confusion and uncertainty following the attack had caught them all off guard. Knowing they had a leader with their best interests in mind, who was focused on the safety of their home country, was a comfort they didn't even realize they needed during this uncertain time.

"I will also have to address the nation before the media does." The corners of Thomas's lips turned down in a frown. "Secretary Andrews, you have three hours. Make the most of them."

The damned biased media were always waiting in the wings to pounce on a news story and run with it. If he didn't get to the public first, who knew what kind of story they would spin? James knew all too well how unflattering public opinion could be used to smear the reputation of the president. Thomas did too. The media seemed to relish stories like this.

Andrews glanced down at his watch, and James cast a surreptitious look at his own timepiece. It was almost nine o'clock on the dot. Andrews returned his gaze to the video feed of the president, and his voice was calm and resolute as he spoke. "Mr. President, I've already ordered our Pacific fleet to alert status, and they are standing by for further orders."

"Very well." Thomas nodded and leaned forward, reaching for an unseen button in front of him. "I'll see you soon."

The president's screen went dark, leaving just the picture of the charred and smoking *McCain* in its wake. Collins glanced up at it, then moved to reach for the keyboard on the wooden table in front of him to turn off the monitor. His hand paused mid-reach, and he kept it suspended in midair momentarily before pulling it back.

James caught the minute shrug of his shoulders as the major reconsidered his actions. Why should he remove the picture of the *Keris* from the screen? Leaving it up served a sobering reminder of what China had just done. It was an entirely unnecessary gesture. James glanced across the room, taking in the stunned faces of the people in the Situation Room. All eyes were fixed on the image on the monitor, wide and dismayed. On the screen, the *McCain* remained locked in a permanent scene of destruction, its body in ruin from the combination of flames and a gaping hole in the side. No, turning off the monitor couldn't undo what they had all just seen.

Nobody, James mused, his eyes playing over the sinking ship of the *McCain, is going to be forgetting what they saw here anytime soon.*

CHAPTER SEVEN

PLANNING

OVER THE DULL ROAR OF the emerging conversations already rising up inside the Situation Room, James could hear the secretary of defense clear his throat. It was a subtle sound, almost inaudible, but it was unmistakable to James's ears. He clearly was not the only person who had heard it, as the overlapping voices in the room abruptly fell silent at the noise. Eyes shifted to Andrews as they waited for him to speak.

"I know I probably don't have to point out to all of you how important this is," he said, his voice carrying over the span of the room, "and I really don't think I need to remind you that we're operating on very little time here. I need suggestions for three military responses, and one of them needs to be a nuclear response."

His eyes swept across the faces in the room, tense and resolute. No further comment was necessary. Immediately, as though his words had broken their stunned reverie, the personnel in the room started to break off into smaller clusters, their faces somber and grim as they grouped up. A few people navigated their way to the door, no doubt already mentally brainstorming their own responses. Andrews turned away from them, his attention now drawn to the two men on either side of him. James recognized them as the deputy secretary and the chief of staff, their broad shoulders bent over the table as they spoke among themselves.

James stepped away from the wall, his hands falling to his sides as he eased his way through the crowd toward Major Collins. His mind raced as he walked, triaging his pressing duties. For starters, he needed to contact his team and let them know what had happened. They would be with the motorcade, waiting expectantly for him to return with a much-needed update about what he'd learned during the briefing. There was no way he would be able to reach out to them over their earpieces from this deep within the Pentagon. The signal would be blocked by several feet of reinforced concrete and steel.

The secretary didn't glance up at James as he walked past him. Andrews's silver head was bowed over his legal pad, his voice a low murmur as he spoke rapidly to the deputy secretary and the chief of staff. James could hear snatches of his conversation as he passed and slowed his pace, loitering behind him momentarily. Andrews had clearly wasted no time in starting a brainstorming session with his executive staff members. While the secretary's voice was overall fairly quiet, occasionally it would crest as the emotional weight of the situation elicited a raised voice.

"We could send an ICBM," the deputy secretary suggested with a raised eyebrow and his gaze fixed on Secretary Andrews's face. "What do you think about that, sir? I suspect if we send a Trident D5 from one of our submarines, it would be a pretty damned clear message. We could return the Spratly Islands back to shallow coal basins."

An intercontinental ballistic missile with a nuclear warhead attached to it would certainly send a clear message to China. James glanced at the deputy secretary's face as he strode past, then at Andrews. The slight shake of Andrews's head told James all he needed to know about his opinion of that particular military response, and the deputy secretary pulled back, a look of both concern and disappointment on his face. Now they were both looking at the chief of staff, their matching expectant expressions boring into the man's strained face. That idea was clearly a no-go, and it was time to return to the drawing board.

It wasn't James's intention to eavesdrop, so he continued his walk across the floor. Major Collins had taken a seat at the chair at the head of the table, and the computer monitor showed another satellite image of the wreckage of the *McCain*. He glanced up as James approached and let out a quiet grunt as a flash of recognition crossed his face. "James."

"Major." James glanced back at the exit to the Situation Room, then back at Collins. "I'm heading back to my office now as I have to get my team ready for the trip to the White House."

"Uh-huh." The major dropped his gaze back down toward the monitor and clicked a button on the keyboard. The image changed. This one was unfamiliar to James, and he wondered how many similar satellite images their intel had managed to gather on such short notice. Collins clicked again, and a fresh frown furrowed his brow as he squinted at it.

"Let the secretary know where I went?" James's voice trailed off as he peered over Collins's shoulder at the images. This one was very similar to the last one in the slideshow he had presented, revealing the black smudge that represented the remains of the Malaysian ship.

"I can do that for you," Collins said, his voice distant and distracted. He raised his eyes up to James once more, his brows raised expectantly. There was a mild flash of annoyance there, as though he was bothering him.

James knew better than to take it personally. Hell, they were all distracted and hyper-focused and didn't blame Collins for acting irritated at the perceived interruption. "Anything else?"

"No, sir. Thank you." James turned away. He could still hear the major clicking away at his computer, the low hiss of his breath through his teeth as he considered the satellite images.

With this task completed, James could now focus on readying his team. The last thing he needed was the secretary looking for him and unable to find him. While it would be assumed James was with his fellow CID agents, he didn't want to be the cause of any needless delays under these circumstances especially.

James moved briskly as he headed toward the exit of the Situation Room. He strode through the NMCC at a steady clip, the heavy steel door on the other side of the room locked in his sights. Once he was on the other side of it, he would finally be able to contact his team. Even though he still had a few hours before he needed to transport Secretary Andrews to the White House, every minute of it would have to be carefully metered so they wasted no time in their preparations. The sooner he got ahold of his team, the sooner he could start the process of preparing for the afternoon ahead.

James glided through the door, his feet carrying him down the hall toward his office. Now that he was within radio distance of his men, he could break the news to them. It was a task that he wasn't looking forward to, but he knew the sooner he revealed the context of the briefing to them, the sooner they could get started on more pressing matters at hand.

Namely, he needed to double check to make sure the Limo was prepared for the journey to the White House. There was no reason it shouldn't be, but James wasn't feeling like gambling with it.

James brought his left hand up to his mouth as he walked, his ear trained for the telltale sound of static to indicate that he was finally within communication range of his team. A moment later, he was rewarded with a burst of static in his ear as the radio connected with the repeater in the hallway. He didn't break his stride as he spoke into the radio, "Team, I'm leaving the briefing now and headed back to the office. Go park the vehicles in the garage and alert the Advance Team to be on standby, then meet me in the CID office."

Marc's voice came back, "What's going on, James?"

"I'll tell you when we meet in the office," James said. Not only was there inadequate time to explain this to his team over the radio, something else stopped him from revealing the details of the briefing to his men. Not a fear that someone might be listening to their radio traffic, though that certainly was a risk, a nominal one at worst, but James felt he needed to be present when he shared the briefing with them. Telling them over the radio seemed somehow disrespectful to the men who had perished in this cowardly attack by the Chinese government. "We have to have a meeting."

"Understood." The normally upbeat man was subdued, and James could hear the weight in his friend's voice.

Good. Marc needs to know how serious this is.

James lowered his hand back down to his side and allowed his arms to swing back and forth as he walked. Walking seemed so inefficient and slow, but his sense of dignity and decorum restrained him from breaking into a sprint. There was no need to rush. Even walking briskly, he suspected he would be getting back to the CID office before the rest of his team. Instead, he picked up his pace slightly, walking faster as he closed the distance between himself and his team. As he moved steadily down the hall, his mind went back to the briefing.

We're going to war with China. From his perspective, there was no other recourse possible. The country had fired upon American sailors and sunk the *USS John S. McCain* while the vessel was operating peacefully in neutral waters. As Newton himself had posited, each and every action warranted an equal and opposite reaction. There was no way President Thomas would allow this evil act to go unpunished.

Going to war with China wasn't the most pressing of James's concerns, though. He was aware that the United States had the Missile Defense Agency (MDA), whose sole purpose was to defend the continental United States from ICBMs launched toward her from an aggressor. This missile defense was very similar to Israel's Iron Dome but more advanced. It was designed to counter ballistic missiles of all ranges—short, medium, intermediate, and long. Since ballistic missiles had different ranges, speeds, sizes, and performance characteristics, the Ballistic Missile Defense System was also an integrated, "layered" architecture that provided multiple opportunities to destroy missiles and their warheads before they could reach their targets. But even with this system in place, there were plenty of areas where errors could occur and one or two missiles could get through and hit major population centers, one of which would undoubtedly be Washington DC.

The garage where the motorcade was normally parked was empty, and James paused at the doorway leading to the CID office. In a moment, the team would be arriving with the Limo and the Chase, and he wanted to be ready for them when they did appear. The location of the CID special agents' office was no coincidence. Being stationed near the motorcade vehicles was an intentional measure. In the event of an emergency situation that warranted a hasty evacuation from the Pentagon, their close proximity would help expedite their retreat.

He swung the door open, then propped it open with a rubber doorstop. There. Now he'd be able to hear them when they pulled up. He threw a final glance into the garage, but there was still no sign of the men arriving with the pair of heavy black SUVs.

James went into the office, circled his desk, then sat down. From his angle, he had a perfect view of the garage. He leaned forward, resting his face in his hands. He wasn't sure how the team was going to take this new intel, but he knew it was his responsibility to break it to them as tactfully as possible. The last thing he needed was a panicky team. While they were typically levelheaded and intelligent, the looming threat of a nuclear war was certainly enough to set the most rational person off.

And, he reminded himself, *I need to make sure they don't go running their mouths to anyone, either.*

He understood firsthand that the temptation to call family and let them know what was going on was a powerful one. He'd experienced it himself, after his own experience in Iraq over a decade ago. Every single fiber of his being had wanted to reach out to Christina from the hospital and tell her how he had almost died, how he had used his wits to stay alive, how his men had rallied around him to save his life…but keeping those secrets, upholding his loyalty to the security of the United States, had probably been the final dying ember of their relationship. But that had been over six thousand miles away, in the Middle Eastern desert. Here, with the threat trained on the US, the stakes were much higher.

James heard the sound of the engines from the duo of SUVs and lifted his face from his hands. His team had arrived. He ran his hand over his face, then sat up and squared his shoulders. His face was blank as he watched the door. The sound of their chatter greeted him before they stepped through the door, but the look on James's face instantly silenced them.

"Uh, James?" Marc said. He exchanged a glance with Charles, then cleared his throat. "We brought the motorcade around. You mind telling us what's going on?"

James considered him. A part of him wanted to keep the news to himself, protect his men from the new reality they were living in. He exhaled through his nose, then brought his eyes up to face Marc. They needed to know. Not only for their own sakes—not telling them would be nothing short of a betrayal, and they deserved better than that—but for the SecDef as well. The threat level for Andrews had just grown exponentially due to the situation, and failure to address the briefing with his team could unquestionably put the secretary's life at risk.

"Yeah," James said. He rose to his feet and walked to the door. With a quick glance through the open door, he kicked the rubber brace that had propped it open. The door swung shut, and he tugged on it until it clicked and then turned back to his team. "Go ahead and grab a seat. I'm afraid you're going to want to be sitting down for this."

Marc moved first, grabbing a chair from across the room. He dragged it over and positioned it in front of James as Aurora snagged the chair next to him and Charles followed suit, imitating the gesture. Liz grabbed the last one, completing a semicircle in front of James.

Marc straddled his chair, his arms crossed over the back of the seat, his face both concerned and expectant. "Spill it. What's going on?"

How could he possibly summarize what he had heard during the briefing in just a few sentences? *Just tell them already.* He hesitated for the briefest of moments, finding his words, then said, "Approximately two hours ago, the *USS John S. McCain* was struck by a cruise missile. The missile was presumed to have come from the Chinese. Major Collins reported that they do have telemetry data confirming the missiles came from Gaven Island in the Spratly Island chain. The Chinese also fired upon a Malaysian ship, a littoral by the name of *KD Keris-111*. Both ships sunk."

Silence.

Of all the reactions James had anticipated from his men, he hadn't expected to be greeted with silence. He met the eyes of each of the team members in the room, allowing them to absorb what he had just said.

"What about the sailors aboard the *McCain*?" Marc asked after a moment's deliberation. His voice was quiet, his thoughts no doubt on the men who had perished in the South China Sea that morning.

James shook his head. "The survivors were picked up by a Chinese vessel. We don't know much about them beyond that. What we *do* know is that the *Keris* was headed toward the *McCain* when it was struck by the missile. It's assumed they were trying to rescue the sailors in the water."

"Holy shit," Charles said, his eyes wide as he glanced at Marc and then at James. "Y'all have any idea why they did it?"

James recalled what he had heard during the briefing. "The top brass believe China finally got tired of foreign vessels navigating in their so-called waters of the South China Sea. And after several years of it, I guess they decided to take action against us. We know they did issue warnings before they fired upon the *McCain,* but we don't know yet what they said in those warnings. That data's been lost, but we've asked Okinawa if they have a copy of it. Still waiting to hear back on that one."

"What about us?" Liz asked as she fumbled into her pocket and produced her phone, then began thumbing on the screen. She glanced down at it, then back up at James.

"The president told the secretary to meet him at the White House in three hours." James's gaze flickered to the phone in Liz's hand, then back to Liz's face. "He's currently working on drafting a military response to the attack."

"This is insane," Liz said. She pressed a button on the screen of her phone, then brought it to her ear.

James lunged toward her, snatching the device out of her hand. "What the hell are you doing?" He thumbed the call button, canceling the outbound transmission. His eyes flashed as he pointed the phone at the stunned woman before him. "Don't you understand? We can't tell *anyone* about this until the president announces it. That means you can't tell your friends or family."

"What the hell, Liz?" Marc shook his head, then snapped his fingers at James and reached for the phone, opening and closing his hand at the senior CID agent.

James took a step forward, handing it to him.

Marc swiftly turned to Liz and smacked her lightly in the arm with the mobile device. "You dumbass."

"Sorry." Liz seemed properly chastised as she took her phone from Marc and slipped it back into her front pants pocket. "That was stupid of me, you're right. I don't know what I was thinking. I guess my first thought was to call Kassie."

"Well, don't call Kassie," James said sharply. "Get that idea out of your head right now. After the president makes his announcement? Yeah, then you can go for it. But don't go spilling any classified information when you do call her, either."

"Point taken. I apologize. I don't know what I was thinking, really." The pointed barb had hit its target, and high spots of color decorated Liz's cheeks. She reached behind her head, tightening her ponytail, then leaned forward in her chair and braced her elbows on her thighs, locking her hands together. "So now what?"

"We're screwed, that's what," Marc said. His thumb went to his nose, rubbing at the crease where it met his cheek. "You do realize China is a nuclear power, right?"

"No shit." Liz's voice was steady, despite the thread of fear evident in it.

"I never got that soda," Charles said after a moment, his voice morose. "And I could really go for some donuts right about now."

"We're going to war with China, and all you can think about is food?" Marc shot an incredulous look at him.

"Well, if we're about to wage a damned war against a nuclear power," Charles pointed out, "I need to keep my energy up."

"You keep your energy up like this," Marc said in a dry voice, "you're just going to get fat."

"Oh yeah? What's your best time on the two-mile run, huh?" Charles countered.

There was no edge to his words, and Marc seemed to take the heckling in stride. Finding something to fuss about seemed to give them a distraction from the real issue at hand, and James couldn't fault them for it. He didn't want to think about a war with China, either. But he didn't have any choice in the matter.

Charles continued, "I don't know about you, but I can at least outrun the enemy. You'll be out there waddling while the enemy gains on you."

"That's real rich, coming from you." Marc scoffed at the comment. Even despite being over fifty years old, he was still in great shape. The man often joined James for his workouts in the gym and even occasionally outperformed him—when James allowed him to, of course.

James turned away from his team, blocking out their banter. Their nervous energy was contagious, and he knew it was far too easy to get caught up in it. He'd let them squabble for a few more minutes, then have to cut them off. For now, they needed to blow off some steam and assimilate what he had just told them. Had he not so much work to do right now, he would have joined them. Instead, he ambled over to his desk and pulled the chair back, sitting down.

It occurred to him that he needed to tell battalion leadership about the briefing. With them involved, he could get some much-needed help in increasing the secretary's protection detail. The unwelcome mental image of Andrews getting pierced through the back by a bullet from a Chinese nationalist turned the corners of his lips down into a frown, and he shoved the picture out of his mind. Yes, he definitely could use extra help protecting the SecDef, but if he did let the battalion leadership become privy to what China had done, then it would be a matter of when—not if—the information spread like wildfire in a California forest.

Was it worth the risk, though? James mulled over this. Yes, there was a risk of someone running their mouths, but the risk was low. Plus, the president would be giving his address to the American people in just a couple hours. How much could they possibly say in such a short amount of time? James tapped his index finger on his desk. The protection of the secretary was of a greater priority. As much as he wanted to keep things under tight wraps, his loyalty to Andrews was paramount.

James turned toward his computer. If he wanted to get ahold of the battalion commander, he'd have to email him through the Joint Worldwide Intelligence Communication System. All messages on the JWICS intranet were carefully encrypted, ensuring that no prying eyes saw something they weren't authorized to see. James typed up his message to the lieutenant colonel quickly, taking care to focus only on the key points he wanted to convey to him. He read over it once, then twice, for accuracy. That would have to do. Satisfied, he clicked send on the message.

James let out a low sigh of relief. That, at least, would help. It couldn't completely guarantee Andrews would be safe, but it was a step in the right direction. He rose to his feet. "Charles?"

Charles stopped mid-sentence and turned toward James. "Hm? What's up?"

"You still want that soda?" James asked.

"Hell yeah." Charles nodded vigorously. "And those donuts. I'm *starving.*"

"When are you *not* hungry?" Marc challenged.

Charles dismissed him with a wave of his hand.

"I want you to take some time and get to the restroom. All of you. If you need to whiz, go whiz. If you're holding it in, let it out." James turned his focus to Charles. "If you're hungry, I want you to swing by the Pentagon food court and pick up some snacks and drinks. Hell, even if you're not hungry, I want you to stockpile yourself a little bit of food, okay? It's going to be a long day, and I don't want to hear any whining about how you're hungry or you gotta go or anything. We need to remain on task today. No distractions, period."

The team nodded back at him. What James was telling them made perfect sense. Conversation time was over. In a moment, they were going to take possibly their last break of the day. They knew to savor it, but not to linger too long. The day was undoubtedly going to be a stressful one and likely to run longer than usual. Quick burning carbs could help keep their energy up through the day, and the caffeine in the sodas could help keep their minds sharp as the day progressed.

"When you're done with that," James said, glancing down at his watch, "I want you to load up the vehicles. I want this done by 1030 hours. Be ready to go, because I want us to be ready for the secretary's departure for the White House at 1130 hours."

There was no need for anyone to reply to his orders other than offer a reply of assent. There was nothing else for them to say. They knew exactly what he was telling them, and giving this brief window of time to relax and make sure they were ready for the day ahead of them was not only a professional courtesy but also a matter of national security. If they somehow were slow-thinking or acting today, it could have far-reaching implications. It could even cost the secretary his life.

CHAPTER EIGHT

THE ADDRESS

THE PRESIDENT HAD SOMEHOW MANAGED to keep his composure throughout the entire briefing. The anger that threatened to bubble out of his chest and cause an unwanted tremor in his voice had remained suppressed. In retrospect, this surprised him somewhat. In all of his years of serving the public, he had never shown a moment of weakness. Today, however, he'd expected his voice to shake with barely restrained fury upon hearing the news of China's attack on the *McCain*. He'd held his composure though, until the moment he turned the video feed off and his face immediately contoured into a livid scowl.

What the ever-living hell just happened?

President David Thomas leaned back in his leather chair and raised his eyes to the ceiling of the West Wing Situation Room. Unlike the ceiling in the Oval Office, this room had no fancy embellishments or glyphs pressed into its surface to divert his gaze. He let his eyes slowly close, and the ceiling overhead faded away while the one in the Oval Office drifted into his mind's eye. It was a markedly distinct surface as the Oval Office itself was largely for show rather than function. In there, the white plaster fresco was stark, clean, and free from stains and blemishes. The pristine plaster surface was quickly proving to be the complete opposite of his term in office, and Thomas knew it.

Could his tenure as president get any worse? He suspected that yes, there was a very strong likelihood of this happening. China had, at least, seen to that. If they would have left the United States alone, he wouldn't need to be compelled to escalate the situation. Now, though, he had no choice. He suspected his advisers would tell him the same too. There was no way this was going to end without bloodshed.

He reflected on the past two years and shook his head. There was a hint of sadness to the gesture. As much as he had tried to keep peace within the country and outside the country, conflict and strife consistently tried to foil his diplomacies. Civil unrest, violence, and ongoing riots seemed to punctuate his residence at 1600 Pennsylvania Avenue and around the country, despite his best efforts to maintain a semblance of peace within the nation's borders. Thomas was, frankly, growing quite tired of it. His efforts felt almost futile, and as much as he tried to keep this country both functional *and* happy, he was wondering what it would take to do that.

The ceiling was the perfect surface for him to ruminate upon as he gathered his thoughts. The seal—*his* seal, the seal of the president of the United States—made for a dramatic centerpiece in the Oval Office. Unlike the office itself, however, it wasn't just a façade. It actually had significant meaning, even if most people didn't realize it.

The eagle, its face turned to the right, held a powerful message in the ribbon held in its beak: *E pluribus unum*. Out of many, one. Thomas was the president of all fifty states and fourteen territories. Despite their differences, he had to remain a steady and respected figure for all of them. They needed him, depended upon him. And now more than ever, he needed to prove his leadership to them.

The first year of his term as president hadn't been an easy one, that was for damned sure. Thomas hadn't been deterred, though. He had methodically passed public policies he sincerely believed would help the American people, even though the Senate had fought him every single step of the way. There were some concessions he'd had needed to make, such as certain Congress members trying to sneak riders into bills that were ready to be passed, but overall, Thomas was proud of his country. His home. His constituents. His diligent work was slowly starting to pay off. The economy was finally recovering from the recent recession and had firmly managed to maintain its position as a global superpower. Civil unrest had finally started to calm down. There were no active military conflicts underway, even though there were still small scale operations in Iraq and Afghanistan. It had been an uphill battle, no doubt, and there was still a lot more work to do.

And then this happened. Damn it all to hell!

One thing many people didn't realize, as he thought about the seal etched into the ceiling in the Oval Office, was what was clutched in the talons of the bald eagle adorning the seal. Sure, the regal bird was the United States' national emblem. Once nearly hunted to extinction, it now boasted a thriving population and was flourishing. The same could be said for the United States too. But like the eagle, his country couldn't have achieved such peace and prosperity without recognizing the importance of bloodshed. One claw clutched an olive branch, but the others held the arrows of war. One could not be achieved without the other.

Thomas had seen enough death during his lifetime and would prefer to never encounter it again, if at all possible. He certainly wasn't keen on going to war or the loss of innocent lives. He had sincerely hoped he would have been able to serve his term as president without a global conflict. It would not, evidently, be so.

Thomas recalled the image of the flame-engulfed destroyer, the *USS John S. McCain*, sinking in the South China Sea, surrounded by the surviving sailors in the water. What had been their fate? Would China surrender them? He exhaled through his nose as the image of the vessel hovered in his mind's eye.

It was no secret that China had been aspiring to become a superpower, and tensions between the United States and the People's Republic of China (PRC) had been steadily growing over the past several years. It wasn't enough for China to become a strong world power, though. They wanted to be an elite global contender, one to be reckoned with, greater than the US itself. That, to Thomas, wasn't a problem in and of itself. There were many other countries that were also powerful—not as powerful as the United States, of course, but they could hold their own—like Germany and the United Kingdom. But Germany and the UK weren't blowing up their destroyers either.

China was now starting their fifteenth 5-year plan, and Thomas wondered—not for the first time—how anyone could not read it and realize that everything in it was a direct threat to the United States and its allies. Every five years, since 1953, the PRC had released such a plan, and there was always something new within it. In March 2025, they had released their most recent iteration of their 5-year plan. Their defense budget had increased to $300 billion, a 7.8 percent increase from the previous year and a staggering 59.6 percent increase over the core budget of $188 billion established in 2020. People's Liberation Army, Navy, and Air Force had amplified its modernization to exceed the US military. It detailed a 12.6 percent budget increase on R&D (Research & Development) for the military and finally cemented the concept that Taiwanese people were Chinese people and would be unified once again in the near future.

There had been several references to improving their development of advanced technologies, including biotechnology and robotics. *Dear God, biotechnology.* China's accidental release of the COVID-19 virus from the Wuhan Institute of Virology back in December of 2019 had clearly demonstrated their commitment to that. The pandemic, as well as the subsequent "vaccine," had been devastating and millions had lost their lives. Yes, it was no secret they were actively pursuing biological warfare.

There had been certain things over the past few years that suggested something like this was coming, and in retrospect, it should have all been red flags for an imminent attack. China taking possession of the Spratly Islands, for instance. The true ownership of the archipelago had been in dispute for years with Malaysia, the Philippines, Vietnam, Brunei, and Taiwan all vying for their stake in ownership while China had unilaterally claimed it as their own. Then there was the other issue of the PRC building military installations on the islands. They hadn't exactly been secretive about their construction of the fortifications, either. Not only had military bases appeared on the Spratly Islands seemingly overnight, but also dozens of hangars and several runways as well. The complete garrisoning of the islands was something they had been planning for several years, but their actions were one of those things he hadn't believed would escalate into a global conflict. At least, not during his term as president.

China hadn't been content to merely claim the Spratly Islands as their own, either. Slowly but steadily, they had been encroaching on other geography in the area. Once they had established the islands as military fortifications, it had only been a matter of time before they set their sights on the rest of the South China Sea within their nine-dash line. China has claimed everything within the nine-dash line for years, but now their claim was justified with military fortifications and the naval force to back it up.

The PRC were smart…damned smart. Thomas shook his head ruefully.

And they had been so brazen about it too. Their taunting of Taiwan, for instance. Boldly flying into their Air Defense Identification Zone (ADIZ), and the PLA pilots actually mocking Taiwan while in their airspace. According to unclassified reports, they had stated to the Taiwanese that it was *their* airspace and they should get used to it.

While flying in and out of Taiwan's ADIZ, their fortifications in the Spratly Islands—among others—had given them a powerful upper hand. The island's location made it easy for them to intimidate the Southeast Asian Nation states, in many cases forcing vessels to leave fishing grounds they had fished for years. And the proximity of the islands could make them a terrifying enemy. From their location in the South China Sea, they could mobilize and engage anywhere in Southeast Asia in an alarmingly brief amount of time.

There was only one thing he could reasonably do moving forward. He needed to speak with Congress to let them know the only recourse for this attack against the United States was a declaration of war. Even though it wasn't some closely guarded secret, many people weren't aware it wasn't within the president's authority to declare war. He certainly could engage in military action, but it was a subtle nuance of a difference. A series of checks and balances helped to prevent a unilateral dictatorship, and Thomas wasn't able to simply press a large red button on his desk and then rub his hands together while announcing, "I hereby declare war."

Because he couldn't officially make a concrete declaration without their authority, he needed to make sure they fully understood the gravity of the situation. If he failed in conveying this urgent message, he would be failing the men who had died out there today. He would be failing the American people. He suspected once he presented the relevant facts to Congress, though, they would not need much convincing. What other option was there?

President Thomas sighed and reached across the desk for the phone. He first called his speechwriter, a thin and wiry man by the name of Dawson. The speechwriter picked up the phone on the first ring and listened silently as the president summoned him to the Oval Office. Dawson assured the commander in chief he'd be there immediately, and requiring no further information, hung up. His second call was to Congress. He needed to initiate a special session in order to present these facts to them, and there was no time like the present to get started on it.

It took less than a half hour to get all of the local members of Congress to agree to assemble together for the SVTC, and the members who were unable to make it—whether they were out of town or busy with other personal matters—would have to be briefed about it later. President Thomas wasted no time presenting the evidence as he knew it to the tense majority listening over the encrypted video teleconference feed. He carefully outlined the events that had occurred that morning, taking care to not gloss over anything relevant in his briefing to them.

China had attacked the American people, he explained to their stunned and disbelieving faces, cementing themselves as the sworn enemy of the United States. The only possible solution, he concluded, was to declare war on the People's Republic of China.

The members of Congress didn't delay in coming to an agreement. After a very brief discourse where they considered the evidence presented to them, they came to an almost unanimous decision to go to war. President Thomas gave a couple of closing remarks and the SVTC was concluded. A few people stubbornly refused to vote aye, and Thomas took a mental note of those who voted nay. Those dissenters could very well be a threat to the American people in the future, and it might be in America's best interest to see if he could sway local districts when it was time for elections.

Thomas had seen their faces as they transitioned through understanding and ultimately processing what he had told him. First, there had been the shock. Then there was the outrage. He was satisfied that some faces had been furious. Good. He needed them to be angry, just like he himself was, if they were to successfully put the rogue country in check for the international community and for the United States. They needed to pay for their violence against the American people.

Throughout history, Congress had only declared war a grand total of eleven times, including its first ever declaration against Great Britain back in 1812. Had they not taken that bold first step, the US wouldn't be the country it was today. Today marked the twelfth official declaration of war. Would today also be a day that would live in infamy? The president didn't doubt it. He had been aware of the mounting tensions between China and the United States and known it would eventually come to this, but he had never anticipated it would come this quickly. Perhaps it had been naive of him, too trusting of the country situated on the other side of the globe, but now he knew better. Such a brazen attack wasn't unprecedented, and the signs had been there.

It was too late to dwell on the what-ifs. That was in the past. Today, President Thomas needed to make sure this attack was dealt with swiftly and precisely. He got up from his seat, spun on his heel in an about face, and stepped out of the room. Walking briskly, he navigated his way toward the Oval Office to prepare for his pending speech to the American people.

The Oval Office was different now, changed in light of the new burden on the president. He cast a critical eye over it, trying to imagine how it would look to the American people. It was pristine, ready for his address. Not a single rogue scrap of paper or speck of dust dared to blemish the immaculate room. Not many people were aware of it, but big decisions rarely came from the Oval Office and the spotless room was primarily for highlighting the importance of whatever missive the president had for the public. The majority of his work was actually completed in the Treaty Room, a handsome room that also doubled as his study.

President Thomas rounded the desk, rapping it absently with his knuckles as he strode past it, and he claimed his seat in the plush leather chair. Any minute now, the process of people coming in to prepare him for his pending speech would begin.

Dawson bustled in first. The president greeted the speechwriter with a nod, invited him to take a seat opposite of him, and started to work on the address to the public. Dawson's fingers flew over the keyboard as he typed up the first draft, then he thanked the president and turned his face down to the glowing screen to start his revisions. While he was a very articulate man, there was a certain artistry that Dawson brought to the speechwriting process, which Thomas privately respected. He would have one more chance to glance over it before it was fed into his teleprompter for relay to the American public.

A makeup artist arrived and went to work powdering his face and dabbing away the bloom of sweat that had formed there. The last thing he needed was for his people to think he was nervous. As she fussed over him, he reviewed the speech one final time and then slid it across the table, back at Dawson. Ready to go, he dismissed the makeup artist with a nod, and she hurried away.

It's time.

President David Thomas met the gaze of every single American around the world. His voice was hushed and somber as he read from the teleprompter streaming his message in front of him. His speechwriter had been efficient in drafting the words in his announcement, and he mentally commended him for being able to write what he'd dictated. He'd only had to make a few minor modifications to the speech to make it perfect. His voice didn't falter, and Thomas hoped he was able to convey the gravity of the situation without sending the American people into a panic.

"My fellow citizens, it is with a heavy heart that I tell you that today, at approximately six-thirty this morning, American and Malaysian forces were brutally attacked by the People's Republic of China. This attack occurred without provocation in the international waters of the South China Seas. I am here to reassure you that our military response to this attack will be swift in order to defend our nation, as well as other nations. We can't be consumed by our petty differences anymore. We will be united in our common interests. We will not be intimidated. We will not bow down to another. We will fight for what is right, for the Southeast Asian Nations, and for the United States. On my orders, we are currently in the early stages of military operations to deal with this new threat…"

Over the next ten minutes, he shared with the American people a condensed version of what he knew. They didn't need to know everything, of course, but they did deserve to be indirectly involved in the decision-making process.

It wasn't his job to convince them that war was the best response to the attack, but he doubted any reasonable person would disagree with such a declaration. His goal wasn't to weigh in on the morality of war, but rather, merely inform them that they had been subjected to an act of war from the People's Republic of China. And, because of these actions against them, the United States would be retaliating. It was a logical, just, and reasonable response, one he and Congress felt was wholly warranted and deserved.

By the time he was done speaking to the American people, President Thomas was sure of two things. One, he knew he would have their staunch support for this unanticipated war. Even the Democrats would be rallying behind him on this. He was confident he had bipartisan support, not only from fellow members of the government but also from his constituents. Who would refuse to stand up for the innocent victims of this attack? One would have to be heartless to protest this war. And two? China deserved what was coming. Even as he delivered his announcement to the American people, the president's belief in this was further crystallized.

The Dragon attacked the Eagle, and now the Eagle must strike back!

CHAPTER NINE

THE AMBASSADOR

T HE PRESIDENT'S THOUGHTS HAD BEEN on his speech when he got the notification that his guest had arrived. He had been reflecting on the anticipated impact it would have on the American people, and he had no doubt they were moved by it. His thoughts went to his wife. The address would have been the first Susan Thomas heard about what had happened, but the slim and soft-spoken woman had long since learned that being married to the president of the United States had its pitfalls. While there were undoubtedly many perks to being wed to the most powerful man in the country, she knew there were still several degrees of separation between what he knew and what she was permitted to know. She'd harbor no hard feelings toward him, at least. It was all part of the job as the first lady. She accepted it with quiet grace, and it was one of the many reasons he loved her.

He knew, though, she'd want to discuss it with him further at dinnertime. She might be a little bit reproachful, and he didn't doubt she'd try to coax more information out of him. Oh, how he wished he could use his wife as a soundboard more often. Susan wasn't only beautiful, but she was also incredibly brilliant, a true equal to himself. Nobody else he knew, not even any of the sharp minds who served as his aides, held a match to her. As much as she'd want to ease more information out of him, she also knew when to pull back and suppress the questions on her tongue. It wasn't just for national security, but also for her own safety. Nevertheless, he wasn't looking forward to the conversation. This might be one of the times she'd be more than a little bit annoyed at him keeping secrets from her.

A rap on the door drew him out of his reverie, and he glanced up at the sudden noise, his concentration broken. "Yes?"

"Mr. President?" A Secret Service agent stood in the doorway of the Oval Office, his brow creased in an uncertain frown. "I was just informed that Ambassador Han Wenjin is here. Are you ready to see him?"

Thomas sat up straight at his desk. His eyes narrowed in anticipation of encountering the Chinese ambassador face to face. Despite the fury coursing through his veins, he nevertheless was acutely aware that this could be a rather interesting conversation. Even though he was not particularly eager to speak with the man, he recognized this was his chance to glean any critical intel from him.

He nodded at the agent. "Go ahead and send him on in, please, Chris. Thank you."

"Yes, sir." The agent turned away, and Thomas could hear him speaking into his radio as he disappeared down the hall.

A minute passed, then two, and then a new form appeared at the doorway. On both sides of the man were Secret Service agents, Christopher Aboy and another man by the name of Daniel Kirkland. Both their faces were blank and expressionless as they presented the ambassador of China to the president. Thomas knew Chris and Dan would be standing guard just outside the Oval Office in case something should go wrong.

The ambassador stepped into the office, and as Chris started closing the door, he looked at Thomas and said, "The SecDef has just left the Pentagon, sir." Chris then pulled the door shut, leaving it cracked open an inch so he could still monitor the meeting occurring inside the room.

The ambassador stood before him, a slim man of slight build, his dark eyes cold and flat beneath black eyebrows. He was dressed in a simple black suit that was clearly tailor-made for his body as it fit his smaller stature perfectly. A crisp white shirt peeked out from beneath the coat, and a thin black tie and matching black shoes completed the ensemble. He bowed slightly, creasing the fabric of the suit with the motion, then straightened his back. He cleared his throat, and in a voice that was entirely unaffected by an accent, he said evenly, "Good morning, President Thomas."

The president gestured toward the chair across from the desk, and the ambassador walked leisurely over to it, then pulled the chair back. He glanced down, then bent slightly at the waist once more as to inspect the seat. To the president's surprise, the ambassador reached into his pocket and withdrew a handkerchief. He reached out and, with the palm of his hand wrapped in the swatch of fabric, swept it across the leather surface.

A spark of surprise flashed across Thomas's face. The insult was slight, but duly noted.

Satisfied that the chair was now clean enough for him, the ambassador eased himself down into it, perched primly on the edge, then crossed his legs slightly at the ankles. He met the president's gaze evenly, but no words came from his mouth. His face was blank and unreadable, his dark eyes locked unblinkingly onto President Thomas's own.

Is this how it's going to be? Thomas thought as he raised a brow at the man. Two could play this game. He pursed his lips, then rounded his desk, lowering himself back into his own seat. Now seated opposite the ambassador, he spread his hands out in front of him in an expansive gesture, inviting discourse between the two men. There was no need to beat around the bush. He wanted answers and had no time or desire to be coy. "Tell me, Ambassador. Why did your country attack and destroy the *USS John S. McCain* and the Malaysian ship?"

The ambassador remained silent, perched lightly on the edge of his chair with his dark eyes focused on the president's face, inscrutable.

Thomas fought the wave of irritation threatening to wash over him and kept his voice calm as he added, "You do know this is an act of war."

"You and your American people," the ambassador said suddenly, and Thomas was surprised to hear a note of sharp resentment in the outpouring of words. "You all seem to think that you can just do anything, and you can do it without worrying about the effect it has on others."

Thomas kept his mouth shut. He had allowed the ambassador into his office because he wanted answers. The last thing he wanted right now was for the ambassador to storm out of the room in a huff before answering his questions.

"You think you can manipulate other countries by giving them millions of dollars of your so-called 'foreign aid' to do your bidding." Wenjin bit off each word as he spoke, his voice rising an octave as he outlined his grievances to the president. "And you seem to also think that you're allowed to strike fear in other countries by using your advanced navy and army to perform these 'training exercises' close to their borders."

Thomas leaned back in his chair, crossing his arms over his chest. His lips were drawn into a flat line, and his eyes narrowed as he glared at the man sitting across from him. He crossed his arms across his chest and wordlessly waited for the ambassador to continue.

"But that is far from the truth, Mr. President." Now Wenjin's voice was growing unsteady.

Thomas was startled to realize the man was physically trembling as well. The diminutive ambassador was literally shaking with anger. Was the anger at the president, at the country, or maybe it was a combination of both?

He raised a hand, pointing a finger at the president. The digit struggled to remain fixed on him, the tremors overwhelming his diminutive frame. "This world? It does not belong to the United States of America. You cannot control and manipulate every country in order to get them to do what you want them to do."

Try me. But Thomas said nothing. He still had plenty of time to entertain his guest. He wasn't meeting with the secretary of defense for another half hour or so, at least. He could afford to be patient with the furious ambassador sitting across from him. Hell, if diplomatic maneuvers in the form of foreign aid kept his allies happy, then who was the ambassador to tell him he was forbidden to engage in them? Despite himself, Thomas found himself growing curious as to what would follow next in the ambassador's monologue.

Wenjin continued his tirade without pause. "The People's Republic of China has noticed how the American government likes to control and manipulate other nations. Oh yes, we have grown wise to your American ways. You think your actions are going unnoticed? I will tell you this now, President Thomas: we will not be one of those nations you can manipulate."

He's still picking up steam, Thomas marveled. He wondered fleetingly if the ambassador had rehearsed his speech in his head several times before he came over to speak with him. Perhaps he practiced it in front of his mirror, admiring his reflection as he imagined himself putting the president in his place with his words. Or maybe it was more impromptu than that. Had the ambassador known about the attack on the *McCain* and the Malaysian ship in advance? The thought made Thomas feel cold, very cold, inside.

"China has a great and long history, a history that is much older than your American history," Wenjin said. There was derision in his voice now. He stabbed at his palm with his index finger as he spoke, pronouncing his words with each jab at his open hand. "Its people are a strong and proud people, and they have a great love of their homeland."

A silence followed as Wenjin's words hung in the air, challenging Thomas to refute them. The ambassador was breathing heavily. His rant had riled him up, and now a flush crept up his neck, rising from the crisp white collar of his shirt.

Thomas accepted the invitation to speak. In a mild tone that contradicted the mounting fury he felt, the president said, "I think you had better get to the point, Ambassador."

The words came out of Wenjin's mouth abruptly, falling from his lips in a fast clip with the first hint of the ambassador's native accent breaking through. "Mr. President, the point is that the People's Republic of China has always claimed the Spratly Islands and the South China Seas as its own. And now we have facilities, and homes, and Chinese families living in those homes. And you? You go and send two war ships into our sovereign territory, and that action threatens our people. In fact, your country has been sending warships through our territorial waters for years now, and we have been patient with your disrespect for long enough."

How deep was the propaganda of the People's Republic of China to have convinced Wenjin of these mistruths? Had the government poisoned the minds of its people so thoroughly that they sincerely believed the peaceful training in combination with Freedom of Navigation exercises could genuinely be identified as a plausible threat against them? Yet, the evidence was right there in front of Thomas. Wenjin seemed to sincerely believe what he was telling him. His voice, at least, was earnest.

"The Chinese Navy gave three warnings to both ships that they were in the sovereign waters of the Republic of China." Wenjin's tone was petulant now. He wasn't apologizing for China's actions. He was justifying them. "Three warnings, Mr. President, that your people ignored. They did not attempt to move away. In fact, they did the opposite. They got within twelve nautical miles of our islands. Our navy had no choice but to protect our people."

A heavy pause followed Wenjin's words, and President Thomas recognized it was now his time to speak. He couldn't let the fabrications continue to pour out of the ambassador's mouth without intervening. He uncrossed his arms and rested his palms flat against the surface of his desk, leaning forward in his chair.

The president's eyes met Ambassador Wenjin's evenly, and his tone matched the steadiness of his gaze. "Ambassador, those waters are international waters, and they have been recognized as such from the entire international community. If you think your great country," Thomas said without letting the inflection in his voice change to note the irony in the words, "can come in and build islands overnight, and put buildings and homes and families on those islands, and then lay claim on those man-made islands and the international waters surrounding them? Well, then you and your government have made a grave mistake."

Wenjin opened his mouth to speak, but the president cut him off with a sharp glare. He closed his mouth once more, but it was evident that he was unhappy to have the leader of the free world overtalking him. His lips turned down in a frown as he let the president continue.

Thomas lifted his right hand and pointed his index finger steadily in the face of the Chinese ambassador sitting across from him. "I want you to pay close attention to what I'm about to tell you, Ambassador Wenjin. You and your government fired upon the United States Naval Ship, the *USS John S. McCain*, and sank her. You killed American sailors! I'm only telling you this once. You are going to arrange for the safe return of the surviving members of her crew within the next twenty-four hours, or I promise you, I *will* lay waste to the great Chinese Navy!"

Wenjin said nothing.

Good. He had finally learned when to keep his mouth shut. The president's voice was a low hiss as he concluded, "The United States and the international community will continue to use the international waters in the South China Sea, and we will enforce that with extreme prejudice if we have to." He didn't add, *whether you like it or not.* It was unnecessary. The message was implied, and he was certain the ambassador had picked up on the subtle hint. "Now go and see to the safe return of our sailors."

A heavy silence descended upon the room. Thomas held Wenjin's gaze evenly, silently daring him to protest a single word he had just said to him. The ambassador, at least, had the good sense to remain quiet. In his peripheral vision, Thomas noticed Chris standing inside the Oval Office, the door wide open. The ambassador's raised voice had drawn him in, and the agent's body language indicated his readiness to react should the need arise.

The president was the first to rise to his feet, and Wenjin followed suit a beat later. Thomas circled his desk, his palm open and extended toward the ambassador in a gesture of exaggerated magnanimity. It wasn't an offer to shake, but rather, a subtle indication that the conversation was over. The hand was aimed toward the exit and the agent standing by the door.

Wenjin glanced down at it, then back at the president, but still said nothing. He turned away slowly, his stride smooth as he moved toward the door. Silence prevailed as he allowed the president to lead him to the door.

Chris threw a glance at the president, then at Wenjin, and then turned his face forward once more. So far, the ambassador was leaving without a fuss. Should the situation change, though, he was ready to intervene and escort him out with as much force as necessary.

Thomas turned away from the ambassador. This conversation was over. His shoulders felt heavy, but he kept his spine rigid.

He was almost back at his desk when he heard the ambassador's voice filter across the room to his ears. "Mr. President?"

Thomas turned his shoulders to face the ambassador and raised a brow at the man standing by the door to the Oval Office.

Wenjin seemed to be savoring the words in his mouth, and the words were almost melodious as he delivered his final message to the president. The accent was gone once more. "You do know that China is a nuclear power."

It wasn't a question. The ambassador may have phrased it as a simple reminder of what China possessed, but Thomas recognized the threat. His lips pursed. *The arrogance of the man!* He tugged upward on the seam of his slacks, then eased into his plush leather chair. His voice was smooth and genial in response. "You know I could turn your entire country into glass, right?"

The ambassador's face was unreadable. The tremor was gone. The man was a statue now, rigid with his hate and anger at the American people and their government. He let his eyes linger on the president for several seconds, boring holes into the eyes staring back at him.

Thomas didn't mind. Let him look. *Remember my face, Ambassador. This is the face of someone who won't bow to your petty threats.* He met the gaze with one of his own, his sun-faded blue eyes icy in the sunny room.

If the ambassador was going to say anything more, he must've thought better of it and changed his mind. He spun on his heel and marched out of the room.

Thomas sighed and leaned back in his chair. His eyes went back to the crest of the eagle on the ceiling. *That was,* he thought, *quite rude of him to leave without bowing first.*

Perhaps it was time for America to teach him—and the entirety of the People's Republic of China—some manners. It was obviously long overdue. The disrespect the ambassador had shown to him that morning, compounded with the attack on the *USS John S. McCain,* clearly proved this to be true. China had no idea who they were messing with, and if it took military force to educate them about their wrongdoings, then Thomas was ready to give them this much-needed lesson.

CHAPTER TEN

TRANSPORT TO THE WHITE HOUSE

DECEMBER WAS USUALLY A BUSY month for tourists in Washington DC, which was part of the reason James had wanted to get the motorcade for the secretary ready a little bit early. The cold and damp snow of the region did little to deter them, and while most of the tourists were fairly well behaved, he had seen his share of clueless people launching themselves into traffic without first checking both sides before crossing the street.

Hell, just last month they had almost run over a wide-eyed and clueless tourist with an evident death wish. Marc had hit the brakes just in time, with barely any room to spare, and the tourist had frozen just long enough to blink, shake his head, and continue his trek across the road. Of course, that hadn't stopped the oblivious visitor to reconsider once he had finished crossing the street and, as a parting gift, he'd revealed his middle finger to Marc and James before vanishing into the crowd.

James tapped his foot impatiently against the carpeted floor of the CID office and glanced at his watch again. They needed to depart in less than ten minutes, but Charles was still in the bathroom and Liz had somehow misplaced her earpiece. Why did these things always seem to happen on days like this? He remembered the last time they had encountered this many snags when trying to ready the motorcade. Some extremist troll had made a remark online about kidnapping the secretary's daughter, and while that threat had never come to fruition, it was still a panicked half hour trying to get the secretary back to his house so he could check on her since she didn't answer her cell phone.

"Hey. Sorry about that." James looked up as Liz approached. The younger woman had her hand at the side of her head and was fussing with her earpiece. "Found it. I had left it in the food court. It was right where I left it."

"Any word from Charles?" James asked. He didn't bother asking Liz why she had taken it out in the first place. Maybe she had been on the phone with Kassie. His eyes went back to his watch.

"Yeah, he texted me. He's finishing up now." Liz shook her head. "From what I could gather, he's not doing too hot."

Marc nodded in agreement. "We warned him about mixing donuts with soda, but the man didn't listen. You should have heard it, James. I could hear him on the other side of the door, it was that bad. Sounded like Mount Vesuvius in there. I actually feel sort of bad for him."

"Spare me the details." James crossed his arms over his chest and leaned against the open doorway of the CID office. His toe continued to tap out a beat on the floor. Eight minutes to spare, and the fourth member of the team was still nowhere to be found. If Charles didn't make an appearance in the next thirty seconds, he would march into the bathroom and personally tear him a new one. That should, at least, facilitate both his movement and his exit from the restroom.

"If he's not here on time, then we should probably just leave without him," Marc suggested. He rubbed the side of his nose as he spoke. His voice was anxious. "We don't have time for this. If we're late, Charles is a dead man."

"Give him time," James said shortly. "We need the full team here."

He didn't need to finish the rest of his thought for Marc and Liz to understand. They had a fairly clear understanding as to what the current threat level was for the secretary, and the thought of something happening to him—whether it was due to their own negligence or any other reason—was an entirely unsettling one. If something were to happen to the secretary, it would be an international incident with serious ramifications for whichever country was behind it. As it were, they were already in a very serious global situation. It was an idea too bleak for any of them to entertain. As careless as Charles was acting in that moment, they knew he was still a good man and a valuable member of their team. If he could only get his stomach to settle, then he'd be the very picture of a perfect CID agent.

Charles strode down the hall briskly as though on cue. "I'm here. What did I miss?" His hands brushed against the front of his dress slacks as he walked, drying them off. His voice was breathless, and his cheeks were flushed.

James noted the beads of sweat dappling the upper lip of the agent, and a small square of white paper clinging to his shoe.

Liz cast a pointed glance down at his foot, then turned toward James, raising a brow at him. "We ready, then?"

"Come on. Seven minutes until rendezvous. Let's move it." James snapped his fingers, then pointed toward the garage.

The agents didn't require any further prompting. They moved toward the pair of black SUVs and claimed their respective seats inside it. Marc claimed his seat as the driver of the Limo, but the passenger's seat remained vacant, ready for James when he returned with the SecDef in tow. Liz and Charles moved to the Chase, where Audra was already sitting in the back seat of the idling vehicle. She, at least, had no trouble being on time.

Marc fastened his seatbelt, then turned the ignition key and lowered the volume on the radio. He eased his foot down against the accelerator, and the Limo surged to life. The clock on the dash read 1023 hours, and they would be making it to the Pentagon's north entrance within their allotted time. Fortunately for them—and for Charles's stomach—they had planned ahead for this, which was why they were leaving an entire hour early. It was far better to wait in the SUV for an hour for the secretary, rather than rush around at the last minute.

But the Limo pulled up to the stairs of the Pentagon north entrance with plenty of time to spare. The short stretch of road connecting the Pentagon garage to the north entryway was reserved for high-level executives, making the traffic-free jaunt quick and painless. With the team stationed outside of the north entrance and a whole hour to pass before James and Andrews would emerge, they found themselves relaxing somewhat. They may as well make the most of this downtime, as they all knew the rest of the day would be considerably more hectic. Small talk passed between the two vehicles as they waited.

James could hear them chattering back and forth in his earpiece as he walked toward the elevator that led to the secretary's office. The amiable banter between the Limo and the Chase served as background noise as he stepped into the elevator. He pressed the corresponding button, the elevator doors closed, and he felt the familiar lurch as it brought him to the main floor of the Pentagon. A moment later, they opened again and he navigated his way down the hall, moving toward the SecDef's office. Andrews was still in a meeting, and James didn't doubt he would remain so until precisely 1130 hours.

James paused in front of the doorway, then turned his back toward it, positioning his arms behind his back in a comfortable at-ease pose. Now all he had to do was wait for Andrews to come out. He turned his face forward, nodding at the various personnel who occasionally traversed the hallway. The hour passed at a surprisingly fast clip as James kept an ear on the conversation inside the SUVs. He occasionally responded to questions but remained mostly silent as he stood outside the door. Then, at long last, he heard the door behind him open. He glanced over as Andrews stepped out. Punctual, as usual.

"Sir." James nodded at him, and Andrews returned the nod. He fell into place beside the secretary, and they walked side-by-side toward the north exit of the Pentagon. As they moved down the hallway, James spoke into his radio. "Cobra coming out."

"Roger. Standing by," Liz replied in his ear. Then, with a note of disgust, she added, "You're not going to believe this, but Charles is eating again."

"Are you serious?" James shifted his eyes briefly to the secretary, who seemed indifferent to the one-sided conversation coming from his PSO. His mind was clearly on other things. James lowered his voice, his impatient message for his team's ears only. "Tell him to put it away. He had a whole hour to eat, and now he's got exactly ten seconds before we step out that door. You know the secretary is always on time. What were you thinking, Charles?"

There was a pause, then a hiss of static. "We're good now."

"Sorry," came Charles's muffled voice.

James shook his head. In a way, he understood Charles's behavior. Like himself, Charles worked out regularly, which was bound to make him hungry. Furthermore, the man was built like a tank, not unlike the up-armored Limo. Unlike James, though, Charles was a stress eater. James could go hours without even thinking about food when he was working under pressure. Charles, however, reached for junk food when his adrenaline was pumping. The man seemed to operate entirely on nervous energy and caffeine. It reminded James of another friend he'd had when he was in Delta, a wiry redhead by the name of Ginger. *To each their own.*

James pushed the heavy door open, stepping out first, then held the door open for Andrews. Andrews stepped through, and James let it fall shut behind him once more. He never left the secretary's side as they moved toward the stairs. Next to the rear passenger wheel of the heavily armored Limo stood Liz with the right rear passenger door fully open. With Andrews now visible and being escorted by James, she retreated back to the Chase vehicle and took her seat as the shift leader in the front passenger seat.

The SecDef descended the stairs steadily, one at a time, his head slightly lowered to ward off the spitting snow drifting down from the sky. His pace was brisk but not rushed, and his face was calm despite the turmoil that lurked beneath. James could see the thumb of his right hand fold down to his ring once more. Andrews was feeling the anxiety too. As he approached the Limo, James fell behind slightly, watching closely as the man hoisted himself into the black SUV. Satisfied, he swung it shut, then opened the door to his own front passenger seat and climbed in.

"Thank you, James." The secretary sighed and leaned back in his seat, resting his head against the leather surface. Damp flecks of snow clung to his shoulders, melting into droplets of water in the heated SUV. "It's been one helluva morning, that's for damned sure."

"I believe it," James said. He didn't encourage the conversation, but he also didn't discourage it. While making idle chatter with the secretary was frowned upon, James recognized Andrews's autonomy. If the man wanted to talk, he was good with it and enjoyed having discussions with him. A part of him wanted to coax more out of him, but he suppressed it. If Andrews wanted to elaborate, then he would. "How are you doing, sir?"

"I've been better." He sat upright. "But I'm sure I could say the same for everyone this morning, eh? Better move on out, Marc. We've got an important date with the president, and we don't want to be late."

Marc glanced back over his left shoulder, checking to make sure a vehicle wasn't approaching, and started out of the parking lot. He eased the Limo into drive and started across the lot, then down the ramp, then out past the Pentagon Force Protection Agency guard shack. It was a six-mile drive to the White House, but with the lunch hour rush starting and the freshly renewed snowfall, it was expected to take them the better part of a half hour to get there without the use of emergency lights.

James heard a crackle in his ear, followed by Liz's voice. "Shift Lead to Advance Team, how are we looking right about now?"

"Not bad, Shift Lead," the voice came back.

James recognized Catherine Parks's voice, a soft-spoken but keenly intelligent woman. Kat had earned her role on the Advanced Team through both her sharp observation skills and experience. "Traffic is a little heavy, and there was some construction going on near the Lincoln Monument but no traffic obstructions."

"Thank you, Advance Team. Are you in position?"

"Yes, we are." There was a moment's beat of hesitation, then the voice continued, "We are at the West Gate. Secret Service at the West Gate was advised of your pending arrival, and they're all prepped and ready for your arrival."

"Thank you, Advance Team. Hey, Limo, did you get all of that?" Liz's tone shifted as she addressed James directly. "Traffic's looking pretty heavy, but not bad. You want me to turn on the lights?"

"Stand by, Shift Lead." James met the secretary's eyes in the mirror. "Sir? There's a lot of traffic. Do you want us to activate the emergency lights?"

Andrews shook his head. "You know better than to ask me that. I don't like having people to move on my behalf. Just drive as usual, please."

"Understood." James met Marc's gaze, and the man shrugged. If that was what the secretary wanted, then that's what they'd do.

Historically, it was routine for the Limo to turn on the emergency red and blue flashing lights and sirens when transporting the SecDef from the Pentagon to the White House. Not only did this get the attention of motorists and pedestrians, but it was also effective for getting people to move out of the way. James remained astounded at how indifferent some people were in the DC metropolitan area to the vehicle's emergency lights, as though they thought their commute was more important. But motorcades were an everyday occurrence here, so they got accustomed to it.

Andrews had established during his first week as the SecDef that he didn't think he was better than anyone else. Suffering in traffic was humanizing, and he wanted to not only relate to his fellow citizens but to coexist with them. James respected that about him. If only more people were like this, the world would perhaps be a better place.

James thumbed his radio. "Shift Lead, Cobra says it's a no-go on the lights. It's only six miles, and we should make it with time to spare."

A few minutes later, Liz came over the radio, "Advance, we are approximately ten minutes out."

Kat answered the message. "Roger that, Shift Lead. We'll see you in ten."

⸙ ⸙ ⸙ ⸙ ⸙

Unlike James and the rest of the CID agents waiting at the Pentagon, the Advance Team had gotten an earlier start on their short jaunt to the White House. They had been waiting at the corner of E Street and 17th Street for the better part of an hour. While their job could undoubtedly appear boring from the outside, it was one they took seriously. Kat had a unique talent for picking up on patterns of behavior and was often the first person to comment if anyone had gotten a haircut or switched colognes. The woman's observation skills were second-to-none, which made her an invaluable asset to the Advance Team.

At precisely 1030 hours, they had secured their position near the intersection and parked their black SUV there. They made mental notes of the traffic, checked the DDOT report for any closed lanes or construction, and scanned the pedestrian flow for anything that might seem out of the ordinary. Nothing did, and traffic was moving steadily, albeit slowly in the winter weather. With nothing else to do for an hour, they unwrapped their sandwiches and pulled soft drinks from a cooler from the back seat and started eating while they watched the slow-moving stream of traffic traveling both north and south along 17th Street.

A less patient person would have fidgeted or grown irritated with sitting in the heated SUV in the blustery December chill, but Kat didn't mind. There was something strangely relaxing about watching the people of the nation's capital do their day-to-day business. She felt a certain fondness toward them, one that likely arose out of her youth. A southern gal, born and raised, Kat had spent most of her childhood in Georgia. While a slight, soft drawl had lingered in her voice, her time in DC had all but banished her country accent. Nevertheless, she felt an immediate kinship with the nation's capital and loved it just as much—if not more—than her tenure in the Deep South.

The bustling energy of the capital city invigorated her. She genuinely enjoyed seeing the annoyed and harried politicians and businesspeople hurrying down the streets, their faces buried in their phones as they navigated the sidewalk in their impractical shoes. The tourists, too, were part of the charm of the area. The wide-eyed wonder of visitors to the region reminded her of her father. She sincerely hoped that they too loved the city and, despite all of its quirks, might one day be motivated to move there.

One tourist seemed to be taking his time on the southwest corner of 17th and E. Kat smiled at the young man as the stranger raised his Nikon camera to his face and snapped a picture of the Old Executive Office Building in the background. The fresh blanket of white snow, not yet polluted by foot traffic, allowed the stark off-white building to stand out in sharp relief, and it made for a gorgeous photograph. The buildings lining the street added to the appeal of this stretch of the road. It certainly did make for a nice photo montage, and Kat had no doubt that the man would be flipping through the images later and be content with the memories he had made in DC.

"Up ahead," Brandon Claridge said suddenly.

Kat glanced up in the direction that her partner was nodding. Ahead, the Limo was pulling up to the intersection. The light turned red, and she could see Marc's face turn down in a frown through the windshield. "How about that. Perfect timing."

"And at the worst possible intersection too." Brandon shook his head as he unfastened his seatbelt and reached for the door handle. "I keep telling Marc and James, just use the emergency lights. You won't have to stop at red lights, and you'll make better time. But Marc said that the secretary refuses."

Kat nodded absently as she reached for her own seatbelt. Directly ahead and to her left, her tourist was now fiddling with his camera. She took note of the slim Asian man as he jammed his thumb against the back of the Nikon. He turned away from her, and Kat could see the young man's black backpack sagging down low on his shoulders. Whatever was in it, it was heavy. A stainless steel water bottle was strapped to the side of it, but the tourist hadn't taken a single sip from it the entire time he had been standing on the corner. And, to Kat's calculations, it had been the better part of an hour.

Huh. Weird.

She hopped out of the black SUV, joining Brandon as he maneuvered over to the corner of the intersection to intercept any pedestrian traffic that might try to interfere with the Limo's passage. However, her eyes went back to the Asian tourist with his backpack now slung low on his pelvis. There was nothing unusual about him, nothing that made him stand out from the crowd. The young man was dressed casually, wearing a plain blue sweater, an insulated puffy vest over it, and faded blue jeans. The outfit was perfectly appropriate—albeit maybe not warm enough, for the DC weather—and plain white tennis shoes completed the outfit. A red baseball cap with the Washington Nationals' trademark "W" logo on it kept the majority of the snow flurries out of the man's face. This hat was now turned down toward the camera, and Kat could see the wan sunlight bouncing off the digital screen as the tourist fussed with it.

"Ah, there it goes," Brandon said.

Kat followed his gaze with her own.

The cross-street traffic slowed to a trickle, and he could see the traffic light switching from green to yellow. In a moment, it would turn red, which would mean that the Limo and the Chase would be passing them. "A lot faster than usual. Son of a gun, they just might make it on time after all. I'll go ahead and let the Secret Service know to expect the secretary's Limo."

"Hey," Kat said, and her hand shot out, grasping at Brandon's coat as he turned away.

He stopped mid-stride, turning back to face her with a quizzical expression on his face. The tourist had evidently given up on his camera. He bent at his knees, placing the camera on the sidewalk. Kat silently willed him to pick it back up. Not only was the sidewalk coated in a grimy layer of filthy snow, but an eager thief could easily snatch it off the ground and sprint off with the camera before the tourist even realized what happened. But the man seemed oblivious to his camera now. He shrugged out of his backpack and brought it around to his front.

"What's he doing?" Brandon said, apparently noticing the tourist for the first time. His message to the Secret Service seemed to be forgotten, and he lingered on the sidewalk next to Kat, squinting at the Asian man. "How long's he been there? Wasn't he there when we got here an hour ago?"

"Yeah," Kat said slowly, her voice trailing off. The tourist was now holding the backpack in front of him, his arms extended away from his body.

Both agents watched in silence as the tourist glanced around, first to the left and then to the right, and hurried up the northbound side of the pedestrian sidewalk. He paused within eight feet of the Limo, his satchel still held out stiffly before him in his hands. Then, without preamble, he drew his elbows in and then extended them forcefully in the direction of the Limo. The bag flew from his hands and skidded across the icy street, spinning to a stop beneath the undercarriage of the black SUV Limo. He spun on his heel and, without hesitation, broke into a full sprint west down E Street.

With horror, Kat realized the man had what appeared to be a detonator in his left hand. It swung back and forth as the man's arms pumped on both sides of his body while he ran. *Good God, it's an IED!* The words clanged hollowly in her head. How had she failed to notice this? She heard a shout in her ear and realized it was Liz's voice screaming frantically into her radio. "Limo! Somebody just tossed a bag underneath you! Get the hell out! *Get Cobra out of there!*"

But it was too late. Kat knew it, and her stomach sank as she watched Marc's eyes grow wide at the warning. Any moment, the so-called tourist would depress the button on the detonator. If he succeeded in doing so, she knew everyone in the Limo could be killed in an instant, including the secretary of defense. And, Kat knew, it would be her fault. This would be a burden she would have to bear for the rest of her life. From her position on the sidewalk, Catharine Parks watched powerlessly as she witnessed her friends trapped helplessly in the two vehicles, unable to escape the bleak fate that awaited them.

CHAPTER ELEVEN

THE BACKPACK LANDED ON THE road, then skidded to a stop beneath the Limo. The passengers inside the up-armored black SUV had no idea that at any second, they could all be dead. Then Liz's voice tore through the radio, echoing what Kat had just witnessed with her own eyes. There was no doubt about the nature of the weapon, and the Asian man sprinting down the street behind them only verified Catherine Parks's darkest fears. The nondescript vinyl fabric betrayed the bag's contents—most likely a carefully packed container of blocks of C-4 with an extra parting gift of ball bearings and nails.

"We need to stop him." Brandon's voice was taut with tension as he spoke his thoughts aloud.

From her position on the curb, Kat stood frozen in her spot, her eyes wide as she stared at the Limo. He followed her gaze to the up-armored SUV in the intersection. It was locked in place, unable to move forward in the gridlocked traffic, the lethal IED tucked securely beneath it. Even though the light had just turned green, a light blue Sport Utility Vehicle blocked them from their escape, the driver either oblivious or impervious to what was unfolding behind them. His fingers were wrapped tightly around his steering wheel, his knuckles blanched and his gaze fixed on his rearview mirror. If it didn't move soon, they could all very well become collateral damage in the explosion.

Brandon glanced at Kat, then back over his shoulder. Kat didn't seem to hear him, but he couldn't delay any longer. Any attempts to help usher the personnel from the SUVs would be both foolhardy and dangerous, as staying within the reinforced vehicles—even with the explosive beneath them—was safer than trying to evacuate them. His only other recourse, then, was to try to stop the terrorist. From his experience in law enforcement with a small municipal police department in California long before he became a CID special agent, he was acutely aware that it was imperative to catch him immediately. He needed to move *now.*

He shot one final glance at his partner, then turned away, his heel slipping slightly beneath him as he stepped off the sidewalk. Brandon staggered momentarily, his left hand reaching for Kat's arm to steady him, then regained his footing. The icy sidewalk was slippery beneath his feet, but this lack of traction could also be in his favor. The icy conditions would probably slow down the terrorist too. Brandon lowered his head and launched himself into the stalled traffic. Despite the slick film of ice glazing the surface, he allowed himself to pick up the pace.

Please, dear God, don't let me slip, he prayed silently.

As soon as he'd issued the request, his rubber-soled oxford skidded on a patch of ice, launching him farther down the street. His arms pinwheeled at his side as he regained his footing, and someone pressed on their horn as he ricocheted off the front end of their vehicle. Then he increased his tempo, emerging onto the other side of the street, and broke into a sprint as he headed west down E Street.

The terrorist was fast, but Brandon was faster. He held one hand out in front of him, extending it not unlike a quarterback charging through a sea of football players. Around him, the handful of holiday tourists moved aside, making way for the pair of men suddenly headed their way. Their faces were frozen in surprise as the Asian man darted past them, shortly followed by the sharply dressed man in a suit barreling down the sidewalk behind him.

The intersection fell behind him as he moved rapidly down E Street. The space between the terrorist and motorcade grew steadily wider as he narrowed the margin between himself and his target. Only a dozen yards separated Brandon from the Asian male, and the broad-shouldered CID agent was steadily gaining on the fleeing man. His eyes were locked on his quarry, his legs pumping rapidly beneath him. His breath came out of his lungs in short bursts, a hazy plume jerked out of his mouth by the prying wind as he sprinted toward the man steadily moving down the sidewalk.

"Brandon!"

He heard his name behind him and recognized Kat's voice. The wind blew her words away, making the normally resonant voice almost faint and distant. Then it came again, louder this time. Kat was gaining on him. Brandon felt a surge of relief and even a hint of pride at the younger agent trailing behind him. They were a team, after all. She had his back. Hell, in a moment, he'd possibly have the terrorist's back too. With her behind him, their chances of capturing the suspect had doubled.

Even with Kat's help, though, he knew saving the secretary's life wasn't guaranteed. If he did manage to capture the man darting down the sidewalk, there was no measure of assurance that he wouldn't just activate the detonator anyway. He knew this and that his chances of actually capturing him were slim, but he still had to try. He couldn't just let someone attack the secretary of defense—but also his friends—and get away.

Such a death would be so abrupt, so cruel. It would be no doubt a piss-poor end to such a respected and prolific career, and the thought of seeing such a respected figure reduced to a human pincushion caused a fresh surge of adrenaline to course through his veins, pushing him to go faster. Andrews deserved better than this. Hell, his friends in the motorcade deserved better than this.

Brandon steadily closed the distance between himself and the Asian man. In a few more seconds, he might actually be able to overtake him.

A tourist stumbled to the sidewalk, and Brandon ventured a glance back over his shoulder to confirm his partner's position. Kat's muscular, petite shape was only a handful of paces behind him, and like himself, her arm was outstretched. Despite her smaller stature, she was almost haphazardly pushing the loitering tourists off the sidewalk. He could hear a few shouts of surprise and pain as Kat rushed past them. Now Brandon could hear the woman shouting instructions at the tourists, telling them to get down. Yes, that was good advice. *They* should *get down,* Brandon thought distantly. If that backpack IED were to explode while they were still this close, they could be seriously injured.

And, in that instant, the IED behind them detonated. Heat—overwhelming and oppressive—enveloped them, wrapping them in a thick and tarry shroud of smoke and caustic fumes. The percussive force of the blast made the gusts of December wind seem like a mild breeze in comparison, and Brandon could hear the screams of victims rising over the roar of the explosion. Pain, fear, and outrage all mingled in a deafening crest. Brandon could see bodies collapsing to the ground around him, their faces and bodies marred by flying shrapnel and fresh, weeping wounds.

He had been too slow. Despite their best efforts, the terrorist had nonetheless succeeded in evading him. Agonized shrieks of pain and fear radiated from the intersection like a second shockwave, and he stumbled back from them involuntarily. The pounding in his chest had nothing to do with the exertion of trying to stop the terrorist. Each thud was a reminder that he was alive but others no longer were. They had perished because of his failure. He had failed not only his friends, but he had also failed the innocent bystanders who had the misfortune of being in the wrong place at the wrong time. It was a burden of guilt he would never be able to reconcile, and one he'd undoubtedly carry with him for the rest of his life.

—✶——✶——✶——✶——✶—

Chief Elizabeth Springer had fought an uphill battle to be in the passenger seat of the Chase vehicle, but despite the obstacles she'd faced throughout her fifteen-year military career to get there, she had proven time and again that she was undoubtedly the top candidate to be the shift lead. While her own team had never doubted her capabilities, she endured scrutiny from virtually everyone else. To them, it didn't matter that she was a top agent working the protection detail for the secretary of defense. They somehow couldn't overlook the fact that she stood at a fairly diminutive five-foot-two, weighed a max of a 110 pounds soaking wet, and happened to be in possession of female reproductive organs.

Liz wasn't the type of person to let these kinds of things hold her back, and in a way, they worked as fuel to drive her unwavering commitment to her job and gave her a strong competitive edge. She was arguably one of the most observant people on the team, which was why she was the first person to notice the Asian tourist hoisting the heavy backpack at the Limo. It took her just a couple of seconds to assimilate what was happening, and her eyes widened in horror as she recognized the threat unfolding in front of the Chase vehicle.

"James! Somebody just tossed a bag underneath the Limo! Get the hell out! *Get Cobra out of there!*" Liz's voice broke through the radio, alerting them all of the pending danger unfolding before them. But they weren't reacting. It was almost as though a dumbfounded shock had frozen them in place. Time seemed to slow down, and Liz couldn't be certain if it had been seconds or minutes since she had issued her order.

What the hell is taking them so long? From her seat, she could see an oblong object in his hand. With something like dismay, she realized it was most likely a detonator. Then the would-be assailant turned away from the Limo, his legs carrying him rapidly down the block. She estimated that when he had a wide enough distance between himself and the Limo, he would press the button on the detonator. They were living on borrowed time.

A chill had taken up residence in the base of her spine, and she couldn't conceal the mounting fear growing inside her. Despite her warning, the Limo still hadn't moved far enough forward to clear it from the threat. Ahead of them, she could see Brandon run past the Limo and then the Chase in the direction of the fleeing man. Her gaze followed him momentarily, then she returned her attention to the scene ahead of her. Why did she have to be so damned short?

"Shit," she muttered. Pressing her feet against the floorboard of the Chase, she hoisted her body up so she could see the traffic. Beneath her, the body armor she was using to raise her height a few inches above the dash shifted, then settled beneath her. It was admittedly a piss-poor booster seat, but even Liz had to admit it was better than the alternative.

Suddenly everything made sense to her. The Limo was trapped. Ahead of it, a bulky, older-model SUV blocked the intersection, its driver apparently oblivious to what was unfolding behind him. She could see him staring unflinchingly back at them in the rearview mirror of his vehicle, his expression unreadable from this distance. Why was he looking at them like that? Damn it, his careless curiosity was going to cost them all of their lives. He seemed indifferent to the impatiently honking horns behind him, as Liz watched, his eyes shifted to the Secret Service checkpoint. Not even Kat seemed to register on his radar as the CID agent threaded herself between the two vehicles a moment later, in her pursuit of her partner and the Chinese terrorist.

"Lights," Liz said suddenly, the words falling out of her mouth in a rapid clip. Her mind raced as she tried to make sense of the chaos unfolding around them. "Charles, turn on the lights and sirens. This jackass ahead of us isn't moving, and we need to get the hell out of here."

Ahead of them, the Limo seemed to have the same idea. The words were barely out of her mouth before they were cut out by the high-pitched whine of the siren on the heavily armored vehicle ahead. Charles nodded and, without hesitation, moved his hand to flick on their own SUV's lights and sirens. Now a repeated pulse of blue and red coming from low-profile emergency lights of the Chase added to the chaos, and their own vehicle's siren rose to meet the wail of the one emanating from the Limo.

There. That should, at least, get the damned driver to do something.

It had worked. The sudden output of flashing lights and piercing sirens seemed to successfully wake up the driver in the powder blue SUV. After what felt like an eternity—but perhaps was no more than three or four seconds—the driver's side door opened and a tall, slim figure leaped out. The driver turned to face them, the December wind pulling his dark hair out of his face long enough for Liz to see the flat expression in his almond-shaped eyes. Then, without preamble, he started sprinting north on 17th Street as if he was exactly aware of what had just occurred.

Something seemed to click as the reality of the situation registered inside Liz's mind, and her eyes widened in horror. The driver of the blue SUV wasn't just some reckless tourist obstructing their frantic attempt to escape from danger. He was working in coordination with the guy who had tossed the backpack under the Limo to assassinate the SecDef, and if the rest of the passengers in the Limo and Chase were taken out as collateral damage, it was all the better.

Her voice, however, was surprisingly steady as she cried out into her radio, "Push through! I repeat, push through! Push through!"

No reply from the Limo was necessary. From all the times they had practiced this maneuver in their executive protection training, they had never truly expected to have to use it. An instant later, Liz saw the Limo move forward, bearing down on the older-model blue SUV. Its tires spun on the ice, squealing audibly, but their efforts were futile. The SUV wasn't budging.

"Charles, listen." She turned her face toward the man in the driver's seat. "We have to help them. That damned SUV isn't going anywhere, and the Limo can't push it on its own. We've gotta help them push it out of the way."

"Yeah. I got you." In the driver's seat next to her, Charles nodded. He tore his gaze from the fleeing man, and his foot shifted from the brake pedal to the gas pedal and pressed down lightly against the accelerator. The normally jovial man was now tense and subdued as he glanced sideways at her, nodding once more as he turned back to the road and focused his concerted efforts on clearing the Limo of danger. Slowly, the Chase vehicle edged forward, closing in on the heavy black SUV in front of it.

Inside the vehicle, the tension was palpable, and in the rearview window, Liz could see Audra in the back seat. Her cell phone was to her ear, her lips moving quickly as she spoke into it. The woman's pupils darted back and forth as she broke down the scene around them to Pentagon Communications, as their training dictated. Then the call ended, and her eyes locked with Liz's. Yes, she was also afraid, but she was refusing to reveal it. To Liz, though, it was unmistakable.

Would their efforts be enough, though? Liz watched with wide eyes as the nose of the Chase SUV nudged against the rear bumper of the Limo. Ahead of them, she could see the Limo using its bulk to nudge the powder blue SUV forward. Now the Chase's fender was directly on the rear bumper of the Limo. Beside her, Charles kept his foot pressed on the accelerator, his eyes fixed on the pair of vehicles ahead of them. His knuckles blanched as they gripped the steering wheel, and as Liz glanced down at him and then up at his set jaw, she realized she was holding her breath.

She wanted to scream, Fucking *move* already! But it wouldn't have made any difference. She gripped the dashboard with her right hand, and the side of the leather seat with her left hand. Charles kept his foot pressed resolutely down upon the gas pedal. The rear tires spun futilely on the slush-covered asphalt, but they were making it move. Marc seemed to be aware of the Chase's efforts, and from her vantage, she could see the rear tires of his own SUV rotating in its own icy trap, spinning but unable to propel him forward with much enthusiasm.

The nose of the Limo was wedged firmly against the bumper of the pastel blue SUV, and inch by inch, it seemed to be gaining more ground. At first, the vehicle resisted the hulking weight of the Limo pressing against it, but Liz let out a low sigh of relief as the vehicle was slowly forced out of the way. It rocked slightly, fighting back against the efforts of the vehicle behind it, the locked brakes trying to secure it in place on the roadway. Then the Limo was moving, the ice somehow facilitating them instead of hindering them, and so was the Chase. It had worked. Charles's efforts in assisting the Limo were actually working.

Liz let the air out of her lungs. They just might make it. In the distance, the man with the detonator was nearly a quarter block away now. She could see the bright red blur of his hat as he wove in and out of pedestrian traffic. In just a few moments, he'd round a corner and be completely clear of the blast radius. People spun out of his way, throwing their arms up in surprise as he careened past them.

The Limo inched forward first a foot, then another. It crept steadily forward, distancing itself from the IED. The Chase matched its pace, and Liz found herself struggling to not implore Charles to floor the gas pedal. Even if he did, it wouldn't actually accomplish anything because of the ice-slick road.

We got this. We can do this. C'mon, Charles, get us out of here—

⁕——⁕——⁕——⁕——⁕

There was an IED beneath the Limo. The realization of this new threat raced through James's thoughts, completing their journey in the span of a heartbeat. There was an IED beneath the Limo, and they were trapped in a damned traffic jam at 17th and E with a powder-blue SUV holding them hostage at the intersection. How the hell had they managed to get themselves into this predicament? And more importantly, how was he going to get them back out of it?

"Drive, damn it," James said abruptly, the words breaking through the stunned silence in the vehicle. "*Drive!*"

"I'm fucking *trying*,"_Marc shot back, his voice almost a snarl and entirely uncharacteristic of the normally easygoing man's demeanor. His foot leaned on the gas pedal, and the Limo inched closer to the blue SUV ahead of them.

Even with the Limo inches away from hitting its bumper, though, the driver of the vehicle still refused to budge. The light had turned green several seconds before, and he somehow seemed unaware of the change in the flow of traffic, his focus on his rearview mirror and not the traffic signal in front of him. It was both infuriating and baffling, and the outraged expression on Marc's face matched the one James felt on his own.

James braced his arm against the dashboard and turned his body toward the Chase SUV. The dark tint obscured a clearer view of the three passengers, but he could see Liz's hands moving animatedly in the air as she issued some unheard instruction to Charles. He nodded, his lips moving soundlessly as he offered an equally frantic reply.

Behind him, Secretary Andrews's hands were frozen in place, holding onto the stack of paperwork in his lap. The action plans were forgotten as he looked first at James, then at Marc. Despite the urgency of the situation, there was a dry note of irony in his voice as he spoke. "Marc, I believe now would be a good time to turn on those lights."

"Yes, sir." Marc reached down and, without taking his eyes off the intersection ahead of them, turned on the emergency lights and sirens. The keening shriek of the siren rose in the midday traffic, adding to the steady cacophony of strident horns and the confused shouts of the tourists. "What the *hell* is this clown doing?"

In front of them, the driver's door of the blue SUV was opening, and a tall, wiry man slipped out. He turned as he emerged from the vehicle, and his gaze lit momentarily on the Limo. The hate emanating from it was unmistakable, and despite himself, James felt oddly unnerved by the unrestrained fury behind them. Then the door swung shut, and James pried his eyes from his and allowed them to sweep over the man, taking in the rest of his appearance. His sallow skin and jet black hair seemed to be far too much of a coincidence. As James locked the pieces of the puzzle together in his mind, the man took off in a sprint north on 17th Street.

"They're together," James said flatly. The words sounded hollow in his ears. How many more terrorists were within proximity to them right now? Would someone start opening fire upon them at any moment? His eyes swept the roadway, but just like the traffic was at a standstill, nobody else seemed to be moving with any sense of urgency. That needed to change. The IED was literally a ticking bomb beneath them, and the longer they loitered there, the greater their chances were of being in the blast radius when the terrorist ultimately detonated it.

A voice in his ear broke through his thoughts, and he recognized Liz's voice calling out, "Push through! I repeat, push through! Push through!"

A moment later, a sudden jolt behind him made him turn back in his seat once more. The Chase SUV was now pressed against the heavily armored Limo, its bumper nestled against their own bumper. Behind him, Secretary Andrews swayed forward from the motion, and his arm shot out to brace against the headrest of the seat directly in front of him. In that moment, James realized the man was not wearing his seatbelt. How the hell did he manage to overlook this when Andrews had gotten into the Limo? Normally he had it securely fastened, as damage to government property was a fairly severe offense in the army. And, undoubtedly, Andrews was an article of property of high value.

Shit! Could anything else go wrong today?

James felt the Limo sway again from the force of the Chase SUV pushing up behind it. Next to him, Marc's hands were tight on the steering wheel, keeping the vehicle steady as he eased it forward. The Limo moved again, and in front of them, the blue SUV steadily inched toward the intersection. The Chase SUV supplied the extra force necessary, assisting the Limo forward. James couldn't conceal the relief he felt as the vehicle moved forward. The knowledge that he might be killed by an IED didn't unnerve him half as much as the thought of Secretary Andrews dying.

Ahead of him, the powder blue SUV was now pushed out into the intersection. With this obstacle cleared from their path, their escape route was evident, if not still slightly hindered. If Marc could just navigate away from the backpack, then they'd finally be out of harm's way with the vehicle's armor being enough to protect them. But the bag had been tossed beneath the nose of the Limo, and now it was probably somewhere near the rear of their vehicle or right around the front of the Chase vehicle. Despite their efforts, they had only managed to gain a couple meters of forward distance, and if it exploded now, it would very likely be all over for them.

In the distance, James could see the Asian man with the detonator plowing through the crowd of tourists on the sidewalk, and Brandon and Kat trailing behind him. The sea of visitors parted, then closed again, once more obstructing his view of the terrorist.

"Marc," James said, giving his friend's name a note of warning in his tone. The single word had numerous other meanings hidden within it. It was a plea. It was a command. It was a question. They both knew what James was trying to communicate, and he didn't need to say anything else.

Marc didn't look at him, nor did he reply to James's comment. His face was a stony mask. There was no reason for him to take his eyes off the road and glance over at James. His shoulders were tense, and his spine was rigid. The man was the embodiment of unflinching focus. Until he had navigated them to safety, he would not reply to James's words. Right now, all that mattered to him was getting off the X. Marc had the power to save the secretary and themselves, but only if he could successfully put enough distance between the Limo and the threat beneath them.

No pressure now, buddy. C'mon.

The SUV moved forward another foot, then another. The Limo had managed to clear the backpack completely now, and they just needed to create a wide enough berth between the Chase and the IED and they'd both be out of any immediate danger of the blast. For the first time since the explosive had skidded beneath them at the intersection of 17th and E—had it really only been less than two minutes before?—James allowed himself to start to believe they would actually be able to escape this situation.

CHAPTER TWELVE

THE AFTERMATH

J AMES FELT HIS BODY LURCH forward and realized with detached wonder that the Limo was airborne. The city block faded as the vehicle launched forward several yards, its fire engulfed rear wheels high in the air and spinning futilely as they still tried to gain traction despite being completely airborne. For a moment, it seemed as though the laws of gravity had been forgotten. But just as quickly as the Limo tried to master these new acrobatic maneuvers, it slammed violently back to the road, rupturing the tires upon impact.

Bright white splotches blotted out James's vision, and his teeth snapped painfully together as the vehicle slammed down. His body jolted forward, a limp ragdoll in the SUV, then fell back against the passenger seat. Then the Limo was still.

The damage, however, had only just begun. Flames licked out of the rear of the Limo, working their way up the body of the hefty vehicle. In a few minutes, the SUV would be completely engulfed in flames. The passengers would also be consumed by fire if they didn't escape the vehicle quickly.

While the harm inflicted upon the Limo was severe, it paled in comparison to the Chase. Behind James, the SUV was practicing its own attempts at mastering a twirl. Thanks to its position directly over the IED and the lack of armor, the relatively weaker vehicle bore a much greater brunt of damage.

Liz's efforts had been nothing short of heroic. Thanks to her quick thinking, she had managed to assist in clearing the Limo from over top of the IED, reducing the amount of damage being sustained to the passengers inside. Sadly, the same couldn't be said for the passengers inside the Chase. By forcing the Limo forward, she had managed to relocate the backpack from beneath the entirety of the Limo and instead reposition it to the first half of the Chase's engine block. While her actions had been a valiant attempt to save the secretary—as well as the rest of the team inside the Limo—they'd had devastating repercussions for the Chase vehicle and its occupants.

The magnitude of the explosion was significant enough to launch the Chase into the air. It soared high above the street, completing one revolution before landing nose-first onto the road. Fortunately for Liz, she was unconscious before the vehicle crumpled like a ball of aluminum foil against the asphalt. It stood suspended in the air for a moment, a precarious balancing act that defied gravity, before tipping over and falling onto its roof. The windows had fractured from the explosion, and the impact from the collision with the ground was more than the glass could handle. Sharp, glittering shards rained down, spraying out from the vehicle in all directions.

Hungry flames erupted almost immediately upon impact, enveloping the SUV in lethal heat. Liz hung suspended from the passenger's seat, her body hanging laxly against the seatbelt. Next to her, Charles dangled lifelessly in the driver's seat with his head cocked at an unnatural angle, his eyes wide and unseeing. His death had been instantaneous, a small mercy. Audra had no such luck. She was alive but unconscious as the flames found her body. Fortunately, her neck had snapped in the explosion and she felt none of the fire consuming her. It was a paltry blessing, though she'd never have the opportunity to utter a word of thanks.

Liz had never been one to let mocking comments about her gender or her height hold her back, but she couldn't deny the fact that being a petite woman did make it harder to do her job. In order to help her see more clearly from vehicle seats, she had always made herself a booster seat out of whatever was handy. Tucked beneath her this time, her body armor had absorbed most of the concussive force when the explosion occurred. Combined with the newly issued body armor she was wearing underneath her suit, she'd been protected from the majority of the shrapnel. A jagged wedge of metal later identified as part of the oil pan had embedded itself in the chest plate of her vest. Because of this, she had the dubious honor of becoming the sole survivor inside the Chase vehicle.

Around the pair of SUVs, chaos and disarray had erupted. The closest tourists and bystanders, all of whom had been watching the events unfold with bemused interest minutes before, were now laying in crumpled heaps on the sidewalk. Most, if not all of them, had sustained severe injuries. Limbs lay on the icy road, separated from their owners, and bloodied faces stared out blind and unseeing. A few let out pitiful groans, but even more were silent and still. Around them, the debris—paperwork, shrapnel, nails, and shards of glass—rained down upon the frozen December ground.

It was a fairly safe assessment to say that most of the people within thirty feet of the blast had perished, were in the process of dying, or were critically wounded. A second wave of tourists and locals, those who had been fortunate enough to be greater than forty feet or more away from the explosion, had also sustained wounds, but the majority of them survived. They wasted zero time making a hasty retreat from the blast site, the shock and horror of the situation propelling them away. Understandably, they seemed to be in shock, and beneath the screams of anguish and pain, a disjointed conversation moved between them, echoing the sentiments that they all shared.

"What the hell happened?"

"Dear God, where is my leg?"

"Somebody help me!"

The road and sidewalks had been refinished in a thick layer of blood, making it difficult to distinguish hunks of flesh from debris.

While the morning had started with the SUVs transporting four CID agents, an air force communicator, and the secretary of defense, those numbers had just been tragically reduced. And the death unfolding before them was only the start of similar actions unfolding across the country. Before the day ended, hundreds more lives would be claimed by the actions of agents working on behalf of the People's Republic of China.

⸺ ✖ ✖ ✖ ✖ ✖ ⸻

Kat had watched as the terrorist vanished in the crowd. From her position on the sidewalk, her partner's body pinned beneath her, she felt completely helpless. It wasn't a feeling that she particularly cared for, and as she watched the assailant vanish in the crowd, she decided she never wanted to feel like that again. Even as the attacker escaped by vanishing around the street corner, it clearly did not occur to any of the tourists on the street to try to intercept or block him.

"Kat!" From behind her, Brandon tugged on her suit sleeve.

The sharp yank on the fabric caused her to pivot her head toward the sound of his voice. The agent had somehow managed to wrench himself out from beneath her and stand up. He extended his arm, and Kat took it, letting him hoist her to feet.

Brandon said matter-of-factly, "He's gone. We need to check on the SecDef and the rest of the team."

The grim simplicity of his message seemed to jolt Kat from her haze, and she didn't hesitate as she fell into step behind Brandon. Both agents hurried back to the motorcade, moving as fast as the icy, debris-coated roadway would allow them to move. The sight that greeted them caused them both to momentarily freeze on the edge of the sidewalk. Both SUVs were fully engulfed in flames, and within each were the limp, lifeless bodies of the personnel assigned to the secretary.

Then Kat saw stirring from the passenger's side of the Limo, and renewed hope surged inside her. Brandon had been right. Someone may have actually survived the attack. She darted toward the Limo as he set off in the direction of the Chase. She had no idea what her partner would find in the inverted SUV, but she had a bleak feeling it wasn't going to be any better than what she was going to find in the Limo. There was something uncanny about the vehicle's appearance, and it seemed to be strangely tilted on the icy road. As she moved closer, she realized the rear of the SUV was sitting lower than the front. A glance down confirmed that the rear tires had ruptured in the explosion, the heat and force of the explosion causing severe damage to them and the rear of the up-armored SUV.

She approached the passenger side of the vehicle, her breath trapped in her throat as she scanned its interior. She grabbed the front passenger side door handle with both hands and tried to pull it open, but it was still locked. She looked inside and could see James turn his head to face her. At that moment, he looked down and unlocked all the doors of the SUV.

Kat tried the door again and was surprised at being able to get it open with relative ease. "James, you good?"

"Yeah, I'm good," he muttered as he rubbed the back of his neck with his left hand.

Kat glanced over at Marc in the driver seat and noticed he was seatbelted in and still breathing but unconscious. Satisfied with her findings, she returned her attention to James. "Are you sure you're okay?"

He offered her a slight shake of his head in acknowledgment, a grimace flashing across his face as an invisible jolt of pain shot through him at the motion. She then noticed blood trickling down his nose, but other than that, he seemed surprisingly unblemished in the attack.

"I'm fine. Check on the secretary. He wasn't wearing his seat belt," he said. Coughing, he jerked his thumb toward the back seat and shook his head back and forth at the alarm on Kat's face. *I'm okay*, his expression read. *Don't worry about me.*

The words didn't seem to register at first, and Kat stared blankly at James for several heart beats before she realized what the senior CID agent had told her. She spun hastily on her heel, her shoe slipping on the icy road, and turned toward the rear passenger seat. Even before she opened the door, she could see the lax, lifeless body of Secretary Andrews propped against it. His head appeared flopped forward, his silver hair falling down into his face. Kat reached down and grabbed the door handle and pulled the heavy armored door open, then stepped back, her arms extended and ready to catch Andrews.

"Sir?" Kat couldn't conceal the waver in her voice. The secretary's body was a heavy burden, limp and lifeless in her tense grip. "Secretary Andrews? Sir? Can you hear me?"

Dread twisted in her stomach, and her pulse pounded loudly in her ears as she held the warm, heavy body in her arms. The secretary wasn't responding, and as his weight shifted, his body slipped down. A bright crimson streak marked her suit coat, then was quickly absorbed into the fabric.

Oh, dear God, he's dead.

Just as the thought crossed her mind, though, it was banished by a low groan coming out of Secretary Andrews's mouth. The fear and grief that had already been burgeoning inside her gut were quickly replaced by tentative hope, and she found herself releasing a breath that she had no idea she had been holding. He was alive. He had somehow managed to survive the explosion.

"Secretary Andrews, sir?"

"Kat!" A cry from behind caused Kat to jerk her head up, and she glanced back at the direction of the shout.

Brandon was rising to his feet, his hand waving frantically over his head, beckoning the woman toward him.

She gently hoisted the secretary back into the SUV, taking note of the deep gash on his forehead, then carefully shut the door. She closed it gently, not allowing it to click. The smoke coming from the back of the Limo was growing thicker, and while she didn't want Andrews to tumble out of the vehicle, she also didn't want him to suffocate. "James?"

"I've got him," James told her in a hoarse rasp as he opened the heavy passenger's side door by reaching back from inside.

He lowered his feet to the road. His legs were unsteady, and she had no doubts that adrenaline was making him impervious to the pain he surely felt. Or, perhaps he was carefully ignoring it, knowing Kat was needed elsewhere. Already the SecDef was stirring in his seat.

James waved the back of his hand at her, dismissing her. "Go, check on the team in the Chase."

Kat didn't need to be told twice. She let her fingers slide against the metal door of the Limo as she rounded it. In the distance, she could hear the siren wails of first responder vehicles arriving to the scene. She glanced back over her shoulder as she rushed to Brandon's side, but none of the flashing red lights were visible yet. She turned her face back to the flipped SUV and Brandon was her partner kneeling on the icy road, a fire extinguisher by his side.

He glanced up as Kat approached, his eyes flat and expressionless. "I was able to get most of the fire, but I now need you to help me get Liz out of there."

"The paramedics are coming," Kat said. She lowered herself to the ground next to Brandon and turned her gaze toward the unconscious PSO in the passenger seat of the Chase SUV. From where she squatted, she could see the woman was not moving. Her eyes were shut, and her skin was coated in a thick film of blood. It was almost as though she were bleeding from every surface, her normally tan skin coated in crimson blood. Trails of the viscous substance trickled from her nose, her ears, and even from her scalp. "Holy shit. This is bad."

"The others didn't make it." Brandon glanced at Kat's face, then back inside the vehicle. "I know the paramedics are coming, but this vehicle is getting hot. I don't think the gas tank is going to blow, but I don't want to risk it. There's no way in hell she can breathe in there. And those flames are moving quick. We need to get her out of there."

"If we move her, we could hurt her more." Kat's voice was uncertain. As far as she could determine, Liz was in terrible shape. She could have a broken neck or spine. If they shifted her and tried to hoist her out of the Chase, they could permanently disable her. If they didn't, she could very well suffocate inside the vehicle before the paramedics arrived. She could hear the wails of the rescue vehicles closing the distance. They would be there in less than a minute or two.

"Yeah." Brandon scooted back, then reached for the door handle. He paused, his fingers wrapping around it, then he shrugged. "Cool to the touch. For now. Help me open the door. Get some air in there. All the other windows are busted out, anyway, but I don't think she can breathe. All we need is to buy a minute or two for her, until the paramedics get here."

"What?" Kat said, then she paused. She didn't want to ask the question loitering on the tip of her tongue, but she needed to know. "What about the others? Are you sure they're dead?"

"I'm sure." There was no inflection to Brandon's words. He raised his eyes to Kat's, then back at the door of the battered SUV. "Help me. Please."

"Yeah, sure. Of course." Kat brushed her hands off on the wool fabric of her slacks and, without a final glance back at the drawn face of her friend and partner, gripped the door handle. Behind Liz, through the thick black smoke congesting the body of the Chase vehicle, she could see a vague hint of the outline of Charles's body. Brandon had been correct. There was nothing they could do for him. She didn't dare glance into the back seat to confirm Audra's death. Brandon had already shouldered that burden for the both of them.

As the metal door pried open, screeching an inhuman shriek that blended in seamlessly with the chaos already unfolding on 17th Street, Kat found herself mourning the loss of life before her. It was such a damned waste. Not only were Audra and Charles incredibly good people, but they had also been her good friends. Charles had his sarcastic and self-exaggerating wit, and Audra? She was a career air force woman with a husband and two teenagers at home. Somebody would be coming home to an empty house that night. Her son and daughter would have to learn what it was like to grow up without their mother. But what they lost almost paled in comparison to what the handful of determined, ruthless Chinese agents had stolen away from the rest of the nation that day.

The attempt on the secretary of defense's life was a catalyst leading to an almost domino-like effect immediately following it. After the IED exploded beneath the Chase SUV, the Secret Service also exploded into action, thanks to the instantaneous, automatic activation of the White House Emergency System following the explosion.

President Thomas's PSO sought him out and quickly briefed him as to what had transpired just a couple hundred meters away from the White House, then ushered him to the Presidential Emergency Operations Center (PEOC). It took only minutes for the vice president, first lady, and other essential personnel to join him in the White House bunker. There they would remain sequestered until the all-clear was given. The bunker had its own command-and-control center, so they could arguably remain there and run operations from within with no issues.

President Thomas nodded distantly. The words barely registered to him. First the attack on the *McCain*, then this. He didn't even know yet if Andrews was still alive, much less the fate of the CID agents assigned to his detail. The lack of information was almost as infuriating as the attack itself. His thumb and forefinger rubbed together automatically as he leaned on his desk, his eyes fixed on the wall opposite of him. They better damned well catch the perpetrator. He could even admit that he wouldn't mind interrogating the bastard himself. While he knew this would be a luxury never afforded to him, it didn't change the sentiment. Cold vengeance settled in his stomach.

Back at the scene of the attack, chaos and disarray seemed to be the new normal. Just as Secret Service Personnel had scattered across the White House in order to secure it, another team descended upon the blast site with similar intentions. Not only did they need to close off the block, but they also needed to check on the secretary of defense—the primary target of the attack—and the remaining survivors. The survivors were ushered away from the scene, with the exception of a handful of witnesses who were pulled aside to collect statements.

Within minutes of the attack, a perimeter crime scene had been created. Several streets running in both directions away from the attack were closed off, and the DC police set up an impromptu barrier to maintain the perimeter and crowd control. The ATF and the FBI followed suit, launching the primary investigation to determine the origins of the attack and track down the suspects. While nobody actually believed they would be able to successfully capture them, at least not within any reasonable distance to the blast site, they still wanted to carefully comb the area for any evidence that might lead back to them.

Throughout the nation, a series of explosions had erupted, killing over a thousand innocent men and women. While the attacks primarily occurred at military locations, the victims weren't exclusively soldiers or military personnel. Numerous civilian bystanders also perished in these cruel, premeditated attacks.

In Tampa, Florida, an agent working for China had managed to sneak onto MacDill Air Force Base in a seemingly benign white van with "Chen's Flowers" inscribed on the side in fading letters. It had been no ordinary vehicle, though. It had not come bearing gifts of fragrant blooms, but rather, tightly packed explosives. The vehicle-borne improvised explosive device (VBED) had parked itself right outside the entrance to the DEFAC at MacDill Air Force Base, its engine idling in the shadow of the building. Considering how closely guarded the perimeter of the base had been after the attack on the *McCain*, it clearly pointed to an insider threat.

One eyewitness recounted seeing an Asian man of slim build casually walking away from the vehicle minutes before the explosion. His presence wasn't necessarily out of the ordinary as MacDill AFB was an international base, but his attire made him stand out somewhat. The observer noted he had been dressed in a long-sleeved shirt and a heavy knit hat, which was uncommon attire for the sunny region.

The loss of life in this particular attack was perhaps the largest that day. Over three hundred people—men and women, soldiers and civilians—had been congregated at the dining facility and other nearby buildings when the VBED detonated. The percussive force from the explosion managed to demolish not only the DEFAC but several surrounding facilities as well. The majority of the people inside the DEFAC, including active duty personnel, retirees, and civilians, perished.

Another dozen attacks were executed that day, the majority of them occurring several hours after the assault on the secretary's motorcade. While the initial body count was approximately one thousand men and women, this number would rise as the days passed and additional people succumbed to their injuries. December 01, 2025 had been one of the largest coordinated domestic terrorist attacks in the country in decades and would go down as one of the greatest losses of life in American history, second only to September 11, 2001. It would not be soon forgotten, which was exactly what the operatives behind the attacks had wanted.

But there had also been another side effect of the widescale assault, one that the Chinese terrorists had failed to anticipate. While they had indeed succeeded in their goal of driving fear through the hearts of the American people, patriotism surged in the immediate hours following the attacks and a renewed mutual adoration for their home country instantly followed. Such levels of devotion and unity hadn't been seen in over two decades, since 2001. The strikes had been designed to cripple the country, weaken their morale and their resolve, it had the complete opposite effect.

A rally cry arose from the rubble, one that was echoed on the lips of the American people with earnest candor. "If you mess with us, you will pay." That devout patriotism—which almost veered onto nationalism for many—was, at least, something that the terrorists could never take from them.

CHAPTER THIRTEEN

INTELLIGENCE ON CHINA

THE CIA'S ANALYST TO CHINA'S military affairs was a short and slim man, barely above five and a half feet in height. His eyes were a piercing and alert shade of hazel, which he hid behind wireframed glasses. He peered around the room with those intelligent eyes as he waited for the briefing to begin. Edgar Montgomery's brow wrinkled as he met the president's gaze, and President Thomas returned it with a nod of his own. The gesture was meant to be encouraging, but the tension continued to linger there as Edgar waited for permission to disclose the information written down before him.

A low murmur coursed through the stuffy room as the Cabinet members waited for the briefing to begin. The morning meeting had already been delayed due to the attempt on the secretary of defense's life, and a thrum of impatience seemed to generate its own source of energy inside the Cabinet Room. Throats cleared, feet shuffled on the floor, and quiet glances were exchanged between the personnel occupying it. Already they were guaranteed to be short one essential party, the SecDef himself, who was currently in recovery at Walter Reed. The official report on Andrews had been largely positive, indicating he was well on his way to recovery. However, getting the Secret Service to allow them to host the meeting in the Cabinet Room instead of the PEOC had been a task in and of itself. With the pushback they had faced to even hold it in the first place, they weren't about to start without the vice president.

As if on cue, a door opened and the vice president ducked his head and stepped through it. There was an apologetic look on his face as he crossed the room. The eyes in the room momentarily shifted from Edgar to Vice President Nicholas Roth and back again. Roth took a seat next to the president, and as he settled into the high-backed wooden chair, his lips went to President Thomas's ear to whisper a quick apology for his tardiness. Thomas dismissed the explanation with a shrug. What mattered was that he was there now, and his meeting with the president of Zambia to discuss humanitarian aid was secondary to this. The people in the room shifted impatiently in their seats. With everyone now present, they were officially ready for the briefing. Edgar could finally begin.

"Mr. Montgomery?" President Thomas cleared his throat, and a hush fell over the room.

All the Cabinet's eyes immediately fixed upon him.

He nodded briefly in acknowledgment of the polite silence, then continued, "I understand you have some intel about China for us."

"I do, Mr. President." Edgar rose to his feet. Despite his diminutive height, he had a strong bearing to him, one that made him appear taller than he truly was. He pushed his glasses up his nose, then lifted his chin, positioning his lined legal pad at arm's length from his face. His eyes swept across the room, lingering on each individual seated inside the briefing room. "I'd like to begin by reminding everyone in this room that what you're about to hear is classified Top Secret and cannot leave this room."

Heads nodded. This reminder was redundant. They already knew this. They hadn't earned their position in the Cabinet by running their mouths or betraying the nation's secrets, for crying out loud. The notes were clearly of high value, though, and his reminder reinforced the gravity of the situation that the nation had found itself in. Someone coughed, and another person tapped their fingertip on the table impatiently. The unspoken message was loud and clear. *Just begin, already.*

"Here's what we know," Edgar said, glancing up from the handwritten notes in front of him for a beat before returning his gaze to it. "As far as we can determine, China has been steadily moving forward with what they call 'China's New World Order.' What does that mean? In short, global domination. China has increased its research and education funding exponentially every single year since 1976."

If anyone was surprised by this information, they kept it to themselves.

Most, if not all, of them knew about China's increased spending. That was no secret, and anyone with a modest amount of interest in the nation had a fairly modest understanding about their education budget. However, the terminology for it, calling it a New World Order, might have been a revelation to some of them. If it were, nobody was ready to admit it. Nobody commented. Nobody uttered a word. Eleven pairs of eyes bore into the CIA analyst, silently prodding him to continue speaking.

Edgar didn't pause to wait for their reactions. Questions would come after the briefing. For now, he merely needed to get the words out, to share this vital intel with the people in the room. He added, "China has multiple programs in place, each designed to strengthen their foothold in the East. None of them, however, were more successful than the Thousand Talents program."

In the back of the room, a hand started to creep up. Edgar ignored it, and the hand slowly descended back into the lap of the secretary of transportation. Marilyn Whittier glanced sheepishly around the room, but nobody else seemed to currently have any questions for the CIA analyst. If she wanted clarification on anything, she would have to wait for the end of the briefing. She picked up her pen and tapped her notepad with it, a chagrined scowl on her face.

"If you're wondering what the Thousand Talents program is," Edgar said, casting a pointed glance at the secretary of transportation briefly before resuming, "it's one of the many programs China has initiated to enhance the technological and military advancements of the country."

In the room, a low murmur started to crest, steadily growing louder. Questions lingered on the lips of the Cabinet members, but nobody dared speak them aloud. Instead, they waited for Edgar to reveal what the Thousand Talents program entailed. He had lingered long enough, and a collective mounting impatience was mirrored on the faces of the men and women in the briefing room.

"It was designed to recruit people from around the world and have them bring in research and technological advancements from other corporations and governments." Edgar nodded as he read these words on his notes, as though affirming them either to himself or his audience. "They'd then give these discoveries to China at great monetary reward. This information that they divulged included proprietary and classified government technology.

And as it turns out, this program has been highly successful for China in increasing their military technological advancements."

Ah. So that's what it was. President Thomas leaned forward, capturing his chin in his hand as he listened to Edgar speak. His eyes narrowed. *Who sold them out? Does Edgar know?* Icy wrath pulsed through his veins, and he found himself fighting—and resisting—the urge to direct his irritation toward Edgar. After all, the man was merely delivering the intel. He wasn't to blame for what China had done to them. He waited for the CIA analyst to continue.

"Of course, the Thousand Talents program isn't the only one that has been lucrative for China. There's also been one other, which has also proven to be very rewarding to the Chinese government." Edgar swiped his index finger across his tongue, then turned the page of his notebook. "That program would be their cyber intrusions and cyber warfare programs. Because of their continuous success in cyber activity, China has invested quite a lot of resources to make their own cyber program one of the best in the world."

How powerful is their cyber program, exactly? President Thomas leaned back in his chair, crossing his arms over his chest. The depth of careful planning by the Chinese was astounding. How long had they been working toward this goal? No doubt, it had been for at least several years. Perhaps even decades. *What exactly have they accomplished so far?* The thought shot through his mind, and he briefly entertained it before returning his attention to Edgar. He didn't doubt that he'd soon find out.

"In the last ten years, they have broken into more than twelve defense contractors' networks. At least, those are the ones we're aware of." Edgar cleared his throat and pushed his glasses back up his nose. He didn't look up from the notepad in front of him, but the stiffening of his spine indicated that the ripple of outraged murmurs rising in the room wasn't lost on him. "They've been able to access thousands of gigabytes of corporate and government advanced proprietary technological data, most of which they've reengineered to work better and faster."

Ah, there it was. They had added the proverbial insult to injury. Not only had they found a back door to sneak in through to access their hard-earned, proprietary technology, but they actually had the knowledge to revise it to make it work more efficiently. Since what they had taken from them had not met their specific needs, they had then taken the liberty of modifying what they had taken to improve upon it. Then, as the icing on the larceny cake, they had used it against the very people from whom they stole the information. Thomas's lips settled into a firm line. *The bastards.*

"I hate to say it," Edgar said, and his voice genuinely sounded remorseful, "but within the last few years, we've seriously lost the technological advantage we used to have. There are many reasons for this, but it is, in part, that over the last fifteen years, China has become more geopolitically involved. They have an impressive business and political involvement in South America, Central America, and even a large presence in several African countries. And because of this involvement, their economy has prospered."

That was, without a doubt, an understatement. Anyone who had been keeping tabs on current events could have attested to that. China's exports, for instance, had grown exponentially in the last twenty years. These days, it was all but impossible to purchase an item without a "Made in China" sticker. Mainland tourists, suddenly nouveau riche, had flocked to areas that were once inaccessible to Chinese visitors. Reports of rude behavior from these guests were often dismissed as in poor taste, as nobody wanted to be the person who called out an entire demographic for being disrespectful guests. And, of course, the majority of technology and manufacturing seemed to come from China these days. It would, therefore, only make sense that the country was becoming handsomely rich.

"China's economy produced $29.3 trillion in 2024 according to the International Monetary Fund," Edgar told them.

Eyes around the room grew wider at this number. They had known it was a vast amount, but none of them had fathomed it would be this large of a number.

"That number's based on purchasing power parity, though, which takes into account the effect of exchange rates. For those of you who don't know how this works, doing it this way makes it the best method for comparing gross domestic product by country. That also, interestingly enough, makes China the world's largest economy."

Someone from the back of the room let out a low whistle, followed by a dumbfounded, "Holy *shit.*"

Heads craned back to peer at the source of the voice, and a flush went up the collar of the secretary of agriculture. He shook his head and offered them a rueful grin and a shrug. He had merely been echoing the sentiments everyone else in the room happened to be currently thinking. At least the remark hadn't come from the secretary of commerce. Marilyn Whittier shook her head at him reproachfully, and he shrugged again, an unrepentant gesture.

Edgar waited patiently for the room to fall quiet again, then returned his attention to the sheath of papers in his grasp. "As I was saying, China's now the world's largest economy. If you're wondering who is second, I hate to disappoint you, but it's not us either. That goes to the European Union, at $27 trillion. And finally, we eke by in third, producing a comparatively paltry $24.5 trillion."

"Listen," President Thomas drawled, his voice breaking through the pause in Edgar's monologue. "That's all fine and dandy that you know all that information, but it doesn't help me one lick here. What I want to know is how we compare militarily. That's the number that matters to me right now. Can you give me that information, Edgar?"

Edgar lowered the pad of paper in his hands, and the sigh that came out of his mouth seemed to come from the deepest recesses of his lungs. The look on his face was stark and naked, and he stood silently at the front of the room, his eyes trailing first over the president and then the rest of the Cabinet members. At long last, he said, "It's not looking too good, sir. I'll be honest with you, China's got us outnumbered. They have 3.3 million active duty personnel at most recent count."

"And?" President Thomas prompted. "What about us?"

Edgar met his gaze steadily, unblinking. "We have almost 1.3 million active duty personnel. But that's not it, sir. China also has approximately eight million reservists too. We have just a little over eight hundred thousand of our own."

"You mean to tell me that they've almost got us outnumbered four to one?" President Thomas raised a brow at the CIA analyst. Edgar hadn't been exaggerating. They weren't just a little outnumbered. They were grossly outnumbered.

"That's correct, sir." His Adam's apple bobbed in his throat as he swallowed. He reached for a bottle of water on the table before him, unscrewed the cap, and took a sip before continuing. "For man to man, China has us beat. They could lose four men to every one of ours, and they'd still win. But that's not it. There's more."

It was like a never-ending infomercial of terrible news. President Thomas rubbed his thumb and forefinger together and waited expectantly for the rest of Edgar's missive. It didn't matter if the news itself was unpleasant. He still needed to know what they were up against. Knowing was, after all, half the battle. He trained his eyes on the CIA analyst and waited.

"As you already know, this is going to be mostly a war between navies. As it stands, China has three aircraft carriers, plus one more that was in production and is now undergoing sea trials. So I'm going to have to say that yes, they do have a total of four aircraft carriers in all." Edgar extended his hand, counting the information on his fingers as he spoke. "But when we look at what we have, we're not looking half bad. The United States has ten active carriers, five of which are in the Pacific. The other half are currently in the Atlantic."

President Thomas nodded slowly, taking this in. "Okay, that's good. You're right, that's not half bad. We can work with that." He seemed as though he wanted to say more, but the sound of the door clicking open directly to his left drew his attention upward. He turned his face, a stunned expression crossing it as he stared at the man standing in the doorway. "Well, I'll be a son of a bitch."

"Language, Mr. President," came the dry retort from the secretary of defense as he strode across the room, carefully ignoring the eyes boring into him. Secretary Andrews's gait was steady, and except for a carefully bandaged square of gauze affixed to his forehead with surgical tape, he looked remarkably alert and uninjured. He circled the back of the room as heads craned to observe him crossing the room. As he walked, he spoke. "The five carriers we have in the Pacific are the *USS Nimitz, USS Carl Vinson, USS Theodore Roosevelt, USS John C. Stennis,* and the *USS Ronald Reagan.*"

Mouths moved, working as they struggled to find words to direct at the new arrival to their meeting, but none came out. Instead, a low rumble of whispers passed through the room as the Cabinet members tried to make sense of this unexpected development. As far as they knew, the secretary had been in serious condition, being treated at the hospital. The rumor mill had spread fast, and the fact that he hadn't been wearing his safety restraint had quickly traveled across the White House. Even President Thomas, who had been given the most detailed update on his condition, hadn't expected to see him so soon. None of them, however, were bold enough to ask him directly what he was doing there.

Immediately to the president's left was Nicholas Roth, the vice president, but the chair directly next to it was still vacant. This was the secretary's reserved spot. Secretary Andrews paused behind it and pulled the chair out from underneath the table, then carefully eased himself into it. "Unfortunately, the *USS Nimitz* is currently in Refueling and Complex Overhaul, so it's currently out of commission for the time being." He then folded his hands in front of him on the table and shifted his weight, turning to look at the president. One of his eyebrows went up, as though he were waiting for a reply on his current assessment of their naval carriers. His presence in the room was, to him, entirely unremarkable. A benign smile rested on his face.

President Thomas gazed at him in frank wonderment. The secretary of defense was already starting to sport the telltale purplish bruises around his orbital bone, which was sure to develop into a nasty black eye by the end of the day, and there were several minor lacerations on his face. The largest one was hidden beneath the gauze pad, and already the first hints of blood were starting to seep through the sanitary cotton material.

"Michael, what are you doing here?" President Thomas reached across the table, resting his hand on top of the secretary's. "You shouldn't be here. You need to be in the hospital."

Secretary Andrews slipped his hand out from beneath the president's. His voice was level as he spoke, and his eyes didn't waver from the president's own gaze. "Mr. President, I was a marine for over twenty-five years. I've had cuts from *shaving* worse than this. And," he added, glancing around the room at the dumbfounded faces of the Cabinet members, "I apologize for being late to the meeting. I had a little traffic delay."

"Well, then," President Thomas said, tapping the butt of his pen against his note pad. His voice was a barely audible scoff as he muttered beneath his breath, "I hope I never cut myself shaving like that."

"They let you out?" Vice President Roth asked as he drew back from the secretary, his thick gray eyebrows drawing together as he considered the man. "I thought they advised you to stay at Walter Reed overnight for evaluation."

"They may have advised it," Secretary Andrews said crisply, "but that doesn't mean they were right, or that I have to listen to them. Are we going to play Twenty Questions, or are we here to work?"

Roth exchanged a glance with the president. David Thomas said nothing, but his own face echoed the expression found on Roth's countenance.

After the explosion, the paramedics had managed to get the secretary and the three surviving agents out of the SUVs. Liz had been airlifted to Water Reed, her condition reported as critical, and James had chosen to ride in the same ambulance as Andrews. Marc had gone in a separate ambulance. The prognosis for Liz was poor, and James had been informed there was a strong likelihood that she wouldn't survive the night. He promised to let Kassie know. Marc had a large contusion on his forehead from slamming it against the steering wheel, since the driver side airbag failed to deploy. James, on the other hand, had somehow managed to walk away from the explosion relatively unscathed.

As for Secretary Andrews, it was a fairly straightforward diagnosis: he had contusions, a couple of lacerations, and minor whiplash. He received treatment for the injuries. The doctor had strongly recommended that all three of them remain overnight for additional tests and observation, but Secretary Andrews had other pressing duties that demanded his attention. Going against medical orders, he'd declined further treatment and checked himself out of the hospital. Additional CID special agents from Fort Belvoir were called in and had reluctantly ushered the secretary to the White House for the meeting, transporting the SecDef in a secondary up-armored SUV.

Secretary Andrews opened his briefcase and pulled out several red folders. Their surface was emblazoned with a stamped warning on both the top and the bottom of them. "Top Secret//NOFORN." He slid the folders across the table one by one, pushing them in the direction of each of the Cabinet members in attendance.

They accepted them wordlessly.

"Mr. President?" The secretary turned to President Thomas, reaching across Roth to hand him his own folder directly. His hands were steady as he extended them to the commander in chief, and the president took them from him wordlessly. "Here are the battle plans you requested."

CHAPTER FOURTEEN

T HE ROOM THAT HOUSED THE Pentagon Force Protection Agency was a largely forgotten, almost haphazardly converted conference room that had seen better days. In the lower-level quarter of the building not far removed from the basement of the Pentagon, there were no windows to be found and so no natural sunlight could beam into the dim, poorly lit room. A strip of flickering fluorescent bulbs ran from one end of the ceiling to the other, casting a wan, yellow glow onto the personnel stationed inside.

The scarred and stained white plastic table was now closer to a dingy shade of gray, and various scuff marks and ink doodles blemished its surface. A wedge of paper had been shoved beneath one of its legs once upon a time in a futile attempt to prevent it from wobbling, but every time one of the weary officers leaned on it during the morning roll call, it shifted, leading to a mad scramble to grab pens and Styrofoam cups of coffee to keep them from toppling over and rolling off the edge. For the eighteen officers and their K9 companions congregated inside the room, a seat at the table was considered a luxury while a handful of agents had to settle for the duct-tape repaired couch against the side wall. Despite the less-than-welcoming accommodations, the men and women of the PFPA didn't seem to mind. It wasn't like they spent much of their time in the room anyway. Once they received their assignments, they would bid farewell to it and seek out their duty stations for the day. No, it wasn't the most hospitable or nicely decorated room of the Pentagon, but that didn't really matter. It served its purpose and little more.

"I also just got wind of a pretty nasty fender bender off I-395 near South Joyce Street, which is probably going to cause some traffic issues this morning," Sergeant Chi droned on, his Boston accent lending an almost nasally quality to his voice that seemed almost out of place with his sallow skin and almond-shaped eyes. He lifted his gaze up from the clipboard in his hands and looked around at the officers in the room. Nearly fifty, the only hint to his age was the first traces of silver forming at his temples and the lined bifocals perched on the tip of his flat, broad nose. "You know what that means. Pentagon employees are going to be driving like a bat out of hell to make it to work on time, so for those of you who have been assigned to parking lot detail, I want you to be alert and stay visible. I don't want any of you getting hit by speeding cars this morning."

This comment led to a low murmur of agreement and a few chuckles. These officers were no strangers to the packed Pentagon parking lot and erratic driving of the employees who worked there. It was even worse this time of the year as well, when the holiday tourists descended upon the Pentagon City Mall in hopes of securing a good deal at the overpriced shopping center. The bright yellow police vests they wore helped somewhat, but everyone assigned to parking lot patrol had done their share of dodging late-model vehicles and harried Pentagon employees in their time.

"Also, a word about Officer Miller. Most, if not all of you, have probably worked with him at least once in your time here. Well, he's retiring with twenty-four years of service underneath his belt. As you all know, he was one of the first officers hired with PFPA, and he will be missed." Sergeant Chi paused at this, the expression on his unlined face respectful and almost reverent as he relayed this to the officers gathered in the briefing room. "His retirement ceremony will be next week, and we have a card for him here, so please be sure to sign it when you come in on your break."

"Will there be cake?" a voice piped up from the back of the room.

Sergeant Chi's eyes narrowed as he followed the source of the interruption. A short and stocky man with close-cropped black hair and a wide grin splitting his face and a raised hand in the air was the offending party.

"Yes, Tim." Chi removed the cap from his pen, positioning it on the butt end of it. "Let me take a note real quick about your inquiry. What flavor do you like, just so I can know and pass it onto the baker?"

"Chocolate," Tim Schmidt replied, and the quip was followed with another round of laughter. "With lots of chocolate frosting too, of course, and those fancy little chocolate curls on the top."

"Great." The sergeant scribbled a note in the margins of the paper, then capped the lid once more. "Carrot cake with cream cheese frosting it is. Anyone else have any questions about the cake, or can I get back to the briefing?"

A louder volley of laughter filled the room, and both Chi and Schmidt joined them. No harm, no foul. These officers had been working together for many years, and even the newcomers were like family among them. It made sense, really. The extensive background checks on all of the men and women had proven their dependability and trustworthiness, and all of the officers in the room embodied these positive characteristics. After all, working as a Pentagon Force Protection Agency officer meant you always had to be confident that your partner had your back. Over their time with PFPA, these eighteen officers had trained together, worked together, and of course, laughed together too.

"Okay," Chi said after the last laugh faded away to shuffling feet and loud sips from foam coffee cups. He brought his clipboard back up to his face and wrinkled his nose briefly, shifting his glasses farther up its bridge. "Your post assignments for the day, then. Tim, for your remark, you're now working on south parking patrol. Have fun playing *Frogger* out there this morning."

Another round of laughter filled the room. They knew the assignments had already been decided long before the morning briefing, and Schmidt's comments had no bearing on where he would work that day. The unfortunate coincidence, though, made it all the more amusing. Nobody particularly cared for parking patrol, but a job was a job and each was treated with the same level of importance between the officers.

"James Jay, we've got you on the south gate this morning. Mark Duvall? You're with James on the south gate as well." Chi's voice continued on for the greater part of a minute as he assigned out the day's duties.

Nods followed each assignment as the officers confirmed receipt of their tasks, and once the briefing ended, the men and women rose to their feet, dusted off the fabric of their crisp blue uniforms, and—for those who had K9 units, they called their dogs each their own way to alert their four-legged partners they were heading out—and turned away. They filed out of the room in a slow trickle, the K9s padding out behind them. Some of them lingered in loose clusters, finishing up incomplete conversations, and a handful of them blocked the door as they chatted among one another.

Near the front of the room sat two officers, their own heads bowed in a private conversation with one another. The focus of their chat was not about their assigned duty station that day, which happened to be Pentagon rover, but rather, the football game the night before. While Officer Hong and Officer Sung weren't brothers, they were quite close, especially since they had joined PFPA at the same time and undergone their twelve-week training period together. As long-term members of the force, they could often be found dining together or even at the other's house on weekends. Last night, however, neither of them had had the chance to hang out at the local watering hole due to the attempt on the secretary's life closing down their favorite pub, so the majority of their discourse had instead been through text message. Because of this, Hong's voice was particularly loud and even somewhat irritable when he said, "Yeah, but Heinicke's fumble caused the turnover, and that's what led to them losing the game. You can't expect him to carry the entire team on his shoulders if Scherff's going to be out there picking his ass and not covering him like he should."

"I still blame Sweat for that tackle in the third quarter. He looked like he was out for blood, and he almost dislocated Heinicke's hip with that stunt. He's not a rookie anymore, you know. He's already in his thirties. Plus, the Eagles have been playing pretty damned well this year, and it's not looking too hot for Washington so far…" Sung's voice trailed off, and his eyes flickered to Chi, who still lingered at the head of the table. The sergeant had rested his clipboard on the plastic table and was now giving the pair a thoughtful look. "Uh-oh, looks like it's time to head out. Chi's giving us that look again. Finish this up at break?"

"Yeah." Hong moved to rise to his feet, but a subtle shake of the head from Chi kept him planted to his chair. He raised a brow but kept his mouth shut.

Chi glanced over the pair of officers' shoulders, and the two men followed his gaze to the door where the last of the remaining officers were filing out. The black-tipped tail of the final K9 officer in the room wagged as he slipped through the doorway and then out of sight. They were now alone in the PFPA office, and if they didn't get moving soon, they'd wind up being late to their assigned stations.

"Look alive," Officer Sung murmured.

Officer Hong turned his head back toward the front of the room.

Sgt. Chi was now moving toward them, his eyes alternating between the pair of officers.

"Good morning, Sergeant," Hong said cautiously. He exchanged a glance with Sung, but the other man was now tight-lipped and the previous animation had fallen from his face.

"Morning, Hong. Sung." Chi's New England accent was just as prominent in a low whisper as it was when it was booming across the room, and the nasal intonations made the agents' names seem even more foreign, if that were even possible. He reached down and rapped on the table between the two men with his knuckles, then glanced once more at the back of the room. They were still alone. "Listen, I got the both of you assigned to Pentagon rover for a reason. I want the two of you to meet me at the Pentagon Nail Salon in ten minutes. Do you understand?" A single camera in the corner of the room was the only surveillance in the PFPA office, but it was enough to make the senior officer remain vague in his directives to the two men.

"Yes, Sergeant." Hong nodded at him, the gesture terse and short. The previous good cheer was gone from his voice, and last night's football game was now a distant memory.

Sung's face matched his, his eyes distant and his lips turned down in a distracted frown at the instruction.

Sgt. Chi turned away from the men and, without a final glance in their direction, strode out of the room. His slim form rounded the corner, and the sound of his polished loafers faded away as the senior officer took his head start to the salon.

Both men rose to their feet in unison and, wearing matching blank expressions, followed the sergeant to the Pentagon Nail Salon. Stationed on the second level of the Pentagon, near the mall entrance, it saw its share of military wives and civilians on a daily basis. Owned by a matronly Chinese woman in her mid-40s who evidently spoke no English—or evidently preferred not to use it around customers—the salon still drew customers to it in droves. The wealthy wives and tourists didn't seem to mind that idle chatter was kept to a minimum, just as long as they had the shiny, pretty lacquers on the end of their fingertips to make up for it.

The petite owner seemed to be working that day, as well as a younger employee who was seated in one of the salon chairs and turning the pages of a Chinese edition of *Vogue* magazine. As they stepped through the door, the bell above the door tinkled, alerting her to the arrival of the two Pentagon officers. She cast a sidelong glance at them but didn't let their presence stop her monologue with the sergeant. The Mandarin words fell from her mouth in a rapid clip as she addressed Chi, then with a final glance at Sung and Hong, she fell silent.

Chi nodded at her, and she seemed satisfied with his gesture. She reached into the front pocket of her apron and fished out a set of keys, then approached the door, sliding the key into the lock and turning it. While the salon itself wouldn't open to the public for a few more hours, that didn't seem to deter a fairly sizable portion of patrons who nevertheless would test the door despite the CLOSED sign and darkened interior.

With this task now complete, the salon owner plucked a rag from behind the front counter and busied herself with polishing the laminate finishes, a public display of indifference to the trio of men now inside her salon. Sung glanced at her, then at Chi. Next to him, Hong shrugged. Chi turned to the men and took a step toward them. With a jerk of his head, he turned away once more, moving toward the back of the salon. A wooden divider separated the front of the salon from the back part, and his silhouette was visible behind the white parchment paper covered in a faded cherry-blossom motif.

The owner of the salon ventured a glance upward as Hong and Sung fell into step behind the sergeant and slipped around the divider. Beyond it were two doors, both of which were closed. One had the universal sign of male and female stick figures against a blue background, indicating the presence of a bathroom. The other was nondescript and unmarked.

Chi crossed his arms over his chest and, continuing the conversation in Mandarin, said, "Do you two know why I asked you to meet me here?"

Both men remained quiet, neither of them daring to answer. Whatever it was, it probably wasn't to discuss their plans for New Years' Eve or weigh the pros and cons of the Patriots over their favored Washington football team. Chi might have had the poise to carry himself with quiet dignity as a PFPA officer and a sergeant, but they both knew he had a hot streak running through him. While he wouldn't strike out at them for their ignorance, the glower of disgust on his face would be more than enough to make them wither. It was best to remain silent and let him speak.

"The secretary of defense survived the attack yesterday," Chi said flatly.

Both men nodded. They knew this. It had been all over the news the day before.

"This means it is now upon us to finish the job, as per our duty to the People's Liberation Army and our motherland."

A chill coursed down Sung's back. So that was why Chi had called them there. He had often privately wondered if they were ever going to be given a role greater than glorified crossing guard since they had initially received their placement to the PFPA nearly five years before, and now, it seemed, their hard work and training would finally be put to use. Next to him, Hong stood up straighter and squared his shoulders. He, too, was ready for his assignment.

"Listen to me carefully and do not ask any questions until I am done," Chi said, his dark eyes flashing coldly at each man standing before him. "We are going to go into the secretary of defense's office and kill him ourselves since the fool who was supposed to do it yesterday was unable to do this very simple task asked of him."

Both men remained silent as Sergeant Chi outlined the plans for assassinating the secretary of defense. As they listened raptly to the instructions, they found themselves nodding along with him. It made perfect sense, especially since there were no executive protection agents in the office area where the secretary worked. It would be a remarkably simple task overall, one that they knew they were well suited for. The honor of being summoned for such a responsibility wasn't lost on them, and the surge of pride welling up inside Sung's chest made it hard for him to keep his expression calm as he mentally routed the senior officer's instructions inside his head.

The best part of the plan, of course, was the genius simplicity of it. There was no need to rappel into the Pentagon or try to sneak into the office behind smoke bombs or other diversions. They would be able to simply stride in under the cover of their uniforms, and nobody would pay them any attention. The People's Republic of China was clever like that, and having three sleeper agents working under the same roof of their targets was admittedly nothing short of brilliant. Hong felt the same crest of pride inside him, and his eyes never left Chi's face as the sergeant revealed the blueprints for the assassination.

Finally, after several minutes of near-endless speaking, the words pouring out of Chi's mouth trickled off to a lengthy pause, signaling the end to his plan. Chi locked the two men in his gaze, his face betraying none of the passion that was evident in his words moments before. "Now you may ask me your questions."

Silence followed, almost oppressive behind the room divider inside the nail salon. From where they stood, they could hear the younger Chinese nail technician bring her index fingers to her mouth to lick it, then turn the page of the glossy magazine in her lap. The rustling of the paper was deafening in the quietude.

Hong cleared his throat, then said in Mandarin, "I do have a question. When are we to do this, Sergeant?"

"Today." Chi let the words linger in the air for a moment, then added, "When the secretary of defense gets into work this morning, that is when we will do it."

If they were surprised by the short notice, both officers kept it concealed. While Sergeant Chi's plan was an intricate one, it wasn't exactly something outside of their scope of capabilities. They had no doubt they would be able to successfully pull it off, even on such short notice. After all, they had trained for this day extensively and honed their skills to needle-point precision. Today, tomorrow, or even next week—it did not matter, as they were very well-trained agents, acting on behalf of the PLA.

Hong pursed his lips, then stole a glance at Sung. The man was staring at Chi and seemed oblivious to any external stimuli. He was a statue, obedient and submissive to the senior officer and his home country. To him, all that mattered was the mission. Hong took a deep breath, then let it out. He nodded, then said in English, "Let's do it, then. For China."

"For China," Sung echoed.

"For China," Chi concluded. His words were as bland as his face, and despite the fervent speech he had delivered to the two men a moment before, he hadn't even worked up a sweat. The matter was settled. They would be killing the secretary of defense today. He spun on his heel, stepping past the divider.

The salon owner didn't look up as Chi strode past her, and the other employee very deliberately turned the page of the magazine once more. As far as the three officers were concerned, the two women hadn't heard a single thing. Even though both had uttered the words "For China" with firm conviction, audibly enough to be heard in the front part of the room, that mattered not to them, as they spoke little to no English—at least, if anyone ever tried to interrogate them about the conversation, that would be their story and nether would ever waver from it.

Chi turned the key in the lock, then pulled the door open. With a slight bounce in their steps, which somehow seemed to betray the gravity of the task that would be unfolding in the next hour, the three officers stepped out of the salon and into the Pentagon's promenade. The bell above the door jangled one final time, then was quict, as though it dared not interrupt the agents of the PRC on their way to work.

The Pentagon was still quiet, but the employees were starting to come in to start their day. The somber atmosphere was appropriate. With all three of them on the task, there was no way the secretary of defense would live to see the end of the day. The thought of it pleased the trio of sleeper agents very much. And despite themselves, a faint ghost of a smile lingered on each of their faces as they made their way back to the other side of the Pentagon to finish the dark job that had been started the day before. The idea of succeeding at this responsibility made them happy, very happy indeed, and the glory they would receive from their homeland would be more than any reward they would earn for it.

After all, Sung mused, his fingers grazing against the pistol at his hip as his feet led him back into the bowels of the Pentagon and to the secretary of defense's office, *wasn't the best reward a job well done?*

CHAPTER FIFTEEN

THE AMBUSH

0700 HOURS

J AMES WAS BEING FOLLOWED. HE glanced in the rearview mirror of the Limo, briefly taking in the superficial lacerations on his face and the slight swelling and mottled discoloration near his chin, then directed his gaze through the rear window. The pair of heavily armored SUVs behind him confirmed his suspicions. He had a tail, and they weren't exactly being subtle about it, either. Actually, they had their emergency lights on, and all three black SUVs were driving a tight formation. He couldn't see the drivers' faces too clearly through the darkly tinted rear window, but he had no doubts that their expressions were as tense and drawn as his own on this brisk December morning.

Hell, James couldn't fault them for following him so closely—even being allowed back in the PSO seat for the secretary of defense was nothing short of a privilege, one he was privately grateful for. Even then, he knew it only afforded based on two caveats. One, his long-term relationship with the SecDef afforded him this privilege. The second was the somewhat startling realization that James had emerged from the attack the day before almost entirely unscathed.

At Walter Reed the afternoon before, James had been poked, prodded, and given a thorough examination by the surprisingly young and muscular doctor on duty. Even despite a clean bill of health, the battalion commander had been initially reluctant to allow James to return to his detail, but the doctor overseeing him had unexpectedly come to his defense. The BC, a stern-faced man with a no-nonsense bearing and deep lines etched into the sides of his blue eyes, had arrived at the hospital with the goal of assessing the survivors of the attack and pulling them all from their details. Rest, he had concluded, was what they needed most. He even discreetly suggested, in his own circumspect manner, that James seek out a conversation with the chaplain to determine whether he was still suited for his duties.

James had reacted with nothing short of barely restrained outrage, but he'd kept his voice calm as he made his counterpoint to the BC. "Sir, you know me as well as the rest of them out there. I feel fine. I *am* fine."

The doctor, who had been standing behind him and quietly watching the exchange, took that opportunity to speak up. "James is telling the truth, sir. According to my notes and all of the diagnostic tests we've done on him, he's actually doing amazingly well, all things considered. Just a few bumps and bruises, but nothing that a little ibuprofen won't take care of for him."

The BC had shrugged, and with a final critical glance over the CID agent sitting upright with his legs dangling over the side of the hospital bed, said, "You're the boss."

Putting James back on Secretary Andrews's detail hadn't been without some additional precautions, however. After the attack, they weren't going to risk a similar incident from occurring again, and so the morning drive to the Pentagon now looked slightly different. For instance, Marc wasn't in the driver's seat. And none of his friends—the ones who had survived the attack, of course—were in the other corresponding roles. The shift lead, Chase driver, and communicator had all been replaced by faces James barely recognized by more than a passing acquaintance.

Furthermore, a Tail car had also been added to the motorcade. The extra agents had clocked into their shift that morning fully prepared to prevent any other unanticipated incidents, and the driver and three agents inside the Tail now bore Heckler & Koch MP5 submachine guns in addition to their standard-issue Sig Sauer M18 pistols. If they had been able to conceal a Phalanx SeaWiz on the belt of their trousers too, James had no doubts they would have attempted to carry one of those as well. As it were, the morning conversation had been muted, and there was no chatter to be heard either in the Limo or the other SUVs behind it.

The clock on the Limo's dash revealed 0700 hours as it rolled past the Lincoln Memorial Gate to the stairs leading to the secretary's entrance to the Pentagon. James waited for the Limo to stop, then glanced through the darkened window to verify the positions of the other agents. They poured out of their corresponding vehicles and claimed their stances around the three SUVs, their hands positioned close to their sidearms. James reached for the door handle, ignoring the quiet sear of heat shooting up his arm, and stepped out. His loafers met the slick ice, and he tested his traction before lowering his other foot to the sidewalk. The last thing he needed was for his ass to kiss pavement after campaigning so hard to remain on Andrews's detail.

He turned toward the passenger side of the Limo and pulled on the handle. Secretary Andrews peered out at him, a polite but distant smile on his face, and lowered himself out of the SUV. As he fell into place behind James, the wind whipped his silver locks away from his face, revealing a single beige bandage on his forehead. Beneath it were precisely three stitches, a thank you gift from the headrest when his face had collided with it in the attack the day before. Combined with dappled red pinpoints of blood below the surface of his skin and just enough swelling to cause a squint of his left eye, the man was also relatively unscathed. His gait was steady as James led him up the stairs, and he indicated no hint of discomfort as he walked. If Andrews was in any pain that morning, he was keeping it to himself.

James nodded at the young PFPA officer holding the door open for them as he approached, and she nodded back. Like the others this morning, she seemed tense and on high alert. Her eyes swept past him, moving over Secretary Andrews, then to the CID agents surrounding the SUVs. James stepped past her, then stopped in the doorway. His head turned first to the left, then to the right, and then straight down the hallway. Clear. Behind him, Andrews slipped through the open door, his briefcase clutched in his hand as he let the officer close the door behind him.

The hallway was empty this morning, fairly standard for this time of the day, and James allowed his stride to match Andrews's gait as they moved down toward his office. The door was shut, and he pulled on the handle, tugging the heavy wooden door open. Andrews stepped through it first, then James allowed his feet to carry him over the threshold. His hand never left the door handle, and he tugged on it, drawing it shut behind him once more. The scent of coffee, strong and welcoming, greeted his nose.

"Hey, James," Andrews said in a low voice with his sun-faded eyes lit on the agent standing behind him. "There's something I want to talk to you about today. Maybe later this afternoon, once we get back to the house?"

"Yes, of course, sir." James nodded. The aroma of coffee was stronger now, and in his peripheral vision, he saw the secretary's administrator standing in the doorway with a coffee cup in her hands. Despite already having two cups that morning, James realized he wouldn't mind a third. "I'll get with you then, when we get settled back at the house."

"Sounds good. Thank you." Andrews turned toward his administrator.

"No problem, sir." James cast a smile at the woman standing in the office.

Michelle Clarke was a slightly heavyset woman dressed in a plain green sweater and tan slacks, her salt and pepper hair braided and pinned at the nape of her neck. Despite her somewhat plain attire, the woman had a ready smile and naturally rosy cheeks, both of which matched her warm personality.

"Is that for me, Shelley?" the secretary said with a kind smile.

Like clockwork, she had anticipated their arrival and prepared for it accordingly. No doubt, the steaming mug in her hand was freshly brewed and had exactly two creamers and two sugars, just how Secretary Andrews liked it.

"You know it, sir." Shelley passed the mug to Andrews, her eyes sweeping over his face as she relinquished it to its rightful owner. A slight frown line appeared between her eyebrows as she made a mental note of his injuries, but if she had any questions, she kept them to herself. Like virtually everyone else in the city, she too was aware of the attack. It was neither her place nor her station to ask the secretary probing questions about his presence in the office that morning, and so she pursed her lips and said nothing.

"Hey, you got one of those for me?" James jutted his chin toward the cup in Andrews's hand.

"When you become the SecDef," Shelley replied tartly with a smile on her face transforming into an easy grin. "I'll be happy to make you some coffee. How's that?"

"Fair enough." James matched her grin with one of his own, the gesture causing a subtle jolt of pain in his jaw. He pushed it to the back of his mind. The bruise on his face was nothing, and he refused to even acknowledge it, especially compared to what his friends had suffered. They were either recovering at home or in the hospital or cooling in the hospital morgue. An aching neck and jaw paled in comparison, and he knew he was fortunate to have sustained such relatively minimal injury in the attack.

He turned away from Andrews and Shelly, back to the heavy door that separated the office from the hallway. After stepping through the door, he pushed it closed and listened to it click behind him. With it now shut, the scent of coffee faded away. James threw a glance back down both directions of the lengthy corridor. Still alone. He depressed his microphone and said quietly, "Cobra is in the henhouse."

That was all the signal the remaining agents in the motorcade needed. Satisfied that both James and Secretary Andrews had made it safely inside with no further incidents delaying their arrival to his office, they climbed back into their SUVs to begin their drive to the Pentagon garage.

Another turn of his head confirmed he was still alone in the hallway, and the jolt of pain that followed the motion caused him to draw in a sharp breath. Damn it, the last thing he needed was an annoying injury trying to distract him from his duties. It was nothing a massage couldn't work out, though. James lifted his right hand to his neck, craning his head slightly to the left, and let his hands knead the tense knot he found there. The relief was almost instantaneous, and he let out a low hiss from between his teeth. Yes, it was nothing that a hot soak and a couple of Tylenol when he got home couldn't knock out.

Motion out of the corner of his eye drew his head up, his dark eyes squinting suspiciously at the two new arrivals rounding the corner at the end of the hallway. At this distance, nearly fifty yards away, he couldn't make out their faces. However, their distinct PFPA uniforms—neatly pressed blue pants and gray button-down tops with the radios on their shoulders and brass insignia on the front—were unmistakable. His brow creased. Seeing the two officers in this hallway wasn't particularly unusual, as some of the officers used it to get to their posts, but at this hour? They should have been at their assigned duty stations already, not traversing the corridor.

James let his callused hands continue to work on the ache in his neck as he craned his chin upward, rotating his head in a slow circle. If he could just get it to crack, the knot might successfully fray and the pain could finally become a distant memory. A brief flash of light drew his eye to the opposite side of the hallway, and James could see a slim, fairly short silhouette in the doorway to the Washington Memorial entrance. As the door swung shut behind him, the shadow covering the new arrival's face fell away, revealing a third PFPA officer. This one's insignia indicated he was a sergeant, and James realized with acute certainty that he knew the man from somewhere. But from where?

On any given day, he encountered a vast number of personnel—military, civilian, and police—and while his memory was keen for faces, names sometimes evaded him until he heard them speak. Still. He couldn't shake the feeling that he knew the sergeant from somewhere and had encountered him sometime recently. But when? Like a thought perched on the tip of his tongue that he couldn't quite articulate, the gap in his memory bothered him more than he cared to admit.

The sergeant's hand was reaching for his pocket, and James stood up straight, his eyes narrowing. But it was just the officer's cell phone, which he was returning to his pocket. The man's stride was easy and confident as he ambled down the hallway toward James. Even though he was approaching James, his eyes seemed to be focused on the two officers on the other end of the corridor. He followed the sergeant's gaze, and with the distance now reduced somewhat, James could see that like the new arrival, the other two PFPA officers were also Asian.

James's hand shot down from his neck to his hip, his fingertips brushing over the leather holster of his Sig. The face. All at once, the pieces of the puzzle connected and he realized he knew where he recognized the man from. It wasn't in the canteen or in mere passing during the sergeant's patrol. No, the face—which James could now see was contoured in a rictus of loathing, the thin lips drawn down in a bestial snarl—was the very same as the one belonging to the owner of the powder blue SUV in front of him the afternoon before.

Oh, shit!

James could feel his heartrate pick up as his fingers closed around the cool metal of his sidearm. The sergeant was closer, but the other two PFPA agents were also steadily closing in on him. In a few seconds, they would be on top of him, affording them an advantage in numbers that James did not particularly feel interested in seeing unfold. He was outnumbered three to one and needed to act quickly. The sergeant—who was now only a handful of yards away from him—was clearly the more looming threat of the three men. As the officer closed the gap between him, he seemed to realize that James had recognized him, and his own hand went for his weapon.

In a singular, fluid motion, James withdrew his Sig from his duty holster and raised the weapon. His thumb released the safety, and he ducked his head, launching himself backward toward the closed door leading to the secretary's office. As his left hand grappled with the handle, he felt something sweep past his face. Just above his right temple, the door jamb splintered, and a rain of wood cascaded down upon him. He threw his weight against the door, and it reluctantly swung open, affording him access to the office.

Five more rounds in rapid succession followed the first. A dull *thunk* greeted his ears as each embedded into the oak surface of the door. The door buckled with each bullet colliding with it, but it wasn't enough to fully stop their lethal journey to its target. Only moderately stifled, they were still unrelenting in their thus-far failed attempts to break through James's flesh. Above his head, he heard the distinct peal of glass breaking as a bullet found a framed picture, and he jerked instinctively away from the glittering shards as they fell to the carpeted floor around him.

He lifted his firearm, training it on the man in the hallway. His fingers squeezed the trigger, and two rounds flew from the chamber at the sergeant looming before him. His backward trajectory, however, jolted his arm up. The man barely flinched away from the rounds as they flew high and harmlessly over his head, meeting the wall behind him. The stone-faced sergeant did not bother to glance over his right shoulder to track the rounds, though, or check on the two other PFPA officers as they ducked out of range of the crossfire. He was on a mission, his target was just beyond the CID agent firing upon him, and he wasn't going to stop until he completed the task he had set out to finish. The malice never left his face as he tracked James with his firearm.

James wasn't about to wait around to see if his aim was any better next time. Keeping his body low, his left arm guarding his neck and the back of his head, he let his legs carry him into the administrator's office. Inside, Shelley was gazing at him in wide-eyed horror from behind her desk, her mouth open and her jaw slack. Her lips seemed to be moving, but no words came from them. Her coffee cup was poised in her fingers, now forgotten, as she watched him tear through the door. They flickered from James to the sounds of Chinese shouting and gunfire beyond him, and now James could hear the almost inaudible squeak coming from her throat.

Now was not the time to start barking out orders to the stunned and terrified woman. His body, propelled forward by the momentum, ricocheted off her desk. Paperwork, a vintage lamp with a green glass dome, and an assortment of pens and other debris scattered across the floor. The lamp shattered as it landed, and emerald shards of glass bounced off the rug and settled in a haphazard pattern on the floor. This seemed to break Shelley from her trance, and she rose to her feet, pushing away from the desk. The coffee fell from her fingers, the hot beverage sloshing across its surface as the mug joined the rest of the clutter on the floor.

James spun away from the desk, his hip ramming against it as he turned, and he pushed forward once more. He breathlessly captured the edge of the door with his fingertips and slammed it shut. It rattled against the jamb, then latched into place. While closing the door wouldn't necessarily keep them safe against the assailants in the corridor, it might afford them a few extra seconds of precious time to keep the sergeant and other two PFPA officers at bay while he regrouped and organized his thoughts.

"James!" Secretary Andrews's voice was taut and uncertain from his position in the doorway leading to his office, and James could see the matching look of surprise on his face. "What the hell is going on here?"

James shook his head, drawing in a breath as his fingers turned the lock. Adrenaline surged through his body, heightening his senses and making him acutely aware of every motion and every sound in near proximity. The secretary was staring expectantly at him, and James realized he somehow needed to condense the currently unfolding events into just a few words. He glanced at the door—a relatively ineffectual barrier overall, but it would have to do for the time being—and back at Andrews.

"Sir," he said evenly, and despite the urgency of the situation, his voice was calm and his words metered, "there are three PFPA officers out there, and I believe they're here to kill you."

A myriad of expressions seemed to cross Andrews's face all at once as the reality of the situation flooded over him. Yes, he had anticipated another attempt on his life, so the fact that there were more assailants after him so soon after the initial attack was not surprising. However, the combination of the attackers finding him in his office—and coming in under the guise of the Pentagon Force Protection Agency even—had rendered him somewhat flatfooted.

This wasn't just an improvised explosive device thrown underneath the Limo, a bomb addressed to "Whomever it may concern," flagrantly taking out civilians and special agents, yet somehow missing its intended recipient. No, this was a highly coordinated and alarmingly intelligent attack on his person, one that was clearly premeditated, and his life was now in grave danger once more.

On the other side of the door, rising shouts wafted into the room, only moderately muffled by the heavy oak door. James trained his Sig onto the door, his ears straining as he listened to the men talk among one another. He couldn't make out the words themselves, as they were in some dialect of Chinese, but their tone was certainly evident. They were furious, unhinged, and determined to break down the door so they could access their quarry on the other side of it. The doorknob rattled back and forth on its spindle, and the litany of words on the other side of the door grew louder as the three attackers realized it was locked.

"Sir," James said over his shoulder, "I need you to take Shelley and move back into your office right now. That lock won't hold for very long. And make sure you lock the door behind you and call 911!"

Neither party answered his instruction, but James could hear the door swing shut behind him, followed by the sound of the lock latching. It was a piss-poor barrier, but it was better than nothing. If—rather, when—the Chinese officers managed to break down the door, it would afford a modicum of security and might even buy them some time until backup finally arrived. That was, of course, until they took down Andrews's office door as well. It was up to James to prevent that from happening, and he would be damned if he was going to let them get past him.

He stepped aside, keeping his Sig aimed at the door, and justified a quick peek over his shoulder. His neck flashed angrily at him for the sudden movement, but he shoved the pain aside and returned his focus to the slab of wood separating him from the would-be assassins. There was nowhere he could take cover. The office had been decorated with a focus on aesthetics and comfort, not to become a bunker should the secretary of defense ever get ambushed. James made a mental note to have a firmly worded discussion with the Pentagon's interior decorator.

Two shots rang out, drawing his attention forward once more. The metal faceplate on the lock had buckled. Three more shots followed, shattering the wood around the lock. With sharp clarity, James realized he probably would not be able to keep them at bay on his own. He needed backup—*now*. There was no way he would be able to ward them off on his own for much longer, and based on the current state of the lock, they would be storming through the door in the next few seconds.

Without lowering his weapon, James lifted his left hand to his mouth and pressed the transmit button on the microphone. There was a slight beep in his earpiece, the only indication that his message would relay to his team if they were even within range, but it would have to suffice. In a strained but clear voice, he spoke into the mouthpiece, "I need you in the secretary's office now! We are being fired upon by three PFPA officers. I repeat, I need you in here *now*!"

Silence followed.

Had they gotten his message? There was no time to pause and dwell on it. Even if they had, it would still be another minute or two before they made it upstairs from the garage to find him cloistered in the SecDef's office. For now, it was on him to hold the assailants off. He craned his neck, glancing around the room for anything he could use as cover, and his gaze landed on Shelley's desk. It was more ornamental than sturdy, with handsomely carved inlays on its outer perimeter, but it would have to do.

He took a cautious step backward, not removing his focus from the door. Moving quickly, he rounded the desk and positioned himself behind it. With a firm kick from the flat of his foot, he knocked it over. The remaining paperwork slid to the floor as the desk listed, wobbled, then fell on its side with a loud crash. James lowered himself to a crouch behind it, his heel slipping on a rogue paperweight, then righted himself.

He gritted his teeth as he threw a glance at the door, his Sig propped on the carved edge of the desk. "You have *got* to be fuckin' kidding me. I feel like I'm back in the Middle East!"

Behind the door, there was another bellow from the PFPA officers, then a booming crash as what sounded like a foot slammed against it. The lock tumbled to the ground, and on the other side of the door, the shouting of the three officers came once more with renewed vigor. Their cries were now triumphant, smug with the knowledge that they had managed to break down the barricade separating them from the man keeping them from fulfilling their mission. Once they killed James, nothing would be able to stop them from getting to the secretary of defense.

A man stepped through it, and although James didn't recognize his face, the light coming from the overhead fixture glinted off the name badge on his right pocket. His attacker's name was Sung. James had no time to make sense of this new knowledge, as Sung's sidearm was pointed at him, his finger curled around the trigger of the matte black Glock 23. Shots rang out, loud and reverberating, as he fired several rounds. They collided with the wall above James's head, and James felt a chip of plaster fall on his shoulder and bounce off to the floor.

It was close, too damned close for his comfort. James's eyes lit on the officer, briefly taking in his form as he reloaded his weapon on the other side of the room. This was his chance. Without hesitation, he squeezed the trigger, releasing five rounds in rapid succession at his chest. Officer Sung's body jerked like a crude marionette in the doorway as the bullets tracked their way up his torso. The first round buried itself in his abdomen, and like ants marching steadily upward in a line, the four remaining ones slammed into his chest. The last one hit his left shoulder, and both Sung and his weapon fell to the floor.

The sound of James's breathing was loud and ragged in his ears, and he sucked in a deep lungful of air as he listened for any indication of the next attack from the two remaining Chinese officers. He lifted himself slightly, assessing the scene in a single glance. The man on the floor was no longer moving, and a pool of scarlet blood was steadily spreading around his lifeless body. *Dead. Good. One down, two to go.* Maybe he *could* do this by himself after all. The radio in his ear was oppressively quiet, and for the first time since his urgent message to his team, he wondered if the thick reinforced walls of the Pentagon garage had prevented it from reaching them.

Shit. He would *have* to do this on his own. He didn't particularly savor the idea of being killed in a firefight, but he had no other recourse. No matter what, he needed to prevent these two officers from getting to the secretary and Shelley. A flash movement caught his eye, and James caught the blurry shape of a head peek around the door jamb. He fired off a round, and the wooden jamb surrendered a few more splinters of wood onto the carpet. James was fast, but they were faster. Just as quickly as the head appeared, it had vanished once more behind the doorframe.

The sentry's quick peek had done the job, though. James's location had been betrayed in the millisecond it had taken for the officer to glance into the room, and he knew their next shots into Shelley's office might not be so high or erratic. Her desk might suppress a few rounds, but the next series of rounds would have his name on them, of that he was certain.

James bounced himself lightly on the balls of his feet, testing the heft, then shoved off the floor. He launched himself into a standing position, then pivoted his body, angling it toward the other side of the desk. Moving rapidly, he sprinted around the desk, and the momentum carried him across the room in mere seconds. As he approached the far wall, he reached out, steadying himself as he skidded across the rug. He eased into a stop against the wallpapered surface, his shoulder pressed against it, his Sig raised at chest level. The last thing the officers would expect was to find him flush with them, and at this point, all he had going for him was the element of surprise. He certainly didn't have an unlimited amount of ammo or the much-needed backup he had requested.

A hand snaked through the doorway, and from his position against the wall, James could see the long, slender fingers curled around the trigger of a Glock. Despite himself, James found himself counting the rounds fired from the chamber and into the upended desk. One shot, two, three… Eleven shots flew from the barrel of the weapon, and no less than eight of them met against the soft walnut surface of Shelley's desk. It had been designed for taking transcripts and office work, not holding off bullets, and it shattered against this newest volley of rounds. His hunch had been correct. Had he still been hiding behind it, those bullets would have been in his flesh now and the fight would be over.

His fight, rather, would be over. Shelley and Secretary Andrews would have been left on their own, trying to protect themselves without his aid against the ever-encroaching Chinese PFPA officers. As much as he respected the secretary and knew he could take care of himself, he knew the man lacked the skills James had. His odds of survival were significantly greater as long as James remained alive, and it was those abilities that had been the reason he was assigned to Andrews's protection detail in the first place.

James's eyes didn't waver from the doorway as he reached down to his hip with his left hand, where his dual magazine pouch rested. His fingers plucked a full magazine from the nylon pocket and in a steady motion, he raised it up to the Sig clasped in his right hand. The thumb of his right hand found the mag release, and the partially spent magazine slid smoothly from it and fell to the ground. Using the flat of his palm, he slammed the fresh mag into the well, locking it into place even before the ejected one finished its downward trajectory to the floor. The thought of having a full sixteen rounds ready for a firefight was a small comfort.

Again, a dark-haired head darted into the room, and James barely had time to register the simmering hate in its eyes as they locked on him before vanishing around the jamb once more. This clearly was not the work of an amateur, and it was becoming evident the officer had undergone some sort of either military or police training. For the first time since the firefight had started, James wondered if their uniforms weren't simply just a costume, some haphazard ruse designed to get them into the secretary of defense's office. That these men might actually be real military or police personnel further escalated the threat. If they were agents working on behalf of the People's Republic of China, flying undetected underneath the radar, how many more of them were out there?

"I am done," James said, gritting his teeth as he aimed his firearm at the space where the head had been an instant before, "playing cat and mouse with you two."

He squeezed the trigger, firing off a round at the doorway. No shout followed it, indicating it had missed its target. That was irrelevant, however. He was not going to just cower down inside Shelley's office any longer, waiting for them to storm the room. If they wanted a fight, well, then he'd bring the fight to them. With a fresh mag in his Sig and one more in the chamber, he had more than enough ammunition to fight them off. Whether or not he survived the barrage remained to be seen, but he wasn't going to sit around and wait patiently for them any longer.

A second round followed the first, and James took a step away from the wall, moving his body in an axis around the entryway. With each step he took, he fired another shot through the open doorway and into the hall. It was almost as though his body was moving along the face of an invisible clock, and the Sig clutched in his grasp was the hour hand. The tactic, known as "slicing the pie," helped to maximize the chance that he could hit a target while still minimizing his own risk of being on the receiving end of a bullet.

If he timed his shots correctly, James could hypothetically fire one round per second at the two remaining agents on the other side of the door. Quick mental calculations pointed toward affording him a grand total of sixteen seconds—one for each of the rounds in his Sig—which was more than enough time and ammunition to get him through the doorway. Even more importantly, it also left him several rounds to spare, should he need them once he got there. He didn't doubt the likelihood of that occurring, though he also didn't look forward to it with any particular relish.

Round after round flew from his weapon and through the doorway, the suppressive fire guiding his steps as he moved in an arc around the room, until he found himself facing it completely. His eyes were alert as they peered through the doorway, straining for any sign of his targets. He had spent a total of ten rounds so far, leaving him with only six remaining bullets to take out the two surviving attackers. His aim needed to be precise, unwavering, and direct. If his margin for error had been slim before, it was even more scant now. One errant shot could leave him critically short on ammunition and compromise his chances of succeeding.

As James approached the open door, his field of vision broadened, affording him a wider view of the hallway. A sliver of blue a few feet away from the entryway, just down the hall, caught his eye as he turned his head. Another step forward granted him a better visual, and from where he stood, he could see it was the bottom half of one of the officer's right legs. Evidently the man had flattened himself against the wall in anticipation of James stepping through it, ready to fire a shot at the CID agent as he stepped into the hallway. While it wasn't a chest or back or some other ideal target, the leg would have to suffice. He squeezed the trigger, and the round sliced through the air, cutting through the blue fabric encasing the opponent's leg.

The PFPA officer let out a high-pitched shriek as the round met with his knee. He collapsed to the floor, his body hitting it with a weighty thud. He sat slumped, doubled over in the hallway, his wounded leg sticking out straight in front of him. The shrill wail coming from his mouth didn't wane as he clutched the bloodied and shattered knee with both hands. The fabric around his knee was tattered, the exposed flesh a bright scarlet, coating the officer's hands in the viscous fluid. With the uniformed body now fully in his line of sight, James could make out the insignia on the officer's sleeve. This was the other officer in the pair, and not the sergeant.

The Chinese officer turned his face toward James, his eyes wide and round as he clasped his injured knee. Despite the evident pain he seemed to be in, though, his glittering eyes never left James's face. The hate was more pronounced now, and with his mouth open wide and the unrelenting scream coming from it, it was almost as though he blamed the CID agent for the anguish he was now in.

James was not the type of man to allow needless suffering. It was clear the officer was in agony, completely incapacitated by his ruined knee. In a swift motion, he trained his Sig on the downed enemy and squeezed the trigger. The two rounds fired from the chamber, one after another, following a clean and straight path toward the man. The first one glided smoothly through his right cheek and the second one pierced his right temple. The malice finally fell from the officer's face as the skin around his eyes ruptured from the impact of the bullet entering his cheek. A red mist flew from the opposite side of the PFPA officer's head, and clotted pink matter sprayed the wall behind him.

There. Now you are no longer in pain.

With this attacker now out of the picture, James could turn his focus onto the final assailant. Deduction indicated the last remaining officer was the sergeant himself, and as James took another cautious step toward the open doorway, he was acutely aware that the man may have undergone even more intensive training than the first two to allow him to rise through the ranks to become a sergeant. He needed to remain on alert—even more so than he already was, if that was even possible—when he finally faced him down.

There was a limited number of places the sergeant could be, and James knew it was highly likely the officer was lurking on the other side of the wall, but farther down the hall. Had the material of the wall been oak like the door, shooting straight through would be the simplest, safest, and easiest way to neutralize the man. But, James recalled, the walls throughout the Pentagon had been designed for both aesthetics and durability. That meant the thick granite material would not permit passage of the rounds through them, and any shots he fired would be wasted. He would have to face the man head on.

He had only four rounds left in the Sig's magazine, which meant he needed to be especially careful as he stepped through the threshold. Each bullet was now a precious commodity, one he needed to spend with exact precision. James drew his weapon closer to his body and away from the open doorway, minimizing his real estate as much as possible. He was tense, ready to react, as he inched his way closer to the entry in a slow arc. Less than a half of a foot's distance now separated him from the hallway, and as he stood there gauging his next step, he froze. On the other side of the doorway, just within his field of vision, was a sliver of a uniform jacket sleeve. Like the deceased officer on the other side of the door, it also bore the distinct PFPA patch.

Got you now, you bastard.

This was it. It was finally over. James felt no relief—only a cold, calculating sense of finishing this duty—as he aimed his weapon at the officer to deliver the final, lethal round.

As he tightened his index finger around the trigger, mentally calculating the bullet's trajectory into the shoulder, a sudden onslaught of deafening shots broke through the tense silence. With a single, lateral step, the sergeant positioned himself opposite of James in the hallway. As he stood nearly diagonal to him, approximately twenty feet away, he took advantage of James's vulnerable position, firing shot after shot in his direction. Despite all of his care in calculating his enemy's location and his diligence in approaching the open doorway, James realized with dismay that he was completely exposed and under direct fire.

CHAPTER SIXTEEN

MISTAKEN IDENTITIES

SHIT! JAMES SWORE UNDER HIS breath as he moved back and dropped to the floor. Even though he had known the Chinese officer would be on the other side of the wall, the sudden onslaught of bullets had still taken him by surprise. As he squatted, one leg shifted slightly farther behind him to help maintain his center of balance, he realized the sergeant had decided to slice the pie as well. The rounds sailed over his head, peppering the wall and the doorjamb with holes. The last vestiges of the door's frame didn't have much material left, and as each round pierced it, large hunks of wood exploded and fell to the ground. One wickedly jagged splinter bounced off the side of his head on its way down, and as he took a step back, James knew he had dodged a bullet—several of them, in fact, quite literally.

James retreated rapidly, stepping over the dead PFPA officer and jumping over Shelley's overturned desk, then turned, positioning himself to face the open door. Behind the pockmarked desk, he drew his limbs tightly to his body, making himself as small as possible without compromising his aim. He raised his Sig over the ragged side of the desk, aiming it at the doorway. The sergeant's rounds were relentless as they peppered the wall to his left, the rounds getting closer to James and leaving deep scars at chest-height in the stone surface.

It was clear the sergeant was done playing around as well. He was ready to end the fight and finish the job he had set out to do that day. As he charged into the administrator's office, his Glock pointing forward in his outstretched arm, he let out an almost inhumane roar. The noise coming from his throat, however, was overshadowed by the sound of him squeezing round after round from his firearm at the agent behind the desk. The first two rounds flew wild and high, missing their target and sending shards of granite falling to the floor.

The officer paused, his slitted eyes lighting on the agent crouched behind the desk.

James met his gaze evenly, and as the officer lowered his weapon to aim at his head, James returned fire.

A round jetted out from the barrel of the Sig and soared through the air, cutting off the battle cry coming from the sergeant's mouth instantly as it accidentally ricocheted off his firearm. The sergeant staggered but didn't move. Without hesitation, James fired again, slightly adjusting his aim on his target even as he pulled the trigger. This time, the round went higher, landing squarely in the sergeant's shoulder. It glided smoothly through the fabric and the flesh behind it, piercing his body just a handful of centimeters above his PFPA badge. The officer's body pivoted left from the impact, with a single, stumbling step backward. The weapon tumbled from his open fingers, thudded harmlessly to the ground, and skidded away from him.

To James's displeasure, the man was still standing. Neither the round that had struck his Glock nor the one that had hit his shoulder had managed to drop him. He continued to linger in front of the doorway, his legs wide and his body twisted slightly away from him, as the dark stain of his blood spread across the front of his navy-blue PFPA jacket. As he stood there, the realization of the new hole in his body seemed to dawn on him, and his right hand flew up to it. Even with his palm clasped over it, the crimson fluid seeped out from between his fingers and oozed down the back of his hand. Despite his injuries, though, the officer was somehow still alert. His dark eyes darted toward the black metal of his sidearm on the rug less than two feet away from his polished loafers, and James could almost see the mental calculations in the injured man's head as he followed his gaze to the damaged weapon.

"If you want to live," James said evenly, his weapon recentering on the sergeant's forehead and his index finger tightening around the trigger, "don't even *think* about it."

"James?" A new voice broke through the tense standoff.

James recognized the familiar baritone of the secretary and threw a glance over his shoulder with a flash of alarm and even annoyance jolting across his face. Why the hell had the SecDef stepped out of his office, and *now* of all times? Andrews's eyes flickered from his PSO to the Chinese officer standing across from him, and even as he stood there, it was evident he was trying to find some way to assist James against their common enemy. His eyes swept the room for a weapon, any weapon, he could use on the wounded sergeant.

"Mike!" James barked, formalities momentarily forgotten. Could he not see that the threat had not yet been diffused? He could apologize for snapping at him later. For now, he needed to keep the SecDef from getting killed. "Get back in the office! *Go!*"

In his peripheral vision, a sudden blur of movement drew James's attention back at the sergeant. The Chinese agent had sensed his window of opportunity provided by the distraction and leaped forward. He reached for his weapon with his bloodied, outstretched fingers, his eyes locked on the Glock on the floor. James had no time to think or assess the situation. In a second or two at the very most, the sergeant would have his fingers on the firearm. Once he had it, he would not hesitate to use it on first Andrews, then James himself.

Moving on impulse, James shifted his aim slightly, as the top of the sergeant's head revealed itself when he was going for the gun. He squeezed the trigger twice, not daring to pause between shots. The first round flew from the chamber and embedded itself into the top of the officer's head with a wet, splintering *crack*. The second shot, however, caused the slide to lock to the rear of the Sig, and the weapon jerked in his hand. Unlike the first round, this one was futile, the chamber empty. That didn't seem to matter, though. The first bullet had done the job. It had buried itself deep within the sergeant's skull, and there it would remain until the medical examiner took the liberty of removing it. The officer fell forward wordlessly, his body prone and lifeless on the floor.

James's breath was heavy and ragged as he fished the final magazine from the pouch on his hip. The spent magazine fell to the floor, landing inches away from the fallen sergeant's head. He reached up, the fresh magazine gripped in his fingers, and slid it into the reservoir. With a firm rap from his palm, he locked it into place, ready to fire another sixteen rounds at whatever target needed further attention. He took another step closer to the PFPA officer, his finger braced against the Sig's trigger guard as he stood over the corpse. The weapon in his hand remained firmly locked on the sergeant's back as he considered the body.

"James?" Andrews said quietly, and despite the violent scene that had just unfolded before him, his voice was calm and even almost gentle as he addressed the agent. "I think he's dead now. You can put your weapon down."

"Hm?" James blinked, his head turning slowly toward the secretary standing in the doorway. He could see Shelley beyond him, her eyes wide and shocked as she peered back at them. The pain in his neck was now a dull throb, a subtle reminder of everything he had been through in the past twenty-four hours. His eyes went back to the corpse lying face down on the floor and, seeing the spreading pool of blood beneath the lifeless form, reluctantly nodded at the secretary. "Yeah, I think you might be right."

Andrews seemed to have something more to say, but an unexpected shout from the other side of the door caused them to both jerk their heads up. They cocked their heads in the direction of the words coming to them from the hallway, listening. Unlike those of the three PFPA officers James had just taken care of, these new words were in English. It was almost refreshing, given the circumstances.

"Police! Come out with your hands up!"

James cast a glance through the entry, but no movement caught his gaze. The officers must have been standing well clear of it. He exchanged a glance with Andrews, and with an almost imperceptible shrug, the secretary raised both of his hands into the air. He took a step toward the door, but a sharp jerk of James's head stopped him in his tracks. The CID agent raised his left palm in the air, his right hand still holding the Sig. Instead of being pointed at the sergeant on the floor, though, it was now pointed at the open doorway.

"Mike," James said briskly, his voice low and rushed, "listen to me. I just shot and killed three Pentagon Force Protection Agency law enforcement officers. I really don't think you should go out there just yet."

Andrews seemed to consider this. After a beat, he lowered his hands back down to his sides and nodded. "Good point. Yeah, I think you're probably right. But…do you think they're real PFPA officers, or were they just dressed up like them?"

"I had the same question myself, honestly." James turned his attention to the corpse of the sergeant on the floor, nudging it with his shoe. It lifted slightly off the floor, revealing the glassy, unseeing eyes of the Chinese officer. "But look at him. The uniform fits him properly, he has the same type of pistol as they assign to PFPA officers, and even the radio is the same standard-issue radio PFPA officers use. It's even on the correct frequency."

Andrews gazed down at the body on the floor, seeming to listen to the faint crackling of distant chatter on the sergeant's radio. "Damn."

"If they're not real officers," James concluded, pulling his leg back and allowing the body to flop back down on the rug, "then they did a damned amazing job of looking just like them. Listen to me, sir. I want you to go back into your office with Shelley and wait for my signal. Let me figure out if these guys are interested in shooting at us as well, okay?"

"She's probably half scared out of her mind," Andrews said almost as an afterthought. "I sort of just left her in there alone. Yeah. I'll go back in there and wait with her. But, James? I want you to be careful."

"I will." James brought his left hand up to his forehead, wiping absently at the bloom of sweat that had formed there. A small streak of blood followed the pattern of his hand, a souvenir of the recent firefight vanishing into his hairline. "I'm trying, believe me, sir. I thought I had left all of this behind when I left Delta. It's almost like the shit storm finds me, though, no matter where I go."

"Yeah." Andrews glanced at the door, then back at James. A line of sympathy creased his brow, and he nodded at him one last time, then turned back to his office door. He opened it and slipped through it, and a moment later, James could hear the lock latching behind him.

Alright. James sighed and turned his attention back to the door. As though on cue, another shout drifted in from the hallway. "I said, this is the police! Come out with your hands up, or we are going to have to send in the K9!"

That, James knew, was highly unlikely. The Pentagon Force Protection Agency's K9 units were bomb-sniffing dogs, not patrol dogs. If they had tried to send in such a dog to suppress him, the poor dog would not know how to proceed after determining James was not, in fact, a pile of explosive material.

"Look," James called back at the splintered door, "I'm Special Agent James Chase. I was just attacked by three uniformed PFPA officers. How do I know you're not going to shoot me if I step out?"

A moment of silence followed this as the officers on the other side of the door seemed to weigh his message. After several seconds, the original voice called back unconvincingly, "You're just going to have to trust us."

James shook his head. *Yeah, I don't think so, buddy.*

He glanced around the room, his eyes sweeping over the destroyed office. Paintings, furniture, and even a vase had been reduced to nothing more than shards of glass and rubble on the floor. The room itself was smoky with floating debris, dust, and gunpowder. His gaze landed on the office phone resting on the floor by the desk. It must have fallen during the fray, and in doing so, the handset had slipped from the receiver. Kneeling carefully without lowering the firearm he had trained on the doorway, James flipped the phone over. He pressed the switch hook with his index finger and, with his left hand, brought the headset to his ear.

There was a dial tone.

"Hey, listen." James raised his voice, lifting it so the officers could hear him clearly as he spoke. "I'm coming right out, okay? Just give me a second."

There was a shuffle of feet on the other side of the doorway, but no reply. Like James, they too could be patient. For now. But how long would it be before they would start shooting through the entryway just like the three officers who had attacked him a few minutes before? Time was running out, and James needed answers, clarification, any tangible indication that it was safe for himself and the secretary—and poor Shelley too—to emerge from their impromptu barricade in his office.

Pressing the buttons quickly, James dialed the number for the CID office in the garage from memory. From somewhere below him in the bowels of the Pentagon, someone picked up the line on the second ring.

A crisp voice spoke into the headset, "Agent Foshee, how can I be of assistance?"

"John!" James recognized the agent's voice instantly. Despite himself, anger seeped into his voice as he hissed into the line, "Get the entire team to the SecDef's office *right now*. There was a shooting!"

If visibly blanching had a sound, the shocked gurgle in Agent Foshee's voice was the audible representation of it. "Yes, sir…Chief. We're going right now."

James lowered the headset to the carpet and rose to his feet, turning slowly toward the broken door. He took a cautious step forward, then said, "Okay, listen to me. I'm going to toss out my gun. I just…I don't want any mistakes, okay? I'm doing it right now."

He leaned forward and, not removing his focus on the entryway, slid his fingers across the rug until they grazed over the fallen sergeant's Glock. With a low, underhanded flick of his wrist, he tossed it through the open door. It skidded across the threshold, skidding to a stop in the hallway. Hopefully, the officers on the other side would fail to notice it wasn't a standard-issue CID agent firearm, but it was a risk James would have to take. There was no way in hell he was going out there unarmed, especially after apparently three PFPA officers had tried to assassinate the secretary of defense on his watch.

The presence of the weapon in the corridor was enough to send the officers into another hushed frenzy of chatter as they tried to make sense of it. The voices rose and fell over one another, then just as they started, they were cut off by a new sound: heavy footsteps running down the hall followed by even louder shouts. James let out a breath he had no idea he was holding as he realized he recognized the new voices. From the time he had placed the call to the arrival of his agents down in the Pentagon garage, less than a minute had transpired.

In the hallway, an argument broke out. James turned his head slightly, listening to the new shouts of "Stop!" and "Lower your weapons!" and "Stay away from that office!" as the special agents and the PFPA officers met each other in the corridor. Just as the voices crested into shouts, though, they quickly dropped once more into metered tones. A dull murmur of conversation could be heard through the open door, though the words themselves were imperceptible and hard to distinguish.

"James?" a new voice spoke up after a moment's pause, calling out to the agent in the office. "Hey, are you in there? It's me, Agent Foshee."

Relief, long overdue, washed over James, and he felt his shoulders slump at the arrival of the CID agent. With John out there, James knew—as well as he could know, at least—that he was finally safe. Andrews was safe, and Shelley too. His arrival signaled that the threat had successfully been eliminated and verified the men on the other side of the door were indeed friendlies.

He cleared his throat, then said, "John? Yeah, it's me, James. I'm in here."

"It's okay." John's words were reassuring as he spoke to the CID agent within the administrator's office. His tall, broad-shouldered shape filled the doorway, and the light of the hallway spilled around him like an ironic halo as he squinted into the smoky room. He waved his hand back and forth in the entryway, trying to clear the haze. Recognizing the futility of the gesture, he slowly lowered it back down to his side. "I'm out here with several PFPA officers. It's safe. You can come out now."

"Okay, John. Yeah." James slipped his pistol into the holster, then lifted his hands slightly, letting the palms face outward in a gesture of submission. "I'm coming out now."

His feet carried him across the office toward the man standing in the doorway. His body was almost spectral as it materialized through the dust-congested room and glided toward the agent in the doorway. As James approached, John took a step back, then another, giving him a wide berth to exit. The door itself hung on its hinges like a broken tooth, its surface bearing more holes than actual wood. His dark eyes lifted toward the hallway as he stepped through the battered entryway, and his eyes widened slightly at the sight that greeted him.

Never before had he seen so many PFPA agents in one place. But, James knew, there was a first time for everything. Yesterday had been the first time he encountered a domestic terror attack on his home turf. Today he had been engaged in a shootout with three Pentagon Police Officers, all before lunchtime. And now, seeing the hallway choked with literally dozens of stunned PFPA officers set another new precedent.

It's almost enough to make you wonder, James thought wryly to himself as his gaze landed on John Foshee standing front and center of the pack with a baffled frown on his face. *What fresh new shit is in store for me tomorrow.*

He wasn't particularly looking forward to finding out, but for now, it would have to wait. He had more pressing things to attend to first, such as letting Secretary Andrews and Shelly know they were out of harm's way. The rest of his day was already spoken for as well, with the witness interviews he'd be giving to bland-faced FBI and PFPA agents as they tried to fit together the pieces of the puzzle that had led to the morning ambush. The remainder would be dedicated to completing an incident report for CID. And in the meantime, they needed to get to the bottom of whomever had arranged this attack to determine how the PFPA had been compromised—and ultimately determine if these three agents were part of an even larger cell of sleeper agents waiting in the wings for their own chance to attack.

CHAPTER SEVENTEEN

THE TRAINING EXERCISE

UNDER THE COVER OF A starless night and beneath the watchful eye of the People's Liberation Army Navy (PLAN), the *Fujian* glided through the frigid waters of the North China Sea. The flight deck of the Type 003 aircraft carrier bustled with activity as the sailors and pilots aboard it readied the next fighter jet for takeoff, their faces drawn with determined concentration as they worked. These men and women had been up since the day before in anticipation of the upcoming maneuver, but if any of them felt any of the first hints of fatigue as they readied the jets, they kept it to themselves. A powerful surge of adrenaline coursed through their veins as they labored aboard the vessel, keeping their focus on their task razor-sharp.

From the flybridge, Admiral Wu's dark eyes swept over the flight deck as he surveyed the jets taking off one and sometimes two at a time. The training exercise had been going on since 0030 hours, just shy of twenty minutes, and showed no signs of stopping. The aircraft continued to take off in a steady rhythm from the vessel, and the sky over the *Fujian* grew more densely packed as yet another plane took off and joined their prospective squadron. While the first few jets had already completed their takeoff and landing circuit and were idling on the flight deck, landing procedures for the ones currently circling the carrier had since been suspended. With so many of them already on the flight deck, and more planes coming off the elevator by the minute, there simply was no remaining place for them to land.

A tall and lean man of fifty, Admiral Sun Wu had been serving in the PLAN his entire adult life with unwavering loyalty, and it was his dedication to the PRC that had invited President Liao Hui to single him out for this exercise. The officer who had given him the command responsibility to oversee the operation had been brief and to the point, remarking only that the instructions had come from Liao himself. His shoulders had been squared as he relayed them to Wu, his eyes glinting with unconcealed pride as he said, "In order to strengthen our position against the United States, we need to turn to our nearby allies for assistance. Through this relationship, we can further broaden our position here in the Pacific and ensure our victory against America."

A commotion to his right drew Wu's attention to the flight deck, and he glanced over to the pair of launching catapults on the port side of the ship. A cluster of sailors stood there, waving their light wands slowly back and forth in the air. Another jet was ready for takeoff, and he nodded approvingly at the seamless transition. Overhead, no less than three dozen similar planes already loitered in the air, moving in an oblong pattern in the sky as they waited for their chance to land. As he watched, the sleek body of a Shenyang FC-31 sped down the runway, gaining momentum as it traversed its length. Just as it seemed the twin-engine fighter jet would slip over the edge and plummet into the churning waters below, its nose turned up and it vanished into the void beyond the carrier strike group (CSG).

Very good. A faint smile turned up the corner of Wu's lips. His sailors had been preparing for this exercise for weeks now, and seeing them work together like this was incredibly satisfying. Their efficiency, as well as their capabilities, reminded him as to why he had such a deep love for his homeland. The People's Republic of China was nothing if not the best, and the combination of their elite military forces and advanced technology only served to reinforce his fondness for it. He turned away from the flight deck, shifting his body to face the officer standing next to him. General Deng Yunsheng, the other commanding officer aboard the vessel, bore a similar expression of contentment on his own face.

"We are making exceptional progress tonight," Wu said, the smile on his face broadening slightly as he spoke. "At this rate, all of our jets should be airborne within the next half hour."

"Very good." The general's gaze was on the flight deck, and even as he spoke, another jet launched down the runway and out over the North China Sea.

Another down, and just another twenty to go. As one became airborne, another quickly followed it down the flight deck, a seamless and well-choreographed maneuver. They were successfully launching four jets per minute now, and the sky above the CSG1 was almost as full as the waters around it. A number of vessels kept pace with the aircraft carrier *Fujian*, a sort of envoy guiding it through the North China Sea. Nearly a third of the PRC's destroyer fleet, twenty in total, flanked it on each side. The same could be said for their frigates, and of the nearly ninety in their possession, thirty of them held a place in the CSG. Finally, fifteen Jiangdao corvettes completed the party. The aircraft carrier *Guangxi*, or CSG2, boasted similar numbers, a well-rounded flotilla on the opposite side of the island.

In the distance, some hundred miles southwest of them, lay Taiwan. The PRC's routine training exercises were more than familiar to the smaller breakaway province by now, as they had been performing them with increasing frequency in recent years. At first, Taiwan had been alarmed by the maneuvers, but now the presence of two carrier strike groups off their northern and southern borders was no more unusual than the side of rice they ate with their dinner in the evening. Like the grain itself, it was expected, routine, and almost even boring. Knowing the aircraft carrier *Guangxi* was performing similar training approximately hundred miles due south of Taiwan with their own fifty-nine jets in the air, similarly was no cause for concern.

The first hint of dawn's blush was still over five hours away when the final fighter jet sped down the runway on the *Fujian's* flight deck and joined the rest of them in the sky. The air space above the nearly thousand-foot-long aircraft carrier now boasted an assortment of J-31 and J-15 jets, as well as a few KJ-600 radar early-warning aircraft to round out the collection.

As Wu watched the last one takeoff over the bow of the vessel, a sense of warm contentment settled over him. Things were finally falling into place and, with all of their jets now in the air, he could initiate the next stage of the evening's clandestine task. He pivoted on his heel, his eyes scanning the bridge until they landed on the communications officer stationed at the ship's radio. "Communications Officer Lieutenant Yang, contact the *Guangxi*. Tell them we are in position and ready to begin."

The lieutenant nodded, and a momentary burst of static spilled out of the radio, then was quickly followed by the sound of his voice relaying the command.

A moment later, the words of the other carrier strike group communications officer could be heard, crisp and loud in the flybridge. "*Fujian*, this is the *Guangxi*. We are also in position and ready. Dispatching our pilots now. Over."

"Lieutenant Yang," Wu said, the smile on his face inching up farther, "please alert the pilots to move into position. We are ready to proceed."

He turned slightly, facing the window to peer out at the flight deck and the blackness beyond. From where he stood, he could see the lights on the jets blinking in the distance as the pilots changed direction after Yang delivered the message. Their glowing navigation lights dipped and swirled as all sixty-one pilots eased their jets closer to the surface of the North China Sea. As he watched, the lights slipped below the lip of the stern, then faded out on the horizon as they barreled toward the island in the distance. At a fairly modest Mach 0.85, or just half of their top speeds of some 1,300 miles per hour, they would be reaching Taiwan in just under twenty minutes. This was more than ample time for him to send a welcoming party ahead of them.

"Lieutenant Yang." Once more Wu turned toward the man seated at the radio. "Contact the Liancheng Air Base. Tell them Operation Taiwan Unification is now underway."

"Yes, sir!" Again Yang nodded, then depressed the button on the radio, delivering the message as instructed. "Liancheng Air Base. This is *Fujian*. Operation Taiwan Unification is now underway."

On the mainland, in the Eastern Theater Command of the PRC, the base's communications officer listened to the incoming message. Wu kept half an ear on the relays and nodded in approval when the transmission ended. Their messages had been brief, crisp, and to the point. However, despite so little being said between the two men, the first of Wu's gifts to Taiwan were now en route. From the Liancheng Air Base stationed in the Fujian Province—the eponymous namesake of the aircraft carrier he was currently commanding—two hundred J-20 stealth fighters were taking flight. Also in tow were an additional twenty Xian H-6 stealth bombers, each fully equipped with air-launched ballistic missiles. And if that wasn't enough, Wu had one last thing in store for Taiwan.

His eyes never left the endless yawning stretch of black beyond the vessel as he spoke. He had one last message for Yang to deliver. In many ways, it was the most important relay of the evening. "Lieutenant Yang, contact the missile destroyers and have them fire their missiles at their designated targets."

Outside the aircraft carrier *Fujian*, the darkness lingered for only a moment longer and then suddenly lit up the sky in a brilliant orange glow as the first missiles departed from the ship's HT-1E universal vertical launch system (VLS). One after another, the missiles rapidly flew from the VLS, cresting high in the air before settling into a dedicated trajectory toward Taiwan. The pilots flying close to the ocean watched as scores of missiles flew quickly overhead, heading in the same direction they were going. The missiles, clocking in at speeds greater than Mach 3.5—or nearly 2,700 miles per hour—would be arriving at their destination in the next three minutes.

Without fanfare or preamble, and deliberately hidden beneath the cloak of the witching hour's darkness, the attack on Taiwan came from nearly all sides. The day had been predicted to be cool and sunny, just another Sunday, no different than the many thousands before it. Around the country, families lay asleep in their beds, blissfully unaware of the threat looming ominously on the horizon. The only ones unfortunate enough to be awake for the unexpected assault were either working the nightshift or insomniacs.

Inside the subterranean Heng Shan facility, the tri-service military command center in the Zhongshan District of Taipei, stood the watch commander responsible for detecting this precise situation. First Lieutenant Peng Li-jie gazed at the wall-mounted monitors with mounting dismay, the cup of coffee in his hands suspended in the air mid-sip. His shift had been routine up until five minutes before. Until that point, the PRC had been engaging in routine training exercises almost identical to dozens of other similar exercises since his appointment to the command post the year before. At first, he had almost doubted the display on the AN/FPS-11 Precision Acquisition Vehicle Entry Phased Array Warning System (PAVE

PAWS). But now, as he watched the radar display of incoming fighter jets headed toward Taiwan, his mind struggled to make sense of it.

Disbelief and fear competed for control within his mind. As soon as the PRC's planes had changed their route on the PAVE PAWS display, Peng reached for the red phone mounted on the wall next to his workstation. His fingers had felt numb, almost as though his body was miles away, as he dialed the number for Heng Shan's base commander. If there had been any notes of annoyance in the commander's voice at the interruption when he answered it, they were gone by the time the young lieutenant had finished his frantic briefing.

Somewhere else inside the building, the base commander was now sending out the alert to Tsai Chih-ming, retired army general and recently appointed defense minister to Taiwan. Once he completed this call, he would next notify all of their air bases across the country to rally the pilots for immediate action. Even as Peng stood there reflecting on the possibilities of the upcoming minutes and hours, the Heng Shan's base commander was already in the process of dispatching their F-16As, F5s, Mirage 2000s, and F-CK-1s. The pilots on night duty would immediately launch into action, their training making them a concise and well-oiled fighting machine even at this hour.

Despite moving as quickly as they could, it would still take them nearly twenty minutes to get the first of them into the air. With the enemy aircraft speeding toward them at nearly six hundred and fifty miles per hour, that window of time was almost exactly the same amount of time as they would need to ready their pilots for the invasion. By the time they managed to get the first wings into the air, the enemy pilots would already be flying over the coast. Even if the defense ministry used all of their resources to counter the incoming fighter jets, Peng was acutely aware of the stark imbalance of what each brought to the fight. Would it be good enough? It bothered Ping more than he cared to admit that he did not know for sure.

And now, as he stood there, he reflected quietly on the past few years and the increasingly strained relationship between Taiwan and the PRC. The People's Liberation Army Air Force (PLAAF) had been dipping in and out of their Air Defense Identification Zone (ADIZ) for several years now, flying too close to their island during their so-called training exercises. The PLAAF had even gone so far as to relay both mockery and thinly veiled verbal threats during these encroachments at the Taiwanese military. After the PRC had abolished the median line in the Taiwan Strait several years before, both sides had known this day was coming. Today was, apparently, that day. In a curious sort of way, it was almost a relief.

The odds against them were great. Peng knew that. The very foundation of Taiwan's Overall Defense Concept had been built on those self-aware principles, underscoring the very stark reality of how uneven the potential conflict between the two countries would be. Even with Taiwan doubling down on its defense budget, having invested over $11 billion in fortifying the island in recent years, it still paled next to the PRC's annual budget of greater than $250 billion. If they stood a chance of defending themselves against an invasion, they would have to find a way to put their limited military assets to use. Not only could they not match them blow for blow, but their victory depended largely on whether or not they could even survive the first attack and hold on long enough to fight back.

Knowing the appallingly narrow window of time they had been given to react and recognizing the sheer volume and scope of the incoming aircraft, Peng took one look at the information from the PAVE PAWS display and shook his head. With something like a hundred and twenty enemy aircraft speeding toward them from approximately ninety miles out, there was no way this night could get any worse.

Cold fingers of fear stroked at Peng's brain as he gazed at the radar display. Something else was now moving toward them from the PRC's two carrier strike groups. Too fast to be jets, the PAVE PAWS identified them as incoming missiles. As his mind scrambled frantically to identify the potential targets of these incoming missiles, the blips vanished from the display just short of making landfall. The screen showed their termination somewhere over the sea, and in a flash of clarity, Peng recognized the reason why: their naval and coast guard patrol vessels that had been assigned to patrol the waters surrounding Taiwan had been targeted.

The PRC's carrier strike groups were not quite done with them yet, though. This initial barrage of missile indicators on the PAVE PAWS display had evidently been just the beginning. As he stared at it, a continuous stream of missiles now poured from the two CSGs on both the north and south sides of the island, far more than Peng could calculate in a glance. Hundreds of them moved across the display, white pinpoints of destruction soaring over the body of water separating the two CSGs from Taiwan. Beneath his gaze, the first of the radar blips targeted the 131st Naval Fleet just offshore of Keelung City. While he couldn't say for certain how many of the fleet's ships had been in the surrounding area, as any number of them could have been on patrol or in dry dock, the score of missile indicators were likely more than sufficient to sink all the ships.

At the same time that dozens more targeted the 146th Fleet in and around the waters offshore of Magong City in Penghu, missiles targeted the anti-stealth radar station and the Tien-Kung III Surface-to-Air Missile Systems (SAMS) on the island. Farther east, even more missiles met their targets as shown by disappearing dots on the feed. Peng knew the 168th Fleet in Su'ao was no more. And finally, the last and most devastating blip came from the south. Moving in a steady trajectory, its target was clearly none other than Kaohsiung City, the second most populous city in Taiwan and home of their fleet headquarters. As he watched, the rain of missiles successfully obliterated not only the naval academy, but also the 124th Fleet, the amphibious 151st Fleet, the 192nd Minesweeper Fleet, and most of the 256th Submarine Squadron.

And with its untimely end, the LCC-1—a vintage tank landing ship on lease from the United States—concluded its prolific eighty-one-year career. The vessel had been fitted with a Sea Oryx short-range air defense system eight years before, and as the enemy missiles had sped toward it, it had fired off its own counterstrike. The Sea Oryx was able to intercept two of the four missiles speeding toward it, but the other two missiles hit their target. Both the LCC-1 and the Sea Oryx now settled into their new home on the bottom of the bay. While Peng had been able to observe the port's destruction from his position inside the command center, the city's three million residents had been awakened to a front-row seat to the devastation.

As another onslaught of enemy missiles took aim at their remaining defensive systems across the island, including ones guarding both Ching Chuan Kang Air Base and Chiashan Air Force Base, the best—or worst— was yet to come. Taiwan was now reduced to just one anti-missile defense system: the CIWS at Leshan Radar Station. However, unlike the other two close-in weapon systems at the air bases, this one had been dragged to the top of Mount Lu Chang over a decade before to serve a greater purpose.

The modified defense system, with its attack range of just over three miles, was also the primary guardian of their PAVE PAWS radar system.

Positioning the PAVE PAWS on the mountain had been no coincidence. At an elevation of greater than 2,600 feet, it had the ability to detect threats from as far as three thousand nautical miles away. Its antenna array were their eyes, and the system could arguably afford them a six-minute warning to any incoming ballistic missile attack. Without it, though, Taiwan would be blinded, forced to fight back with the equivalent of a mask over its eyes. And now, the geometric array watched objectively as eight missiles moved toward both itself and the nearby CIWS, dutifully relaying this warning to Peng in the command center. As he watched the display on the PAVE PAWS, he knew the life expectancy of both systems was coming to an end.

The missile indicators inched closer and closer to Mount Lu Chang nearly eighty miles south of Peng and the command center, an unrelenting dot matrix blinking its way steadily across the display. Upon detecting the surface-to-surface missiles (SSMs) speeding toward it, the CIWS had unleashed a barrage of armor-piercing tungsten projectiles at a rate of more than fifty per second. The stream of rounds pouring from its turret vaguely resembled weld spatter as it promptly destroyed three of the missiles, a fiery show of profound defensive measures. On the display, however, it was nothing more than three blips falling from the screen. As much as the close-in weapon system had tried its best to defend itself and the radar array against the incoming missiles, and despite succeeding in destroying the SSMs, its efforts had ultimately been in vain. No grandiose spectacle on the PAVE PAWS's display heralded its destruction as the five remaining missiles collided with the mountain. Instead, there was only a final flash and then the screen grew dark. And with no other way to keep tabs on their enemy, the show was now officially over for both the watch commander inside the Heng Shan Military Command Center and the rest of Taiwan.

CHAPTER EIGHTEEN

THE INVASION

DEEP UNDERGROUND INSIDE THE HENG Shan facility, Peng stared at the blank display of the now lifeless PAVE PAWS system. With its glassy black screen gazing back lifelessly, the only clues as to what was going on in the world above his head was now limited to the large monitor on the command center's back wall. The infrared cameras kept an unblinking eye trained on various points across the country, allowing him a less precise—but no less vital—view of the invading aerial forces on the screen. The display was sectioned into nine sections, and his eyes flickered from screen to screen, his lips moving silently as he quietly calculated the number of jets headed their way. Even with his roughest estimates, there had to be close to two hundred enemy aircraft headed their way…possibly more.

Like many Taiwanese citizens, Peng had frequently entertained the idea of what might happen when the PRC finally invaded their country. It had been a fairly common narrative in his childhood and hushed conversations around the dinner table, punctuated by cautious glances at the sky every time an airplane departing from Taoyuan International Airport had seemed unusually loud. It was this pervasive uncertainty, the fear of a sudden invasion, that had spurred his motivation to enlist in the military when he had turned eighteen. Even though the official mandatory conscription had ended back in 2018, he would have volunteered for service regardless. And why wouldn't he? He believed in his country, believed in its values, and believed in its ability to put up a solid fight against the PRC.

And now, in the belly of the Heng Shan Military Command Center, the expanding and uncomfortable doubts regarding their possible success clanged loudly between his ears. With their naval defenses gone, their anti-missile systems destroyed, and the destroyed PAVE PAWS now unable to keep track of the incoming enemy, the reality of the situation was becoming abundantly clear. Without these vital military resources, and with only their smaller air force to fight back against the barrage of jets headed their way, Taiwan's chances of a victory against the PRC were growing increasingly slim by the minute.

Even though he was just a first lieutenant, Peng was arguably one of the more knowledgeable soldiers among his peers, especially when it came to strategic relations and their ongoing conflict with the PRC. He had his eye set on climbing the ranks in the upcoming years and, in preparation for it, had dedicated his life to learning everything he could about the mainland country positioned only a hundred miles away from them. This was also part of why he had jumped at the opportunity to become part of the watch command here in Taipei. Because of this, his patriotism was strengthened by a steady dose of grounded reality. Regardless of the challenges they would be facing today in their fight against the PRC, he knew their military would not simply roll over and play dead.

Sure, their navy was paltry in comparison, but it was all they had. From his time working in Heng Shan, he had picked up a thing or two about his country's resources and how they could use them. Even right now, as he waited for the defense minister to arrive, he knew his commanders were actively gathering up every resource they had in their power to defend Taiwan. Despite the PRC all but destroying their naval assets, they still at least had their air force to fight off the incoming military. Preparing the Taiwanese fighter jets for dispatch and assembling the pilots for takeoff generally took at least twenty minutes, maybe more. By now, most of their pilots would already be strapped in and going through their takeoff checklist. In another minute or two, the first of them would be taxing down the runways from the three different points on the island, ready to meet the People's Liberation Army, Navy, and Air Force (PLANAF) in the sky above Taiwan.

Up against over two hundred aircraft steadily closing the gap toward them, growing closer by the second, the Taiwan Air Force had a fairly formidable 320 jets on their side to help them counter it. While that was no scant amount in and of itself, actually getting their pilots up into the air in time to fight back would be an entirely different story. According to the digital clock on the wall, only ten minutes had passed since the PLANAF had shifted its position midair and turned toward Taiwan. And only six of them had occurred since the missiles had taken out their navy and the island's defense systems. It seemed so much longer than that, as though a small eternity had passed in this relatively narrow window of time.

Thanks to the ongoing taunts from the PRC's armed forces, as well as the steadily increasing breaches into their Air Defense Identification Zone (ADIZ), their pilots were on constant standby for dispatch at Ching Chuan Kang Air Base, Hsinchu Air Base, and Chiashan Air Force Base. However, the PRC was not going to wait idly by for them to assemble their counterstrike. Already the first wave of incoming PLAAF pilots had released air-to-surface (ASM) missiles at key landmarks on the island, and the guided ballistics had wasted no time in destroying key targets across the island. One video display, its camera trained directly overhead on Taipei's Zhongzheng District, showed the flattened ruins of the Presidential Office Building and the eight-story main building of the Ministry of National Defense headquarters.

A commotion at the door to the control room drew Peng's attention away from the video monitors, and he turned his head to face the source of the noise. The sounds of men's voices, loud and overlapping one another, cut through the recirculated air filtered throughout the base. The heavily reinforced steel door opened, and eight men strode through. Leading the group was the base commander, Dai Kuan-lin. Behind him were three other men, tall and broad in black suits. Behind this trio stood none other than the defense minister, Tsai Chih-ming, and following the party included three additional security agents. As they entered, the trailing security detail resecured the steel door behind them, then returned his attention once more to the defense minister.

Peng stood at attention as the men strode into the room, his eyes locking forward at an invisible spot on the wall, and the commander dismissed him with a distracted nod. His attention was divided by the words coming out of the defense minister's mouth and the monitors behind him, and Peng allowed himself to follow his gaze to the wall.

Dai's words were abrupt as he said, "On the bottom screen, there. You can see it, at Hsinchu Air Base. Our pilots are now taking flight. At this rate, they will be meeting the enemy forces just as they reach our coast. Estimated contact in approximately five minutes."

Tsai acknowledged this with a slight nod of his own as he trained his eyes on the screen closest to the floor. "Very good. Were there casualties when the Leshan Radar Station was hit?"

The corners of Dai's lips turned down, and he shook his head slightly. "Yes, sir. Not as bad as it could have been, fortunately. But yes, there were casualties."

"Hm." The expression on Tsai's face was unreadable as he continued to glance from screen to screen. It lingered on a video feed in the center of the panel of monitors, then paused. "That display right there, middle right, with the view of Taoyuan City. Can you make that bigger? I want to see it."

"Yes, of course." Dai turned to Peng.

The lieutenant nodded, then stepped toward his desk where the computer controls for the screen rested on the slate gray surface and tapped a few buttons on the keyboard with his right hand. A click of his mouse later and the image grew wider until it spanned the entire breadth of the wall-to-floor monitor.

"Thank you." Tsai's dark brows knit together as he peered at the stretch of coastal land on the western side of the country. "Based on our analyses, there are fewer than fourteen possible beaches where the PLAN's marine corps may land. However, with Taoyuan being a coastal city and the airport directly behind it, we have determined this one to be one of the first targets for a possible invasion. This means their paratroopers will arrive first to lend ground support."

A faint glint on the peripheral side of the display drew Peng's eye toward the left of the feed, and he bit back a quiet gasp as the image materialized into view. Even as they stood there discussing the potential landing site for the PLAN marines, he could see the lights of the first squadron arriving. Tsai's eyes narrowed as he too spotted the growing influx of incoming Chinese planes. Chu-wei Beach was no longer a hypothetical possibility. The jets were coming in rapidly, and in the next sixty seconds or so, they would be soaring over Taiwan. These fighter planes would slow their speed as they approached Taoyuan International Airport, and no later than an additional minute after that, countless enemy aircraft would begin releasing their pay-load of hundreds of paratroopers onto the runways below.

The invasion had officially begun.

⊁⊁ ⊁ ⊁ ⊁ ⊁

Sergeant Hao ignored the bolus of unease twisting in his stomach and instead, allowed his thoughts to go to the mission ahead. Around him, over a hundred other PLA Airborne Corps infantrymen stood nestled together inside the Shaanxi Y-9 transport aircraft, their faces bearing a rainbow of expressions ranging from the stretched grins of candid excitement to the more reserved scowls of vague unrest. Sgt. Hao's own face was a mixture of the two, and his apprehension of the upcoming drop was not quite fear, but rather a churning combination of anxiety and exhilaration. It wasn't so much that he had doubts about their impending battle, but he was more than ready to get started.

Behind him, the static line stretched the length of the plane, and ahead of him, another half-dozen men waited at the mouth of the open cargo bay door. The green runway lights of Taoyuan International Airport unfolded in the distance, and his pulse quickened slightly at the sight of them just over a thousand feet below. This was it. They were now flying over their target. In a moment, the booming voice of the company commander would ring out inside the body of the Shaanxi Y-9, and they would begin shuffling forward to leap out the rear of the aircraft. Even at reduced speeds of just a hundred and fifty miles per hour, the chilly winds buffeted his face beneath his camouflage green Kevlar QGF03 combat helmet. He turned his body toward the bay door and gazed out at the open landscape below.

A shout rang out behind him, and even though he couldn't make out the individual words, he recognized it as the company commander barking out their orders. In front of him, the camouflage green shoulders of the paratrooper took a step forward, and Hao took one of his own, matching his stride step for step as he inched closer to the open door. The wind was blinding now, and he scrunched up his face, trying to protect his eyes from it as he moved closer to the exit. His booted feet now stood at the lip of the bay door, and he could see the Type 07 uniform of the paratrooper ahead now plummeting down into the darkness below. Then it was his turn, and he stepped over the edge, into nothingness.

As the night sky rushed up to greet him, the static line attached to his deployment bag unthreaded his parachute, pulling it taut before releasing it. With the transport plane now behind him, his body was in freefall, plunging down toward the ground at a rate of greater than twenty feet per second. One second passed, then two, then three, and *four*…then a sharp yank caused his body to recoil as the canopy of his parachute billowed open. He could hear it fluttering overhead as it fanned out, reaching its full breadth at the end of the lines. Now he was falling at a more conservative rate of thirteen miles per hour, the ground drifting up toward him at a significantly more comfortable pace.

The air over the landing zone was choked with dozens of infantrymen, a dense fog of human bodies floating down over the terrain. The night sky concealed the paratroopers' positions as they fell slowly from the sky. When they landed on the ground, they would be within two klicks, or 1.25 miles, from Chu-wei Beach—a key site of the incoming PLAN marines—to provide them much-needed ground support. Across the country, similar teams of paratroopers were also jumping from their aircraft, an invisible and deadly assault from above. Overhead, Sgt. Hao could hear the roar of the Shaanxi Y-9's engines fade away as it vanished over the horizon, its task of releasing its cargo of paratroopers completed.

The descent was almost serene, and he felt his body relaxing as he drifted down. The landing zone was less than two hundred meters below him, and he would be on the ground in less than thirty seconds. A sudden tug on his parachute, however, drew his attention away from the ground below and to the circle of nylon above his head. It fluttered ominously in the draft, and as he squinted up at it in the darkness, he could see several new holes now puncturing the material. Another jerk on the parachute followed the first, and he realized with mounting dread that he was falling faster now, speeding toward the runway at a rate that far exceeded what he might comfortably call a safe one. He wasn't spinning out of control just yet, but another round or two from below would likely be more than enough to escalate it to those levels.

Somewhere directly above him, he heard a scream, shrill and agonized. Then, as quickly as it began, it abruptly cut off. The Taiwanese infantry had found them, and now hundreds of rounds sliced through the air from down below as the Guandu Area Command soldiers discharged their T91 assault rifles at the falling paratroopers. Sgt. Hao's pulse quickened as he hoisted his own QBZ-191 assault rifle in his grip and trained it on the ground below. He couldn't run, he couldn't fall faster, and he couldn't avoid the onslaught of bullets raining up at him and his company, but he damned sure could fight back. The intermittent burst of muzzle flash guided his aim as his index finger closed around the trigger, and the weapon jittered in his hands as he fired upon the threat beneath him. Around him, more screams broke through the air, some lingering longer than others but all thick with pain.

The sight of the runway just a handful of meters below was a welcome one, even despite the relentless fire from the Taiwanese soldiers surrounding him. Sgt. Hao drew his feet together, bending his knees slightly, and tucked his chin down to his chest in preparation for his heavy landing. His elbows drew into his sides, and he let his body drift to his left side as the runway loomed directly beneath him. The balls of his feet hit the blacktop a bit faster and harder than they should have, and he saw a momentary surge of light in his vision as his teeth clacked together from the impact. He stumbled, his ankle bending slightly beneath his body as gravity shifted his weight to the side. His calf collided with the runway, then his thigh, and finally his hips. He rolled, allowing momentum to propel his body over until he was lying on his back. The night sky overhead was blotted out by the still-falling paratroopers, and he had only a moment to register this as he rocked onto his side once more and pushed himself to his feet.

He took a cautious step forward, testing his ankle gingerly, then let the air out of his lungs as the joint accepted his weight without complaint. Some twenty feet in the distance, he could see the lifeless shape of one of his fellow soldiers slumped on the ground, one of the unlucky victims of the Taiwanese's attack. He forced his eyes off the body and his thoughts away from wondering about the corpse's identity and reached for the harness strapped around his shoulders. With the landing completed, he could focus on properly defending himself against the enemy. He reluctantly loosened his grip on his rifle and quickly unbuckled the parachute, releasing it. It fell away, and he stepped away from the now useless scrap of fabric. His rifle raised once more, he again tightened his finger around the trigger as he aimed it at the Taiwanese soldiers in the distance.

Even on the ground, it was difficult to see the enemy firing upon him, but their cries of anguish were more than enough indication that his aim was solid. Around him, he could hear the shouts of other PLAAF corps soldiers as they made their landings, and the sounds of rifle fire grew increasingly louder as they joined him in defending the landing zone. Seconds turned into minutes, and as Sgt. Hao began to wonder if they would even make it to Chu-wei Beach on time, a shout of "Cease fire!" rang out. In the distance, one of his fellow corpsmen had his fist raised in the air, and without another word, the soldier turned away. Around him, the night was quiet and still once more.

With this immediate threat no longer looming, he could now move onto the next stage of his mission. Sgt. Hao fell into a brisk trot behind the men as they moved into position. From the airport, it was nearly a ten-minute journey to the beach, and they needed to get there before the marines arrived to not only secure the perimeter but also provide much-needed support. He moved into formation as he navigated the stretch of land separating them from Chu-wei Beach, and his legs felt strong—as though he could keep this pace up for miles—as he made his way toward it. A few roads cut through the landscape, but the area between the airport and the landing site was largely industrial, peppered with large stretches of flat green plains. As the distance between the two sites narrowed, Sgt. Hao became more alert, his ears straining as he listened for any sounds of possible Taiwanese combat troops.

As he rounded a hill, he paused and scanned the stretch of water in the distance. From the briefing he had been given the afternoon before, he knew the strip of Chu-wei Beach just off the bustling city center of Taoyuan City was normally a popular tourist hotspot. With the active Zhuwei Fish Harbor to its north and the Taoyuan International Airport just a couple of miles inland, it wasn't just a beautiful vacation destination but also the best strategic location for the incoming marines. It was arguably one of the only possible ones where they *could* land, in fact, as the majority of the country's coastal topography was aggressive with craggy outcroppings and a combination of natural and man-made barricades. Today, though, there were no tourists on the beach—only the PLA Airborne Corps and the Taiwanese Army waiting for them.

Hulking shapes loomed on the horizon just before the beach beyond it, and the sergeant let his gaze move along the length of the inlet. Off to his right, another soldier stood on the same hill, his body rigid as he too made sense of the blocky forms in the distance. Taiwan's tank force had apparently arrived in advance to greet them and now lined the coast on both sides as far as he could see in either direction. He turned his head slowly, left to right, taking in the scene. Hundreds of armored vehicles blocked their access to the coast, and he knew they would have to somehow find a way to get past them. The paratrooper in the distance seemed to come to the same conclusion, and almost in unison, they dropped to a crouch on the crest of the hill.

The radio at his hip provided a comforting weight, and he reached for it, depressing the transmit button as he brought it to his mouth. "This is Sergeant Hao, 127th Airborne Infantry. I am in position at Chu-wei Beach, but we do not have access to the marine landing zone. There are greater than one hundred tanks standing between us and the beach. Do you copy?"

A crackle followed his message, then a voice broke through the hiss of static coming from his radio. "Copy that, Sergeant Hao. We see them. Initiating an airstrike now."

The voice on the radio fell silent.

Sgt. Hao's eyes moved back and forth, taking in the silhouettes cast in stark relief of the ocean backdrop. In the distance, the sounds of jets grew louder, and he ventured a glance upward. Against the starless sky, it was impossible to see where they were coming from. A moment later, the high-pitched whoosh of a missile streaking through the air cut off the sounds of tanks moving on the sand and an armored vehicle some fifty yards in the distance seemed to spontaneously erupt into orange smoke and flames. Another whoosh followed, and then another, until the sounds of the missiles were blotted out entirely by the even louder din of tanks exploding on impact.

The air-to-surface missiles could not have come at a better time. As tank after tank became flying shrapnel on the beach, the PLAN's Type 071 amphibious transport dock ships materialized on the water. As they got closer, the marines aboard the blacked-out ships fired at the remaining Taiwanese mechanized army on the beach. The sounds of their weapons seemed amplified as they echoed over the waters of the strait. On the shore, the remaining 234th Mechanized Infantry Brigade returned fired at the incoming vessels, but the People's Liberation Army Navy Marine Corps

(PLANMC) was evidently unflustered as they cut down the infantry positioned on the beach. The beach was littered with an assortment of both modern M1A2T Abrams and vintage M60 combat tanks with gaping holes that were spewing fire. As the gaping maws of the PLAN ships swung open, no less than eight hundred troops poured out in a seemingly endless stream. They too had come prepared with their own armored vehicles in tow, and the marines were more than ready to use their ZTZ-99 battle tanks to advance their position.

The marines with their armored tanks flooded the shores of Chu-wei Beach firing at the battered 234th Mechanized Infantry Brigade. The armor-piercing shells sent vast arcs of wet sand pluming into the air with each impact, flying high before raining back down onto the soldiers below. As the firefight continued around him, one single rifle round found its way to Sgt. Hao, slicing cleanly through his neck before emerging on the other side. He gurgled, then fell forward, his staring eyes no longer seeing as the life seeped out of his body. The last sound in his ears was the echoing boom of another artillery round exploding into the dune next to him. For Sergeant Hao, his mission was finally over.

But for the Taiwanese tank battalion and the PLANMC, it had only just begun. To the outside eye, the scene unfolding on the beach could have vaguely resembled a snapshot that might not have seemed out of place in 1944 Normandy, albeit somewhat less noble than the goals of Operation Neptune. Beneath the vast and seemingly endless night sky, tank met tank on the shores of Chu-wei Beach, the dueling forces ruthless and unyielding in their attacks. The churning sand beneath the continuous tread readily gave purchase to the PLAN's armored vehicles, propelling them inexorably forward toward the city in the distance.

CHAPTER NINETEEN

A NEW NORMAL

THE IMAGES ON THE SCREEN painted a bleak picture, and as Tsai gazed at them, he felt the first inklings of doubt settle deep into the base of his skull. One display on the monitor featured the *Ma Kong*, one of their four guided-missile destroyers. The vessel sported a new hole in its stern and, as the briny waters of the Pacific Ocean poured into the gaping wound, it listed precipitously to its port side. In a few more minutes, she—as well as the last of the surviving crew aboard her—would be slipping down beneath the burning surface of the South China Sea. The *Lee Kung* had already predated her in its farewell voyage to the bottom of the Philippine Sea to the right of the island country a half hour before.

Things weren't faring much better on the other displays, either. To their credit, they had put up a solid resistance. At least, they had at first. The dogfight between their air force and the PLANAF had been nothing short of impressive, and seeing their pilots swooping over the coast and meeting the enemy fighter jets had instilled a deep sense of national pride in Tsai. But for every Shenyang J-15 they shot down, more than double that amount of their F-16 Fighting Falcons and Northrop F-5 plummeted to the ground. The waters around their country, as well as the craggy mountains, were littered with the smoking ruins of these downed jets.

It wasn't as though they had been shut out entirely, though. Another video feed showed the fairly new *Nanning* warship, one of the PRC's dozens of naval destroyers, smoldering from its position in the Taiwan Strait. Whether or not it would eventually sink was irrelevant, as their own missiles had successfully destroyed the vessel's vertical launch system. Even if it did somehow manage to stay afloat, it would not be firing any more projectiles at them anytime soon. Then there were the things he could *not* see on the screen, such as the single nuclear and three diesel engine submarines they had managed to hit and sink with torpedoes from their submarines. Unfortunately, shortly thereafter, all the Taiwanese submarines were hunted down and sent to the bottom of the ocean.

It had been a good fight. Tsai couldn't argue with that, but despite their valiant efforts, things were drawing to a close for them. The video feed had shown the Leishen Commando Airborne Force dropping from the sky near the base of the Dazhi Ya Nan Mountain nearly twenty minutes before. Dressed head to toe in black and wearing matching balaclavas, the highly trained and incredibly elite special forces soldiers had wasted no time infiltrating the Heng Shan Command Center. Even with guards posted at every entrance and ever-changing security codes adding an extra element of protection, the lofty reputation of the Thundergod unit had not been earned in poor faith. A screen in the center of the video display had been transmitting the relay from the security cameras throughout the interior of the command center. As the PLAAF Special Operations unit grew closer, moving ever-steadily toward them with each room they penetrated, Tsai felt his unease also grow.

Next to him, Commander Dai stood in an informal at-ease, his hands folded at the small of his back as he regarded the monitor somberly. "We did our best, sir."

"I know." There was nothing more Tsai could say.

This was on him as much as it was on the base commander. Despite their joint efforts and the efforts of their combined military forces, they had not been able to overcome the invading PRC armed forces. With the arrival of the Leishen unit, it was all but over for them. He had held out a tiny sliver of hope when the commandos had taken longer than usual to get past the initial barricade, but once they were inside the mountain base, he knew none of the subsequent checkpoints would be able to stop them. Yes, while they still stood inside the command center and out of the commando unit's grasp, they were still technically free men. But once the special forces got to them? Their fate was going to be the same, regardless.

Just as their soldiers had not gone down without a fight, neither would

Tsai. Yes, they were grossly outnumbered, nearly two to one. And unlike the commando unit steadily working its way closer and closer to them, he was not a young and able-bodied man. Hell, he had nearly fifteen years on Dai, and the commander was already squarely in the middle of his fifth decade. Back when he was younger and still in his prime, he might have been able to take on two or three of the commandos before succumbing to them. But as a man with more silver in his hair than black? It would be a farce. He would be damned if he didn't at least try though.

The steely faces of his security detail told a similar story. Had they been equally matched in numbers, then they might have been able to take on the incoming forces. Then again, maybe not. Despite the fact that his men had undergone extensive training in preparation for becoming his bodyguards, both physical and mental, they were no match for the PRC Thundergod Special Forces. Nevertheless, like Tsai, they would not let the soldiers take them down without at least putting up a fight. Even Peng, despite the evident fear in his eyes, had a firm set in his lips that indicated a similar sentiment.

There was no inflection in Dai's voice as he said, "They have arrived, sir."

Once more Tsai nodded.

The video feed showing the throng of men standing on the other side of the heavy steel door was almost redundant, as he could hear the muffled shouts and noisy rattle of weapon fire hailing their arrival. Unlike the other doors they had managed to get past, though, this one was going to take them a little bit longer. When the special operations forces had landed, the military personnel inside the command center had dispersed, quickly moving to what they perceived to be the points of most vulnerability. No less than fifteen Taiwanese soldiers stood on the opposite side of the door in anticipation of their arrival, a last-ditch effort to protect the men inside. Now, as the sounds of shooting faded away, Tsai could not avoid the truth any longer. They were next.

His security detail stood by the door in a semicircle, just beyond the reach of its opening swing, their weapons trained on the entrance. A lull followed, and the oppressive calm seemed to stretch on for an indefinite period of time. Then a thunderous boom ripped through the silence, and Tsai had only a moment to register the sound of a DZJ-08 launcher firing before the steel door buckled from the impact of a high velocity rocket. The thick, heavy-duty material seemed to be made of nothing more than tinfoil as the 80mm projectile slammed against its metal surface. It bulged out and the door swung open, lifting off its hinges in the process. It spun momentarily in the air, then landed on the floor with a weighty thud.

Through the acrid haze of debris and smoke filling the room, the vague shapes of the special operations unit moving in the hallway seemed almost ghostly. A low clatter drew Tsai's attention downward, and all at once he understood why the Special Forces had not yet advanced into the command room. An oblong canister just over five inches in length and no more than two inches in diameter skidded across the floor.

Tsai had only an instant to register the metal shape as it rolled into the room, and his voice was strained as he cried out, "Cover your eyes!"

His warning had come just a second too late. In a deafening explosion, the M84 flash grenade detonated and a blinding white light filled the room.

Tsai's vision faded out as the photoreceptors in his eyes were flooded with the overwhelmingly bright flash, and almost instantly, a high-pitched keening filled his ears. He took a stumbling step backward, his hands instinctively coming up to shield his face. Around him, Peng and Dai also turned away, their faces contoured in a grimace of pain and shock. Fluorescent stars danced before his eyelids, and he felt a churning knot of bile twist in his stomach, rising up unbidden. He swallowed hard—there was no way he was going to do something as undignified as vomit in front of these invading forces—and forced himself to stand upright.

Tsai blinked rapidly, trying to clear his sight, and peered blearily around the room. It was enshrouded in a fog of whiteness, but he could still see the vague shapes moving in the doorway as the Leishen commando soldiers poured into the room in a thick stream. As they braced themselves in the doorway, occupying the far wall of the command center, the sound of a weapon being discharged cut through the room. The report was distant and muffled in his ringing ears, and through the haze, Tsai saw a body fall to the ground. Was it one of the Leishen commandos taken out by a well-aimed shot from one of his security detail? No. Even with his vision only reluctantly starting to return to him, it was clear the body on the floor was that of one of his own men.

A voice rang out in the room, and in a heavy mainland accent, one of the black-clad men spoke. "Drop your weapons and raise your hands where I can see them. Now."

In front of him, Dai turned his head, his eyes sweeping around the room as they tried to lock on the defense minister. Twin trails of tears cut tracks down his cheeks, but he seemed unaware of the dual streams of water pouring from his bloodshot eyes. "Sir?"

"I said, drop your weapons and show me your hands."

As the commando officer spoke again, Tsai realized he could make out the shape of the weapon grasped in his hand. The QSZ-92 semi-automatic pistol was trained directly on him, and it was evident the elite soldier was not taking any chances. If they did not comply, he would be the first to be killed. "Do not try to resist. Come with us peacefully, and we can guarantee you your life. Try to fight us, and we will shoot you on the spot."

"Sir?" Dai tried again.

"Do it." His resignation was thick with sorrow, and Tsai found himself facing a new emotion as he let his own sidearm clatter to the floor. As he struggled to make sense of it, he realized what it was. Disappointment. He had not only failed his men and his country but also himself. It was almost as foreign as the invading forces in the command center with them.

One by one, their weapons fell to the concrete floor of the command center. His security officers were the last to relinquish them, and only after a sharp look from the defense minister himself had prompted them to do so, but they also joined the growing pile of firearms on the floor. Now unarmed and defenseless, the men had no choice but to comply with the commands of the special operations force standing opposite them. Tsai allowed his hands to lift slowly, bringing them up to chest level. The faint tremor in his fingertips, he was sure, had to be nothing other than an optical illusion from the lingering vision impairment.

As the Special Ops closed around them, guiding them toward the open door like well-trained shepherds, Tsai realized distantly that he was no longer the defense minister of Taiwan. Had the president also been captured? He didn't doubt it. She was likely one of the first people taken by the PRC forces. Of all the possible outcomes of his tenure as Defense Minister, this specific scenario had never occurred to him. Death by assassination? Yes, it was certainly a likely outcome. But surrendering to the masked special operations unit now holding him at weapons point rather than giving up his life to uphold his ingrained notions of independence and freedom? That was somehow unforeseen.

And, just as Tsai's role as Taiwan's defense minister had begun only a few months before in a private swearing-in ceremony at the Defense headquarters a few miles away from where he now stood, it just as summarily ended for him. This time, however, there was no quiet ceremony needed to hail the changing of power. Instead, it was simply the anticlimactic shuttling of Tsai and his men through the carved tunnels of the Heng Shan Military Command Center, guiding them into their new roles in the PRC-controlled puppet government.

⁕ ⁕ ⁕ ⁕ ⁕

Even though the People's Republic of China would never admit it neither on the record nor in private conversations, the fight the Taiwanese military put up against their forces had been nothing short of heroic. While Taiwan certainly had the heart and conviction to try to ward off the military invasion, they unfortunately lacked the same level of power and sheer volume as the PRC. Had they been fighting on even terrain, so to speak, they might have been able to stave off the assault. However, without their radar systems to guide them and their missile systems to defend them, they had no other recourse. Instead, they were forced to watch helplessly as their lifelong enemy swarmed their country and took out one target after another until the entire nation succumbed to the invading forces.

The PRC had been incredibly efficient in the use of their time. Within the first hour, all of Taiwan's key naval assets and airfields had been destroyed. Within three, the PRC had infiltrated and overtaken all their military bases, summarily subduing the majority of military leaders within them—barring, of course, the rare but necessary casualties. And within five hours, just as the sun was rising over the island, the sound of artillery fire eventually died away as the Taiwanese government reluctantly surrendered to the PRC. An oppressive calm descended upon the country, thick and choked with the caustic stench of smoke and burning oil. The war between the two nations was already over, and it had taken less than a single workday to complete it.

As the sun rose higher into the sky, trading the night's darkness for deceptively bright and cheerful daylight, the damages of the battle became evident. Of Taiwan's initial forces, no more than 30 percent of them now remained. Of their destroyers, only the *Su Ao* and the *Tso Ying* remained afloat, but the rate of smoke pouring out of the *Tso Ying's* hull indicated it wouldn't be too much longer. Seventeen frigates, one submarine, and 102 of their 137 dispatched fighter jets had survived. The rest were in ruins, either sunk beneath the waters of the sea surrounding Taiwan or in shatters on the mountainous terrain. Conversely, the PRC had lost only one destroyer, three frigates, four submarines, nearly three hundred aircraft, and a total of 2,841 sailors and soldiers.

With their mission completed well ahead of schedule, several smaller segments of PRC troops broke apart from the main groups and made their way to the various news stations scattered across the island. These included the more popular TTV outlet in Shandong and CTV in Taipei, as well as the smaller, less viewed ones. They had already conquered the land, but gaining media control was the next step in winning over the minds of the Taiwanese people. There these soldiers waited, thick sheaths of paper in one hand and their firearms in the other, for the reporters to arrive. The morning crew took one look at the armed soldiers standing in their newsroom and, with resigned sighs, accepted the scripts without comment.

As the reality of the morning events moved through the population like a muffled shockwave, they turned to their television sets and huddled around them for updates. The familiar faces of the morning newscasters were still there to greet them, but there was something strange and wooden about their presentation. Their voices were flat and hollow as they relayed the morning broadcast, and the stunned Taiwanese people listened as the newscasters reported only the briefest of details about what had transpired overnight. This was, the anchors informed the public tonelessly, for their own good. Together, under one leadership, they would be much stronger. It was clear the news reporters were nervous as they spoke, and despite the lack of obvious panic in their voices, the occasional stammer nevertheless broke through. As they talked, their eyes seemed to shift frequently to the side of the screen. It was almost as though there was someone standing behind the camera, ready to pull the feed if any of them deviated from some pre-rehearsed script. Their words were a stark contradiction to their body language, a sharp juxtaposition that only the most oblivious of people missed.

Life was to go on as normal, the newscasters told them, and these changes would not interrupt their usual daily routine. Men and women would still go to work just like before, and children would also continue to play among one another outside. They were also to disregard the flurry of new activity that would soon be going on around them in the coming days, which would be the PRC installing some important safety technology on the island to help protect them from the Americans. The smiles on their faces seemed unnatural and strained, the opposite of reassuring, as the reporters finalized their morning broadcast. Before the screens went dark, they promised their viewers that their political leaders would also be addressing them soon to reaffirm these claims.

What the reporters' scripts didn't say, however, was left for the 23.5 million formerly-Taiwanese—and now PRC—residents to infer. Their politicians would indeed be endorsing the broadcasts later that day. If they didn't, they would be quietly taken away and simply disappear. Their military forces, all of whom had fought so bravely that morning, were already being issued a one-way ticket to reeducation camps. The safety equipment the PRC was installing would be the new radar and missile defense systems to replace the ones taken out by their missiles hours before. Even as reporters addressed the public, PRC personnel were moving across the island to place over 200 DF-100 anti-ship cruise missiles and greater than 350 long-range stealth fighters in strategic locations, as well as numerous surface-to-air missiles to round out their arsenal. Soldiers had already started laboring beneath the cloudless sky to repair the damaged military bases and airfields. By the time they were done with their work, over three thousand mines would have been dropped into the waters 100 miles to the east of the island to block, or at least slow down, the United States. Under the Taiwanese government, the country didn't have the resources or the budget to serve as a viable military threat. But now, under the PRC regime, their unification would make them stronger.

Yes, life could go on for them, though it would no longer be identical to how it was before. In the coming days, the residents of the island nation would wake up to find a handsome stipend deposited directly into their bank accounts, a bribe disguised as a thank you gift from their new government. Children would continue to go to school, and if any of them stopped to gawk at the soldiers working on the military reinforcements in the December sunshine, they would be quickly shooed away. Nevertheless, they continued on as they had little other choice. For them, it was a violation of their independence and autonomy. For the PRC, however, it was the long overdue union of the larger mainland and the smaller rogue province. And with them finally merged under one government, they would finally be able to take on the United States…and win.

CHAPTER TWENTY

PREPARING FOR ACTION

J AMES PULLED HIS BLACK OVERCOAT closer around his body and ignored the questing fingers of the wind trying to get purchase on the heavy garment. Overhead, the sky was gray and overcast, heavy with dense cloud cover. Already a flurry of snow was spitting down upon them from above, and the weather forecast had warned them that the snow would continue on through the afternoon. The insistent howl of the wind made it harder to focus on his surroundings, but he forced himself to remain upright, his ears and eyes alert to any unexpected or sudden movement. The wind wouldn't be getting the best of him today.

The gusts were significantly worse on the west side of the White House, and James felt a momentary flash of annoyance at the bitter wind buffeting his hair. At least good fortune had been on their side this morning. While securing one of the rare and coveted parking spots at the West Wing entrance parking area was typically no easy feat, the protection team assigned to the secretary's detail had somehow managed to spot a couple of them by the north end of the parking area during their approach. After the security team had dropped off James and the SecDef by the entrance, they'd sped off as fast as they reasonably could to stake their claim on these valuable parking spots.

Three high-ranking military officers flanked Andrews as they approached the West Wing entrance, their bodies huddled together as they spoke quietly among each other. On the secretary's immediate left stood a marine general by the name of Howard Wilbur. Wilbur's close-cropped hair was tucked firmly beneath his olive-drab cover, but if he were aware of the wind trying to pry it off his head, he was outwardly indifferent to it. To his right, Army General Malcolm Cohen and Navy Admiral Blake White also kept pace with Andrews, matching his stride with their own. While James didn't know them as well as he knew the secretary, they were still familiar faces to him, as Andrews often consulted these trusted advisers on a number of strategic military matters. Today would be no different.

James wasn't the only one on high alert that morning. The word about the pair of assassination attempts against Andrews had been the second most popular topic on the evening news this past week. The anchors seemed to take a macabre sort of delight in having several sensational things to divulge to their viewers, and the assassination attempt had somehow managed to supersede everything else that had transpired in that twelve-hour window, including the attack on the *McCain*, the acts of terrorism that had erupted across the nation, and the declaration of war on China.

James took note of the additional Secret Service Uniformed Division officers loitering around the building. Their black-clad shapes were almost spectral as they stood watch, their faces bland and expressionless as they maintained a continuous observation over the White House. Each officer bore a Heckler & Koch MP5-A3 submachine gun, the satin black bodies of their firearms stretching out across the chests of each officer. Overhead, James could hear the rotors of the Secret Service helicopters that were also maintaining a vigilant watch over them. The US government was not going to take any risks on an attempt on the president or vice president.

Unlike the more common north entrance to the West Wing, the west entrance to the White House had no posted marine sentry to let them in. As James approached the door, the conversation between Andrews and his advisers trailed off. He turned the handle, pulling on it, then stepped through the doorway. Even at 0800 hours, the White House was already bustling with activity. James's eyes swept the length of the hallway. From where he stood, none of the personnel seemed to pose an immediate threat. The hate-twisted faces of Sergeant Chi and his officers lingered in his memory as he moved aside for Andrews and his advisers. They nodded briefly at him as they stepped through, and the door fell shut behind them once more.

The men continued down the short corridor of the West Wing, then paused at the small office leading to the Situation Room. One of the president's interns was already waiting for them there, and as Andrews approached him, a courteous but sincere smile settled on the young woman's face.

She extended a hand toward the secretary, and Andrews shook it briefly. "Good morning, Secretary Andrews." Her eyes lit on each man in acknowledgment as she spoke. "It's a pleasure to see you all this morning. Please, come on in."

"Thank you." Andrews didn't glance back as the intern guided him and his entourage into the Situation Room. His focus was now on the task ahead of him, and everything else was ancillary.

The intern pulled the door shut with a click, then turned to James, sizing him up. She was new to the White House, and the badge on her lanyard was turned toward her sweater, concealing her name from him. The smile was now more reserved, but no less cordial. "There's coffee in the navy mess, if you want any."

James shook his head, and with a shrug, she slipped out of the room. His eyes moved around the small waiting room, taking it in. A few chairs were pushed against the wall for the comfort of its guests, but he ignored them, instead positioning himself close to the closed door of the Situation Room. He kept his spine straight and his body tense as he considered the meeting unfolding. Even though Andrews hadn't divulged any of the details of its nature to him, he knew it had something to do with the upcoming war against China. No matter what it was, however, he had no doubts their decisions this morning would unquestionably have vast and far-reaching consequences for the entire nation.

⁂

The Situation Room had recently been remodeled, and the scent of earthy mahogany still mingled with the sharp odor of fresh paint. Secretary Andrews glanced around the room as he stepped through the door. It was admittedly a rather handsome room, outfitted in shades of tan and navy that were quite fitting for the duties of the personnel who occasionally congregated within it. Much smaller in dimension than what people might generally expect of a room with this level of importance, it spanned some twenty-eight feet in length and another fifteen feet in width. The décor was understated but elegant and, save for a single analog clock on the left-hand wall, the room was free from any unnecessary ornamentation or embellishment.

A single, rectangular wooden table ran from the north end to the south side of the Situation Room, occupying a majority of the room's already somewhat cramped dimensions. Only a few feet of access on each side allowed for passage around it. The south wall boasted a six-foot by four-foot digital monitor, and four smaller monitors clung to eastern and western walls. Two security cameras, each enclosed within a black glass bubble, peered down upon the actions of the personnel stationed around the table. One lingered by the doorway, closely monitoring whoever came and went. The second was stationed next to the monitor on the southern wall, keeping tireless minutes of the activity inside the room.

Secretary Andrews circled the table, pausing at the head, and tugged on the chair tucked beneath it. It rolled back with ease, and he lowered himself down into it. Leaning against the headrest, he glanced up, casting an expectant glance at his security advisers. They nodded, then claimed the seats directly next to him, creating a chain of high-level military personnel in a row to his left. They sat patiently at the table, not fidgeting as they waited for the meeting to begin. Wilbur glanced down at his watch, then compared the results to the clock on the far wall. It was thirteen minutes past eight, and their meeting was scheduled for a quarter past.

Andrews leaned over and, grabbing the handle of his briefcase, hoisted it onto the table. He unlatched it, then reached inside. His hand closed over a sheath of paperwork, and he withdrew it, resting the paperclip-bound stack on the desk in front of him. Satisfied, he folded his hands together on the table and waited. The long hand of the clock on the wall moved to 0815 hours, and on the other side of the room, the door swung open. President Thomas and Vice President Roth stepped through, their eyes sweeping the room as they entered. Everyone had arrived. The meeting could now begin.

"Good morning," Andrews said as he and each military member stood up from their chairs. He jutted his chin up in greeting, and they returned it with a nod of their own.

"Good morning, gentlemen. Please sit." President Thomas approached the table, stopping directly across from the secretary and his advisers, then pulled the chair out. He eased into the plush leather surface, then glanced up at the vice president. Roth followed suit, scooting his chair forward to rest his elbows on the table next to his boss. Silence prevailed until the steady metronome of the clock ticking in the background became overly noticeable.

Finally, the president said, "So, Michael, you called this meeting because you wanted to give us an update, and you mentioned you also had some concerns as well?"

"Yes, that's correct." Secretary Andrews cleared his throat, then trained his gaze onto the president. "As you already know, at approximately 1200 hours yesterday, or around 0100 hours China Standard Time, China invaded Taiwan."

"Yes, I heard about that." President Thomas shook his head in disgust. "They're sneaky sons of bitches, aren't they? Coming in after them in the middle of the night, pretending it was just a training exercise until the last minute."

"They are," Andrews agreed. He had seen the aerial images of the country following the attack, the smoking ruins of Taiwan's defense infrastructure. Curiously enough, the loss of life—both military and civilian—had been relatively small, especially with the sheer amount of force used against them. "But all things considered, it shouldn't have been too surprising. They've always claimed Taiwan as part of their own country. To them, this was just them taking back what they thought was already rightfully theirs."

"True." Thomas cast a glance at the stack of papers on the table in front of Andrews, then back at the man sitting behind them. "Anything else we know about it yet?"

"A little." Andrews held out his palm, counting off the points with the fingers of his other hand as he spoke. "As far as our sources can confirm, the Chinese military is currently repairing all the damage they did to Taiwan's military installations during their invasion. They're also moving thousands of military personnel and assets into the country, giving them a much bigger advantage now than ever before against our upcoming naval assault."

"They're covering all their bases, then, so to speak." Thomas sighed. Andrews had been right. The actual invasion itself wasn't altogether unexpected. It was the damned inconvenient timing of it, though, that was certainly culpable for the tension headache that had made itself at home in his head the afternoon before.

"On the plus side," Andrews said. "I do have a small bit of good news."

"And that is?" Thomas raised a brow at him.

"Our ships are ahead of schedule and should be in position in two days. Unfortunately, though, that still gives China more than enough time to turn Taiwan into a formidable defensive point." Andrews let his eyes meet the president's across the table. There was no distant glint of optimism or hope to be found there. Today, he was just the messenger, the bearer of bad news.

"Great." Thomas's voice lacked conviction, and the corners of his lips turned down as he contemplated the implications of China's actions. "What does that mean for our plans, though, now that China has control of Taiwan?"

"Not much, really. We'll just have to take the island first, on our way into China. But that brings me to my next point. As you already know, it's been well over seventy years since two major powers have fought." Andrews paused for a beat, waiting for the president to acknowledge this.

Thomas nodded.

He continued, "Now, this fight between our navy and the Chinese Navy is going to be very different from naval battles in the past."

"This is true," the president replied. He glanced at the secretary's advisers, then back at the secretary himself. "But what does that have to do with anything?"

"Hear me out," Andrews said, and he held a finger up in the air. Nobody else would have been allowed to speak to the president of the United States like this, but instead of bristling, Thomas waited patiently to hear his friend's perspective. "Unlike naval battles in the past, this is going to be technological, precision-guided warfare, along with cyber warfare mixed in. And we've gotten some intelligence information that the Chinese Navy also has new, precision-guided weapons that are equal to, if not technologically better, than ours."

"Uh-huh," President Thomas said. Either he already had a suspicion that this was the case, or he genuinely didn't seem fazed by it.

"I just want you to know that this isn't going to be like Desert Shield where we go in and have full control in a week." Secretary Andrews tapped the table with his index finger, punctuating his words as he spoke. "It could end up being very costly to us, with ships, and with men."

President Thomas leaned forward, his eyes guarded as he captured the secretary's gaze with his own. "What exactly are you trying to tell me, then? That we shouldn't go to war with China? That we could lose a war with China?"

"No, sir." Andrews shook his head vehemently. He shifted his weight, breaking away from the president's intent expression. "That's not what I'm saying at all. What I'm saying is that we will win, sure. The odds are in our favor. But it'll just be very costly in the end. At this point, though, we're not sure *how* costly."

"I see." President Thomas reclined in his chair, his gaze drifting to the blank monitor on the opposite wall as he considered this latest information.

"Here, look. I brought some of the latest intel with me, which is specifically related to China's total number of ships and latest advancements on naval ship weapons." Andrews pulled a sheet of paper from the top of the stack in front of him and, as he spoke, slid it across the table to the president. The words TOP SECRET//SCI/NOFORN were emblazoned across the top and bottom of the page. He pulled four more identical sheets from the top of the stack, then passed them to the rest of the men at the table. His advisers already knew what was printed on the paper, but they took it from him regardless. "Go ahead and take a look at this."

"What am I looking at here?" Frowning at the paper in his hands, President Thomas reached into his front suit pocket and withdrew a pair of reading glasses. He stuck the temple into his mouth, extending the arm, then slid the spectacles onto his face.

"If you look it over, you'll see it supports everything I've been telling you so far," Andrews said. He reached across the table and tapped the top corner of the paper in front of the president. "But in short, it's an overview of all of China's total numbers and the types of ships they have compared to ours."

The president's lips moved as he skimmed the document in front of him. "So you're telling me that China's Naval assets pretty much blow ours out of the water."

"Probably not the best choice of words there, sir," Andrews said through pursed lips.

The president cast a sharp glance at him before returning his eyes to the classified document.

"But yes, you'll see that China has four aircraft carriers, and one hundred and sixty aircraft on those carriers. They've got fifty-two frigates and thirty-three missile destroyers. They have forty-two corvettes, seventy-six submarines, and one hundred and ninety-two coastal patrol ships."

"And where are we on this page?" President Thomas's eyes scanned the length of paper in front of him, trying to pinpoint this data on the sheet in his hands. "What's our assets?"

"Middle of the page." Andrews slid his finger down his own paper, and Thomas glanced over, verifying the location on the sheet. "Look here."

"Ah, yes. I see it now. Thank you." The president referenced the paper in front of him as he spoke. "It says here that our naval assets in the Pacific include four aircraft carriers, and I see one is in drydock for repairs. Any idea how long before it's ready?"

"The estimated refit and repairs on the *USS Nimitz* are scheduled to be done in March 2026," Andrews replied. "The supercarrier has been at the Puget Sound Naval Shipyard for the Refueling and Complex Overhaul (RCOH) for nearly eleven months, and even if we try to rush it for an earlier completion, which I don't recommend, it'd only push it up by a few weeks at most. So no, that one won't be ready in time."

"Got it," the president replied. "This means we have just four carriers. But we have a total of three hundred aircraft for the carriers. And I'm seeing eleven battle cruisers, thirty-one destroyers, three frigates, and five mine-sweepers. We've also got…seven attack subs and two support ships. That's not bad."

"Yes," Andrews replied after a moment. "But go ahead and flip that page over. You'll see that China has conventionally armed medium-range ballistic missiles too. That's the DF-21D anti-ship ballistic missiles, or the ASBMs. They also have the DF-100s, the ones that sank the *McCain* and the *Keris*. These missiles have been appropriately dubbed the 'carrier killers,' and I'll tell you why."

"I can take a wild guess," the president said dryly. He turned the page over and scanned the words the secretary had spoken aloud. The line between his eyebrows deepened as he followed along with the dismal intel printed on the page.

"These carrier killers are hypersonic missiles. Their range exceeds a thousand miles, and even worse?" Andrews's voice was somber as he spoke.

"They're also armed with a maneuverable warhead, which makes it extremely difficult to get a target lock and destroy with interceptor missiles."

"I don't like the sound of that," President Thomas said. He reached up, pulling his glasses off, and rested them on the paper in front of him. His fingers pinched the bridge of his nose. A pained expression had settled on his face, and he looked at the secretary with troubled eyes. "What else?"

"Well, they've also got the smaller, twin-engine Shenyang J-31 fifth-generation fighter," Andrews told him. "As you probably already know, this fighter bears a striking resemblance to the Lockheed F-35 Joint Strike Fighter, which we suspect has the same capabilities. The key difference between the two, though, is that it doesn't have a cannon for close air battles."

"And?" the president prompted him.

"They also have five operational nuclear ballistic missile submarines, or SSBNs." Andrews didn't look at the paper on the table. "These are the new, eleven-thousand-ton Jin-class Type 94 boomers, which are the equivalent to ours. They've also got this new integrated air defense system that has multiple surface-to-air missile systems that can detect stealth aircraft, as well as unmanned aerial vehicles, or UAVs."

"Tell me more about those," the president said. His fingers were still firmly positioned at the top of his nose, and now his eyes were starting to close. The frown on his face had deepened.

"For starters, they're Russian," Andrews answered him. "Those are the new S-400s. And they also have manufactured their own as well, called the HQ-19, which are based off the S-400s but technologically more advanced."

"I see." He lowered his fingers from his nose and allowed his hand to drop back down onto the table. "Let me get this straight, Mike. What I'm hearing from you here is that China's pretty much got us beat on all fronts. I mean, where do we stand in all of this?"

"I'm glad you asked." The secretary cast a sidelong glance at his advisers, then back at the president. "Our analysts believe that even though China's made significant advancements over the years, our own technological battle systems still outpace theirs. For instance, our radar, sonar, and most importantly, our jammers are better. Then we've got our EA-6B Prowler Tactical Jamming Aircraft. It's extremely comprehensive, operating over a wide range of frequency bands, which should make it extremely difficult for their radar systems to lock onto our ships and fighter jets."

"That's something, at least." The discouraged note was no longer in his voice, but even still, Thomas's expression remained dubious.

"There's more," Andrews said briskly without breaking his verbal stride. "We've also got our radars, like the SPY-6. They're used to perform air and missile defense on seven different classes of ships and have several key advantages over older legacy radars. For instance, they've got a significantly greater detection range, increased sensitivity, and more accurate discrimination. They're also integrated, which means they can simultaneously track and defend against virtually any threat, such as ballistic missiles, cruise missiles, hostile aircraft, and even surface ships. And finally, we've got our Integrated Undersea Surveillance System." A hint of pride crept into Andrews's voice now as he detailed the final asset in their arsenal. "That sonar system can locate any enemy ship, no matter where it is in the Pacific."

Thomas leaned back in his chair once more, his face quiet as he reflected on this last wedge of information. Throughout this entire conversation, the secretary's military advisers had remained quiet, allowing Andrews to do all the talking. President Thomas glanced at them, but they still seemed to have nothing to say. He looked back at the secretary. "It sounds like we'll win this war with China, but we're going to get a little bruised up in the process."

"Yes, we will get a little bruised up," Andrews admitted. "I figured you'd want to know what our situation is before the fighting starts. Do you have any questions for me?"

"No, I don't." The president shook his head. "I appreciate your candor and giving me your assessment of the situation."

"Gentlemen, you have anything you want to mention?" Andrews turned back to his advisers.

One by one, they shook their heads in the negative. They already knew this information, as they had been integral in helping him acquire it. There was nothing new they could add. The president was now better informed of the situation and better prepared for the possible losses in personnel and ships.

"Well, on a positive note, I've got my own good news for you all today." A ghost of a smile spread across the president's face, stopping before it creased the corners of his eyes. "There were a few countries that decided they want to support the United States in this war effort, militarily."

"Oh, that *is* good news," Secretary Andrews agreed. Next to him, his advisers murmured a note of assent. "We've got some support on our side, huh?"

"We do," President Thomas confirmed. The darkly pleasant smile remained on his face. "That said, we've decided to not let any other countries get involved. Too much political risk, if you think about it. If Japan or India joins us, it could possibly drive Russia and Pakistan into wanting to join China. Then it'd be this domino effect, and we could find ourselves in a nasty World War situation. We obviously want to avoid that, so we've requested that no other countries get involved between China and the United States."

"That makes sense," Andrews said with a nod. "I can't say I blame them for wanting to help out, especially since China's been encroaching on their territory in the South China Sea for years now. And since when haven't China and Japan been at each other's throats? Territorial disputes aside, though, Malaysia is the only country that has any real reason to join us, with what China did to the *Keris*."

"Precisely my train of thought." The president pointed an approving finger at the secretary, then brought his hands back down to the stack of paper in front of him on the table. "We told Malaysia we understand where they're coming from, and they have every reason to want to join, and we're angry on their behalf. But we've also warned them to not get involved, either, as the risk of a global conflict is far too high. Malaysia begrudgingly agreed, so that settles it. This war is between us and China, period."

"Very good," the secretary said. He leaned back in his own chair, folding his fingers over his abdomen. His eyes went first to the president, then back to his advisers. Overhead, the clock continued to count the seconds with a steady tick. "Anything else you want to discuss with me today, or are we done here?"

President Thomas glanced at the vice president, then around the room at the men seated at the table. Mouths remained shut. It was settled, then. The show would go on as planned. The president reached forward and scooped up the stack of papers, rapping the bottom of the papers against the table. "Well, I guess that concludes our briefing today, then. Thank you all for coming. And thank you again, Michael, for the intel and giving me your assessment. Have a good rest of your day, gentlemen."

Without another word, President Thomas rose and strode out of the office. Vice President Roth followed, trailing behind him. They let the door swing shut behind him, leaving Secretary Andrews alone in the room with the two generals and the admiral.

Secretary Andrews reached forward and gathered up his documents, then directed his gaze to his advisers. "That went better than expected, don't you think?"

They peered back at him, their faces calm and quiet. Nobody could disagree with him.

It had indeed been a productive meeting. What better conclusion to their morning briefing could they possibly have asked for? Andrews couldn't imagine any alternatives, and so, with a final glance across the room, he pushed away from the table and exited the Situation Room. With the meeting now over, they could finish their planning of the war effort.

He had been honest with the president in the briefing. He did believe they could win, but it didn't change the nag of doubt that loitered in the back of his mind. Winning the war wasn't absolutely guaranteed, but he was going to make damned sure that even if they didn't win, they put up a solid fight. It was the least they could do for the sailors held hostage in China, the lives lost in the terrorist attacks across the country, and yes, Andrews had to be honest with himself, having someone try to assassinate him—*twice*—definitely made him more than a little bit emotionally invested in this war. He just hoped that his careful optimism wasn't misguided.

CHAPTER TWENTY-ONE

WASHINGTON DC WAS STARTING TO look a little bit like a ghost town. While the Pentagon was still bustling with activity as the United States prepared for its imminent war with China, the China Embassy itself had been fully evacuated seemingly overnight. Ambassador Han Wenjin, as well as all of his staff, had slipped back to China on an undisclosed flight earlier in the week. A stark and un-inhabited embassy now stood at the corner of International Drive and Van Ness, a sprawling concrete fortress against the District of Columbia skyline.

The word *empty* could also be used to describe the response the United States had received for their request to have their captured sailors returned to them. The Chinese government seemed either disinterested in relinquishing their captives, or conversely, highly interested in holding them in continued detainment to use as a bargaining chip. Despite the president making it abundantly clear what the repercussions were for keeping them as prisoners, no actions had yet been taken to bring the survivors of the *USS John S. McCain* back home. China's silence was response enough, and on the other side of the world, the American carrier strike groups began moving into position.

Inside the Pentagon National Military Command Center, the room was alive with activity. Tense energy moved around the cramped room in a sinuous wave as the various personnel inside the NMCC monitored the Chinese naval ships, as well as all visible military activity in and around the country, on the numerous displays inside it. Each screen glowed with its own unique scene, depicting from geostationary satellites what was happening near the East China Sea, Spratly Islands, Taiwan, and China. In addition to revealing their own forces, the feeds also showed the Chinese CSGs too. The enemy's northern fleet was already venturing ominously close to the US bases in South Korea and Japan, and the others were equally menacing from their own positions in the water.

From where he stood near the back of the room, James could see the entirety of the cramped room in a glance. Every workstation was also occupied, creases of concentration on each agent's forehead as their eyes moved back and forth at the private screen before them. Occasionally one of them would look up and announce an update from their feed before resuming their close observation of it.

A handful of paces away from James stood Secretary Andrews and his Joint Chief of Staff, William Miller. Their arms were crossed over their chests as they regarded the main screen affixed to the front wall, matching expressions of concentration on their faces.

To the untrained eye, the satellite feed on the ten-foot-wide monitor looked like another aerial view of the ocean, a vast and stunningly turquoise stretch of calm waters. A US Navy Carrier Strike Group moved across it, the angular body of the lead destroyer portrayed in remarkably high resolution. The bottom left side of the screen displayed the words CSG (Carrier Strike Group) #3—USS *John C. Stennis* (Celebes Sea) inscribed in block print. The clarity of the image made it easy to see all the vessels on the screen, down to the white caps of the waves lapping against the vessels as they sliced through the water. The clarity of the image was so sharp, so vivid, it was almost as though he were down there with them. James suspected if he closed his eyes, he would be able to feel the cold spray of the subtropical waters and smell the sharp bite of the salt water. The flight deck of the *Stennis* was heavily laden with numerous naval aircraft. Their triangular shapes huddled together on the deck, ready to launch when the order came through, and many more remained out of view in the hangars below. In total, the aircraft carrier was responsible for approximately ninety aircraft, if not more, greater than double the amount most other countries could claim.

Several vessels surrounded the *Stennis* on all sides, arranged carefully within the strike group. They varied in their roles and function, but from where James stood, he could make out the distinct shapes of guided-missile cruisers, destroyers, and frigates. And those numbers were only what he could visibly see on the screen. As far as what he couldn't see, he knew there were several submarines lurking well below the calm water's surface. The US Navy had come prepared, and most of its resources had been rallied together for this moment. An unholy hell was about to be unleashed upon China. They just didn't know it yet.

CSG #3 had been traveling throughout the night, and at 0935 local time, it was now almost in position. Their current position had them traveling northwest in the Celebes Sea, with Borneo to their Southeast and the Philippines to the north. The distance between their current location and their desired position at China's nine-dash line was rapidly narrowing, and based on their current rate of speed, it wouldn't be long before they closed in on their mark. Once the formation approached this hotly contested boundary, they'd be verging into territory claimed by the People's Republic of China within the South China Sea. While the rightful ownership of this territory—which included the Paracel and the Spratly Islands—was still up for debate, it didn't change the fact that China had planted military installations upon those archipelagos. No doubt, the personnel aboard the aircraft carrier were maintaining a careful watch in their approach into enemy territory. There was no question that China would go on the offensive once the CSG glided over this invisible line of demarcation, and James suspected their progress was already under close scrutiny from the PLAN.

As James watched, the screen blinked and momentarily turned dark. Then a new image replaced it, as crisp and vivid in clarity as the first scene. James paused, considering it thoughtfully. It looked no different than the first image displayed on the screen, but a glance down at the bottom left corner confirmed that the image had indeed changed. Now, instead of denoting the *Stennis* on the monitor, the words read, CSG (Carrier Strike Group) #1—*USS Carl Vinson* (Java Sea). He squinted at this new image, trying to determine what differentiated it from the original. Perhaps the number of vessels was slightly different, but without the footer denoting the new destroyer in the center of the cluster, it was all but identical.

The image panned out, giving James a wider field of view of the strike group as it navigated toward its target. This one, unlike the *Stennis*, was in the heart of the Java Sea. The water was the same deep shade of teal as the one in the other satellite image, the sky overhead sunny and cheerful, almost jarring in contrast to the somber tasks being performed by the vessels coasting across the open body of water. Unlike the *Stennis*, which was near the Spratly Islands in the Celebes Sea, the *USS Carl Vinson* was maneuvering its way through a stretch of water tucked somewhere between Indonesia and Borneo.

"Major Collins?" Secretary Andrews's voice cut through the low thrum of conversation in the room.

The commanding officer in charge of the NMCC glanced up sharply at the sound of his name, craning it around to face the secretary.

Andrews glanced down at him, then back to the screen, gesturing toward it with his right hand. "Is there any way we can get a split-screen image of all four carrier strike groups? I want to be able to see them all at a glance, if that's possible, please."

"Yes, sir." Major Collins leaned forward and tapped a button on his computer without hesitation. A few keystrokes later, the image on the screen flashed and then split into quarters. "How's this, sir? Any better?"

The secretary nodded. "Yes, much better. Thank you, Major."

Now the monitor revealed four images, broken into perfect quadrants across its surface. Each image was approximately five feet wide and five feet high, and despite being much smaller now, it still afforded the viewer with a complete view of all four CSGs as they churned through the glasslike water of the ocean. In addition to the *USS John C. Stennis* and the *USS Carl Vinson*, there were also the *USS Ronald Reagan* and the *USS Theodore Roosevelt* too. The *Reagan*, which had CSG #5 printed beneath it, was positioned in the Philippine Sea, somewhere between the Philippines and the Palau archipelago. The *Roosevelt*, which bore the label of CSG #9, was in the East China Sea, between South Korea and Japan.

"Sir?" A tense voice cut through the room, and James followed the source to its owner. One of the staff officers seated at the Missile Defense Agency workstation had a hand in the air and his eyes fixed on the screen in front of him. He turned and faced Major Collins, and for the briefest moment, James saw the stark look of stunned disbelief on his face. "The MDA has detected multiple intercontinental ballistic missile launches with the Space-Based Infrared System (SBIRS) satellites. They're reporting seventeen missiles have just been launched from China."

Secretary Andrews cast a sharp glance at the young man, a first lieutenant by the name of Turner, and James could hear the note of concern in his voice. "Do they have a trajectory for those ICBMs? Are they headed toward the United States?"

"We're getting that information from the SBIRS now, sir," Turner said. He returned his focus to his computer station, his brows drawing together as he gazed at the screen. He tapped on the keyboard, and a look of triumph momentarily replaced the barely concealed fear on his face. "There we go."

Major Collins leaned forward and clicked his own keyboard, and the image on the main screen flashed bright, then changed. The carrier strike groups were no longer on the monitor, instead replaced by an image of China and the surrounding territory. All eyes turned to the screen as a series of seventeen red dots seemed to radiate away from China, up toward space. There was no question what they were all looking at.

Well, James thought, and the words clanged hollowly in his mind, *this is it. China's launched a nuclear strike on the United States.*

It was over for them. Seventeen nuclear missiles, all aimed directly at the United States. James wondered fleetingly which cities would be the target of this attack. No doubt, Washington DC would be high on the list, as well as New York City. What else? Los Angeles? Chicago? Tampa? His thoughts went to his children back home in Florida, and a flash of fear jolted through his mind. It was a foreign sensation, unpleasant and unwelcome. Fear wasn't typically in his DNA, but this wasn't fear for his own life. It was for his family. His hands curled into a fist at his side, and he opened and closed his grip, flexing it.

"Sir?" Turner said abruptly, his voice trailing off. All eyes in the room were on him as he spoke. He cleared his throat, and the words coming out of his mouth when he spoke again seemed somehow distant and hazy. "I have a trajectory for the missiles, but it's not showing as hitting the United States."

James watched as the seventeen red dots navigated steadily across the monitor and spread apart, relentlessly progressing toward unknown targets. Relief washed over him, momentary and fleeting. His children were safe for now. Thank God. He issued a silent prayer heavenward, a brief murmur of thanks to the Big Guy who was looking over his family. But if the missiles weren't headed toward America, where exactly *were* they going?

"Well, where are they headed, then?" Secretary Andrews couldn't conceal the concern or the impatience in his voice. "The CSGs?"

Lieutenant Turner huddled over his monitor, his face intent as he tracked the progress of the seventeen missiles from his workstation. The blue cast radiating from it made his dark skin look almost wan and sickly. Even though his eyes were hidden in shadows, stark fear was evident on his face as he gazed down at his workstation's digital monitor. The concerned expression on his face matched the drawn and anxious looks on the majority of the faces of the personnel inside the NMCC.

"I'm checking, sir," Turner said with a note of confusion in his voice. As he reviewed the readout before him, the look of fear on his face subtly shifted into surprise, then he said, "The trajectory is not showing a path toward the carrier strike groups, either."

"Okay," the secretary said, his face unreadable.

James exchanged a glance with him, but whatever Andrews suspected about the destination of those missiles, he was keeping to himself for the time being. *Well, then. This is going to be interesting. What do you know, Michael?*

James turned back toward the large main monitor at the front of the room and shifted his body, locking his arms behind his back in a casual at-ease position, then tried to encourage his eyes to see the map from a fresh perspective. Perhaps he could glean what the secretary was thinking by reviewing the map more closely. The dots continued their journey higher, steady and unyielding. What target justified such a heavy arsenal of ballistic missiles to be used against it, were it not the United States or the CSGs?

"Sir, it appears as though the missiles are headed toward..." Turner trailed off, the bewilderment more evident in his voice than before. The telltale fear, at least, was gone. His voice lifted in a puzzled inflection as he finished his sentence. "They're headed toward our reconnaissance satellites in space?"

"Ah." Secretary Andrews let out a quiet grunt at this update. His nonplussed expression didn't change. If anything, renewed contemplation seemed to linger behind his eyes at this latest report.

"I'm getting more reports of additional activity from MDA," Turner added abruptly. He raised his face to the secretary, and Andrews paused, allowing the officer to continue. "Based on this information, they've also deployed their ground-based and space-based anti-satellite missiles too. And it would appear that our laser warning receiver has picked up on activity from their ASAT lasers in Xinjiang."

"That makes sense," the secretary said. He moved forward, taking a step down the angled stairs leading toward the monitor displaying the missiles. "Honestly, I'd be surprised if they *didn't* try to disable our reconnaissance and GPS satellites or attempt to use their anti-satellite lasers to destroy the optical sensors."

So that's what it was. James nodded knowingly to himself as he gazed at the missiles working their way across the screen.

It was a wonder it hadn't occurred to him sooner. Of *course* they would want to wipe out the United States' reconnaissance satellites and take out their global positioning systems. Without their GPS, not only would they lose their primary navigation system but would also struggle with knowing where they were and where they needed to be. And since this war was to be waged largely through advanced technology in space, land, and sea, blinding the enemy would take away one of their greatest advantages. Why wouldn't China want to cut off their visual feed? *Blind the enemy so they can't see you.* Their opponent certainly wasn't stupid. Impulsive, yes. Reckless, for sure. But foolish? No, they knew exactly what they were doing.

Miller fell into step behind Andrews. "Correct me if I'm wrong here, Secretary Andrews, but you *expected* them to shoot down our eyes in the sky?"

"Well, yes. I did." Andrews glanced back at him and shrugged briefly before returning his focus to the monitors. "But we have a plan in place for this exact situation, so I'm not too concerned by this."

"What is this plan, sir?" Miller asked. He descended the rest of the stairs, only stopping when he stood next to the secretary once more. They lingered a mere five feet from the screen, both gazing at it as the cluster of dots flickered and moved across it.

"Simple." Secretary Andrews glanced at him, then back at the screen, a hint of a smile playing at the corner of his face. "We've got the MQ-4E Triton UAVs, among others, on our side."

While he should have suspected that China might go for their satellites, it seemed as though Secretary Andrews hadn't overlooked this key consideration. Having the unmanned aerial vehicles in position would help level the playing field once more, compensating for what would be taken from them once the missiles destroyed their reconnaissance satellites. James searched his memory to dredge up what he could recall about the Triton UAVs. The MQ-4E Triton was an exclusively designed, high-altitude, long-endurance aircraft created specifically for the US Navy to serve just one job: monitoring other countries to provide real-time intelligence, surveillance, and reconnaissance. While the Tritons certainly weren't a replacement for conventional satellite surveillance, they were still an indispensable asset.

The chairman of the Joint Chiefs of Staff seemed to consider this information. He didn't take his eyes off the screen. Finally, he said, "And you believe that should be adequate?"

"Yes, absolutely." The secretary glanced over at Miller and raised a brow at him. "All of the carrier strike groups maintain, and will deploy, the MQ-4E Triton UAV to provide the intelligence, surveillance, target acquisition, and reconnaissance information the reconnaissance satellites provided."

Miller seemed to consider this. The Tritons were undoubtedly a valuable asset and would be more than capable of delivering the necessary intel the American Navy required to maintain the upper hand in this battle. While they wouldn't be able to remain in the air indefinitely like the satellites, they would at least be able to remain airborne for greater than twenty-four hours at a stretch. They were piloted remotely, which meant no lives would be endangered if the UAV were targeted and destroyed by the enemy. Furthermore, they could gather said intel at an impressive distance, which meant they could also remain largely undetected.

"No, it's not the same as having those satellites in place, but that's not necessarily a bad thing. In fact, it's a damned solid alternative, if you ask me." Secretary Andrews offered him a vague shrug. "I'd even venture that they'll give us a view of the battle space, with comparable quality that our satellites could have given us."

Miller nodded. This answer seemed to satisfy him. While he had risen through the ranks as a general officer in the US Army, which made the operational capabilities of the navy somewhat out of his grasp, he understood the basic principles of the UAV and how it related to the current mission. Having it spelled out so matter-of-factly seemed to have dispelled any remaining uncertainty he had about the UAV's abilities. Its ability to provide them with vital ISTAR information—intelligence, surveillance, target acquisition, and reconnaissance data—made it a priceless asset.

Contemplative silence settled upon the room. The only sound inside the NMCC was the quiet whir of the computers operating in the background and the occasional intermittent beep from the monitor as the image on the screen refreshed. It was as though a collective hush had descended upon the occupants of the room, and they had all silently made a uniform decision to hold their breaths in anticipation of the strike.

All around James, the NMCC was suspended in animation as every individual in the room waited for the attack to be completed. Once it did, it would be the end of one chapter of the war and the beginning of the next. China thought they were disabling their enemy, but instead, they were giving them the opportunity to adjust and adapt—and ultimately continue—the fight. While tensions were still high in the command center, they all seemed to mutually understand the implications of losing their satellites, as well as grasp what the landscape of the war would look like without them. Having Triton UAVs monitoring China didn't automatically ensure a guaranteed victory, but it was certainly significantly better than having no means to track their enemy.

The contents of the monitor were practically nondescript, almost boring without context. The seventeen red dots, the only indicators of the missiles making their way from the PRC to the satellites, steadily worked their way across the screen and skyward to the satellites hovering high above Earth. They inched closer and closer to the satellites, dogged in their persistent pursuit of their target. Then, without preamble, three of the screens on the wall flickered and went black.

The missiles had found their mark.

CHAPTER TWENTY-TWO

A S THE SCREENS ON THE wall flickered and faded to blank emptiness, the silence in the room broke. James heard a low gasp off to his right and turned his head in the direction of the sound. An air force captain rose to his feet, his eyes sweeping across the room as though to confirm if anyone else was seeing what he had witnessed. James craned his neck, and the officer's monitor edged into his field of view. Like the three monitors on the far wall, it was also a blank and glassy surface, no light or image reflected upon it. Another soldier to James's right was also moving into a standing position, and a glance in his direction confirmed that his screen had blinked out too. In the first row of the NMCC, one final screen was a black and gaping hole in the line of steadily glowing monitors.

"Sir?" A voice broke through the silence, and the sound of the young female officer's voice seemed to interrupt the alarmed murmur in the room.

James glanced in her direction. She was another lieutenant, this one by the name of Marquez. Her hair was pulled into a tight bun at the nape of her neck, and her eyes were sharp and intelligent as she rose steadily to her feet to address the secretary of defense.

"The Department of Homeland Security and Cyber Command are reporting that several primary information gateway network servers on the West Coast are being overwhelmed with data by a DDoS, and it's more than its bandwidth can sustain."

A distributed denial-of-service attack? James's eyebrow raised at this, and he turned slightly, facing the young officer directly. *What the hell is China doing now?*

A DDoS attack on these network gateways meant the enemy was trying to shut these servers down by flooding them with internet traffic. Such an attack on the western portion of the United States wouldn't just wipe out all of the networks west of the Rocky Mountains. It would also spread into parts of Mexico and Canada, all but destroying their internet communication systems. This wouldn't just block access to the world wide web, either, but all internet-dependent technology would also be taken out by the DDoS attack. Anything ranging from fairly basic applications to the significantly more complex ones would no longer work. For instance, something as simple as placing a call on a cell phone, or even withdrawing, depositing, or transferring money from a bank account or ATM would be impossible, rendering their basic infrastructure useless.

Not to mention more devastating impacts on the country like crippling air traffic control, meaning the US would be effectively grounded. Water distribution plants and power plants would also stop working, cutting Americans off from access to clean water and a warm home—a must in these frigid winter months. Anyone receiving treatment in a hospital would also be endangered, as the life support systems would stop functioning. And of course, their Pacific Theater Forces were also largely dependent upon network communications. Without it, they would not be able to operate at even the bare minimum of efficiency. Such an attack would propel them back decades in time, technologically speaking.

"What do you know so far?" Secretary Andrews asked Marquez.

"According to the report here in front of me, it's increasing, sir." Her dark eyes were wide as she read the information aloud from her computer terminal. She glanced up from her screen. "Cyber Command has stated they're in the process of terminating the ports that the data is entering from, but I'm not yet sure how long this will take."

"Have Cyber Command start Operation Athena," Secretary Andrews said shortly. He exchanged a glance with Miller, then returned his focus to the screen.

"Yes, sir." Marquez nodded and lowered herself back into her workstation's chair. She was already typing before fully settling into the seat, and rapt focus occupied her face as she worked.

A moment later, the first flickers of life sprang back onto the screens, flooding them first with static before replacing them with a steady blue glow. Marquez glanced up at it, then at Andrews. He nodded, then turned to Major Collins.

The commander had been loitering next to a workstation in the corner of the room, and while he had been tracking the progress of the attack on his own screen, he now alternated his gaze between Lieutenant Marquez and the secretary of defense. An expectant look seemed to linger on his face, as though he had anticipated the pending instructions from the secretary.

"Major Collins, please go ahead and bring up the map of the South and East China Seas on the main screen for me. And I want you to present the current locations of the carrier strike groups for me as well."

"Yes, sir." Collins barely glanced up from the screen. He manipulated the keyboard, typing in a command into a dialogue box, then straightened his back. His eyes went to the monitor expectantly, and a moment later, the image on it changed. Now the main monitor displayed a map of the South and East China Seas in high resolution.

"Thank you, Major." Andrews took a pace back, then crossed his arms over his chest. His blue eyes swept over the new image on the monitor, taking in the updated display with a frown of concentration.

At the bottom of the screen was the Indonesian Islands, a sprawling collection of land—including Java, Sumatra, and Western New Guinea—that ran as far east as Indonesia and as far west as the lower tip of Malaysia. Lingering near the center of the map was Borneo and Malaysia and the waters that surrounded these island countries. Near the center of the map was Vietnam, Cambodia, and the other small countries nearby. Above them was China, the South China Sea to the right, and the Philippines in the farthest reaches of the projection. At the very peak was the East China Sea, both North and South Korea, and a vast portion of Japan.

James let his eyes trail over the cluster of island nations on the map and the CSGs in these waters. The carrier strike groups were finally in position, ready to begin the job they had begun that morning. The instructions to start Operation Athena had been issued. Everything was a go. All they needed to do now was actually win this damned war. How hard could it be?

"Mr. Secretary?" Major Collins's voice broke through the silence in the room. "The MQ-4E Tritons are up and ready, and we should be getting a visual on the battle space in just a few seconds."

This was it. In just a couple minutes, the battle itself would finally commence. Nearly two weeks of detailed planning had led them to this moment, when the Dragon and the Eagle would meet in battle. While there was a certain disconnect from what was currently unfolding on the screen before the personnel inside the relative safety of the NMCC, it didn't undermine the reality of what was occurring across the ocean or make it any less real. Their sailors on the combat ships, as well as the pilots inside the fighters, would be risking their lives in the name of freedom today. They would be maimed, disabled, their lives permanently changed due to their heroic actions.

Today, people would die. Not only would numerous American men and women die in this battle—this was another inevitability of war, James knew—but there was also the indisputable fact that they could still lose. China was playing to win, and they weren't simply going to let the American forces breeze in without a furious battle. He knew what kind of assets the PLAN bore and what type of weapons they would be employing. They had multiple advanced missile systems. The fate of the *USS John S. McCain* attested to that.

The American Navy wasn't going in unprepared, though. In recent years, they had developed their own arms to rival their enemy's arsenal. Among these technologically advanced weapons was the AGM-158C LRASM. This long-range anti-surface cruise missile had recently completed its final stages of development and been waiting since 2018 for its opportunity to be put to use. Designed exclusively for the United States Navy, it had been dubbed "the ship killer" by those who knew of its precision-guided capabilities. Each missile came fully equipped with the tools to completely obliterate enemy ships, including an anti-jamming communications system and a reach of greater than nine hundred miles. In addition, not only could it avoid areas with active radar, but once it was just a few miles from its target, it could fly low to the ocean to avoid detection from the ship's defensive systems.

And what if they did happen to lose this battle? James didn't like thinking about it, but he also knew there would be nothing stopping China from landing their own military forces on American soil. The likelihood of their 2.5 million-strong army immediately expanding their reach in an effort to claim the country as their own would be considerable. Maybe they could secure it in one swift action, with the nuclear missiles he had no doubt they could just as readily use. Or perhaps they would infiltrate the White House and plant a puppet government, just like they had done in Taiwan. President Thomas would not give up his seat without a fight, but James had no misgivings about China's ability to use lethal force on US territory should they feel so inclined.

Oh yes, this war was very much real. It was certainly real to the men and women who were ready and in position on that side of the world. Just because these men and women were standing in the slightly dimmed interior of the NMCC, far away from the combat action itself, it didn't make the scene that was about to appear on the screen any less genuine. It might as well have been in their backyard, because if they didn't win this battle, their neighborhoods could very well be the location of where the next battle would unfold.

"Here it goes now," Major Collins said, and he lifted his face from his personal monitor to the bigger screen on the wall. "The Triton UAVs are now in position."

The screen blinked, then the image changed to feature a video feed of the carrier strike group. Large white swells lapped at the side of the vessels as they churned through the vibrant blue waters of the South China Sea. The video feed seemed to linger on the monitor for several seconds, then the image shifted and changed. It broke into four smaller pictures, with each feed revealing a live video feed of each of the CSGs. It was a formidable sight, one that James privately hoped made their enemy nervous when they witnessed it. They deserved to experience fear, just as the men aboard the *McCain* had felt when they were so ruthlessly fired upon by the PRC's Navy.

"All the CSGs are in position," Major Collins announced, his eyes following the progress of the aircraft as they took off. "And they are preparing to launch their carrier squadrons now."

"What kind of delay are we looking at with this video feed, sir?" Miller asked.

Secretary Andrews answered without glancing up from the screen. "This is almost completely real time, Bill. We're seeing what the CSGs are seeing, just with a delay of about thirty seconds. Of course, our view of it is aerial, so we're seeing things from a slightly different angle, but the delay is marginal at most."

"Interesting," Miller remarked, and fell silent.

The technology of the Tritons was nothing short of impressive. Having the satellites wiped out by the missiles had been a significant loss, but it wasn't as though they couldn't regain their footing, albeit on slightly less level ground. And no doubt, any advantage they could gain from the UAVs, no matter how small, would put them one step closer to securing a victory in battle. Not only could they watch the battle at almost the exact same time as the crew stationed out in the middle of the ocean experienced it, but they could still issue commands and expect them to be followed within a reasonable amount of time as well. While it wasn't the same as their satellites, it certainly was better than nothing.

As James watched, the triangular gray bodies of the FA-18E Super Hornets and the F-35C Lightning II jets moved into position on the flight decks of three of the aircraft carriers. From this distance, the yellow jerseys of the aviation boatswain mates vaguely resembled frantically moving golden dots in stark contrast against the matte surface of the flight deck. The decks were bustling with the activity of personnel hurrying around, trying to get the fighters into position for takeoff. Each screen showed various states of their preparations, and as James watched, it was the *USS John C. Stennis* that bore the privilege of launching the first fighter plane into the air.

The aircraft locked into the catapult, and the petty officers in charge of preparing it scattered away from the fighter plane. Without warning, the jet shot forward down the three-hundred-foot runway like a round from an M4 carbine. It rapidly gained speed, moving faster as it flew forth from the steam-powered catapult. In the two seconds it took for the jet to reach the end of the deck, it clocked speeds nearing 170 miles per hour. Right when it seemed as though it would plummet off the edge of the *Stennis*, its nose turned up and the FA-18 was airborne.

Back on the flight deck, another FA-18 moved into position on the parallel runway alongside the first runway. It locked into the catapult, and a few moments later, the fighter jet joined its companion in a holding pattern above the *Stennis*. The battle had officially commenced, and these first two American fighter pilots were now flying into position to face their opponents. They would not be lonely for long, though. One by one, the remaining jets sped along the twin runways of the carriers, steadily gaining momentum as they traversed the length of their vessels. It didn't take long for the sky around each CSG to grow thick with fighter jets.

It wasn't just the FA-18s and the F-35Cs taking to the sky. While the pilots of the fighter jets readied themselves for the air battle, their rotary-wing aircraft were also getting ready to move into position. On the other side of the carriers, a half-dozen Sikorsky SH-60 Seahawks started spinning their rotors, then eased into the air to provide vital assistance to the fighter pilots. While they would not be flying with the jets, they would be able to perform other key duties such as hunting down China's submarine fleet. Should the need arise, they would also provide medical evacuations and combat search and rescue if and when pilots got shot down.

Finally, a handful of UAVs claimed their position in the sky, high above the flight formations moving toward the enemy. Hidden from the risk of possible detection by soaring at an altitude of nearly eleven miles above the ocean, the Tritons had already gotten a fairly solid head start on the fighter jets. These additional unmanned drones would serve as the eyes of the squadrons, assisting in target location and tracking.

Collins said, "What you're seeing here is ninety aircraft in total, with a fairly even split between the FA-18 Super Hornets and F-35 Lightnings. The remaining ten aircraft are Seahawks and the UAVs."

"That's one hell of a greeting we're going to give them," Secretary Andrews remarked.

Collins nodded but didn't answer. A hint of a smile played at the corner of his lips, but his professionalism won over. It was quickly replaced by a stern frown as he watched the battle on the quad-screen monitor, an expression more appropriate for the actions unfolding on the screen before them.

If each carrier strike group held a total of ninety aircraft, then it meant there was an approximate total of 240 fighter aircraft heading into battle at the same time. It was a striking offensive display from the squadrons. Again, James found himself hoping that the Chinese collectively pissed themselves upon sight of the welcoming party slicing through the air toward them. A man could dream.

Sending out the carrier squadrons was more than just a practical decision, though. Yes, it did look fearsome, that was for damned sure. And it certainly made the US Navy seem like an indomitable force. But this wasn't a war that was going to be fought exclusively in the waters. Gaining air superiority was integral to making sure they maintained the upper hand during this battle. If they were somehow unable to claim control of the skies, then that could very well put them at a grave disadvantage. Even parity against the Chinese forces could lead to a stalemate. If they could secure air supremacy, though, they just might maintain the much-needed advantage over the Chinese forces.

The images on the screen shifted as the MQ-4E UAVs flew overhead, taking in the route of the fighter jets on their way to the battle space in the South China Sea. Their cameras recorded the path of the jets like an unblinking eye, broadcasting them back to the screen in the NMCC. Despite their position several miles overhead, they still were able to capture remarkably clear footage of the squadrons. The incredibly sensitive and highly refined optics allowed for the impressive clarity of the squadrons, more than making up for its distance above them. Even though the drones were still approximately a thousand miles away from the Spratly and Paracel Islands and the nine-dash line, the Chinese military would not hesitate in taking any opportunity to shoot them down. Fortunately, the UAVs also came fully equipped with an electronic system to allow them to avoid detection by the enemy's radar systems at that distance.

The procession of American forces in all four battle spaces occupied both the water below them and sky above them. Overhead, the fighters continued steadily onward, moving toward their target at an impressive rate. Below them, the CSGs also closed the gap between themselves and the PLAN. In the East China Sea, the *Roosevelt* and its squadrons continued pursuit of their northern fleet as it moved south toward mainland China. With its multiple squadrons in the air and its fast-moving attack subs in the water, not only would it hunt for the carrier strike group, but it would also defend their allies and US forces stationed in Japan and South Korea. Farther south, the *Vinson, Stennis,* and *Reagan* remained on track to meet the other three Chinese carriers and their own battle groups. Even though their pace toward China-occupied Taiwan wasn't as rapid as the fighter jets, they still coursed through their own battle space of water at a remarkable thirty knots, or thirty-five miles per hour.

This didn't mean that the battle would officially begin when the CSGs arrived at their destinations, though. According to the latest intelligence,

James knew that the PLAN was waiting patiently for them in both the South China Sea and the East China Sea. Their decision to maintain a defensive posture in these two locations was a strategic one, allowing them to have two carrier battle groups positioned within each location. Furthermore, their carrier battle groups would also be able to rely upon support from their forces in mainland China and Taiwan, further increasing their defensive and offensive capabilities.

Even as the jets were coursing through the air toward their targets, they also had an ally below them. Deep beneath the calm waters of the South China Sea and East China Sea were numerous *Virginia*-class submarines. Many of these nuclear-powered subs lurked in wait, inching ever closer to the Chinese CSGs. Once they were close enough, they would launch their upgraded Block V Tomahawk cruise missiles to take out specific vessels in the Chinese CSGs. Others remained closer to the American CSGs, hunting any Chinese submarines that might try to target their ships.

On the monitor, the images of the carrier strike groups seemed to shrink, and James realized the UAVs were zooming out. While they had been close enough to show the almost frantic activity on the flight decks as the FA-18s and F-35Cs launched from the carriers, now the view offered a wider angle of the CSGs below. The aircraft carriers steadily diminished in size until all of the fighters were visible on the three monitors. Not only could he see all the fighters as they moved toward the enemy battle space, but he was also granted a clear visual for several miles on all sides of the fighter jets. The carriers faded out of view as the UAVs tracked the fighters moving relentlessly toward their targets. If anything happened to penetrate that battle space, they would detect it.

Minutes ticked past. The room was locked in a state of suspended animation, and all chatter had stopped as eyes remained locked on the screens before them. The silence seemed to stretch on endlessly until Major Collins cleared his throat. The sound jarred the men and women out of their quiet contemplative observation of the monitor, and all eyes shifted from the screen to the source of the sound.

Major Collins turned his face toward Secretary Andrews and Chairman Miller, and his voice was surprisingly serene as he stated matter-of-factly, "Gentlemen, our fighters have just made radar contact with their fighters."

CHAPTER TWENTY-THREE

T HE MIDDAY SUNLIGHT SPARKLED OFF the dazzling blue waters of the South China Sea, lending an uncanny aura of good cheer to the morning. Lieutenant Leon Anderson gazed out into the distance, taking in the stunning vista. In a moment, he'd be taxiing down the narrow, angled runway to meet their enemy somewhere over the middle of the ocean. For now, though, he would appreciate the views while he still could.

Anderson heard a crackle in his ear and recognized the voice of the air traffic controller hailing him. He sighed, then lowered the dark visor of his helmet. It was warm inside the domed cockpit of the F-35 Lightning II, and the lieutenant was certain it was more than just his heavy Nomex flight suit causing the trickle of sweat to work its way down the back of his neck and spine. There were no certainties today, and he was keenly aware that he may die in battle. Surprisingly, he found he wasn't afraid of this possibility. Anxious? Hell yes. But fear? No. A tranquil calm descended upon him, allowing him to evade the cold grasp of dread that reached for him with wintry fingers.

"I said, Firefly, you are next for launch." The AC's voice was tense, echoing the sentiments Anderson felt himself. "Do you copy?"

"Copy, AC," Anderson replied.

"We need you to be alert out there, Firefly." There was a note of reproach in the AC's voice, and he acknowledged it silently. The petty officer first class was also clearly feeling tense, and Anderson didn't blame him for the sharp remark. He deserved the chiding for letting his thoughts wander. He squared his shoulders, squinting out at the horizon through the dark shield of his visor.

The headset crackled again, and he could hear the AC chattering in the background. The petty officer relayed his response to the catapult officer, also known as the "shooters," on the deck below. A moment later, Anderson could see the yellow and green jerseys on the flight deck in front of him moving away from his jet. They, too, bore matching strained expressions. To his left, the catapult officer ducked out from beneath the wing, scurrying away from the jet like a hunchbacked troll on the deck. That meant only one thing. The F-35 had been successfully secured to the catapult, and once the steam filled the pistons, Lieutenant Anderson would be launched down the runway and into the air above the South China Sea.

The AC continued, a low drone in his ear that was barely audible over the sound of Anderson's heart thumping in his ears. "Wind coming south, southeast at twenty-two knots. Firefly, you are clear for launch. Godspeed."

He had been on several missions before, as well as over a hundred launches, but this one felt starkly different. The weight of this mission was almost as heavy as the four-transverse Gs of force that would be bearing down on him any moment, when his F-35 was flung from the catapult.

Below him and to the left, he could see the pointing index and middle finger from the yellow jersey perched on the gray flight deck, his signal to take off. He returned it with a thumbs up of his own, then braced himself in the cockpit. Even with over a hundred launches, the sudden acceleration still made him a little queasy. An instant later, there was a loud *whump!* as the catapult released the F-35 from its grasp and spat the fighter jet down the flight deck. Anderson's body pressed firmly against the thickly padded leather cockpit seat, and he made no attempt to pry himself off the flat surface. Even if he did try to move his body, he would be unable to.

Then, just as quickly as he was stuck to the seat, he was released. His body jerked forward, and he felt the familiar weightlessness as the F-35 lifted off the deck of the *USS Carl Vinson*. The ocean opened up in a gaping yawn below him, inviting, blue and glassy. Around him, he could see the other jets that had taken off before him, each holding its position in the sky close to the aircraft carrier. Behind him on the flight deck, another pilot would already be in the process of getting strapped into the catapult to join them. Once the entire carrier wing was in the air, they would only then begin their pursuit of their enemy in the middle of the deceptively serene-looking ocean.

A burst of chatter in his headset moments later confirmed the last fighter's launch, and he let himself fall into the standard four-finger formation with the rest of his squadron. In the F-35C to his left, his flight wingman—a young lieutenant named Carl Patrick—nodded at the element leader directly across from him, who returned it with one of his own. Twenty-four squadrons totaling ninety-six individual aircraft now zipped toward the enemy. At top speeds of over a thousand knots, or just over 1,100 miles per hour, it would take less than an hour to close the 900-mile distance between himself and the Chinese squadrons. This gave him ample time to reflect on not only the day ahead of him but also his possible fate. He had been thoroughly briefed on his assignment earlier that morning, including the approximate number of enemy planes and ships waiting for him, the aircraft they'd be flying, and even their onboard weapons, as well as the mission's objectives and its potential outcomes.

Anderson felt acutely aware of his own mortality as he flew over the South China Sea, and his thoughts went to the slip of paper hidden in his uniform. In the old days, fighter pilots had black and white photographs of childhood sweethearts tucked inside the control columns of their aircrafts. With no such place to hide his picture of his wife and kids, Anderson had to settle with a digital printout in the front breast pocket of his olive flight suit. He took a moment to press his hand against it, then promptly—almost guiltily—he lowered it back down to his thigh. Even though nobody could see the subtle gesture, he still felt slightly embarrassed about it. The picture in his left breast pocket wasn't just everything he was fighting for, but to him, it was also a talisman. It was what was keeping him alive during this mission, both literally and figuratively.

As the miles slipped past them at a rate of more than a thousand feet per second, time also passed in a steady, blue haze. The minutes accumulated, and as the largest portion of the hour passed in an indeterminable block of time, Anderson found himself almost surprised to witness the PLANAF forces suddenly materialize on his radar. In one moment, the black screen of his active electronically scanned array was unremarkable, and in the next, it was teeming with white triangles. Every single one of the geometric shapes on his feed indicated the presence of a Chinese fighter plane, and Anderson found his pulse increase at the sight of the new arrivals.

The Dragon and the Eagle finally meet in battle.

He blinked and lifted his eyes from the display mounted on his control panel, peering through the cockpit's reinforced windshield. Despite the presence on his radar feed, no visible threat loomed on the horizon just yet. The enemy jets were still nearly 250 miles away. Even when he did eventually narrow the gap between himself and the PLANAF, being within visual range didn't necessarily guarantee a sighting, as anything from the brilliant sunlight to his own proximity inside the battle space could impair his ability to see them with the naked eye. He silently hoped his own heavy ordnance of AIM-120 and AIM-9X Sidewinder missiles would be enough to effectively pick off the incoming fighter jets before he got close enough to see the proverbial whites of their eyes.

Anderson found he couldn't remove his gaze from the fleet of triangles on his radar screen. Their sheer numbers were staggering. Even though he had known this moment would come, now that it was finally happening, it was somewhat surreal. Who would make the first move? A twinge of uncertainty rose in the back of his mind, a fleeting and unwelcome flash in his thoughts, and he suppressed it as immediately as it appeared. He realized he was holding the air in his lungs and let it out slowly. The exhalation dissipated any lingering doubts, and he followed it with another deep breath for good measure. In his ear, he heard the tense voice of the squadron captain—Lieutenant Colonel Marvin Cooper—reporting their findings back to the aircraft carrier.

This is it. It's time.

"Okay, now listen up." Lt. Colonel Cooper's booming voice cut through their earpieces, and to Anderson, it sounded almost as though their squad captain was inside the cockpit with him. "We've got a radar tally on the enemy, which means it's now time to show those bastards how bad they fucked up by attacking the *USS John S. McCain*. Fire when you have radar lock, remember to stick to your wingman and, most importantly, show no mercy!"

The rally cries of his squadron filled his ear as they responded to Cooper's impromptu speech. Brief, and without any flowery prose embellishment, it was all they needed to remind them as to why they were out there on this picturesque December morning and not back at home with their families. In that moment, Anderson knew there was no other place in the entire world he would rather be. Deep pride swelled up inside his chest, blotting out any last vestiges of apprehension. The words flew from his mouth, joining the resounding call of the courageous men and women on all sides of him, "For the *McCain*!"

Anderson's right hand had been gripped around the control stick the entire time, and the matte black material was warm beneath his gloved palm as he controlled it to maintain his altitude and trajectory. Now he slid his hand up the stick and, not taking his eyes off the fleet of enemy fighters bracketed on the radar screen before him, he carefully placed his thumb over the weapon release button on the top of it. Once the radar display revealed a range of eighty-five miles between him and the enemy squadron, he would be within the maximum effective range of his AAMs. When his jet skimmed past this invisible boundary, then and only then would he release a pair of advanced medium-range AIM-120D air-to-air missiles from the weapons bay to eliminate their chosen targets.

Somewhere off to his right side, Anderson caught a glimpse of something moving swiftly in his peripheral vision. Even though the object was coursing so rapidly through the air that it was already almost out of his line of sight, he didn't have to take a guess to determine what the white, oblong cylinder was. Someone had just released their own AAM payload. He glanced down, verifying his distance was within the missile range and nodded to himself. This was his cue to begin. He let his thumb close over the release button on his control stick, and there was a barely perceptible groan from beneath his jet as the bay doors opened. The AIM-120D missiles floated in the air for a beat as they dropped from their stations, then abruptly darted forward toward the horizon.

Anderson watched the display as the missiles zeroed in on their target, carefully tracking their path in his radar array. Even moving at Mach 4—or slightly over three thousand miles per hour—the seconds between their release and its impact stretched out indefinitely. Ten seconds faded into twenty, then the J 20 on his readout vanished in a nondescript blip. The delivery of his deadly message had been successful. Still, there was no time to pat himself on the back. This was just one jet out of scores of Chinese fighters, and many more waited in the distance. All around him, he could see plumes of smoke as his squadron released their own AIM-120s at the enemy aircraft. At this distance, nearly eighty miles away from the enemy squadron, it was still too far to see the results of their handiwork. Perhaps in another minute or two, though, he might have a visual on them and the view from his seat would change.

His squadron had happened to move near the front of the formation during the battle, affording Anderson a front-row seat to the deadly air-show. While the majority of his attention had been on firing his first volley of AIM-120s at the enemy jets, he could now see hundreds—and perhaps even thousands—of white streaks in the sky all around him. Not only was his squadron firing their missiles, but the PLANAF were also firing their own missiles. He shifted his gaze from his radar display to the electro-optical distributed aperture system (EO-DAS) inside his helmet. Unlike the archaic missile detection systems pilots had used in the past, this one afforded him a 360-degree view of the sky around him. Its infrared search-and-track abilities allowed him to see possible threats from all angles.

As he watched, his computer's missile detection system activated, alerting him to one of these threats. A red indicator light on his console blinked urgently, and at the same time, a high-pitched beep filled his cockpit. On his display, a Chinese PL-12 air-to-air missile wove its way toward him, an unassuming yet lethal cylinder of death in the distance. Anderson's gaze never left its trajectory as he pressed the button on his console to initiate the onboard Electronic Countermeasures (ECM). He shifted the steering side-stick, and the F-35 responded instantly to his touch. Its engine thrummed audibly as he guided himself away from the incoming missile. Now unable to lock onto him, the PL-12 appeared to be momentarily baffled, then it corrected its path. Seemingly no longer interested in Anderson or his plane, it locked onto another target beyond him. Anderson's missile alerts ended as quickly as they had begun.

He could hear the quiet chatter of his team in his ear, but it was a distant sound, muffled and strangely muted. The battle around him felt curiously amplified, as though his senses had elevated since they'd arrived at the airspace, heightening his focus to acute precision. Around him, a combination of US and Chinese missiles trailed dense plumes of smoke across the sky as they streaked by him on all sides. There were more missiles than fighter planes in the air, choking the battle space with their lethal shapes.

One soared directly overhead, and his face jerked up to track it through his canopy as it rushed over and then vanished behind him. An instant later, he felt the shockwave blast as one of his squadron's jets became the unwitting recipient of the PL-12 missile. Somewhere to his right, another missile found a different F-35 in his squadron and a blinding burst of light filled the sky from the impact, momentarily blotting out his field of vision.

It was kill or be killed, and Anderson knew instinctively which option he preferred. While his ECM might safeguard him from most missile attacks, it wasn't a guarantee of his salvation. To survive this battle, he had to also do his part to reduce the enemy's numbers. On the screen, his onboard computer locked onto a J-20 in the distance, bracketing it in a white square. He wet his lips, darting his tongue over the chapped skin, then moved the control column in his right hand. The enemy pilot didn't know it yet, but he now had a missile with his own name on it. Anderson's thumb closed over the release button once more, and the last two AIM-120 missiles dropped from the F-35 and soared toward their target now a mere fifty miles away. He didn't have to wait as long this time to determine that his aim had been true. Another triangular blip vanished from his tactical display, one less threat to worry about.

His radio crackled, and he heard a familiar voice filter into his ear. "How's it going over there, Firefly? Enjoying the fireworks show?"

"Not bad, Smiley. Not bad at all." As he uttered the words, Anderson realized they were the truth. Things could be better, of course. But then again, they could also be worse. "What about you? Kicking some ass over there?"

"You know it," Patrick replied. Even as he spoke, another missile soared out from beneath his wing toward some unseen enemy in the distance.

"Save some of the action for the rest of us, man." Anderson grinned at him from behind his visor.

"Not my fault you're too slow," Patrick said, then fell silent, his focus returning once more to the battle.

Ahead of him, Anderson took note of the burning clouds of smoke and debris dotting the skyline. When they had arrived, there were dozens of enemy jets obstructing their access to the Chinese CSG. While their numbers hadn't matched the American forces, it was still a formidable battery. Yet as he glanced down at his radar array, something seemed to change on the feed. As he watched, the Chinese forces—which had slowly been starting to diminish thanks to the concerted efforts of Anderson and his squadron—suddenly seemed to revert back to their previous levels. The white triangles poured onto his display, clotting the feed with their growing numbers. The readout now showed greater than double the original ranks, possibly to the tune of an additional hundred fighters, if not more.

What the hell? He blinked, then looked up, peering through the windshield of his canopy. Around him, he could see the turning heads of his remaining squadron as they also checked to see if anyone had noticed these new arrivals. As much as he had hoped otherwise, their presence clearly wasn't a figment of his imagination. They were so densely packed on his radar array, it was almost as though they were overlapping one another. The only logical conclusion he could deduce was that they had come from the mainland, as there was no way any single PLAN aircraft carrier could hold so many jets in its hangars. And if they had been so able to send another hundred into the battle, what would stop them from sending a hundred more should those numbers get depleted?

A moment later, his wingman's voice spoke into his ear once more. Despite the threat accumulating in the distance, Patrick sounded calm. "Hey, are you the jackass who invited these unwanted guests to the dance? I don't remember sending out engraved invitations this morning."

"Wasn't me," Anderson replied, the levity in his words countering the growing anxiety blooming inside him. "So what we're looking at here is a bunch of party crashers, huh?"

"Sounds about right," Patrick agreed. "Well, I guess we better show these bastards what we do to people who show up unannounced. Lucky for them, I planned ahead and brought enough party favors to share. I wouldn't want anyone to feel left out."

"Very generous of you," Anderson said with a nod.

He, too, had his own party favors to share with the incoming enemy fighters. With his AIM-120 reserves depleted, he would have to instead rely upon the pair of Sidewinder missiles affixed to the hardpoints beneath his jet's wings to defend himself. A glance at his radar array confirmed his distance from the enemy squadron, and he nodded to himself. While incredibly powerful tools, the Sidewinders also had their own limitations, namely how far they could travel. However, with Anderson now closing in on just under twenty miles between himself and the PLANAF's forces, there was no time like the present to test their effectiveness in battle. He nudged the weapons control column forward, and the computer display in front of him paused, then highlighted the AAM missiles on each side of his jet. A tap on a button beneath his finger finalized his selection.

The Sidewinder clung to the weapons pylon beneath the wing of his aircraft, waiting for his instruction to proceed. The computer's display calibrated, then bracketed yet another one of the J-20s on the horizon. Anderson's thumb closed over the release button once more, and the long, slender missile launched obediently toward its target. He watched as it flew through the sky, carefully tracking its route through his windshield. Once it vanished from his sight, he'd switch his focus to the radar feed.

Through the cockpit canopy, a sudden and brilliant flash of light filled the sky, and he blinked in disbelief at the radiant fireball in the distance. Something had obstructed the Sidewinder's path, and as a rain of shrapnel fell from the sky, he realized what had happened. It had collided not against a fighter jet but instead had been accidentally hit by another Chinese incoming missile.

Anger, along with the first tinges of fear, coursed through Anderson's veins as he guided his jet out of the mist of debris. He stole another glance over at Patrick. *C'mon, man, give me* some *sign that you saw that. You're killing me here, buddy.* With the intensity of the morning battle surrounding him on all sides, he craved the camaraderie between himself and his wingman, even if it were a simple nod or an upright thumb in his direction. The two men had been through much of their training together, and having Patrick assigned as his wingman had been no coincidence. He had played a key role in giving the cheerful son of a bitch his callsign. Sure, Smiley was a lame one, but so was Firefly. He had to admit, though, that marveling at the glowing exhaust and comparing it to the ubiquitous lightning bug did warrant his new name. Neither of them would ever live it down.

Patrick, however, had his own developing concerns to worry about. As Anderson watched, his wingman's jet lurched, then pirouetted in the air.

Anderson blinked. *That isn't right. What the hell is going on?*

Then the F-35 was engulfed in a blinding flash of light, and where his friend once was, a fiery plume of heat and destruction had replaced him.

An expletive flew from Anderson's mouth, but he was only distantly aware of it. His wingman, his friend, was dead. As he watched, the remains of his jet rained down onto the deceptively calm waters below.

But how? Anderson's mind raced as he tried to make sense of what he'd just seen. He hadn't observed any missiles coming toward him. And yes, he had been watching the EO-DAS closely. Hell, he had been looking *directly* at the man, and there had been no such threat from ahead of him to indicate that Patrick had been in imminent danger.

As he widened the gap between himself and his friend's remains, he realized what must have happened. The missile couldn't have come from the enemy squadron ahead of them, which meant that it must have come from below. His computer readout only showed an endless expanse of sapphire blue water, but that didn't mean the ocean wasn't hiding its own malevolent secrets. Somewhere down below them, either a Chinese submarine or even one of the PLAN's surface vessels had played a role in killing his friend. And if they had successfully killed Patrick, then that meant there could be a missile on its way already to get Anderson too. The enemy must have employed a surface-to-air missile from one of their own frigates or submarines, and his wingman had been unable to dodge it.

As though to validate this revelation, one of his squadron's missiles in the distance seemed to spontaneously detonate as another SAM found it. Despite having been built with advanced jamming technology to confuse enemy missiles, the Chinese Navy still had managed to thwart its defensive systems. Sending out imaginary targets had done little for the missile that had just exploded before Anderson's eyes, and it had also done equally poorly for Patrick.

Anderson made a mental note to say a prayer for his fallen wingman later. While he himself was not a man of faith, he knew Patrick had been a devout Protestant. His own talisman, the gold cross he wore around his neck, was probably a melted scrap of metal on its way to the bottom of the ocean. He thought of the photograph in his pocket. Would it really keep him safe? A slip of paper had no power against a missile. He had been foolish for believing in it. Even as he felt the first whispered fears of a possible defeat rise in the pit of his stomach, tasting of acid and bile, he couldn't dismiss its protective properties just yet. He was still alive. Patrick may be gone, as well as numerous others. Leon Anderson, though, still had some fight left in him. The men in his squadron, as well as the faces of his family in the picture in his pocket, were counting on him to continue.

Even as he locked onto his next target, he couldn't shake the sense of foreboding threatening to distract him. While the war itself had only just begun, already so much had been lost. The People's Liberation Army Navy had no doubts they would win today, and it was up to Anderson—as well as the rest of his squadron—to prove them wrong.

CHAPTER TWENTY-FOUR

Inside the Pentagon National Military Command Center, a hush fell on the room as the personnel watched the main monitor with rapt interest. Three out of the four displays showed the American flight wings traversing through the air. As the pilots approached the PLANAF in the skies over the South China Sea, their fighter jets seemed momentarily suspended in midair, locked in a fleeting repose as enemy planes materialized in the distance. Then within the span of no more than thirty seconds, they began their offensive maneuvers. The sky immediately grew heavy with white columns of smoke and oblong missiles as both sides launched their payloads, and the abrupt transformation from transient quiet to a full-scale battle seemed almost coordinated in its suddenness.

James's eyes moved from screen to screen, taking in each of the different squadrons on each monitor with a glance. The squadrons of FA-18s and F-35s fired a seemingly uninterrupted cascade of Sidewinder and AIM-120 missiles at the Chinese fighter jets, and streaks of thick smoke flew out from beneath them as they continued their relentless barrage at the PLANAF. The only display that didn't show any combat activity was the bottom right-hand side of the monitor, where the *USS Theodore Roosevelt* glided serenely through the tranquil waters of the East China Sea. Recent intel from their UAVs had placed China's northern fleet in this region, and the carrier had just launched her squadrons in preparation for the upcoming battle. He had no doubts the carrier would begin her own offensive measures once she came within range of the enemy vessels. From this vantage, though, the lack of immediate action seemed oddly inconsistent compared to the other three monitors.

A sudden movement on the screen featuring the *Stennis* caught his eye, and he shifted his gaze from the battle to the display on the left-hand side of the main screen. The last time he had glanced at it, the crew aboard the aircraft carrier had just finished launching its air wings. Now the sailors seemed to be moving frantically aboard the flight deck, and multicolored dots rushed across her surface toward the hatches. He frowned as he regarded this new activity. Something had evidently worked them into a panic, but what?

Andrews seemed to have the same question. "Major Collins, can you connect us to their communication feed, please?"

"Yes, of course." Collins leaned forward and tapped a button on the keyboard, then clicked the mouse. "Give me one second to link it, and… Okay, there. That should do it."

As Andrews straightened his back once more and returned his focus to the screen, the sound of the crew's voices filtered into the command room from the wall-mounted speakers. The urgency of their words matched their frenzied actions aboard the flight deck, and as James listened, he realized what he was hearing. The *Stennis's* radar system had picked up on an incoming missile, and her personnel were in the process of launching their own missile from the onboard RIM-116 missile defense system. Based on the increasingly louder voices shouting commands back and forth on the bridge, the threat was coming in fast. The six missile destroyers in the CSG were also firing their own vertical launch systems, an amount that would total no less than twenty Standard Missile-3s from the half-dozen ships, in a desperate and unified attempt to try to protect the aircraft carrier. Yet even as he watched the display and saw the first volley of infrared missiles fire from the *Stennis* and her neighboring destroyers, he could readily see they had all been too slow. Or rather, the incoming missile had been too fast.

The DF-100 slammed against the starboard bow of the ship, then continued its route without interruption, slicing cleanly through it. As it finished its journey through the front of the aircraft carrier, a massive fireball billowed out from the site of the impact, its vibrant orange fingers reaching for the sky above the *USS John C. Stennis*. The display momentarily brightened from the flaming cloud, then dimmed once more as it completed its heavenward journey. With it out of the way, the aftermath of the missile's collision with the vessel was evident. The entire front end of the carrier was enshrouded in a combination of black, tarry smoke and white-hot flames.

As the remaining shrapnel of the longsword missile worked its way out of the ship, the survivors aboard the *Stennis* no longer bothered with readying their RIM-116 missile system. Instead, they scrambled across the burning deck to survey the scope of the damage, weaving through sprays of fire suppressant foam jetting from the island superstructure. The fire blazing on the screen seemed to be reflected in the eyes of all the personnel inside the NMCC, holding their gaze in a macabre fascination. The Chinese Dongfeng-100 hypersonic missile that had just struck the *Stennis* had been the exact same type of missile that had also sunk the *USS John S. McCain*. And curiously, for some reason, the *Stennis* was still afloat. Already the fire was subsiding. Around him, James could hear the quiet sighs of relief. All things considered, the damage could have been worse. Much worse.

Secretary Andrews unfolded his arms and turned toward Major Collins. His voice was grave as he said, "Those sons of bitches have no right wielding such power."

"I think you're right," Collins replied. James couldn't see his eyes, but his tense shoulders and jutted chin clearly hinted at the cold fury he shared with the SecDef. "And now they know how successful this shot was, there's nothing stopping them from trying again."

"Yes…" Andrews trailed off. His brow furrowed and his lips set in a grim line, he turned back toward the screen.

On a different display, seemingly oblivious to the destruction occurring aboard the *Stennis*, the battle between the naval fighter planes and PLANAF raged on. As he watched, another one of their fighter jets pinwheeled out of the sky and plummeted to the turquoise waters below. A moment later, a Chinese J-20 stealth fighter also exploded and joined its fallen comrades at the bottom of the Pacific Ocean. It was an eye for an eye out there, and from where James stood, it seemed as though the Americans were getting hit hard. While it had initially appeared as though the American forces were the stronger contender out there, the Chinese forces quickly proved this assessment to be incorrect. Not only were they methodically culling the American squadrons' numbers, but the attack on the *Stennis* also indicated the enemy wasn't only focusing on the aerial assault.

The fire on the *Stennis* was nearly completely extinguished, thanks to the skill of her highly trained crew. James nodded in private encouragement at the screen. These men and women had not only been on the receiving end of a DF-100, but many of them had also lived to be able to talk about it. As the crew worked on putting out the last flames of the fire, their eyes tore away from the mounds of foam and up to the sky once more. Even from this distance, James could see the unbridled terror on their faces. The voices from the crew members on the bridge were shouting once more, overlapping one another with cries of, "Fire the intercept missiles!" and "It's coming in too fast!" Several intercept missiles launched from their RIM-116, as well as dozens more SM-3s from the nearby guided-missile destroyers.

Almost as though they had been waiting patiently for their opportunity to strike, three more DF-100s cut through the air. A brilliant flash of white light filled the screen, and James had only a second to register the first enemy missile exploding in the sky some two hundred yards away from the aircraft carrier after being struck by an SM-3 intercept missile. This small victory, however, had little bearing on the fate of the *Stennis*. The two remaining missiles bypassed the SM-3s with ease, barreling against the body of the ship in an instantaneous onslaught of devastating power. The first met against her starboard side, not far from the site of the first DF-100 hypersonic missile, and glided smoothly through it. Then, a moment later, the remaining missile met the port side of the *Stennis* in a booming explosion. The sounds of the missiles crashing into the body of the aircraft carrier were deafening, blotting out all noise in the NMCC.

When silence again descended upon the room, there was nothing they could say to articulate the horror on the screen in front of them. The flames spread out across the body of the vessel, concealed by the heavy clouds of smoke enveloping the mortally wounded vessel. Water rushed in to fill the void created by the missiles, cloaking the destroyed ship in its blue embrace. The seawater did little for extinguishing the flames, and where the waves lapped against the sinking ship, the oil-coated surface promptly ignited. Floating bodies were consumed by the fire, then claimed by the waters. The body of the carrier split apart, and for a lingering moment, the *Stennis* seemed to bob uncertainly on the surface. Then the nose of the ship dipped beneath the South China Sea, and a beat later, the stern joined it.

"God rest their souls," Andrews said hollowly.

The faces of the personnel watching the screen seemed to spontaneously age in the aftermath of the sinking, and the dark crescents beneath their eyes deepened as they stared unblinkingly at the screen. On the main monitor, the squadrons that had departed from the *Stennis* only minutes before continued their assigned mission. James couldn't see their faces, but he could easily envision their expressions beneath their polarized visors. The sound of the dying screams of the *Stennis's* crew had made for a bleak final broadcast in their ears. They had no home ship to return to, so instead, they continued steadfastly onward toward the Chinese CSG. To these orphaned squadrons, it was now personal. Their friends, their fellow crew, had perished, and so now the bastards who'd caused their demise would also perish.

Not all of them would survive to see the end of the day, though. As James watched, another American fighter jet vanished in a flash of red flames and black smoke. And then another. The Chinese forces were ruthless, and as the US Navy inched ever closer to the enemy CSGs, their attacks were growing almost feverish in their frequency. While China had not been reserved earlier, their onslaught seemed more furious as their opponents closed in on them. They fired upon the American forces in an unremitting barrage, releasing an unbroken stream of missiles. Despite many of their missiles skirting safely past their targets entirely, several more of them landed squarely on an advancing fighter jet.

It wasn't just the fighter jets that were being steadily picked off by the Chinese forces, either. On another screen, James could see the smoldering ruins of several of their frigates. The water was choked with floating debris, evidence of the carnage of the sea battle. Even though the Triton was far overhead, panning over the destroyed vessels in a wide-angle gaze, the distinct shapes of the floating bodies face down in the water were unmistakable. The *Stennis* hadn't been the only vessel sunk by the PLAN so far, just the largest. But at China's current pace, the likelihood of many more taken out by their enemy before the battle ended was swiftly increasing.

Time seemed to have no meaning within the NMCC, and the only barometer of its passage was another jet tumbling from the sky or another missile striking its target. James reluctantly pried his gaze away from the display, shifting to the clock on the far wall. Somehow, nearly two hours had managed to creep by since the battle had initially commenced. As his focus moved back to the main monitor, a much smaller one several feet away caught his attention. This one had been trained on Shanghai, or more specifically, the Dachang Airbase positioned directly above the coastal city. There was something distinctly wrong about the video feed and, as he peered at it, he realized its normally neon skyline was now flat and dull in the noonday sunlight.

As though on cue, Lieutenant Turner lifted his face from his workstation. His voice broke through the quiet, and heads turned slightly to listen as he spoke. "Sir? I have an update from the Missile Defense Agency. According to my report, there's some unusual activity going on at various missile stations across China, including those at Yumen, Hami, and Jilantai, among others."

"What would that be, Lieutenant?" Andrews asked, casting a glance over his shoulder at the young officer, then returning it to the video display on the wall.

"They're no longer actively firing missiles, sir," Turner said. The bafflement, which was now becoming his trademark state, was back in his voice. "It seems as though they've been shut down."

Andrews didn't reply.

James watched as Turner's eyes moved around the room, waiting for someone to chime in and explain what this new development meant. However, nobody spoke up and nobody offered to clarify. It wasn't so much as an attempt to be elusive, as all of the personnel in the room had known—or rather, hoped—this was going to happen, even if they didn't necessarily know how it would manifest. But the missile stations and silos, as well as the blackout rolling throughout mainland China, meant Project Athena was now in full effect. And by all definitions of the term, it appeared to have been a success.

⸻

The timing of Project Athena could not have been any more opportune. While James and the rest of the personnel inside the command center had been watching the conflict in the South China Sea, China continued to work covertly in the background. From silos across their country, they fired several ICBMs at various sites across the globe. The United States was the recipient of several of those missiles, and their targets included the historic

Pearl Harbor in Honolulu, Hawaii; Camp Humphreys near Anjeong-ri, South Korea; and Okinawa's Torii Station. Other American installations scattered across the Pacific Rim in Guam, the Philippines, and Thailand were also fired upon.

Before they could accomplish their deadly objective, however, the Missile Defense Agency stepped in. From their location in Fort Belvoir, their sensitive Terminal High Altitude Area Defense radar tracking system issued an emergency alert at the lethal threat, and they promptly sprang into action. Within less than a minute of the initial warning, the radar tracking system locked in on the trajectories of the incoming missiles. The Missile Defense Agency then transmitted the tracking data to all of the Aegis Ballistic Missile destroyers and cruisers in the area, and these ships immediately began arming their SM-3s. There were a half-dozen ships in total responding to the threat, as well as additional ground-based interceptors in South Korea, Japan, and the Philippines, each launching their own SAMs to take out these incoming ICBMs.

As effective as these ground-based interceptors were, though, it also had a somewhat limited margin of operation. The defense system could arguably shoot down the ICBMs, but only once the missiles were in their terminal phase. This meant their ground interceptors could not successfully destroy the incoming missiles until they were actively in the final stage of their twenty-minute journey, mere moments before they would engage with their targets. Just as it seemed as though the long-range missiles might actually cause serious and irreparable harm to their targeted military installations and cities, anti-ballistic missiles zeroed in on the enemy missiles and, one by one, they were successfully and safely destroyed midair moments before they would have hit their targets.

The cascading effects of Project Athena were stunning in their sharp simplicity, and its value was underscored by the ICBMs fired from mainland China. In the early hours of the war, James had witnessed the American forces taking serious losses. Between the PLAN outnumbering them from the very beginning to their comparable—and in some ways, even better—technology, their prognosis for a victory was fifty-fifty. Then, all at once, it seemed as though the PLANAF had forgotten how to fight. James watched with restrained satisfaction as the change unfolded on the monitors. The formerly adept fighters went from swooping aggressively toward the American squadrons to falling harmlessly down to the South China Sea below. Where jets once occupied the battle space, now dozens of canvas parachutes holding dangling pilots beneath them filled the sky.

While having the power cut throughout the country had unquestionably been a beneficial result of Project Athena, it had not been the operation's primary objective. Rather, its ultimate goal was to shut down all of China's ICBM missile silos and other military assets. Had they not, the risk of them firing intercontinental ballistic missiles at the United States remained far too great, as demonstrated by the recent attacks on military installations in South Korea, Japan, and Hawaii. But by implementing a comprehensive blackout on all computer systems on the Chinese mainland, the US had effectively prevented them from using any of their powerful weapons on them again. China had already come too damn close to wiping parts of the world off the map once today with its ICBMs—and given the opportunity, they would have undoubtedly tried again.

CHAPTER TWENTY-FIVE

P RESIDENT THOMAS HAD ACCUMULATED HIS share of secrets in his lifetime, and the details of their victory against China would join that ever-growing list. Although he would never admit it to anyone, not even under oath or coercion, it had been no accident that the *USS John S. McCain* had ventured so close to the Spratly Islands. Yes, hundreds of Americans had perished, both in the initial attack and the following battles. But had he not invited the war by authorizing the US Navy to patrol in the South China Seas and instead waited for China to attack them several years down the road, their losses could have been much higher. The term "calculated decision" had never before borne such weight. The president had personally done the math himself and reluctantly determined a little bit of subtraction today was worth it to prevent global division in the future. Only time would reveal if his numbers actually checked out.

The US was still a formidable force to be reckoned with, but its days of being recognized as the "Indispensable Nation" had long since passed. While America was still considered a global military power, the role of being the strongest one had shifted to China. Every year, its defense budget—as well as its threat level—had grown exponentially until it was the largest military force in the globe. Seemingly overnight, China had somehow managed to completely transform itself from a paltry communist nation into a viable threat to all of humanity. Had they been given another few years to expand their military and the PRC then decided it was ready for war against the US, the loss would have been both certain and devastating. Hell, they had already come far too close for comfort even in this current year.

Project Athena had defined a turning point in the battle, all but ensuring their victory against the PRC. But what exactly had made it so successful? In brief, it was a combination of both its forethought and its stealth. The wheels of Athena had been set into motion years before, with credit owed to the ingenuity of a top secret CIA operation to sell computer operating systems with preconfigured viruses to China. Once Andrews had given the command following the DDoS attack, the Department of Defense's Cyber Command Warfare Group had then transmitted a signal through China's internet gateway network servers. When a select few operating systems received it, the signal then proceeded to spread prolifically throughout the nation's networks, servers, and computer systems. Acting like a worm, the signal aggressively wriggled its way into all Wi-Fi, Bluetooth, and cellular networks within the vicinity. Even air-gapped and isolated systems weren't immune. From there, the bug did the one job it had been programmed to do: it corrupted all the computer operating systems and networks within the borders of China, and it did so with great relish.

At 2242 hours, approximately two hours after Secretary Andrews had given the orders, Project Athena overwrote all data from the infected hard drives and then overwrote the BIOS chips within the computers, rendering the devices entirely unusable. As a Fractionated Cavity Code Integration program inside the operating system, locating it on a device would be impossible. The malware code was split into a predetermined number of sections and carefully weaved itself into the operating system code at various locations inside, merging the malware with the OS codes. Their antiviruses wouldn't recognize the bug during any of its sweeps, as it was part of the operating system.

The moment Project Athena began, it was as though a circuit breaker panel in China had been flipped one by one. At first, the residents of smaller towns had believed the loss of power was due to a temporary blackout, as power cuts had been increasingly common in recent years. But as it rippled throughout the nation, entire cities and provinces went dark and they grew suspicious of its origins, especially since the emerging power loss had begun not long after the start of the battle in the East and South China Seas. All buildings—including power plants, water treatment facilities, and even the hospitals—had their plug pulled. Nothing operated or controlled by computers, or any servers with operating systems, were spared. This also included all satellites, airplanes, air traffic controls, and ground-based missile systems.

With China disabled from the cyberattack and its planes successfully removed from the sky, the US Navy could finally concentrate its efforts on the South China Sea and the advancing People's Liberation Army Navy. Without power or computer systems to sustain them, the majority of China's military had been rendered virtually defenseless against the progressive US assault. This didn't mean all of the enemy ships and aircraft had been entirely neutralized by Project Athena, though. While the virus had successfully eliminated greater than 90 percent of the Chinese jets and warships, that still left a substantial number remaining to continue the fight. These uninfected stragglers, although unquestionably powerful in their own right, simply could not sustain their efforts for long without the support of the rest of their fleet.

As the US Navy progressed through the clear blue waters of the South and East China Sea, they methodically defeated any lingering Chinese ships and fighter aircraft encountered. The two surviving aircraft carriers, as well as their surrounding vessels, were not unlike the heavily armored battleships of World War II as they plowed steadily onward. Confident and insuppressible against their enemy, they captured any warships that willingly surrendered to them and unflinchingly subdued any enemy that continued the fight.

The total force losses after the completion of the naval offensive were immense, and the United States had not emerged unscathed. The US Naval assets in the Pacific had sustained a significant loss, and of the four aircraft carriers sent to battle, two had been destroyed. In addition to the *USS John C. Stennis*, the *USS Carl Vinson* had also been sunk. From the eleven battle cruisers deployed, over half of them were destroyed. Six of them were now somewhere at the bottom of the South China Sea. The same could be said for two of the three frigates that had trailed alongside the CSGs. Before the battle had begun, a total of thirty-one naval destroyers had escorted the CSGs. Afterward, only four remained. The minesweepers, conversely, had dramatically fewer losses. Only one of them had been sunk. None of the two support ships had sunk, either.

The losses were not limited to the surface of the ocean. Beneath the waters, two of the seven attack subs sent in to lend support had been taken out by enemy torpedoes. And finally, the aircraft from the three carriers had also incurred substantial losses. Of the 240 fighter planes that had taken off from the three flight decks the morning of the initial battle, only forty-three of them came back. The rest had been claimed by enemy fire and were now floating debris or misshapen shrapnel on the bottom of the ocean. As it turned out, Lieutenant Leon Anderson's photo of his family had not been able to safeguard the young father and husband from enemy missile fire. He had ultimately joined his friend and wingman after all, a tragic reunion beneath the waves.

Despite these vast initial casualties on the American side, China had suffered an even greater loss of both assets and lives. All four aircraft carriers in their CSGs had been sent to the bottom of the seas. The same could be said for the 160 aircraft from their carriers and the fighters that had come to support from China and Taiwan. Not a single one had survived. Every one of their frigates had been sunk, as had their destroyers. Their corvette class warships had also been wiped out, with every one of the forty-two vessels now loitering somewhere at the bottom of the ocean. Their mine-sweepers had faced total loss, with all thirty-three of them destroyed. Their coastal patrol ships, which had tried valiantly to guard the Chinese shore, had sustained a loss of 192 vessels. Not a single one had survived. Finally, their submarines had also been subject to almost complete elimination. The PLAN had started out with seventy-three submarines. Of these numbers, all but three had been destroyed.

Once the oceans had been secured, the US Army had then proceeded to secure several beachheads and move their fight into mainland China. As they'd moved from province to province, they met pockets of resistance from the People's Liberation Army. Unlike the PLA's naval and air forces, however, their efforts against the PLA were somewhat tempered. Largely defenseless with no power, most of the Chinese soldiers had readily surrendered. This shifted the United States' focus from active combat to capturing the PLA's ground forces. These Chinese Prisoners of War now waited for their eventual release from internment camps in Xinjiang. It was also within those POW camps where American troops had discovered the survivors of the *McCain*, half-starved and exhausted but nonetheless still alive.

The end of the war had arrived with little ceremony. It merely *was*. One minute, the Chinese forces were mopping the floor with American blood, and the next, it was game over for them. The US took little pleasure in the battle, and they completed the task with a type of grim determination of someone who knew they had an unsavory task to complete but would not stop until it was done. By the time it was over, China had been converted into a shell of its former self. With no power, no resources, and no fight left, they had no choice but to surrender. And the United States was merciful enough to graciously accept the surrender, keeping their gloating to a diplomatically mandated minimum.

After securing their victory, the American forces had then carefully focused their efforts on destroying all the remaining coastal offensive and defensive missile platforms. They also trained their attention on completely eliminating China's Air Force and, most importantly, all of their ICBM sites. Had China somehow managed to reboot their systems, they would never be able to recover their military equipment. While the United States had required a grand total of seventy-two hours to win the war, it would still take another four months to finish tying off any remaining loose ends. Housing the captured Chinese soldiers would be a logistical nightmare, maxing out supply lines to keep them fed, housed, and clothed within the internment camps.

With the war over, the only remaining thing to do was announce the United States' triumph to the waiting public. Seated behind his desk in the Oval Office, the president of the United States of America was ready to deliver this message. The ceremonial room was immaculate, as always, and the tall, stately president completed the impressive image. Dressed in a crisp, navy-blue suit and a freshly pressed white shirt, a red silk tie rounded out the patriotic color scheme of his outfit. On his lapel was a small enamel American flag, and beneath it was the black and white POW flag for the survivors of the *McCain*. His silver hair was carefully combed and tucked behind his ears, and not a single rogue hair dared blemish his appearance. In front of him, an intern carefully dabbed at his nose with a cosmetic sponge, then leaned back to consider her handiwork. After a pause, she nodded, satisfied. President Thomas raised his almost colorless blue eyes to her, and she met his gaze and smiled timidly before scurrying out of the room. He did not return the smile.

On the oak desk before him lay a sheath of papers. He reached out and brushed the back of his hand against the corner of the stack, brushing away an almost imperceptible speck blemishing the otherwise crisp document. The desk he sat behind, the Resolute desk, had been a gift to the US from none other than Queen Victoria. Named after the royal ship from which its wood had been derived, it summarized his sentiments as he waited for the teleprompter to start rolling. There was a heavy sense of finality weighing down upon him, and he had to admit he was ready for this entire ordeal to be over. His address to his constituents would not only give them the much-needed conclusion to the three-day war, but it would also ideally give him closure for the difficult decisions he had to make leading up to this day.

During his speech today, he would reveal the end of their war with China to the public. This would come as no surprise to them, as the news media had been tracking the war efforts almost as closely as an SM-3 might track incoming enemy threats. At the Department of Defense headquarters earlier that day, Thomas had spoken extensively with the CIA about accomplishing a ceasefire with the enemy nation. His top CIA official hadn't hesitated in suggesting their own Potsdam Declaration, and after considering it for a moment, the president had nodded. It would borrow heavily from the original one issued to Japan back in 1945, when the United States had demanded the unconditional surrender of Japan following World War II. And, like the original, theirs would add in their own non-negotiable terms, citing the original document in its staunch assertion. "We will not deviate from them. There are no alternatives. We shall brook no delay."

It hadn't taken them long to draft the ultimatum documents, outlining what they expected from China. Key demands included limited sovereignty by the PRC, forbidding them from further global expansion and relinquishing their claim on the Spratly Islands and the South China Seas. The proclamation had also included a statement calling for the surrender of all Chinese armed forces, noting that if China refused these terms, they would face an ongoing military occupation until they did submit. Conversely, the US was reasonable, pointing out a lack of interest in annexing the nation and even encouraging them to go on to live peaceful lives after the war. After being thoroughly proofread by several sets of eyes, it was sent to China's president. Less than an hour after receiving the document, President Yong issued his own statement, confirming his agreement with the terms. And, just like that, the final stages of their victory over China had been confirmed.

"Mr. President?" came a voice from directly ahead of him.

President Thomas jerked his head up and locked his eyes upon his press secretary.

"We're about ready to roll. How are you feeling?"

"Me?" The president shook his head slightly and forced a wan smile on his face. "I'm fine. Thank you for asking, Peter." Then, in a voice that was perhaps a little too courteous, he asked, "How are you?"

The press secretary reached out and tapped the stapled, unlined paper on the desk before him. "Can I take this away from you, sir?"

"Go ahead." President Thomas gave it a dismissive wave. He had already read it a dozen times and committed most of it to memory. It would be one of his longer speeches, not quite as long as the address he had given to announce the intent to declare war, but it would be a lengthy one, nevertheless. He had already crystallized the main points, and the teleprompter would help take care of the rest.

Peter Donaldson scooped up the speech, tucking it beneath his arm. He turned away, then hesitated, casting a glance back at the president.

Thomas was preoccupied, his eyes already distant. The moment the camera trained on him, he would transform into the warm and gregarious man his constituents knew him as. Only those who were close to him, like Pete, knew how somber and quiet the president actually was. Yes, he had his moments of passion—his sense of humor was balanced by his fiery temper—but the grandfatherly persona he projected to the public was nothing more than a carefully curated act.

"Help you?" the president asked Peter with a raised eyebrow and an expectant look. There was a flash of annoyance behind his eyes, the expression clearly reading, *Leave me the hell alone, thank you.*

Peter shook his head. "We're going live in one minute. Good luck, sir. And remember," he added, offering the president a wry smile, "you're a hero today."

Thomas gave the man a pursed-lipped smile of his own, and the secretary nodded once more with finality. He was being dismissed, and he knew it. He navigated behind the teleprompter, ready to spring into action to bail out the president just in case the feed became somehow interrupted.

Thirty seconds. Then twenty. The president counted down the seconds in his head, and right as the seconds ticked down, his face relaxed into his trademark warm and sincere mask. *Nothing's wrong*, that face now read. *Everything's fine.*

"My fellow Americans," the president said, and his voice exuded a careful balance of restrained satisfaction and somberness. His eyes locked with every one of his constituents, beaming into their homes during their suppertime. "It is with extraordinary pride and relief that I share with you the ultimate conclusion to the war with the People's Republic of China."

His voice was steady, strong, and confident. The president was a symbolic figure of peace and authority, and he had given his people the most fundamental gift: freedom from the tyranny and oppression of an enemy nation that had been dead set on eventually subverting and possibly overthrowing them. Over the next ten minutes, President Thomas recited the notable facts of the war, pointing out only in the vaguest of terms as to how Project Athena had helped them secure the victory. When he came to the part of his speech where he talked about the casualties of this three-day war, he lowered his voice respectfully, emphasizing not what they had lost but rather what they had gained from triumphing over the PRC. His words focused on how valiantly the American Navy had fought against the enemy forces. He stressed how they had managed to thoroughly destroy all of their opponent's assets, neutralizing any threat they may pose in the future. All of their adversary's military installations had also been flattened, and their ICBM ground and mobile platforms were nothing more than a heap of metal, rebar, and concrete now. When the American people went to bed that night, they would be sleeping peacefully, secure in the knowledge that their elected leader had done everything within his power to help secure democracy and spare them from the tyranny of a malevolent communist regime. Those were the key points Thomas wanted to tuck them in with rather than the uncertainties and what-ifs that would plague his own repose.

He sighed again, a weighty sound, and glanced around the room. Only Chris loitered by the door, patiently waiting for him. He would be ending his shift soon, but for now, the stocky Secret Service agent who served as his PSO was the only man bearing witness to the president's quiet rumination. Thomas pressed his palms flat against the Resolute desk and pushed himself into a standing position. Something in his back twinged, then fell silent as he rose, a subtle reminder that he was an older man now and no longer the spry young politician he once was. He dismissed it with a grimace. Despite his age, he still had plenty of fight left in him. China could also surely attest to this now too.

As Thomas approached the doorway, the PSO cast a sidelong glance at him, then acknowledged him with a nod. He returned it, then paused to consider the younger man standing before him. "You planning on staying the night, eh, Chris? Isn't it about time for you to head home for the evening?"

"And miss out on all of this excitement?" The agent shook his head and grinned. "It was quite a day, sir. Nobody is going to be forgetting it anytime soon."

Chris's assessment was correct. Today would be a day that would linger in the memories of the American people for years to come. It wasn't just the Americans who would remember it, either. In winning this war against China, they had established a precedent. To anyone who might have been watching, their victory was a staunch reminder that the United States was still an insuppressible force, one not to be trifled with—for now, at least.

Thomas's hand came up and absently patted the agent on the shoulder as he slipped past him and moved into the hallway. "That's right, son."

"You're a hero, sir," Chris added, almost as an afterthought.

It was those words again, the same ones his speechwriter had uttered to him not even an hour before. Thomas paused mid-stride, turning his head slightly in the brightly lit hallway to peer at his PSO keeping pace with him. Hell, in a way, perhaps both men were correct. His foresight had anticipated the threat in the East, but the soldiers, sailors, and pilots on the front lines? They were the *real* heroes. Tonight, the president of the United States of America would sleep soundly in his bed with Susan, his arms wrapped around her slim body as he listened to the steady rhythm of her breathing. The same could not be said for the men and women who had given their lives to help secure their freedom from a potentially oppressive regime.

China's attack on the *McCain* had been the catalyst to securing a lasting truce between the two countries. Had the destroyer not been in the South China Sea that fateful December morning, the eventual loss of life in a future war could have been so much greater. His intentions had been genuine when he'd alerted his security advisers to the imminent risk China posed to them, but there was an old saying about a particular road and good intentions. Yet despite the great loss of life and resources, it was the ultimate outcome of this war that would allow him—as well as the rest of the American people—to sleep peacefully in the Land of the Free, both tonight and in the many years to come.

CHAPTER TWENTY-SIX

THE PHONE CALL

JAMES HADN'T BEEN SEATED AT his desk inside the CID office when the president gave his historic speech proclaiming the end of the China-American War. Instead, he had made the executive decision to put on his most comfortable pair of flannel pants and watch it from the comfort of his living room. After he'd arrived home the night before, he had taken a quick shower and promptly slipped between his bedsheets. Even his unconscious thoughts had been too weary to bother him with nightmares that night. He fell into a deep, dreamless slumber and didn't open his eyes again until the sun was high in the sky the next morning.

The days following the ceasefire had been a blur. Christmas had somehow managed to sneak up on him, and he had reached out to his children that night. They understandably had questions for him about the war, and he answered them as candidly as he could without revealing anything classified. For the most part, though, their conversations had been lighthearted and trivial. It wasn't so much about listening to them talk about how they had burned the pumpkin pie or their preference for turkey over ham, but rather, he simply needed to hear their voices. That brief moment when he had thought he was about to lose them back when China had launched their missile strike at the beginning of the war had been sobering. He craved the sound of their laughter and the mundane updates on their lives. The chats had taken up the greater part of his evening, and only when he caught himself yawning behind his hand between replies did he reluctantly end the conversation.

On the same day China signed the Potsdam Declaration, James had called Liz. She was awake and lucid, but she was still recovering in the hospital. She sounded genuinely delighted to hear from him and chatted with him animatedly for the better part of twenty minutes. According to the army physician who had checked in on her earlier that evening, she was recovering quite nicely and on track to be discharged in a few days. She seemed excited about the idea of being back to light duty by the end of January, though he could hear the heaviness in her voice when she admitted it would be difficult without Charles's sarcastic sense of humor and Audra's levelheaded practicality rounding out their team. Near the end of the call, she mentioned how she wanted a fresh start in the next year. He couldn't find any reason to disagree with the sentiment.

James returned to work the next day. He had apparently needed a full two-week break to recover from his exhaustion, but as it turned out, it was more than sufficient. He felt fully rested and recharged for his twenty-four hour shift when he stepped through the door of the CID office, and upon seeing the friendly faces of his team waiting for him, he realized how much he had missed working with them. Secretary Andrews had made an offhand quip about him going on vacation to celebrate winning the war, and James had simply nodded and diverted the topic by asking him how he was doing. If by vacation, he meant resting on his couch for the better part of the time and ruminating on everything that had transpired in the past month, then yes. That was precisely what he had done. Disney would have been better, of course, but the park's elevated ticket prices made that option a no-go for him. Instead, a week at Château Chase had worked as a close second. The food was better and cheaper there, at least, and he hadn't needed to worry about long lines just to use the bathroom.

He quickly fell back into his familiar routine at the SecDef's residence, and as he sat at the computer console inside the basement control room nearly a week after his return, his thoughts went to the night ahead of him. It was turning out to be another routine shift, and according to the reports on the screen, the day had also been fairly slow. A rerun of the *Magnum PI* reboot was on the television on the wall in front of him, the volume turned down low. Marc and Brandon were speaking over the TV audio, allowing their own running dialogue to replace those of the main characters. On-screen, Thomas Magnum was diffusing a tense situation on the screen, and the subtitles revealed he was done negotiating and ready to get down to business.

"I don't care what anyone says," Marc said, his voice rising. Brandon seemed to want to say something in retort, but he held up a hand, silencing him. "No. Hear me out. Sure, this new Magnum is cool and all, but he's not Tom Selleck *cool.* Where's his mustache? He looks like a little kid."

"I hate to break it to you, buddy, but mustaches are out of style." Brandon shook his head vehemently and brought his hand up to his own freshly shaved face. "The ladies these days, they like a clean-shaven man, like me."

"Yeah right." Marc glanced over his shoulder at James and gestured at the screen in front of him. "He's just mad because he had to shave his soup catcher to get this job. What do you think, James? Do you find you're able to get more dates when you're freshly shaven?"

James looked up from the screen and blinked at Marc. "What was that?"

"I said," Marc began, his finger going to his upper lip, "what do the ladies like? Freshly shaven James, or beard and mustache James?"

"The ladies, huh?" James considered the question, then shrugged and turned back toward the computer screen. "I guess I'd say they like me more with a little bit of scruff on my face. Why?"

"Just being nosy, man. C'mon now." Marc leaned back in his chair and crossed his hands behind his head. "All work and no play makes James a dull boy."

"Maybe if you helped out a little bit around here," James countered, but the comment was balanced by the smile on his face. "Why are you watching that stuff, anyway? Haven't you two got anything better to do?"

"Slow night," Brandon said. He yawned, then reached for the remote on the end table next to him. "Not much else to do right now."

"You want to log into ALERTS and take over these reports?" James motioned to the text on the screen, then turned back to the agent. "Be my guest. I'm not stopping you."

"I dunno, man. You look like you've got the situation under control over there." Brandon seemed to want to say more, but the sound of the phone ringing on the far wall interrupted before he could continue.

Marc rose to his feet, his brow creasing as he stepped across the room and plucked the handset from the receiver. "Special Agent Kovacs. How can

I help you?" A momentary pause followed as the person on the other end of the line introduced themself, and James heard the perplexed note in his friend's voice as he said, "Yes, sir, he's right here." He lowered the phone, pressing it to his chest as he crossed the room. At the sight of James's lifted eyebrow, he mouthed, "It's the SecDef," then handed the phone to him.

James frowned as he brought the phone up to his ear. Getting a call from Andrews wasn't particularly unusual, as he regularly made calls down to the control room during the daytime. However, he almost never called past six or seven in the evening, and a glance at the clock on the wall confirmed the time to be nearly a quarter to nine. "Sir. Is everything okay?"

"Yes, everything's fine." Andrews's voice was calm, and there was no trace of urgency to be found. "Say, James, are you in the middle of something right now? If not, I'd like to see you in my study, please."

James glanced back at his computer. The reports could wait. If the secretary of defense wanted to speak with him privately on a matter, then everything else was secondary. "Not a problem, sir. I'll be right up."

He pushed himself to his feet and strode across the basement office to the stairs leading up to the kitchen, pausing only long enough to place the phone back on the receiver before climbing the stairs. The scent of coffee still lingered in the basement kitchen from the cup he had sipped earlier, but if he had been feeling any lingering fatigue, it was now replaced by stark curiosity. What did Andrews want from him that needed to be discussed this late in the evening? He moved through the upstairs kitchen and down the corridor to the secretary's study where warm amber light spilled from the doorless entryway and onto the hardwood floor of the hallway.

James paused at the opening, then rapped lightly on the side jamb with his knuckles and peered inside. "Sir?"

Andrews's study was a cozy and inviting space, simultaneously immaculate and cluttered with thick, leatherbound books. Three out of the four walls bore floor-to-ceiling mahogany bookshelves, and in addition to the hundreds of books placed carefully on each level, a series of globes and even a few marble busts of former presidents resided. The fourth wall had a deep emerald couch nestled against it, its curved back pressed securely against the wood-paneled surface behind it. Two careworn yet well-maintained Victorian style chairs, both in the same style of the couch, completed the sitting area. A scuffed but polished coffee table stood in front of the sofa, and in the middle of it, a silver tray—complete with a matching tea set, a crystal bowl stacked high with sugar cubes, a pitcher of milk, and a canister of tea—gleamed in the lamplight.

"Oh, hello, James. I'm glad you could join me." The secretary glanced up from his position on the sofa, his blue eyes warm as they regarded him over the rim of his reading glasses. A book rested on his lap, but as James took a step into the room, he closed it and slipped the glasses off his nose. Another book already waited on the coffee table, and Andrews leaned forward, setting down the book in his hand and his folded glasses on top of it. Then he nodded at one of the vintage chairs opposite of him. "Go ahead and make yourself comfortable. Do you drink tea?"

"Yes, I do." James approached the chair and, tugging on the seam of his pants, lowered himself down into it. He reached for one of the porcelain mugs. "Thank you, sir."

"Allow me." Andrews's hands were steady as he poured a steaming cup from the pot, then handed the cup to him. "Here."

James accepted it with a quiet murmur of thanks, then reached for the metal tongs from the sugar dish. He dropped three cubes into the cup, chasing it with a splash of milk, then stirred it with the matching silver spoon on the tray. As he brought the drink to his mouth and exhaled on it to cool it down, he wondered again why he had been summoned. Andrews didn't seem particularly stressed or tense, so it clearly wasn't a matter of pressing urgency.

As though on cue, Andrews leaned back in his chair and folded his hands in his lap. His fingers went to the ring on his right hand, twisting it thoughtfully as he considered his next words. Finally, he said, "I've been meaning to talk to you about something for quite a while now, and now that things have finally calmed down, there's no time like the present. Before I begin, I need to let you know that everything we're about to discuss is confidential. It stays between you and me, okay?"

"Of course, sir. I understand." James took a sip from his cup, then rested it on a saucer on the table. His attention was now focused on the secretary, the curiosity visible in his gaze once more as he waited for him to speak again.

"Okay, first of all, let's just stop with all of this 'sir' stuff. I like to think we're friends by now. You can feel free to call me Mike from here on out."

The corners of Andrews's mouth turned up in a grin, and he reached for his own cup of tea. "But I better not catch you calling me that while we're at work."

A matching smile found its way onto James's face. "I won't." The idea of calling Secretary Andrews—or, rather, Mike—by his first name at the Pentagon was too absurd to even entertain. The likelihood of the SecDef slipping and calling him by his own first name was even less likely.

The grin lingered on Andrews's face for a moment longer, then as he lowered his cup of tea back down to its saucer on the table, it slowly faded away. A contemplative expression now settled there, and the tone of his voice was more solemn when he spoke again. "The reason I called you up here is to tell you about this military organization that I'm part of, that's dedicated to protecting the United States and all of her interests. I became a member of it several years ago, back when I got my first star as a marine general. There's also a lot of other influential people who are part of this organization, including a few former presidents." He shifted his gaze from James to one of the marble busts on the bookshelf behind him.

James followed his glance, then returned his focus to the secretary. "Well, I find that interesting, as I've also been part of an organization just like that. It's the US Army, though."

Andrews let out a low chuckle, then shook his head. "It's kind of funny that you'd mention that, actually, because one of the requirements of being part of this organization is either active military service or former service with an Honorable Discharge on a DD-214. As a member of this organization, I'm supposed to recruit anyone who I think is most qualified to be a member." He let these words hang in the air for a beat, then added, "And I personally believe you'd be a great addition to the organization."

James picked up his teacup, turning the warm porcelain in his hands. His interest was certainly piqued, but exactly what kind of organization was Andrews talking about? He took a sip, then lowered the mug back down to the table. "Okay. You've got my attention."

"This military organization is old, very old," Andrews continued. His own cup of tea was forgotten, and all of his focus was on James. "In fact, it was founded way back in 1118."

"That *is* old," James agreed. "That's long before the United States was a twinkle in the founding fathers' eyes."

"Yes, that's correct. It predates it by about six hundred years. I've got another question for you now, though." The secretary's voice grew somber, his eyes almost guarded. "Would you consider yourself a Christian?"

James sat up straight in his chair, his eyes narrowing at Andrews on the couch. He had never been the type of person to publicly advertise his faith, but it was nonetheless something that made up a substantial portion of both his thoughts and his actions. There had been many times in his life where he knew the Big Guy had been watching over him, and while he would never deny his relationship with Him, it just wasn't something that generally came up in conversation. "Yes, I am."

Andrews nodded knowingly and seemed to visibly relax. "I thought you might be, as that's another requirement of the organization."

"Okay, sir. Mike, I mean. I need to know." James clasped his hands together, folding them over his knees as he leaned forward and locked the secretary in his gaze. "What exactly is the name of this organization?"

"This organization takes its secrecy very seriously. I need you to understand that before I tell you anything else about it. And," Andrews said, his eyes meeting James's squarely, "I need to know first if you'd even consider being a member of this organization."

James didn't shift his gaze, nor did he blink. "If this organization is dedicated to protecting the United States and all of her interests, and if you also happen to be a member of it, then I recognize it can't be a bad thing. So yes, I'd say that I'm interested in becoming a member. But are there any other requirements that I need to be aware of?"

Andrews shook his head. "No, just the three that I mentioned: the willingness to protect the US, the ability to keep it a secret, and being a Christian. If you're willing to do that, then I'd consider it a pleasure to recommend you for membership."

"Yes, I'm willing." James allowed himself to blink, but he still didn't look away from the secretary. "But I still want to know more about this organization before I commit to anything. I don't want to get surprised by anything."

Something seemed to shift on Andrews's face, his expression softening as he reached for his cup again. "I'm glad to hear that. Just so you're aware, though, there are also some benefits of being a member."

"Oh yeah? How's that?" A smile spread across James's face as he took a sip from his own cup. The tea was getting cool, but the brew was still pleasantly sweet and strong in his mouth. "You talking about money here? Am I going to get paid?"

Andrews shrugged, the grin back on his face. "Maybe. Depends on the situation, really. But let's just say this organization is very wealthy. It could also have a good influence on possible promotions and duty assignments within the army as well."

"Well, hell. What are we waiting for, then?" A laugh fell from James's lips, and Andrews shared it with him. It was the sound of two men who had shared countless trials and tribulations in their time together and now had the companionable friendship that only came from mutual experience. "Sign me up!"

"On that note, let me tell you a little bit more about the organization," the secretary said as the laughter faded away. "You asked about its name. It's called the Poor Fellow-Soldiers of Christ and of the Temple of Solomon."

"Wait a minute now." James held up his hand, palm out. "That doesn't sound very wealthy to me. You pulling a bait and switch on me here, sir?"

"Well, they also go by a more well-known name, one you might be more familiar with. You ever hear of the Knights Templar?" The words were jarringly casual as Andrews spoke them. "Let's just say they have old money."

James let out a low whistle. While he had heard of the Templars, it had only been mentioned in passing in his studies of world history. At one time, sure, they had existed in large numbers. But now? In a way, they were almost fictional, one of the oldest urban legends in books. "Didn't they get killed off by a French king or something like that?"

"That's partially correct, yes." Andrews's left hand found its way back to the ring on his right hand, and he twisted it back and forth on the digit as he recounted their history. "At their peak, there were probably something like twenty thousand of them, and nearly a tenth of them were actually knights. You probably heard about them from the Crusades. They weren't just good Christians, either. They were also elite soldiers. Sound like anyone you know?"

James let a smile cross his face but didn't reply.

"Long story short, King Philip IV was in quite a bit of debt with the Templars, but when the bill finally came, he realized he couldn't pay it.

He decided to draw up some false charges of heresy and got nearly all of them slaughtered, but a couple hundred managed to escape and went into hiding. Philip thought he had gotten his hands on all of their assets, but the Templars had been smart enough to hide some away just in case that exact scenario ever did happen." A shadow crossed his face, as though the audacity of the long-gone king offended him, then he concluded, "From there, they continued to maintain their secrecy while still quietly recruiting new members. This lasted for hundreds of years, and when the New World was discovered, they saw their opportunity to rebuild. And the rest, you might say, is history." Andrews moved his hand away from the ring as he finished his recount of the organization.

In the low light in the room, James was able to see the details of the ring more clearly now. While the metal itself was black, perhaps some sort of anodized titanium alloy, the stone in the center was glossy white. In the middle of this white crest was a red cross, its symmetrical arms tapered in the center and flared on the ends. As he peered at it, he wondered how he had never made the connection in his mind before. In the past, he might have been able to dismiss its similarity to the emblem of the Knights Templar as a coincidence. With the secretary's words still ringing in his ears, though, its significance was no longer a mystery.

"So, now you know." Andrews clapped his hands together, drawing James's attention away from the ring and back to his face. "Are you still interested in becoming a member?"

James didn't hesitate in answering, "I'll be the first to admit I'm a little shocked that they've been able to survive what they've been through and are still around today, but yes. I'm definitely interested."

"Very good." The smile on Andrews's face was almost paternal, and James felt again the sense of familial belonging as it trained on him. "I'm glad to hear that. With that in mind, there's someone I want you to meet. As a matter of fact, I think you might already know her. At least, she's said she knows you."

"Who's that?" James racked his brain, trying to draw from his memory all the personnel he had ever met who might also know the SecDef. None came to mind. "Where does she know me from?"

"She said she worked with your team a few times, back when you were still part of Delta in Iraq. She was a CIA analyst at the time, and she's actually still in the CIA." Andrews seemed to be enjoying drawing out the mystery of the female operative, and he paused, taking a lengthy sip from his cup of tea before speaking again. "She's part of the Special Activities Division Political Action Group. I believe you already know all about the SAD/PAG, though, and how the group is used for covert political action in foreign countries."

"Wait a minute," James said, holding up a finger. He shook his head, a half-smile forming at the corner of his mouth. "Is she of Cuban descent?"

"Ah, so you *do* remember her?" Andrews returned the smile with one of his own. "I'm sure she'll be relieved you haven't forgotten her after all these years."

"Maria Vasquez!" James leaned back, crossing his arms over his chest, and nodded at the man seated across from him. "Son of a gun. I haven't heard from her in ages. Yeah, at the time, we thought we were the only people of Cuban descent stationed in Iraq. We used to speak Spanish to each other whenever we were in the DEFAC or the office. She'd also join the Delta team when we did our five mile runs."

"Good. She's coming to the Pentagon tomorrow, so it sounds like it'll be a happy reunion." Andrews took the last sip of tea from his cup, then rested the empty cup down on the saucer. "She's been given a special assignment, and I want you to help her with it. She's actually requested you personally, and she's also aware that you're my PSO."

"It'll be great to catch up with her again," James agreed. Vasquez was a tough, no-nonsense woman, and seeing her friendly face once more would be a welcome sight. "What's the special assignment?"

"I'm not sure of the details yet," Andrews admitted. "But I do know it has something to do with Cuba. She's going to brief us tomorrow about it, though, so we'll know more then. Oh, and just in case you were wondering, she's also a Templar."

"Wait, hold up. Going to Cuba?" The stark expression of disbelief and surprise was unmistakable on his face, and the revelation that she was also a Templar seemed to pale in light of this other key detail. "As interesting as that sounds, I don't think my battalion commander is going to agree to that."

"Really now, James? I thought you'd know better by now." Andrews pursed his lips at him, barely concealing the grin trying to take over his face. "All I have to do is make one phone call, and you'll be assigned to the SecDef's Office for Special Investigations."

"The *what?*" Even despite all of his years in service, no such organization registered in his mind. Then again, up until just a few minutes ago, he had also believed the Knights Templar were just a myth. He lifted his gaze to the secretary, his brow creased as he searched for any clue of its existence in his memory. "There's no SecDef's Office for Special Investigations."

"Is that so?" Andrews raised a brow at him as he rose to his feet.

James copied the motion, brushing the creases out of his slacks as he stood. He allowed himself to be led to the doorway, then paused there, one hand on the jamb as he turned to face the secretary.

A faint smile spread across Andrews's face, and as he swept his open hand toward the exit of his study, the cheerful glint in his normally enigmatic eyes was unmistakable. "Well, then. You better start packing your bags and get ready for your new assignment, because there is one now."

TO BE CONTINUED

Thank you for reading. I hope you enjoyed this reading adventure and will leave a review on your favorite retailer to let me know. Please join our mailing list for more information on upcoming books at tonyperezbooks.com

AUTHOR'S AFTERWORD

The story you have just read, *The Dragon and the Eagle*, is a work of fiction. However, the threat The People's Republic of China poses to the United States is considerably less so. In my novel, you were able to experience one potential outcome of a war between the United States and China should it occur in the winter of 2025. At the time of this writing (winter of 2021), China has already rapidly surpassed the United States in several key technological areas and are also on par with us in numerous others. And at the rate they are advancing, it's extremely possible that their military will eclipse ours by as early as 2027—and surely no later than 2030.

As of March 2021, China is on its 14th Five-Year Plan. Within it, they have detailed a vast array of near-term economic, trade, defense, political, social, cultural, science and technology (S&T), and environmental policy priorities, all of which have been designed to coax the country into a greater position of power. One such principle I will touch on here is their so-called "Thought on Building a Strong Military" for a new era, which focuses on accelerating the "integrated development of mechanization, informatization, and intelligentization; comprehensively strengthen training and battle preparedness, increase strategic capability...and ensure achievement of the centennial objective of building a [modernized] military by 2027."[1]

There is no ambiguity in this statement. China is moving quickly on having a modernized military by the year 2027, and they will do so by investing in the development of mechanization, informatization, and artificial intelligence (AI). Yet, how can they move so swiftly on technology that they have done very little research on? In brief, it's largely due to their Thousand Talents Program.

The Thousand Talents Program is one of the most prominent Chinese talent recruitment plans and is specifically designed to attract, recruit, and cultivate high-level scientific minds in furtherance of China's scientific development, economic prosperity, and national security. This talent program seeks to lure in both foreign experts and overseas talent to bring their knowledge and experience to China. In return for their service, the Chinese government will offer a handsome reward to these individuals for stealing proprietary information (and in some cases, classified information) and sharing it with them.[2]

Key details as they exist:

China's Technological Advancements

China's technological advancements are an area of significant concern for the United States and her allies. They already have certain technologies that are equal to what the US owns and furthermore, there are already other technologies in their possession that can readily outperform ours. Just to name a few, some of these include:[3]

- 5G communications
- artificial intelligence
- hypersonic missiles
- laser technology
- nanogenerators
- lithium-ion batteries

As for the hypersonic missiles, these weapons have the terrifying ability to defeat the missile defense systems we currently have in place to protect the United States of America. Those same hypersonic missiles can penetrate through the defensive systems of a Carrier Strike Group (CSG) and easily destroy an aircraft carrier, as well as just about any other US warship.

Proof of Aggression

China has recently taken possession of the South China Sea by building islands out of the shallow reefs in the area. Those islands possess military bases complete with runways, bunkers, command centers, and offensive/defensive missile systems. Whenever US warships travel through the South China Sea under the Freedom of Navigation (FON) Act, the Chinese mili-tary sends warnings to these vessels, advising them that they are trespassing in Chinese waters and ordering them to leave.[4] Presently, China doesn't have the ability to defend itself against US Naval warships, but by 2027? That may no longer be the case. When that day comes, those warnings will turn to threats—complete with the ability to back them up.

Hostilities Toward Taiwan

It won't be long before China decides to forcefully take Taiwan, but this will not happen until they have the naval assets necessary to defend against the United States. In October 2021, China had a total of 125 military aircraft fly into Taiwan's airspace, and 28 aircraft ventured into it on one day alone in June 2021.[5] These transgressions mean the Chinese military is testing how quickly Taiwan can respond to the incursions and are taking note as to what Taiwan responds with. This crucial information is help-ful for when the day comes that the trespass will be an actual takeover of the island. In reality, Taiwan would not be able to last twenty-four hours defending itself against the might of the People's Liberation Army, Navy, Marine Corps, and Air Force.

Should war occur between China and the United States any time after 2030, it will most likely be drastically different from what I portrayed in my book. With nearly an extra decade to prepare, the conclusion will be less clear and more ambiguous. Would an American victory still be guaranteed at that point in time? That remains to be seen. Yes, *The Dragon and the Eagle* is largely a fictional narrative, but its premise isn't going to be quite so improbable when China finally feels as though it has the upper hand. Because of this, it remains essential for us to stay vigilant not only about this emerging threat from the PRC, but also how it grows steadily more dire with each passing year.

Thank you for reading my book, and I wish you the best. God bless.
—Chief Warrant Officer 2 Tony Perez, US Army
www.tonyperezbooks.com

SOURCES

1. Center for Security and Emerging Technology. "Outline of the People's Republic of China 14th Five-Year Plan for National Economic and Social Development and Long-Range Objectives for 2035." *cset.georgetown.edu*, Georgetown University's Walsh School of Foreign Service, 12 May 2021. [https://cset.georgetown.edu/wp-content/uploads/t0284_14th_Five_Year_Plan_EN.pdf] Accessed 10 Nov. 2021.

2. Jia, H. "What Is China's Thousand Talents Plan?" *Nature,* 2018. [https://media.nature.com/original/magazine-assets/d41586-018-00538-z/d41586-018-00538-z.pdf] Accessed 10 Nov. 2021.

3. Ahmed, R. & Whelan, M. "China Knows the Power of 5G. Why Doesn't the U.S.?" *foreignpolicy.com*, Foreign Policy, 17 July 2021. [https://foreignpolicy.com/2021/07/17/china-5g-us-g7-b3w-technology-infrastructure] Accessed 10 Nov. 2021.

Daitian Li, D. Tong, T., Xiao, Y. "Is China Emerging as the Global Leader in AI?" *hbr.org*, Harvard Business Review, 18 Feb. 2021. [https://hbr.org/2021/02/is-china-emerging-as-the-global-leader-in-ai] Accessed 10 Nov. 2021.

Stewart, P. "Top U.S. general confirms 'very concerning' Chinese hypersonic weapons test." *apnews.com*, The Associated Press, 27 Oct. 2021. [https://www.reuters.com/business/aerospace-defense/top-us-general-confirms-very-concerning-chinese-hypersonic-weapons-test-2021-10-27] Accessed 10 Nov. 2021.

Chen, S. "Chinese breakthrough allows physicists to build the world's most powerful laser." *scmp.com*, South China Morning Post, 02 July 2021.

[https://www.scmp.com/news/china/science/article/3139459/chinese-breakthrough-allows-physicists-build-worlds-most] Accessed 10 Nov. 2021.

Luo, J., Wang, ZL. "Recent progress of triboelectric nanogenerators: From fundamental theory to practical applications." *EcoMat.* 22 Oct. 2020. [https://onlinelibrary.wiley.com/doi/full/10.1002/eom2.12059] Accessed 10 Nov. 2021.

Henze, V. "China Dominates the Lithium-ion Battery Supply Chain, but Europe is on the Rise." *about.bnef.com*, BloombergNEF, 16 Sept. 2020. [https://about.bnef.com/blog/china-dominates-the-lithium-ion-battery-supply-chain-but-europe-is-on-the-rise] Accessed 10 Nov. 2021.

4. The Associated Press. "China says it chased US warship out of disputed sea." *apnews.com*, The Associated Press, 12 July 2021. [https://apnews.com/article/china-3e4f399d1b37fc78f84ea549b09d5367] Accessed 10 Nov. 2021.

5. Blanchard, B. & Lee, Y. "China mounts largest incursion yet near Taiwan, blames U.S. for tensions." *reuters.com*, Reuters, 04 Oct. 2021. [https://www.reuters.com/world/asia-pacific/taiwan-reports-surge-chinese-aircraft-defence-zone-2021-10-04] Accessed 10 Nov. 2021.

Wu. H. "China sends record 28 fighter jets toward Taiwan." *apnews.com*, The Associated Press, 15 June 2021. [https://apnews.com/article/china-taiwan-32cca2ef0553cdcfae7f0f82af10056c] Accessed 10 Nov. 2021.

ABOUT THE AUTHOR

Chief Warrant Officer 2 Tony Perez is an American soldier, defense contractor, and now the author of the James Chase book series. His debut novel, The Delta Mission, is inspired by his experience as a soldier during his extensive military career. His notable accomplishments during his military career earned him several awards, including the National Defense Security Award, Army Commendation, NATO Award, Afghanistan Campaign Award, Global War on Terrorism Award, Global War on Terrorism Expeditionary Award, among many others. Perez has a master's degree in Information Technology, specializing in Cyber Security. He currently works full time for a defense contractor in Florida and part time as a CID Special Agent in the US Army Reserves.

You can follow his upcoming projects at tonyperezbooks.com

You can also follow the author on www.facebook.com/author.tony.perez

and

www.instagram.com/tonyperezbooks/